Praise for Dear Dad

Funny, heart-rending and uplifting – a modern-day
'Sleepless in Seattle.'
THE SUN

I have to say that if you enjoy the books of Jojo Moyes,
I think you'd love this one too.
Being Anne

Oh, I loved it! Just the right mixture of tears and humour ...
Baatty About Books

Unashamedly romantic. A great book full of emotion, to
curl up with at the weekend and relax with a frothy
coffee and your favourite pack of biscuits.
Beady Jans Bookshelf

Heartfelt and poignant, Dear Dad is a wonderful book
this is storytelling at its best!
The Book Magnet

Dear Dad is one of those novels that would melt the
coldest of hearts ... a beautiful and heart warming
story that is screaming out to be read.
By the Letter Book reviews

This was a beautiful story, well-written, dealing with some
difficult subjects ... heart warming, inspiring and full of hope.
Kraftireader

I'm so glad that I read this book as it's a charming read and I think would appeal to people who like Matt Dunn's books.
Laura's Good Books

The latest and best yet ... in these times when the world is falling apart it's nice to read a book that makes you smile a smile of satisfaction at the end.
Books with Wine and Chocolate

All in all, a book I couldn't put down ... and I can simply say, it was worth the wait. Very much recommended :)
B.R Maycock's Books

Sometimes you read a book that really melts your heart and you just know that the characters will stay with you long after you've turned the last page. I am going to treasure the time I spent reading this book.
Bookaholic Confessions

Parts of the story are just heart-wrenching and you will want to leap into the pages to stand up for Adam. Other parts contain a fantastic humorous note which lightens the story and ensures that it does not become too over-laden by the serious underlying issues within the book.
The Curious Ginger Cat

I laughed, I cried ... It has been a very long time since I read all night, but I ended up finishing this book at 6.30 a.m., with tears running down my face because it just touched my heart so much.
Monica Mac

GISELLE GREEN

DEAR DAD

YULE

First published in Great Britain by
Yule press
Staplehurst Lodge,
Staplehurst Road,
Sittingbourne, Kent ME10 1XP
www.Gisellegreen.com

A paperback original 2016
1

A catalogue record for this book is available from the British Library

ISBN 978-0-9571152-2-4.

Typeset by Born Group
Printed and bound by CPI Group (UK) Ltd,
Croydon, CR0 4YY

To Julian.

'All who joy would win must share it ... Happiness was born a twin.' Lord Byron.

Acknowledgements

There are times during the writing of a novel when no amount of secondary research can give you the information you're after. It's also often the case that the way the general public (including myself) imagine systems and the law might work is not exactly how things operate in practice. On such occasions, the input of people who work in the field and understand how things are done 'on the ground' are invaluable. My heartfelt thanks go to all those people who took time out of their daily work to answer my questions and explain how a case like Adam's as described in this book might potentially go. Without your thoughts, I wouldn't have been able to bring Adam's story to the conclusion that I did.

I would like to offer my particular thanks to senior family lawyer Mary Raymont also to former Children's Team social worker Michelle Horlocks – you both gave me a lot to think about. Whilst I have sought expert advice where I needed it, any errors I may have incurred in the writing of this tale are mine alone.

Thanks to Catri for editing, to Megan for help with French, and to Carol, Lucie, Emma, Talli and Brenda for your invaluable thoughts along the way.

To Matthew, who not only does all my IT but also allowed himself to be persuaded to design the cover for this book - I love it. Thank you. Emma Graves, you also did a fabulous job. Daniel Knight has done great work with the book design.

Thank you to my twins, Julian and Andrew because you always help me out.

Lastly, my grateful thanks go as ever to my biggest cheerleader Eliott. You are the best.

Nate

'You're ... what do you mean you're *not coming*?' Judging from her voice down the phone, Marcie is furious, as well she might be. I've just ruined the celebratory mood, given her the worst possible news as far as she's concerned. All the noise in the background of where she is, sounds merry. They'll have broken out the champagne at breakfast, I have no doubt of it.

'Listen. This is one of the most prestigious industry events of the year. You're up for the Young Frontline Reporter Award and you ... just ...?'

'I can't, Marcie.' I go park myself on the edge of my sofa, my head in my hands. 'I can't.'

'Why?' A note of suspicion creeps in. 'Just, please, don't tell me that you're hung over young man, that isn't going to cut it.'

'I'm not hung over.'

'What then?' There's a small pause. 'You're sick? If you think you're coming down with something take a couple of tablets, drink lots of water – but get yourself on the next plane.'

'I'm not sick.' I rub at the back of my neck gingerly. 'I'm just ... not coming.'

'Of course you are,' she shoots back. 'All of the industry press are here.'

I know, I can hear them.

'Besides, if you weren't coming,' she adds roundly, 'you'd have rung up and let me know about it hours ago.'

'I tried,' I tell her faintly. 'I tried to leave the house at six-thirty this morning.'

'I'm sorry?'

'I tried again at eight-thirty. Then ... I went downstairs at eleven o'clock. I thought ... if I could get to the airport by 1 p.m., I'd still be in good time.'

'I'm afraid I have no idea what you are talking about.'

'I'm sorry,' I croak. 'I should have brought this up before, I know. I didn't say anything sooner because I never imagined it would come to this.' I'm freelance, but it's Marcie I report to whenever I do work for Smart World Productions. Her earlier comment about me not having rung her up to give her warning has made my ears go red. I've let her down, that's what she's saying. It's about time she knew why.

'I can't leave the house, Marcie.'

'Go on.'

I stick my thumb and forefinger into the corner of my eyes.

'The fact is,' I tell her, 'I have not been able to leave the flat for a good while, now.'

There's a short pause while I imagine her finding somewhere a little quieter to have this conversation, somewhere a little more private. I hear a door shutting at her end and all the background noise of men and women that surrounded her before, all the sounds of people laughing and talking, having a good time in Paris where I should also be, they disappear.

'Is it your leg still troubling you?' Marcie asks more sympathetically, 'I'm sorry, Nate. I was aware that you needed all those appointments at the hospital for physio and so on, after you returned, but I didn't know you were still ...'

'The physio appointments finished a while back. I can walk.' I pause. 'This isn't a physical problem.'

She's quiet for a moment.

'It's not a physical problem?'

'No.'

2

'Then what? Why are you stuck in the flat?' I can feel Marcie frowning. She doesn't understand. Of course she doesn't. Would I, if it had been her telling me this? Would I have had the faintest inkling of what someone else experiencing this was going through, before it happened to me?

'It's something unexpected that's happened to me.' I tell her warily. 'My GP reckons I have the symptoms of ... um ... post-traumatic stress.' There. I said it. I go over and pull up the sash window in my living room, take in a lungful of air.

'No!' She comes back with a little disbelieving laugh. 'How could that happen to you?' I don't answer, and she runs on, clearly confused. 'Well. Why the hell didn't you mention anything to me before?'

'Why do you think?'

There's a silence while she considers this.

'I'm a twenty-seven-year old war correspondent, who's just admitted he can't even leave the house,' I spell out. She knows as well as I do that in many of our colleagues' eyes, what I've just admitted to her could be professional suicide.

'I see,' she says after a while. 'Has this come on because of what happened when you were out on your last assignment with ...?'

'I don't know why it's come on,' I cut straight across her. 'I thought it would get better, Marcie.' I run on, feeling breathless. 'I kept telling myself this would pass, that it would improve if I just kept my cool. But, it hasn't improved,' I confess to her. 'The truth is, day by day, it's only got worse.'

'And you can't get out?'

'I ... I get panic attacks every time I try to leave here.'

'Wow.' I can almost feel her frown from here. 'Does anyone know about this?'

I swallow. 'No.'

'No one?

'No one except my GP. They've offered counselling, but there's a long waiting list for that. Please,' I tell her thickly, turning from the window. 'I don't want this getting out. You know what this business is like. It would ruin my career if anyone even ...'

'How long since you've been outside of the flat?'

'Six weeks.'

'Six weeks! Good lord. How are you paying your bills, Nate?'

I baulk at that, but I tell her, anyway.

'I am not paying my bills. I can't.'

When she comes back to me now, her voice has changed. She's not angry anymore. What I'm picking up in her tone now sounds, far more horribly, like pity.

'It sounds as if what's happened to you is exactly what happened to that other young guy what's his name? The one who used to courier for us?'

My heart sinks into a further pit of despair. She's likening me to him?

'You remember – he was a great young reporter, one to note. He covered an earthquake in China for Smart World Productions one time and got caught up in the aftershocks,' she enthuses.

'Of course I remember Eric Bailey. How could I forget him?' After he came back from China, he was never able to go out in the field again and now she can't even remember his name.

'He was eventually able to go out to work.' She rallies.

As a courier, not a reporter.

'Whereas in my case,' I remind her quietly, 'I cannot even do that. I know you mean well but Eric's story doesn't exactly fill me with hope,' I mutter quietly.

It fills me with a whole host of things; despair, horror, a terrible fear laced with an overwhelming sorrow. But it does not fill me with any hope.

'It should, Nate,' she assures me now. 'Because even though it took a lot of courage for that young man to get back out there again, he did manage it, and so will you. Courage,' she reminds me softly, 'is something that you have in spades.'

'I wish.' I drum my fingers on the windowsill, impatient for her to go, now. 'I have no courage left. If I once had any, it's gone.'

She's silent for a while, considering that.

'They're planning to give you the bravery award tonight, you know. For showing the most heroism in the field.'

I close my eyes, not wanting to hear this.

'Marcie, what kind of hero can't even leave his flat because he's terrified he'll suffer from a panic attack?'

'The kind who's prepared to go out to the world's worst war zones to bring the story home; the kind,' she adds quietly, 'who's prepared to risk his own life to save that of a wounded colleague without a second's thought.'

I close my eyes, tightly, clenching my fists. Why did she have to mention Jim Nolan? Why did she have to mention him?

'I didn't save Jim though. Did I, Marcie?'

I hear her intake of breath.

'Is that why you're being so hard on yourself now?'

'I didn't save his life, and when it came down to it, I couldn't even bring myself to leave the flat long enough to go to his funeral.'

'Nate,' she's aghast. 'Are you still blaming yourself for the fact that Jim didn't make it?'

'What do you …?' I push my hands through my hair, furiously batting back the tears welling in my eyes and throat. Of course I don't blame myself.

Do I?

'The awards body don't see it that way, you know. They didn't judge whether you succeeded or you failed in your attempt to save his life. They only saw what you were prepared to do. It's what all of us here, see. You do have courage, Nate Hardman. More than most. Just remember; even the bravest among us can't win every battle.'

Marcie has no idea. Even one little trip down to the corner shop would be a victory for me right now.

'I'm sorry,' I tell her thickly. 'I can't be there tonight. I've tried everything I can think of to get myself going again and I don't know what else I can do to make this situation better.'

Again, she's silent for a while, thinking furiously.

5

'Let me have a little time to consider this, Nate. Perhaps I can come up with something that'll help you out?'

'Sure, take all the time you need,' I try and make light of it. 'One thing's for sure – right now, I'm not going anywhere.'

Jenna

'I had it. I had it here a minute ago.' I shrug my duffle bag down onto the platform and the ticket inspector looks at me wearily. I've been searching for over ten minutes already. His colleague behind him, a younger guy more my own age, shoots me a sympathetic glance.

'I've got too many bags with me today, everything I own, in fact.' I give a half-hearted laugh, crouching down to feel around in the zip compartment of my suitcase and my jacket slides out of my arms. 'I'm sorry. I've been up since 3 a.m. I've just flown in from Sicily and I'm not … quite …'

'Think that was a call for you just in over the tannoy, sir.' The younger one slides over and interrupts his boss. There are a lot of announcements, all quite unintelligible, coming in over the tannoy.

'Was it?'

'I can deal with this for you, sir, if you like,' he offers. To me, as the older guy leaves, he says: 'It is an offence to travel on the railway without a valid ticket, Miss. Can I ask you to accompany me over to the office?'

'What office? The ticket office? I haven't got the money on me for another ticket.' I feel my face going hot. My bank account – what remains in it – is all in Euros. 'I *did* have a ticket,' I insist. 'I took it out to show the ticket inspector in the carriage and I remember putting it back in my bag.' *Which one, though …?* My eyes are bleary with the last two days. 'Look,' I put in a last plea for clemency. 'I'm sorry. I had to leave where I was in a bit of a hurry and right now I barely know where *I* am, never mind the ticket …'

A middle-aged couple walk past us now, staring curiously. I stare back at them.

'That happens,' he agrees, bending alongside me to helpfully pick up my jacket. 'But regulations say I still need to see a valid …'

'Fine!' my voice goes up a notch. 'I'll try taking every single item I own out of all four of these bags, shall I? I'll do it right here on the platform, till I find it.' I open up the duffle bag and prepare to tip the entire contents out. I did all my packing in something of a hurry yesterday evening. This isn't going to be pretty. He stares down at the three pairs of black cami knickers and the half eaten granola bar that fall out first. I shake my bag a bit more vigorously and out falls a bottle of water and my book on the fourth wave of feminism which I still haven't got round to reading and then, all covered in granola crumbs, my tiny, blue Bertie Bear.

A little crowd is gathering around us. To the left of me, someone has stopped to record this – the amazing spectacle of the disembowelment of my luggage – on her mobile phone.

'Um.' I feel his staying hand on my shoulder. 'We can sort this out without any need for all *that*, Miss.' His eyes flash at me warningly but now I spy a hint of laughter in there too.

'You find my predicament amusing?' I accuse.

'Not at all.'

'You think it is fair to treat *paying customers* like this, especially when they've just explained that they've been up all night and they're tired and they're … hungry and they've got too many other important matters on their mind?' I push.

'Not paying customers,' he agrees with a smile.

Distracted by his cute dimple, I stop ranting at him and stop shaking my duffle bag because it's not making me feel any better, witnessing all my possessions tumbling out onto the platform like this. I turn towards the woman who's still got her phone pointed at me and maybe it's something she sees on my face but she puts it away rapidly.

The ticket Nazi hands me back my jacket. I watch him now as he retrieves all the rest of my gear as well, shovelling it back efficiently into my duffle bag.

'You didn't need to do that,' I inform him. 'I could have done it myself.'

'You're welcome.' He smiles. 'So these are all your worldly goods? Someone expecting you who can give you a hand out there with these?'

'My friend will help me when I get to hers,' I tell him. 'If she's in.' Which she may well not be, because I haven't had an answer to the text I sent her, yet.

'Oh? You might want to ring her and let her know, then. It's bucketing it down,' he points out.

'Damn. Is it coming down that hard, now?' I am going to get soaked. Everything I own in the world is going to get soaked and I don't know if Mags is home or if she'll even have a room free to put me up. And I still haven't found my ticket.

He neatly pulls the drawstring tight before placing the bag squarely in my arms. 'All done here, Miss.'

'You know, maybe you'd be a lot cuter if you weren't such a jobsworth,' I tell him

'Maybe *you'd* be cuter if you weren't such a firecracker,' he comes straight back. 'You are however, I have to agree, a paying customer.'

I gawp at him, pulling my jacket on with what little remains of my dignity. The crowd disperses, a tad disappointed I sense; they'd been hoping for more.

'Well, about time.' I tell him frostily. About time he believed me.

He glances significantly towards the pocket of the jacket he's just handed back to me. Then his face breaks into a wide smile. 'Here you go, Miss,' He gives me back my ticket, the little edge clipped off it now to show I have completed my journey.

'Welcome to Rochester. You be sure and have a nice day, now.'

Nate

'So tell me.' Marcie's back. She's clearly been thinking about my situation overnight. 'Every time you go outside, what happens?'

I draw in a breath. 'Not good.'

'No,' she understands. 'Would you be prepared to show me?'

'How would I do that?'

'Go outside,' she suggests.

'Right *now?*'

'Right now. Stay on the phone to me and describe what happens to you when you do it.'

I drum my fingers on the arm of my chair, then get up and go look out of the window onto Rochester High Street. It is Saturday afternoon and there's a fine sheet of rain coming down outside. There is some sort of activity going on because it is the beginning of May and there are rather more people out there now than there were when I attempted – again – to go out this morning.

'It's raining.'

'They gave you the bravery award last night. You're not scared of a bit of rain are you?'

'It's not the ...' She can't see the face I'm pulling. This is not going to be as easy as she thinks.

'Show me,' she says again. Damn, but she's persistent.

They gave me the bravery award last night. I stare at the phone in my hand. Decision made, I push my feet into some trainers and slide my house-key into my pocket as if I am properly about to go out.

'I won't get very far,' I warn her.

'You don't need to,' she reassures. 'I only want to see your reaction.'

Why? Because she thinks she knows me and she's having trouble squaring the young go-getter guy she admires so much with the frightened man I've become? I take the stairs to the ground floor quickly; pull back the bolt with a grimace.

She's about to find out, isn't she?

It takes only a moment or two before the feeling of dread descends. I can feel it almost immediately, like a bucket of cold water travelling down my spine.

But, fuck it, I'm on the phone to Marcie.

'Okay, I'm out,' I tell her. Outside, with the reluctant sun that's beginning to shine down onto the wet pavement. I can spy some Morris dancers who have started up a routine on the street and a lot of people are milling about. Already, my chest is tightening. I want to go straight back in and close the door. I want to tell her; *forget this, Marcie, I know you mean well but this is not the way. I'm not sure there is any way back from this. I don't want to become your next courier anyway, please go away.* But I don't say that.

'I'm downstairs, just outside the flat,' I tell her. 'And I'm experiencing a chronic shortness of breath.'

'Breathe,' she directs. 'Talk me through it as if you were talking to camera. As if you were on the front line somewhere.'

The front line? I never feel this scared when I am on the front line with a job to do. All I'm feeling right now is a desperate desire to get this outing over with. Not to do it at all, in fact.

'Describe it.'

I rub at my chest, surprised nonetheless to hear myself saying to Marcie,

'My chest is hurting like hell. As if I've been underwater for too many minutes and my lungs are being squeezed, but I'm going to try and get to Moh's corner shop.'

11

'Good lad,' she encourages. 'What's going through your mind right now?'

'That I want to go back inside,' I admit. 'Being out here feels … too exposing. It feels as if something bad – something really bad – might be about to happen any minute.'

'It won't. Can you see the corner shop, yet?'

I can see it. But I stop, turn around and look back at my front door.

'I'm worried I won't be able to make it back to the flat if I go too far.' I feel sheepish even admitting this to her. 'Stupid, I know. It's just this fear I've developed.'

'You feel that,' she agrees, 'but how about you describe to me what else you can see right now, as if you were reporting back on it, live?'

Report back, live. Okay, I can do that.

'There's a group of yummy mummies coming towards me now, power-pushing their buggies back up the High Street,' I say faintly into the phone.

'Where have they just come from?'

'I don't know.'

'You're my reporter on the ground, you *have* to know,' she snaps back.

'They've … been watching the Morris dancers performing their traditional First of May rites.'

'Good,' she says. Then she asks, out of the blue. 'What else? Are any of them looking at you?'

'A couple of them have just smiled at me,' I admit. I don't know why she's asking me that. Automatically, I shoot the women a pained smile in return.

'You're a good-looking guy, Nate.'

'Thank you.' I look back at my front door again. 'I have missed the company of women,' I admit to her. Right now, though, I'm not really feeling it. Right now all I need is the security of my own four walls around me, sick to death as I am, at the sight of them.

'Anything else?'

'Like what?' I'm having trouble concentrating but she's right, I need to focus. 'A toddler has just raced past me with his balloon,' I say slowly. 'It's one of those novelty ones with a face on it.'

'Yes. What colour?'

'Red.' Red for danger. Red for blood.

No, no … red for roses. Red for clown's noses. Red for strawberry jam in doughnuts …

I swallow, *remember I'm live from the front line*. 'It's bumping and rolling along the pavement.' I watch it warily. 'I'm concerned now the balloon is going to pop,' I admit. 'If it pops, I'm worried that the noise … the noise is going to be difficult for me to cope with.' I breathe, slowly, deep into my belly.

'It won't pop,' she reassures. 'Look around you at the rest of the scene. You're making your way to the corner shop, remember? You need to get there. Describe it all to me as you go.'

'I'm passing the arts centre now.' I hurry past it. 'The charity shop has lots of yellow clothes in the front window. I'm feeling a little giddy.'

'Yellow clothes,' she distracts, '… because it's the spring. Keep going.'

'Yellow clothes because it's spring,' I echo back to her into the phone, keeping the narrative going. 'It's spring and the flower shop has a dozen buckets of tulips out the front.' A bicyclist clips past me, riding on the pavement, eliciting an exchange of curses between us. He spooked me with his carelessness just now. Cussing him, I notice the dark, fearful shadow at my back fades a little.

'Nate,' Marcie breathes down the line, 'You okay?'

I'm okay.

'I'm here,' I tell her. She doesn't know it but Moh's corner store is only eight shops down, literally yards from my own front door. I stare at the pavement display of bananas and mushrooms in their tidy little baskets and now I'm aware of another, strangely triumphant feeling sitting alongside the urge to turn tail and head back.

'You did it.'

13

'I did.' I've turned and I'm walking back already. She can't see how fast.

'That was well done, Nate.' Marcie isn't being facetious. She sounds thoughtful. 'It makes me feel that the idea I've come up with, for you, might work.'

'Idea?' My hands are trembling, shoving the key into my front door I can barely turn it quick enough. At my feet, a pile of letters – brown envelopes mostly – have arrived. Bills that I cannot – and will not, now – be able to pay, stare up at me. But Marcie's got an idea. 'What idea?'

'I haven't completely formulated it, yet,' she admits. 'I wanted to see what going outside felt like for you, but I'm going into my office to put something together for you right now. How about I send Hal round to your place with a proposal for this, first thing next week?'

'Sounds amazing.' I try and inject a bit of enthusiasm. Whatever she's planning, if it's as painful as this short outing just was, I am sure I am not going to like it. Not one little bit. But I do appreciate that she's doing this.

'Let me … do some talking to people,' she runs on. 'Let me think about this. See what I can come up with.'

'Okay,' I tell her faintly. I have no idea what Marcie means, what she thinks she might be able to 'come up with' that would be of any use to me. 'Thank you for going out of your way to help me, Marcie.'

'You're worth it,' she comes straight back. 'I know what not being able to attend last night's ceremony will have meant to you.'

It meant everything. She can't know, not truly, how much being there last night would have meant to me. She rings off, and back inside at last, with the door closed, in the safe but too-dark, too cold downstairs hallway, I lean my clenched fist against the heavy wooden door. *Why? Why is this happening to me now, of all the times in my life?* The fear at my back has lifted but it is replaced by the ever-present loneliness I feel these days. I bend to sweep

14

up all the demand letters in my hands. I still have to find some means of paying these.

Especially this one. A forlorn groan comes from deep within my chest.

'*God.*' My landlord, Rezza, already made threatening noises when I failed to pay my rent last month and this'll be the follow-up, no doubt. It'll take a while for anything to actually happen on that score but I know this is … the beginning of the end.

Then I look at the envelope a little closer.

To my dad, it says in large, childish lettering. I stare at it for a moment, choking back a laugh of relief as I see it is not Rezza after all. It is not even for me! On the back, as I turn it over in my hand, someone has written the words boldly in red:

Please help!

Jenna

'My darling.' In the ten minutes it takes for me to walk down from Rochester station, Mags is already waiting to greet me at the door of her flat. She's got a large G and T in hand and she's wearing something flowing in a mustard-coloured silk which is getting spotted dark as she stands outside in the rain, looking magnificent. 'I'm ecstatic to see you here. Truly ecstatic.' I get a kiss on both cheeks before she pushes me inside, dripping wet, with all my bags. 'Now tell me, what are you doing back in the UK?'

I give a little shake of my head and she frowns. Then the penny drops.

'Oh. What's happened?'

'Alessandro and I are through.' I pull off my wet jacket slowly. 'We're done.'

Mags makes a whistling noise through her teeth. 'Why? What about the wedding?'

'It's off.'

'How? I thought you two lovebirds were …' She's perplexed. 'I thought you had finally found what you were looking for, Jenna.'

'So did I,' I admit.

'So what will you do now?'

'Stop looking,' I assure her. She's shaking her head sadly. 'No, really. It isn't worth the trouble and it isn't worth the heartache.' I plonk my jacket on the end of her bannisters, pulling a face at

16

the proffered Gin and Tonic. 'Not for me, thanks. If you happen to have any lagers in there …?'

'None. I do not stock such items in my larder.' As soon as I've kicked off my wet shoes, Mags ushers me straight through and onto a bar stool in her kitchen, plonks herself down beside me, all the folds of her silk garment puffing out. 'Now. Tell me absolutely everything.'

'To be honest, I'd rather not.'

'So – you spend a year getting to understand the foibles of his traditional Sicilian family and then …' Her hands sweep out in a grand 'all over' gesture.

'*And then,*' I echo, shooting her a pained smile.

'What happened?'

I stare at the ground. 'If you must know, he cheated on me, Mags.' Her lip curls in disdain. 'Why would he do that to you?'

'Why do they ever?' I shrug, turning my face away from her, wishing she would change the subject. This is far more difficult for me than she will ever know. 'Because he could. He turned out to be someone other than who I thought he was.' Some people are lucky in love but that's not me.

'The prick. Do you want me to kill him for you?'

'If there is any murdering to be done I will do it myself. But thank you for offering.'

Mags waves her hand and the long sleeves of the kimono-type thing she's wearing waft dangerously near her G and T. 'The man has no taste at all, obviously.'

'Oh, he has good taste.' I swallow down the lump that has come into my throat. 'At least he did it with one of the most beautiful women in Sicily.'

'A consolation, I am sure.'

'A small one. *Hello, Marmalade.*' Her old and battered Tomcat has jumped up to sit beside us on the counter and I'm grateful for the distraction. 'He's kept his glorious, deep orange colour, hasn't he?'

'Marmalade.' Mags shoots me an affectionate look. 'Just like you.'

'These days,' I remind her, 'my colouring is all the rage.'

'It is. And now, like your fashionable strawberries-and-cream colouring, you are back,' Magda muses. 'To stay?'

'That's the plan.' I look around her kitchen with its super-modern appliances, the pale green juice blender and matching cabinet with its coloured crystal cut glasses, everything chosen with impeccable taste, and console myself with the thought that this place isn't really so bad. I may be starting again from scratch but if I'm living here you could hardly call this slumming it.

'Rochester's just a short hop, skip and a jump from London, after all. It could be the perfect base from which to re-launch myself.'

'It could.' She's looking at me thoughtfully. 'It could possibly. If all the conditions were right.'

'Why wouldn't they be?' I glance around at her drinks cabinet. 'Are you *sure* you don't have any lagers stashed away somewhere?'

She shakes her head which today is a mass of glossy platinum curls.

'Lagers are not a woman's drink, Jenna. You should practise being a little more ladylike if you can.'

'Like you?' I shoot her a small smile.

'I do my best. Now, Honey ...' Mags leans in a little closer.

'I like your shoes,' I distract her. She wants the details of my split but I haven't the heart for it today. The shoes are red patent ones, with a Dorothy-esque bow. 'Do you have any trouble at all, getting them in that size?'

'None whatsoever.' She looks down at her feet proudly. 'I'm only a size ten, which is quite teeny compared to some of the other footwear in my catalogue.'

'I bet. You do have dainty feet for a man.'

She blinks, ignoring that. I recall that she doesn't like to be reminded and I mustn't antagonise.

'Look, Mags, you were right about everything, okay?' I lean on her worktop, head in hand. 'You were right. I fluffed up big-time in Sicily. Or he did. Whatever way you want to look at it, I'm back in England to stay.'

She nods, her mind going immediately to the practicalities. 'You have a job?'

'Well, no. Not *yet*. I only found out about Alessandro this week,' I point out.

'A place to stay?'

I gulp. Sit up a little straighter. I was hoping that part might have been self-evident. 'Well, *here*, Mags. I was thinking to stay here. With you.'

Her heavily made-up eyes seem to widen slightly.

'For now, at least?'

'Ah.' She puts her drink down on the counter; her hand goes to her mouth. 'My darling,' she says regretfully. 'I am so sorry, but no.'

'No?' I reach for her vile gin and take a small sip. This day is just getting better, isn't it? 'I can't stay?'

'I have a guest coming over, next week.' Her voice drops to almost a whisper. 'My brother. He's coming over from Pretoria for six months.'

Six months? Her place is definitely out of the question, then.

'How is he?' The gin is leaving a perfumey burning sensation at the back of my throat, God it is foul. I cough. Magda fans her hands in a *don't ask* gesture. So I don't ask. Her brother is a bigoted bore of the highest order, anyway.

'You can stay for the night, of course,' Mags quickly comes back. 'Maybe even a week, at a pinch and if you don't mind sleeping on the couch. You'll soon find a nice little place of your own, though. I imagine you'll have something of a nest egg put aside, by now?'

'How'd you mean, a nest egg?' I stare at Mags.

She touches finger to nose in a knowing gesture.

'Alessandro was a wealthy man, darling. I only met him once, but I recognise a spender when I see one.'

'Ah,' I say. 'I didn't let him lavish money on me the way you think.'

'Why ever not?'

'I didn't want him to feel that I was bought and paid for, did I?'

She throws her hands in the air in a disbelieving gesture. 'That's the trouble with you young romantics, isn't it? You always think that love will tide you through.'

'Not anymore,' I say.

'Self-sufficiency, I find, is a vastly overrated commodity. Just *how*,' she demands, 'do you imagine I could ever have afforded to buy a flat like this one at the tender age of just twenty-two? Shrewd investments in the stock market?'

Twenty-two is pushing it a bit. If she bought this place at that age, she wouldn't yet be thirty. I reach for my handbag to take out a cigarette and then I remember that I quit them. I quit smoking on the day I left my cheating fiancé and if I am feeling antsy at all it is not because I am missing him.

'Oh, well.' She takes a slug of her gin. 'You had your chance. Looks like you're determined to do it the hard way. 'Have you given *any* thought to what you'll be living on?'

I stare at her. I haven't given it any thought. I've only just got here.

'I imagine I'll find a job in a tattoo parlour somewhere, same as I did in Sicily.'

'It's just that tattoo-parlour work is a little bit specialist, isn't it? You won't just walk into a job doing what you've been doing in Catania, up to now.'

'I might do. I was practically running that place before I left. I was their most in-demand tattooist, and I never lacked for clients at all. In fact,' I let her know, 'I even had a waiting list, some weeks.'

'Over there, you did. The problem is that *here*, you are unknown, correct?' She slaps my hand as I'm sneaking it into the peanut-bowl on her counter. 'Forty calories per peanut. Those are for display purposes only.'

'I don't have to worry about calories,' I remind her.

'No, you don't, do you?' She shoots me a disparaging look. 'Lucky you. You do have to worry about income, though.'

20

'*Income*,' I mutter. 'I'll get a job doing artwork somewhere,' I tell her assuredly. 'If not body art then I'll paint murals for the town hall. Or … I'll offer henna tattoos in the market place, or face-painting at children's parties.' What? *What*? Why not?' Why the faint pity in the way she's smiling at me now?

'You artists.' She rolls her eyes slightly, gives a little shrug. 'How happy to be you. How must it be to enjoy so much freedom of the imagination, living your life moment-to-moment, so butterfly-like and free?'

'It's pretty good,' I admit. 'I love my work.'

'I know.' She's regarding me with faint curiosity. 'I know you do, darling. But how do you gorgeous butterflies cope when the halcyon days of summer are over and all the nasty, boring little bits of life like electricity bills and *needing somewhere to live* come round?'

'We …' I swallow. 'We come to stay with our lovely friends, people like you, Mags.'

'And then …' She shoos the cat off her worktop in one swishing movement of her long, elegant sleeve. 'Then you get a job doing something sensible to tide you over. Something you were trained in and which you do very well. Something that will net you a decent income to enable you to set yourself up independently. Because you do, above all, still want your independence, right?'

I slide off her bar stool and go to the kitchen tap to run myself a glass of water. I need to wash away the taste of the gin.

'If you're talking about me going back into primary school teaching.' I give a firm shake of my head. 'It won't be my first choice, no.'

'I imagine it wouldn't. All those lesson plans and after-school meetings and admin forms to see to. Not the kind of thing little summer butterflies are very fond of, I know.' She takes a tiny sip of her drink, rolling it round her tongue to savour every molecule of it before swallowing. 'But even they have to eat, I imagine.'

'I'll find something.'

'It's not going to be that easy starting afresh, Jenna,' she says quietly. 'Don't you see? You had *everything* in Catania.'

21

'I thought I did.' I frown. 'I thought so, and yet I didn't. Not everything.' We both stare through her kitchen window, silent for a bit. Outside, it was pouring when I got off the train, greyed over, and there's still a fine drizzle pattering down on the mews beyond her house. It's the beginning of May already but that's England, I think resignedly.

Magda's looking at me thoughtfully again. 'No,' she agrees, after a while. 'I suppose that is true.'

I had plenty of money at my disposal, had I chosen to use it. I had a glamorous lifestyle with a large circle of people courtesy of my well-connected boyfriend; an engagement ring on my finger. I had a growing and well-paid body-art practice. I had a beautiful house that we shared in the shadow of smouldering Mount Etna and we woke every morning to views of the sparkling Adriatic Sea below. All these things I had but the importance of them vanished in the instant I learned that Alessandro had lied to me. He had been cheating on me all along.

In that instant I saw that I didn't have the one thing that mattered to me most of all.

Nate

'Hey. The "Young Reporter of the Year Award" last Friday,' Hal Daley is saying gently. 'All kudos to you for getting that, man.'

'Thank you.'

Good as her word, Marcie's sent her rescue proposal in with Hal, first thing. They've sent the little bronze award statue along with it, too. My envoy from Smart World Productions leans back against my sofa.

'A lot of people were bummed you weren't able to be there yourself to pick it up,' he adds. Ever since he walked in, Hal's been looking vaguely uncomfortable. As well he might. Hal Daley's a great guy, a couple of years my senior. He's looking smart today, tanned and fitter than ever, wearing his beard closely trimmed, I see. Is that what all the blokes in production are going for, these days? My hands go self-consciously to my own face.

'I would have given anything to have been there Friday, believe me.'

'I know, I know. These things happen, you're not the first.'

'No.' I look at him uneasily. 'It happens to people, but you never hear of it much. Panic attacks. Agoraphobic symptoms – it's excruciatingly embarrassing. Is that because they're all like me – no one wants to talk about it?'

Hal shrugs. 'This work we do – it's tough, right? It takes its toll. For some guys, it's a sign that it's time to get out of this line of work, but for you …' Hal leans in encouragingly. 'You're still young. The company values you and they still want you. You're freelance

23

now, yes, but in a year or two, who knows? You're one of the ones who's been marked for a permanent post. This proposal Marcie's sent you, it's your way back in.'

'I'm thankful for it.' But this … I pick up the proposal he's come here this morning to deliver and make like I'm examining it again.

'Marcie's already filled you in on the bones of it, I take it?'

I nod.

'She wants to put me forward as a candidate to make one of the "real life shorts" that Smart World Productions are preparing to air next season.'

'Correct. The idea is simple. You keep a diary, video-cam everything and that way you can show your recovery to the viewers as it happens, week on week.'

'My recovery, sure.' I'm working to keep my voice even. *Don't they realise that if I knew how to recover from this I'd have done it by now?* Of course not. In the magical world of TV, if I video-cam everything then the recovery must happen, right? I don't know if it will. But I can't exactly tell him that, can I?

I look at him unhappily.

'You're a little reluctant?' He picks up.

'I'm just not sure how thrilled I am about the world and his wife finding out about what's happened to me,' I admit. 'I've deliberately kept a low profile for precisely that reason.'

'I understand completely. But I think the idea's a winner, to be frank,' Hal's enthusing. 'The public are always going to be interested in cases like yours. How does a man go from receiving the "Young Frontline Reporter award," to being someone who's too scared to leave his flat? Let them see that what you want more than anything is to get back to your old self and your old life. And let's not forget,' he inserts craftily, 'that it'll also help *other people*. People who are in your situation who don't understand it any more than you do, they're looking for a way out, just like you are. You're a journalist, an information-weaver and a fact-finder. If you can't find your way out of this maze, then who can?'

'That's true.'

'And to top it all, Marcie's insisting they offer you a handsome advance, too.'

'An advance?' My hand goes up to the back of my neck. I hesitate for a good few seconds, wondering if there's any way I could ring Marcie and beg her for something else – a desk job, research maybe, something I could do from the flat that'd tide me over. I don't want to do this.

I really don't want it. Then again, they're showing a lot of faith in me, with this. And an advance means funds in the bank, and soon. Funds I can't afford to pass up.

'I do need the work,' I tell him.

'I know. More than that. You need *this* work.' Hal leans forward. 'You've wanted this career so terribly much, all your life. Haven't you?' His green eyes soften, take me in now. 'You've sacrificed everything for this career, the chance of an education you could have gone for, the good money you could have made doing a steady job elsewhere.' He hesitates ever so minutely before adding, 'the girl you loved …'

My eyes go to his, startled. 'It's been a year, Hal. I'm over her.' I take a long slug of my coffee.

'You sure?' His eyes crinkle in sympathy.

'I'm … completely sure.'

'I'm glad.' He seems relieved. 'You just … Camille tells me you never replied to our wedding invite, man.'

'I'm sorry?' *Those two are getting married? Fucking hell, I knew he was dating my ex, but when did* that *happen?* I've been out of circulation longer than I thought, clearly. I drop Marcie's rescue proposal back onto the coffee table and it tips his water glass over onto its side. '*Sorry*, man.' A small river of Perrier dribbles onto all the papers. There are a lot of papers. 'Do you need me to get you another glass of …?'

'No. But you might want to …' His eyes go back to the coffee table, where I dumped a load of un-sorted letters just this morning.

Never mind those. I pick up a nearby tea cloth, glad of the excuse to put my head down while I dab at the mess.

'You did get it, right?' He sounds sheepish. 'The wedding invite?' I blink.

'Uh. The truth is, I haven't been opening my mail much lately.'

'So I see.'

'It's too depressing, but … that invite, if it came, it'll be in amongst this lot.' I pick up a wodge of soggy papers and he helpfully picks up the other half. 'It'll be in here somewhere, for sure.'

'It's in a pink envelope. So you didn't know?' He's pulling an apologetic face at me. 'But, now you know – we're good?'

'Of course we're good. She's a free woman. I'm a free man. We're all good.' I look away, feeling a strange mix of happiness for them alongside a little envy that I don't myself, have that happiness, anymore. 'There you go.' I wave the pink letter I've plucked out of the pile, open it up. 'I got your invite, Hal. You're marrying her on the last Saturday in May.' Dammit, but that's soon … I should have known about this. If I'd kept in contact with all our mutual friends, I would have known about it.

'Do you think you'll make it?' He asks.

'I don't in all honestly know.' It's not just a matter of getting there. Hal seems to be aware of a lot, but does he know this; how I've slowly and insidiously isolated myself from everyone who matters because I couldn't bear the thought of them seeing me like this, unable to go out, do normal things that everyone else takes for granted, *be* normal? The fact is there's still a big part of me longing to rejoin the human race, a part of me that misses my friends like crazy. 'I'd like to say yes. Let's hope.'

'Good man.' Hal smiles. Lifts his shoulders up, now. 'Hey. You've got to *trust*, right? We all visit those places, at times, when we're …' He does a little motion with his hands, 'beset with doubts, can't see our way beyond it.'

'Beset with doubts. Yeah.'

'Can I offer you one piece of advice, Nathaniel?'

'Feel free.'

'Moving past these panic attacks isn't going to be easy. Just find one reason for *you* that makes it personal and compelling. Find the person or the thing this represents that'll make achieving this matter more than anything. Don't try and put yourself through this by an act of will, alone.'

'Find a compelling reason. Sure. Thanks, Man.'

My former colleague is reaching over to place his pile of damp letters back on the table when one of them catches his eye. He does a double take.

'Dear *Dad*?' He glances questioningly at me, and I can virtually see his journalistic curiosity kicking in. 'Surely that's not …?'

'Are you kidding me?' I give a small laugh, shaking my head rapidly. 'Definitely not me. The kid's mis-delivered it, whoever they are.' Hal's still staring at me. Not convinced?

'Please help.' Hal reads out loud the words in bold red on the back. He turns the envelope towards me.

'Pretty intense, huh?' I agree. 'I've been asking around, as best I can, about it. I checked with the letting agency for this flat, but the last two tenants before me were female. I have no idea who that belongs to. It's probably some kid's idea of a prank …'

'Have you thought of opening it?' he suggests.

'Me? You think I should open it?'

'There might be a return address inside? Find out who sent it, at least? If there's an address you can explain their mistake.' He stands, now, needing to take his leave. He looks a lot more at ease than he did when he first came into the flat – because he's found out why I never replied to their invite?

'Yeah, sure,' I tell him confidently. 'I can do that.'

That's a task that'll be one hell of a lot easier for me than what he and Marcie have put together in their proposal, that's for sure.

Nate

Looks like I'm not the only one beset by troubles at the moment.

Dear Dad,
    When I asked Nan where you lived, she
told me it was here. I have never wrote to
you before because Nan told me to leave
you alone. She said that was what you
wanted but now I am writing. I hope
you do not mind if I tell you some things
about me and maybe you will be proud?

    1st. I love football. I am not very good
at it. I like to play when I can.
    2nd. I am helpful. I like to help Nan a lot
especially when she has trouble with her legs.
    3rd. I am a little bit fat but I would like
to be thin.
    4th. There are boys at school who say
bad things to me. Sometimes they hit me.
    5th. Sometimes I feel sad.

Please could you write back and also tell
me some things about you?

Love, Adam.
Ps:

Nan is not well again. She cannot come to watch me at Sports Day this year. Please would you be able to come and watch me instead? If you can come I will be very happy.

Hey, I'm sorry, man. My frown deepens as I fold the letter away, wishing I'd never opened it. *There's been a mix-up of some sort,* I tell him in my head. *If your old nan told you your dad lives here then she's got it wrong. I can't help you out, kid. Not because I don't want to, but because I'm not him, am I? The one you're looking for.*

I'm not him and even if I were him – in this place I'm at in my life – I couldn't help the lad. I can't help anyone right now, not even myself. I push the letter back into its envelope, needing to go shove Marcie's proposal and the award they gave me out of sight because, now that Hal's gone, I can't bear to look at them.

Seeing him today has reminded me of a lot of things; all that has gone past, and now, even worse, what is coming up. Hal is getting married. To Camille. I'm glad for them, yes, but I thought at one time that would be me. I imagined I'd be in a very different place in my life by now, not … stuck in a room surrounded by a pile of letters I should have dealt with, weeks ago, people I don't know how to answer, bills I don't know how to pay. For a few minutes I can't even bring myself to move. I just sit there with my head in my hands, feeling sore.

Damn, but I really imagined my life would be a whole lot different to this.

Sometimes I feel sad. Hey, you and me both, kid. That's life sometimes. That's the way it goes.

I get up, abruptly. I don't want to think about this letter anymore, either. For all I know, this kid's already recognised his mistake, forgotten all about it. Maybe anytime now he'll find his father and his problems will be over. I know that mine will not. I wipe at my face with my sleeve and go open up the curtains that I closed immediately after Hal left. The light comes flooding back in, bright swathes of silver washing out the top of my desk while the dark spire of Rochester Cathedral is silhouetted over the way. Five, maybe ten minutes walk from there – according to the address at the top of this letter – is the house at the top of Churchfields where the child lives.

I need to forget about him, let his problem go because it's not mine. All very well for Hal to suggest I reply to the kid, explain his mistake, but this is nothing but a distraction. It's not what I need to do. I go and hold the kid's envelope over the wastepaper bin, all set to rip it in two, chuck it out.

But for some reason, I don't.

Jenna

Okay, enough. We've been at this for three hours and all the other places this guy has shown me have been too old or too dark or too ugly.

'This is perfect!' I smile at the estate agent guy. 'No need to look any further, I've found what I was looking for.'

The man pauses, the key halfway out of his pocket.

'We haven't been inside yet, Madam. And I haven't shown you the other top-floor bedsits we have along The Terrace, either. We can look at them all if you like.'

'No,' I shake my head. 'I won't be wanting any of the others. I've already been sold on this one.'

'But ...'

'In particular, I've been sold on the doorway.' The arched stone doorway, with its old, wooden, metal-studded, green-painted door which it would be so easy to imagine some medieval scene waiting beyond. I let my fingertips brush over the surface of it and it makes me feel ... happy

'This is the kind of door you'd *want* to come home to.' It makes me feel catapulted back somewhere, into a different era. A memory whispers, laughing like a child in the corner of my mind before rushing away.

'Madam?' He's already got a move on, making a show of carefully cleaning his shoes on the mat beforehand and I follow him inside.

'It's bijoux, but highly desirable,' he notes, leading me upstairs to the first-floor bedsit. Bijoux, indeed. In under five minutes, I have seen all that I need to see. 'Newly renovated, close to all amenities ...' he's intoning.

'It's perfect.' I give myself a little hug. This has been even easier than I thought it would be, despite all Magda's dire warnings about *getting a move on with the job-hunting and the flat-hunting because it might not be the walk in the park I'm expecting.* Ha, just you wait till I tell her it's taken me a mere half a day; she won't believe it.

'Let me just check something ...' He puts his head down, tapping in some details on his laptop, now. 'Ah, yes. Sorry, but it looks as if this one might have been taken, Madam.'

I blink, feeling my stomach fall away.

'They can't,' I tell him. I've just fallen in love with the downstairs door. 'This place is going to be my place. I felt it the moment I saw it from the outside.'

'We have some others, very like it,' he begins.

'The others further down don't have the same door,' I point out.

'No. I'm sorry, Madam,' he says, and for a moment I am not sure what else I'm going to do. I shouldn't have let myself fall in love so easily, perhaps? I have to live somewhere. Where the hell am I going to live? Now that I've seen this place I don't want to rent anywhere else.

'*Actually.*' After examining his records a little more closely, he pulls a smile. 'I see this morning's viewers haven't confirmed their interest, yet.'

'They haven't?'

'Not yet.'

'Good.' I sit down at the tiny kitchen table. 'Let's confirm *my* interest, then. Let's fill out the forms, and get it done.'

'Now? Er ... well. It's a little irregular. We'd normally do these at the office.' He sits and pulls up the relevant document on his laptop. 'I'll let you fill in all these fields. We can just as easily do them here if you're in a hurry.'

'I am.' I feel a rush of happiness, like butterflies in my stomach. And relief. I wasn't much looking forward to moving out of Magda's so soon, if I'm honest. But now it's okay because this place is going to be mine, yay! My fingers fumble like thick butterfingers on his keyboard.

After a bit:

'It says here I need to put two months' rent deposit down on this flat, is that right?'

'It is. That won't be a problem, I hope?' He smiles now, a little obsequious, reminds me of the butler in *Upstairs, Downstairs,* but funds are not my immediate problem.

'Nope. By my calculations I can afford to live here on my savings alone for a good three months before I run to ground.'

'Quite.' For the first time, he shoots me a slightly worried look. 'Always good to have a bit put by, in case of emergencies,' he adds, apropos of nothing.

'Yeah.' I shrug. 'Um ... this bit here where it says I have to fill in my current employer, etc, shall I just leave it blank for the moment, then?'

'Not at all, Madam.' He seems put out at the suggestion. 'It's an absolute requirement that you fill in that part of the form.'

I look up from his keyboard. 'You mean, you need me to fill it in, like, right now?'

'Naturally, you must fill it in.' The guy's face falls suddenly. 'You do actually *have* a job don't you, Madam?'

Bugger.

'I ... I will do,' I assure him. 'In fact, I've got an interview for one this very week. Tomorrow, in fact.'

'You have an interview?' He turns his laptop round slowly and stares at it. He's not taking it back, is he? I haven't finished, yet.

'Does this mean that you don't, at this moment in time, actually ...?'

'I don't have a job yet,' I finish for him. 'I do have funds, however. Enough to last me three months like I said, and I am absolutely guaranteed to have something sorted job-wise before then.'

'Ah.'

'... if not actually by the end of tomorrow,' I add, to show him how confident I am about it.

The man sighs quietly.

'In that case.' He glances at his watch. 'Perhaps you'd like to come back to us as soon as the job issue is settled?'

Job *issue*?

'I'd rather not. I have to leave where I'm currently staying, so my friend can get her room back,' I explain, 'and I wanted to get this side of things sorted this morning.'

'The thing is.' He clears his throat, clearly uncomfortable. 'We are going to need to see some proof of regular income, Miss.'

So I'm 'Miss', now. Not 'Madam' anymore?

'Without that, we can't organise a flat-let for you no matter how many funds you may have put by.'

'Oh.' We both look towards the door.

'So.' He turns back to me. 'You really need to get that job, first.'

'I see.'

He stands up now and I stand with him, feeling my face go pink. That's it, we're done, then? Damn. I have the money, I could have shown him my bank details but he wasn't interested. What's his problem anyway?

I pick up my handbag, feeling a little flatter than I did a few moments ago. Sheesh. Mags wasn't kidding about this flat-hunting business being tricky, was she? Downstairs again, I take my leave of him and turn right, heading up toward The Esplanade to get in a brisk, head-clearing walk. There is nothing else I can do now before my interview tomorrow at Smiler's Body Art, which I *am* going to get, despite what this estate agent guy thinks. I'll be the best-qualified person there by a mile, I know it.

At least, I hope I will be.

I think I will.

I just hope they need me to start soon-ish.

Nate

I roll over on the carpet, feeling the burning in my biceps and my belly from the push-ups and abdominal crunches I've done. Over by the window, there's a bright glow of light lining the bottom of the curtains, heralding a crisp new morning. It's been a whole day already since Hal came by with Marcie's video-diary proposal for me. Twenty-four hours that I've spent almost entirely trying to summon up the mental energy to do it.

Turning to face the camera I've placed at eye-level on the floor, I say:

'I am going to try leaving the house this morning.' I pause. 'This used to be something I could do as easily as anyone. Going outside was as easy as pie.' I wince, turning away to wipe my hot face with the back of my hand. Talking to camera also used to be as easy as pie for me. It isn't at the moment, not now that I'm the subject of the piece. But I've still got to do it. I take in a slow, deep breath, reminding myself why: SWP want to see footage of what happens when I go out – just fifteen minutes, and then they've promised to send me through the first part of that advance. I need it. I have no other options left. Fifteen minutes of exposing what's become of Nate Hardman to the whole world and I get paid. I get to keep my flat.

And I don't want to think about what'll happen if I lose the flat.

I pull myself to my feet, picking up the camera as I go. 'I'm pumped. I've just done an hour's high-intensity training but look …'

I stick my hands out to show how much they're trembling. 'This is a physiological reaction. It's nothing to do with what I know, or what I believe in my head. When you're in this situation, it's like your body's made up its own mind you're in danger and it ... reacts accordingly. It's a fear response. Even though there's nothing to ...' I swallow, my mouth suddenly dry. I do not want to talk anymore.

I take a swig of water from a bottle, go pick up the letter I penned late last night to that lad, Adam, explaining his error. I put in a short note for his nan, too. Maybe it's none of my business, but that kid could get into serious difficulties if he's going round asking for help from random strangers, and she'd want to know about that.

I hope she would.

I wave the letter – my immediate reason for stepping out today, my mercy mission – at the camera.

'I'm going, now,' I say, getting a shot of me grabbing my house key. 'I've got this letter I want to hand-deliver. I am going to attempt to go out now and do it. I am going to show you what happens to me when I do.'

At the mirror by the door, there is an infinitesimally small pause while I check out my reflection and groan inwardly. *Let's not think about this, Nate. Let's not think. Just do it.*

'Okay. I'm going out now.' Coming down, I take the stairs two at a time. I need to do this thing quickly – get out while the adrenalin is flowing, while I'm fired up and I still can. *There's been insurgent gunfire heard outside,* I pretend. *It's rounding on a civilian-led stronghold, a hospital, maybe, a waiting room full of elderly people and children. The kind of thing most people would run away from.* Make like you're out on assignment, Nate, and yours is the only lens through which the world has any hope of viewing this desperate scene and if you don't capture it right this moment then nobody ever will.

I'll do a voice-over on this later, I think, explain what was going through my head. At the front door, pausing for a micro-second, the daylight after the dark hall is blinding and I catch that, camera still held at arm's length, me screwing up my eyes, what that feels like.

'This feels pretty intense.' I take stock. 'My heart is pounding, gearing up for action and all I'm planning to do is … walk down the street.' I turn and shut the front door and now – hey presto – it is the big moment. I am standing in the great outside. On Rochester High Street. There are people around, not too many, but some, nonetheless. I swallow, blinking in the bright sunlight.

Okay. I check the camera's still running. It's not mine, and from what I could tell from playing with it earlier, it's a little temperamental. 'So far, I'm good. I've got a slight churning in my stomach but I can handle that. I'm going to walk fast, now. That might be my best strategy. Going slow gives me too much time to think about it.' I put my head down and go for it. 'I'm blocking out all the noises I can hear around me as best I can. I'm still aware of them, though. That tiny dog barking from the doorway of that flat. The woman calling her husband to look at some bargain fruit. That seagull.' I stop, watching it take off from a rooftop suddenly, screeching.

'Everything sounds very loud, it all feels too near to me, but I'm using a technique we used in the field when we needed to focus; I put all those noises in a box and muffle them. I'm thinking of the road I need to get to at the top of Churchfields, just that. I'm not thinking of anything else.'

As I walk, my eyes go down, skimming the pavement and my shoulders hunch. It's hard to keep the camera aloft walking like this so I point it facing forward instead. I tape the scene going on around me instead of me; the posy somebody's placed on the steps by the war memorial; a wide angle shot of the crowd of French kids, day-trippers, laughing and jostling each other outside the sweet shop. I stop talking, because I can't be doing with it when all my attention is taken up with trying to avoid bumping into people because my own body is feeling as fragile and brittle as an eggshell. Man, this feels bad.

Now that I am this far up the High Street, by the pebbled road beside the Cathedral arch, there are more people going about their business. A lot more. Should I go on? Should I? A couple of pigeons launch out of the way of a bicycle now, startling me. The windy noise from their wings *flap, flap, flap*, assaults my ears. I have to stop where I am on the pavement, feeling something deeply uncomfortable and all too familiar starting up in my chest. That pain. The tightness in my lungs. God, no. Not now. I haven't got anywhere near where I wanted to go, yet.

While I hesitate, a guy on a bike, not looking, nearly runs me down. Again.

'Idiot!' The cyclist turns and gives me the finger. Another layer is torched off my already threadbare sense of safety. For a moment I just stand there, shaking. Part of me wants to swear back at him. Pull him off his bike and tear him limb from limb, in fact, and kick his skinny bicycling legs right into the gutter. Another part of me – at the moment, it feels like the stronger part – wants to run straight back home. *You promised*, this part is warning, *you promised that you would only do what you could. You wouldn't push it.*

A couple of older women nearby have stopped their chatting to stare at me. Can they see it on my face, what's going on for me at this moment? I should be taping this, a faraway thought reminds me, I should be getting this – my reaction – all down on camera for Marcie's video but that seems like the least important thing in the world right now. I rub at my chest, willing the tightness to go away, wiling myself to continue on my journey, *just do it.* I still want to deliver that letter, prove to myself that, if I put all my efforts into it, I can do what I came out for.

But I can't. Since the brush with the cyclist just now, the rest of the world seems to have speeded up while I, on the other hand, am going far more slowly.

It is not a good feeling. It is a very bad feeling.

And then the thing that I've been dreading, happens.

'Well whaddya know!' A friendly bloke's voice is at my elbow. 'It's Nate, right? Nate Hardman.' I look up and some guy's face swims before me. Who the hell is this? 'It's Tim,' he obliges. 'From Rochester Rovers.'

I stare at him blankly.

'Footie. Saturday morning friendlies. Up on Jackson's field, you used to come to those, remember?'

'Tim,' I get out. That's just … dandy. That I should venture out for the first time in weeks and someone who actually knows me has to come across me. Like *this*.

'You okay, mate?' He's regarding me quizzically.

I nod emphatically, holding my ribs. 'Breathless. Been jogging,' I tell him. *What else am I supposed to say?* If that blatant lie is on camera I'll have to delete it.

Or maybe not. Maybe it'll be a good illustration of … of *something*.

'Pretty out of shape, huh?' he commiserates. 'Maybe you could come back to training? We're practising on the field this weekend if you're game?'

Can't he see I'm not game?

'Yeah. Maybe.'

'I'll look out for you then.'

'Yup.' I start to limp away from him now and I hear his short, puzzled laugh behind me as I go. He'll think I'm being rude, but I don't care. I just want to get away from him as fast as I can, don't want anyone seeing me like this, but I feel so slow. I must look like a spaceman in his bloody spacesuit making deliberate, wide strides across the surface of the moon. What's he gonna think? This is … it's mortifying. It's why I haven't been out in so many weeks, exactly because of the fear that *this* would happen.

And now, that harsh sound I can hear in my ears is my own breath rasping in my throat. Does nobody else hear it? Can he? My God. My breath sounds like the last dying breaths of an astronaut before he runs out of air entirely. I let out a long, painful groan and the two women, who were staring at me earlier by the corner, mutter something about *young people on drugs*.

I'm not on drugs. I look up at them as I approach, hoping they'll see this but they take a few steps back. Some little voice tucked far, far away in my mind nudges me; I should be pointing the camera at them at this point, taping their reaction, taping my own. But no fucking way is that happening. The pain in my chest twists a little deeper and it's warning me, I know. Like a dog being yanked back on a short, short lead, the desire to run home builds in ever-increasing waves until at last it is terrible, irresistible and non-negotiable. *Go home, go home.* Nothing else will solve it, nothing else will alleviate it, unless I do.

And I have to obey it. I hate that I have to, I hate it more than I can say, that I have to abandon all other plans and just give in to it. *At least,* I tell myself, *I'll have got the fifteen minutes I need for Marcie to release the advance.* I'd hoped to deliver Adam's letter but from my own point of view, keeping the flat is what this outing was really all about, right?

But today is turning out to be one of those times when life just keeps giving.

When I arrive back at my flat and check the camera ten minutes later, exhausted and covered in sticky sweat from the effort, there's another nasty surprise in store.

Nothing's taped.

Jenna

I have got to get this job. No job equals no flat, and staying on at Magda's once her brother arrives is *so* not on the cards. In order not to be late, I left the flat early and in order not to be *too* early, I have been walking up and down The Esplanade for the last twenty minutes. The river breeze has been blowing so hard in my face it could be winter. Jed Miller, owner of Smiler's Body Art, notices it the minute I walk in.

'Rudolph's arrived!' He points to my frozen nose.

'Ha ha,' I say. A joker, this one. His own nose is so large and bulbous you just know he'll have heard this comment before.

'Come right in, Jenna.' He motions me over to the comfy chairs he's got by the window while his assistant brings us over a cup of hot brew. Three clients sitting on regular table chairs are already getting their tattoos done, two of them on their arms and the girl nearest me is having a tiny robin etched onto her ankle.

'We've got some reclining chairs out back for those who need to lie down.' He follows my line of gaze. 'Or for those who might request a little more privacy.'

I nod. 'Do your artists use a thermal fax, here at all? I see that girl's using a mag to trace the initial line-work on by hand.'

He smiles. 'Wonderful piece of equipment, I agree. Ours is currently down for repair, though.'

'Ah.' I give a mental sigh of relief. At least they're not using equipment that's out of the ark, and that's a plus. As we sit, I can't help noticing all the studio designs on the walls. Faeries and wizards and dragons abound.

'You like?'

'I feel like I've stumbled into some Elvish woodland grotto.' I laugh. Then, with the estate agent's words yesterday about *getting a job* still ringing in my ears, I add quickly, 'But I like elves. No problem with elves. And dragons, of course. And fairy princesses. Those long flowing robes can be real fun to colour in ...'

His eyebrows go up a bit.

'Of course, we also keep a different set of design suggestions in the room at the back. People like what they like, it's not for us to judge, is it?'

I think about that for a moment.

'I don't judge, but there are a couple of things I won't do,' I tell him.

'Oh?'

'I don't, personally, ink minors, no matter how on board with it their parents might be. And I don't ink faces, ever. I've seen too many people live to regret it.'

'Fair enough.' He looks thoughtful for a minute and I wonder if he's been put off? Damn. I examine the chip in my nail polish for a moment, not saying anything else. Perhaps I should have secured the job first – and the bedsit – before being so open with him about that? I add, tentatively, 'I'd be very happy to work here, if you want me.'

'You certainly have the experience and the references. From this, I can see you completed your apprenticeship some six months ago and your teacher – Mario Scellini – was pretty happy with you. As for your portfolio,' he enthuses, opening it up in front of him now, 'you have some pretty nifty – nay, exquisite – artwork in here, no question about it.'

I beam, warming to him.

'Thank you.'

'It says here you actually studied at the Royal College of Art.' He sounds impressed.

42

'I did.'

He nods, thoughtful. 'From your C.V. you're also a qualified and experienced art and primary school teacher, and yet … here you are, applying for a job like this?'

I shuffle my bottom a little uncomfortably on the chair. 'It's what I love doing, and it's also how I've made my living in Sicily,' I tell him.

'Why not teach, if it's what you trained to do?' His head is to one side, curious.

I shrug. 'Didn't work out for me,' I tell him.

'Was it the kids? You weren't in love with the crowd-control exercise that modern teaching has become?'

I look at my hands. 'I have no problem with crowd control, Mr Miller. I loved teaching the kids. I loved working with the kids.' I gaze out of the window for a second, away from his penetrating gaze because none of this seems relevant to me. I'm applying for a different job altogether; why does he care so much why I left my last profession?

'If you're worried that I won't be able to handle the more difficult clients …'

'Oh, you'll be able to handle them all right. I have no qualms about that.' Hearing the ghost of a smile in his voice, I turn back to him.

'What then?'

He says nothing for a few seconds. 'I just wondered,' he says, 'Why it didn't work out for you. Will you tell me?' he persists.

'It just didn't,' I say softly, feeling a strange hollow feeling in my stomach, now. I haven't got this job, have I?

At last, he opens his hands.

'Okay. If you want it, it's yours. There weren't any other takers and I see no reason not to give you a try-out.'

I let out a breath. 'Thank you. *Thank you.*'

'You sound mightily relieved.'

'I am.'

'I can offer you work on a commission-only basis, I'm afraid.'

'It's something. It's a start.' I smile. Then I admit, 'Besides, as long as I've got this as a place of employment to put down for the estate agents, at least I'll be able to rent out a flat.'

'I see.' He frowns slightly at that. 'You can quote us as employers if you need to, by all means, only ...'

'Only ...?'

'I'm not sure if this will be enough for them. They might want to see proof of a regular salary going in every month.'

'No kidding?' The last of the tea which I've just swallowed goes down the wrong way and I splutter.

'I think they might. My daughter encountered the exact same problem a while back when she didn't have a regular job.' He gets up and I follow him over to the counter.

'Shit,' I say, wiping my mouth. '*Sorry.*'

'That's okay.' Both he and his assistant give me a strange look, and the hollow feeling returns. Does this mean that the job I've just secured here won't count after all? I feel – deflated. Like all the stuffing has been knocked out of me. Like little Bertie Bear, all saggy and floppy and not able to stand upright by myself. I don't like the feeling.

'You all right?'

'I'm ...' I want to say *yes, yes of course I am okay, I can handle this disappointment, it's just a minor setback, nothing to cry about, right?* But weirdly, no words will come out at all. I wipe at my eyes brusquely as, right on cue, a text from Mags pings in.

Hope flat-hunting's going okay? Edwin's arrived so I've put your gear into the living room for now. See you l8r.

'Great. *Great.* Now I've lost my bed at my friend's house.'

'Not really turning out to be your day, is it, Jenna?' Jed Miller's rummaging about at the back of the till, looking for something. He brings out a little business card with an intricate, Celtic love-knot on the front. 'Listen, I don't know how helpful this will be, but there's this friend of mine – Christiane Finlayson – very well known on the tattoo-circuit, you heard of her?'

I shake my head. 'She owns a shop near Rochester?'

'No, but she does a lot of work internationally,' he informs me. 'She's been looking for an assistant, someone who can draw beautifully. From what I've seen, you'd more than fit the bill, provided you were prepared to travel a bit. Why don't you give her a ring and in the meantime I'll also put in a word for you?'

'Thank you.' I take the card from him, my spirits reviving a little. I like the sound of this Christiane Finlayson and her international travel.

'And if that fails, you can always go back to your teaching, can't you? Whatever it was put you off, you might have a different experience this time.'

I give a small shake of my head. 'That's not a field I'd want to go back into.'

'Beggars can't be choosers.' He shrugs. 'At least you'd never be unemployed.'

I look out of his window and a flurry of rain spatters across the glass. When is it going to stop raining? When will the summer come, finally, so I can feel warm again and settled again and then maybe my life will start feeling like it should do? Perhaps it will, I muse, when I live in the flat behind that solid, green door. Perhaps. I'm going to need a home base soon, whatever it is I end up doing, so I *have* to get that flat.

'They're always crying out for teachers aren't they? Like nurses,' his assistant says helpfully.

'They are,' I agree. Reluctantly, I bring out my phone and pull up the number of the supply-teaching agency Magda so helpfully texted through to me earlier on. I *so* do not want to have to do this.

'They are crying out for teachers all over the place, only …' I leave the last part of my sentence unfinished.

I'm pretty sure they aren't crying out for teachers like me.

45

Nate

Seriously?

Heart thudding, I fast forward through the blank minutes at the beginning of the tape till finally, *finally*, I find there is some footage I managed to take. *Holy crap.* Like a complete newbie all I seem to have captured is the backs of people's heads, some shots of the ground, a few vignettes of myself, grimacing, not saying much. How can this be? How? Maybe I was more nervous than I knew, maybe I wasn't using the camera properly – my own camera is damaged, I used the one Hal loaned me when he came on Monday – but however I managed it, I've got no usable footage whatsoever.

I can't believe I just did that. I lay the camera down on my desk in disgust.

Shaking, I go pick up the letter, thrown to one side as I came in, that arrived in the morning post while I was out. Then I see it doesn't actually have a stamp. This looks suspiciously like it might be another one from the kid. Jeez Louise. Another note? I haven't even dealt with the first one, yet! I don't want to deal with it, either. It's nothing to do with me, *he's* nothing to do with me, so why does he keep sending stuff here? That old nan of his has a lot of answer for and if I ever catch up with her …

Feeling more angry than I should be, I tear open the kid's second note, and it turns out to be a lovingly rendered drawing of a flower-filled field with a green fence down one side. At the far end, he's drawn in just the *ears* of a large brown horse. Not the whole horse, not even the face of the horse, just the ears. What's that about? I stare at it for a moment before turning it over to read the note on the back.

For my dad. Don't forget I am waiting to hear from you. Love from Adam.

Great. Now he's drawn his dad a horse. Part of a horse. But I'm not his dad, so what am I supposed to do with this? Chuck it away? Keep it with the other one? Stick it with a magnet onto my fridge? If I don't get some money in soon, I'll be evicted from this flat and I won't even have a fridge to stick it on.

Camille would have laughed at this, I know; the footage I took this morning that didn't tape or was unusable, the boy who isn't my son sending me pictures of a horse's ears. She'd have said *the universe is sending you a message, Nate!* 'cos that's the way she thinks. But, what's this all about?

I sit down heavily in my chair with a loud groan. If the universe is sending me messages, it's speaking in Sanskrit, it's speaking in Ancient Greek. If the universe is sending me messages, why doesn't it just send them in good, plain old English, which is the language that I speak? *Ears*, for crap's sake. Now, if they were *listening ears*, that might be different, because that is what I wish I had, right now. If the owner of those ears happened to be someone I could share my troubles with, without fear of censure or judgement, then … maybe I really would be able to tell my story.

I walk back over to the camera on my desk. Without thinking, I turn it on now, sit down to face it. *Perhaps*, the idea flies in from nowhere, *that is what this video-diary is really about?* The camera listens, but it never judges; it only captures what is. I failed in my attempt going out just now and that's left me feeling shaken and upset. But perhaps I don't need to go out anywhere to make a start on this video-diary. Perhaps all I need is to sit down and tell my story to the camera?

47

As soon as I think that, there is such a deep sting of sadness in my throat, I don't know how I'll be able to speak. I don't, in truth, even know what it is I want to say. For a moment, I do not speak.

I sit. Silent and still.

'I'm Nate Hardman, a former front line journalist,' I say at last. 'For the last three years I've been a frequent traveller to the most dangerous places in the world.' I pause. 'Four months ago, shadowing insurgents on the Khost-Gardez Pass in Eastern Afghanistan, myself and a fellow reporter Jim Nolan found ourselves under fire from a shower of stray bullets. That incident …' My voice sticks for a moment now, goes a little quiet. 'That was the beginning of a very altered life for me. One where I have become virtually a prisoner in my own home.' I pick up a stone-cold mug of coffee and take a sip. Place it deliberately back down on the desk, biding my time. Man, it is hard, even harder than I'd thought it would be, recounting this.

I push back my hair with the flat of my hand.

'Four months ago, I ended up with a shattered tibia, medevac'd back to the UK while my colleague – he never even made it onto the stretcher alive.' There's another pause now. A long pause while the camera keeps on rolling, a long whirring sound in the otherwise silence of my suddenly sunny, dusty room and I'm staring at the green leather top on my desk, trying to remember how to keep it all together, just tell the story. I take in a deep, silent breath and go on.

'One minute, Jim's sitting on a boulder next to me, drinking coffee, cracking jokes. We'd had a quiet few days beforehand. Word had come through that the army forces had moved North. It was so quiet, in fact …' I pull a sad smile. 'So quiet we'd got round to shooting stills of the landscape.' I indicate a photo on the wall behind my head, now. 'All that yellow sand and those grey rock formations and that bleached-out blue dome of a sky. There's something very edgy about that, the colour of a sky that can be filled at any moment with rocket fire.' I shoot a look directly into

48

camera. Open my hands. '*Time Magazine* cover material.' I swallow. That's what Jim had been joking about when the first volley of shots came our way.

'When the sniper fire started up, Jim followed his instincts. He decided to forgo the first rule of reporting in combat zones – he tracked the direction of fire with his camera. It's always a risk, that. It might have been what drew their attention to our position, because they started aiming at us after that. One of their bullets hit him. I tried to push him to the ground, get him out of their line of sight. I *tried* … but it was no good.' I shake my head now. 'By the time the bullets started hitting me, I knew there was nothing more I could do to help him. I had to get myself away or I'd end up …' I trail off, pull my coffee cup a little closer towards me, cradling it in my hands.

'He died. I survived. He was a courageous man, a *good* man. He still bled out. I couldn't save him.' I look down at my hands clasped tightly together round the cup. 'Before that day I'd always felt protected, invincible. *Safe.*' My voice is shaking but I carry on. 'After I came home I started to wonder if that's what Jim felt just before the bullet took him. I began to ask myself if he ever realised how vulnerable he was, how fragile in an unsafe world? Jim was so focussed on his role as a reporter, maybe he never did.'

'But after that, *I* did. It took a few weeks, but I began to have increasing difficulty going out to places. Everywhere I went, all I was aware of was that I didn't feel safe. In the end, I couldn't even attend the memorial service at the Cathedral which his widow invited me to.'

The memory of that pulls me up, now.

God, what am I doing, sitting here taping myself talking about all this stuff? How I failed Jim and now I'm a pathetic recluse. Is this really what Marcie wants, I wonder now? Is it what Smart World Productions want? I flick off the recording button and I turn away. Who wants to know about this, anyway? Who's listening, who's going to want to hear?

49

After a while, I get up to throw out the dregs of my coffee in the kitchen sink. When I come back with a fresh cup, the kid's drawing of the field – the one with the ridiculous horse's ears – is still sitting on the table.

Don't forget I am waiting to hear from you.

That kid Adam will imagine his dad's ignoring him, I muse. Is he at school right now, sad but hopeful, wondering if maybe he'll get a response today? That one's still at *my* door. I'm really bummed I didn't make it as far as Churchfields, for his sake almost as much as mine. I need to reply. I googled his address but there's no one called Boxley – the name he gave on his letter – listed as having a telephone number, no way I can contact him unless I actually go down there.

And I can't go down there.

On impulse, I pick up the drawing and sellotape it to the fridge. I couldn't help Jim and I can't get as far as this lad's house and I can't stop the landslide that is currently my life but I must, surely, be able to do *something* to get hold of this kid and help to put him back on the right track? I don't know what, yet but …

The one thing I am not going to do is ignore him.

Jenna

Damn it, I am lost. I crumple up the site map of St Anthony's Primary that I downloaded last night and stare at the profusion of site works out the front which I have walked around three times already. I'll admit – this supply job has come in a little sooner than I'd anticipated – I was only at Jed Miller's two days ago – thank heavens I kept my DBS checks up to date. Since my room at Magda's has already been requisitioned for her brother's use, I had to sleep on the couch again last night, and I am not quite awake yet. Nowhere can I spy the way in.

I am lost. And, though it is only 8 a.m., any minute now, I will also be late for my first day supply teaching. In the distance, coming somewhere from the playground out back, I can hear a coach yelling at his football team. They're a keen bunch, obviously. In bright and early this sunny Thursday morning for training because St Anthony's, is *an enthusiastic, modern, equal-opportunities school inspiring excellence in pupils and staff members alike.* They win a lot of medals for this and that and everything, according to their website, so going the extra mile must pay off. The football pitch is a bit far for me to go, however, to ask for the directions I need. There must be someone nearer.

'He don't have no Mum,' a voice coming from round the corner pipes up, now. 'She gave birth to him and died of shock, I heard.'

Uh-oh.

'No wonder his Mum abandoned him. He's a little runt. He can't even walk straight,' another voice chips in.

Pulling my hands out of my cardigan pockets, I round the corner, and there they are, lurking menacingly.

'You lot can stop that right *this instant*.' There are three of them: the lanky, dopey one, the bully-beef barrel of a lad and the smaller, dark-haired boy who'll be the clever one. Then there's the younger kid, fair-haired and red-faced, cowering on the ground, who's totally invisible till you get right up to their huddle. The ring-leader's eyes narrow, not recognising me as anyone in authority, but he's smart enough not to say anything. Not yet.

'Who's she?' Bully-beef turns away a little, muttering under his breath.

'Dunno,' says Lanky. 'His *Mum*?' Snigger.

'He's too ugly for her to be his mum.'

'And too fat.'

'And she's *alive*.'

'Right,' I cut across them. 'You, you and you. Step away from him.'

'We haven't done anything.' The small one turns carefully neutral eyes on me. The other two stop smirking.

I ignore him. 'You, lad,' I address the one on the ground. 'What's your name and form?'

'Adam Boxley, Miss. 4C.'

'You can make your way to your classroom, now, Adam.'

'Thank you, Miss.' A pair of grateful, green eyes come up to meet mine but it is very obvious that he is trying manfully to avoid coming to tears. I wonder: is it because of what they just said about his mum or because – as I can clearly see now – they have tied his shoelaces together? Poor kid. Seeing his attempt to stand sets the three of them off in fits of giggles. It is *so* horribly amusing that lanky and bully-beef bend over double. Even smart Alec can't hide a grin. On me, it has a different effect altogether. They will see.

'Take your shoes off,' I tell him calmly.

'Miss?'

'Let me see them.'

He does what he's told, wincing when he has to slip them off to reveal his pathetic holey socks with his toes peeping out in various places. Okay, I have seen this a hundred times before, socks get holes in them, it's a fact of life. Children from the best homes come to school with holes in their socks sometimes, but to him it's clearly a big deal. I wonder – just who he *does* have looking out for him, at home? I don't know how true it is, what they were just saying about his mum not being around but has he not at least got a father?

'We were helping Boxley tie his shoelaces,' the dark-haired one shows his bravery now, looking directly at me. 'He's so stupid he doesn't even know how to put them on himself. We didn't want him to fall over and hurt himself, did we?' He turns to his cronies.

'We didn't,' the others agree.

'Oh.' I say congenially to them. 'Was that all it was? You were helping him.'

'That's exactly how it was.'

'Why didn't you say?' A slow smile crosses the stout one's face, and I see a sneaky and triumphant look come into his eye. Adults are such pushovers, right?

'Okay. Show me the knots you were helping him to tie.' That confuses them, some. Lanky and bully-beef bend down reluctantly to make some clumsy attempt with their football bootlaces. Dark Hair, as I suspected, is the clever one. So clever, he can't help but show off to me just how very clever he is.

'Fiendish work,' I admire, as he bends down to his own football boots and ties an expert knot in front of me. A hard one. Exactly like the one I've just seen on the little lad's shoes. The kind of knot you'd have to have learnt how to undo. It was his work, no doubt of it.

'But look, if you do *this*,' I bend, and with a few deft moves – a party trick demonstrated to me by a former boyfriend who was once in the merchant navy – I untie Adam's shoes in a trice. 'Those knots will come off easily enough.' Their faces drop. Dark Hair's face grows sulkier. He doesn't say anything.

'You can run along now, Adam.'

'Thank you, Miss.' He beams. He's got his shoes back on and he's out of there like a shot, surprisingly fast for such a heavy guy. The coach's whistle goes in the distance and I sense the others are instantly keen to escape, too. Their heads go up, like hounds hearing the horn, as the whistle goes again – their coach signalling time to get on with their training session, no doubt. He'll have missed them by now, surely? They want to be there. They don't want to be stuck here, dealing with me.

'Now, you three. You're coming along with me to the Headmasters' office.'

'But Miss, we've got training,' Lanky protests.

'We'll be in trouble,' Bully-beef looks longingly towards the direction he wants to go in. 'It was just a bit of fun, Miss. We didn't mean no harm at all.'

'We can't go,' Dark Hair says, stubborn. 'Besides, The Head won't care. He'll send us straight back to training. We've got a fixture at the weekend and he wants us to win.'

But he doesn't know me.

'We'll let him make that decision, shall we? You lead the way,' I insist. Pretty handy I came across these guys really, seeing as I didn't know the way, myself. The entrance which I couldn't find earlier turns out to be hidden behind some building boards where they're having some work done at the front. It's a long way round, a longer deviation than these lads want right now, even though they're hurrying as much as they can. By the time we get to the Headmaster's office, Dark Hair is looking vengeful and spiteful. He's even got some crocodile tears at the ready, I can see, his eyes glittering. He's going to launch into some tale of how this teacher has totally misunderstood how he was trying his best to help that other poor lad and she's made him miss half of his football practice.

The Head will probably agree with him and send them running off to training. But I'm not in the least bit worried about him.

'Thank you,' I say to the three of them, now. 'You three can sit out here until I am done. Someone will be along to see to you in a minute.'

'But ...'

They all look at each other, flummoxed. 'We *have* to be at the training session,' the barrel-shaped one huffs.

'I know.'

I knock on Mr Drummond's door.

'Come,' he says in a deep and authoritative voice. Why do all Headteachers sound exactly the same? Why are they all, always the same, in every way? There must be a factory where they make them, churning them out of little plastic Headteacher moulds so they all blend into one, just like the children they're hoping to produce at the other end of it. I know exactly what will happen the moment I apprise him of the three bullies waiting on the chairs outside his office.

I sigh, letting myself in, 'Jenna Tierney,' I remind him. 'I'm Miss Cheska's stand-in.'

'Ah, yes.' Mr Drummond looks up from the mound of papers on his desk. He looks like a man who's drowning in papers. He glances over at the clock on the wall. I'm late. *First impressions* ....

'Jenna Tierney.' We exchange a perfunctory handshake over his desk. 'Anyone shown you around, yet?'

'I've just got in.'

I hear the smallest sigh of exasperation escape his lips.

'Of course. I'll show you round myself, then.' He shuffles over reluctantly. 'Sorry it's going to have to be a brief one, Miss Tierney. We're a little inundated this week. Terrible timing for the form teacher to be missing.' He indicates the stack of papers on his desk. 'We've got the parent-teacher evening at the beginning of next week, too. I don't know if the agency apprised you?'

'They did. You'd like me to stand in for her, they said?'

55

He seems a little surprised that I've taken that in my stride.

'Well, if you wouldn't mind?'

'Not at all. Miss Cheska has left the children's reports done already, they told me?'

'She has. Well, this is very obliging of you, I must say.' He seems mightily relieved. 'Some supply staff won't do it. You won't know the children by then, how could you? But you can at least go over the reports with the parents, take on board anything they need to tell you and report back to me?'

'I'll be happy to do that.'

'I'm much obliged. Thank you.'

'You're very welcome. Parent-teacher relations are important, right?' I smile at him.

'Very important. I'm so glad you appreciate that.' He's relaxed, now, a weight off his mind.

'Now, if you're ready for that mini-tour before you go to your class …?'

'Yes, please.' I hesitate. If we go through the main office door, he's going to see those lads still sitting out there on the chairs. 'I'd love a chance to see the school from the *other* direction – away from the building works – if that's okay with you?'

'Of course.' He opens his arms, in a good mood now and seeing no problem with that. 'We could use this side door, go round anti-clockwise.'

I content myself with the knowledge that the three little bullies will be kept waiting outside at least long enough to miss most of their training session. If not all of it.

'So that concludes the tour of our school,' Mr Drummond turns to me, fifteen minutes later. We're at Miss Cheska's class already and the playground outside is full of noisy, happy children.

'Oh-oh. *Adam*, isn't it?' He addresses the kid I rescued earlier, who's sitting in the corner of the room quietly, reading a book. 'Why aren't you out in the playground? Come on, fresh air time, go, go, go …' He claps his hands noisily and the lad gets up, looking resigned.

'Forgive me.' I step in. 'I found this boy outside earlier, being badly bullied by a group of older kids. I told him to go to his form class, so it's my fault if he's in here now.'

Mr Drummond looks a little shocked.

'*Bullies?*'

'I sent them to sit outside your door, Mr Drummond. I told them you would deal with them.'

'Well, naturally, I will.' He frowns. 'We don't tolerate bullying in *this* school, Miss Tierney.' He doesn't seem so congenial, all of a sudden. He looks displeased, in fact. With me?

'I'll let you get on,' he says a little stiffly. 'The class TA should be along shortly, if you need anything.'

'Thank you, Mr Drummond.' I watch him turn on his heels and leave. He looks almost affronted.

God. It has started already.

Jenna

When I get back from a quick trip to the bathroom, Adam is still reading his book in the class. He smiles shyly at me.

'Miss Cheska's left you a class work folder over there, Miss.' He points to the teacher's desk. 'You're Miss Tierney, aren't you? It says your name on the folder.'

'That's right.'

'What does the "J" stand for?'

'Jenna.'

He looks thoughtful. 'Jenna. *Jenna*,' he says, trying it out loud on his tongue. 'I haven't heard that name before. It sounds a bit like Leah, my mum's name.'

'I guess it does.'

'Her hair was very bright and shiny, like yours,' he tells me now. 'Nan keeps a picture of her on the mantelpiece, of her holding me as a baby. That's how I know.'

'That's nice,' I say cautiously. Poor kid.

'I used to think, maybe one day she'd come back, you know.'

I come and put my handbag down on the floor beside him.

'*Could* she come back?' Those other boys were taunting him about her when I chanced on them all, this morning, I recall. Is his mum even still alive?

He shrugs.

'You okay?'

Adam nods, silent for a moment and hangs his head.

'They aren't in *this* class, are they, the terrible trio?'

'They're in Year Six.' His intent eyes come up to meet mine.

'Have they done that to you before?' I venture carefully. 'Cornered you and started making nasty comments about your Mum?'

'All the time.' He wipes at his face with the back of his hand. I swallow.

'I am sorry to hear it. But they won't bother you while I'm here.' I sit down on the edge of the little table.

'Will you be here for very long, Miss?'

'Not too long, I'm afraid. A couple of weeks.'

'Oh.' I see the hope die in his eyes.

He knows what that means. It means that there's nothing I can say or do here that'll have much impact in the long term – I'm only here for two weeks. And I mustn't get too involved with the problems of any one particular child. I can't. I mustn't, it wouldn't be fair. This is just a temporary position taken to secure me the bedsit I wanted. In less than a month, I'll be doing something else that I like better. I'll be somewhere else where I would rather be. I go to the teacher's desk now and take a look at the long list of instructions Miss Cheska has left for me to follow in her absence. I sigh. I am here to follow these, and only these, for two weeks and two days only, and then to go.

Unlike unfortunate kids like this little lad, Adam, I, at least, can make my escape.

Nate

'Hey!' I yell out of my window and the kid looks up, startled. He's a sturdy little pudding of a guy with a round face, and short, fair hair. Christ. He's put *another* letter through my door, I just saw him do it. 'Adam. That's *you*, right?'

He looks about him, as if a little wary. Then back up at the window. Gives me the slightest of nods. Well, whaddya know, it *is* him. He's just solved the problem of how I get a message to him, at any rate. I peer down onto the High Street.

'Hold up,' I say. 'I'm coming down.'

At the door, the hinge sticking as it always does in the rain, I beckon him over from where he's retreated to the other side of the street. He joins me cautiously.

'All right?' I smile at him and he nods again, just once. He's a quiet, sensitive sort of kid, you can see that at a glance. The sort of kid a dad might like to take out fishing with him or bird-spotting. A bit of gentle football-kicking wouldn't do his weight any harm, either, but that's not for me to get into.

'I'm Nate,' I offer. He nods again, unsurprised, and my first hope – that he'd realise straight off he'd got the wrong guy – dissolves.

'This for me?'

He watches, clearly anxious as I bend to pick up his latest letter but I don't open it.

'It's some of my schoolwork.' He's got a gruff little voice. 'I got an A for that. I thought you might like to read it.'

I look at the ground. 'You got an "A", that's … that's brilliant. Well, I mean, sure. I'll read it if you like, but …'

'Will you?' His eyes light up, too bright, stopping me in my tracks. I swallow.

'It would be my pleasure to read it,' I say carefully.

His face relaxes into a tiny smile. 'I wasn't sure,' he says. A drop of rain plops off the arch of the doorway now and onto my nose. His smile grows a little wider.

'No, of course I will. You wrote such a lovely letter the other day. And a … a very nice drawing you dropped by, too. You're good at it, right?'

He nods eagerly and I bite my lower lip.

'I'm good at lots of things,' he assures me. 'Good at times tables, and finding lost things and stuff.'

I give a small laugh. 'Finding lost things? I'm always losing things. Even in my tiny flat. When you're older you could hire yourself out to people as a Finder of Lost Things. It'd be a useful service, I'm sure.'

He considers that for a moment, serious-faced, not certain if I'm joshing him or not.

'I found *you*,' he tells me.

'You did. But …' I wipe the rainwater off my nose. I've got to tell him. Now.

'I had to find you.' His gruff voice goes a notch lower. 'Even though Nan didn't want to tell me, I *made* her tell me.' His lower lip trembles. 'I had to find someone who would make them stop.'

'Make *who* stop?' I lift my chin. In answer, he turns towards his left and we both watch as a small group of slightly older boys in the same school uniform make directly towards us, down the street.

'Who, them?' They don't look like too much of a threat to me. One square one, one lanky, and the inevitable short, wiry kid.

'Make them stop doing what, exactly, Adam?'

In answer, he lifts his trouser leg and a rash of angry weals where someone's obviously given him a good kicking are visible on both shins. Christ. I wince. I thought I'd seen the last of this kind of thing. Another time, another school, and this could easily have been my older brother Mo, getting beaten up every single day because he was one of those kids who was always way too loud. Mo never meant any harm, but he never did learn when to keep his mouth closed. He never figured out how to keep his head down and steer clear of trouble, either, no matter how many times I warned him. A wave of sadness washes over me, now.

'They've done that to you after school?'

'They did it this morning before school and they promised me at break they'd get me again tonight.'

'Did they now?' My eyes go back to the apparent leader of the group. Titchy little thing he is, but clearly not in his own estimation, judging by his swagger. Or by the smirk on his face, now he's spotted his prey. That look on his face. My brows furrow and I can feel a tic going in my jaw because I recognise that look. That … anticipation of the chance to pick off some easy prey; to make someone who he sees as being weaker than him, suffer. The thought does something to me, inside. I get a momentary rush of blood to my head, and a partial memory floods back in with it. How, when we were at school, I used to eat kids like him for breakfast every day. I got a reputation for being a troublemaker, a fight-picker, just so they'd all leave Mo alone. It's not a memory that gives me any pleasure.

These must be the boys who he was talking about in his first letter. *Sometimes they hit me.* Little fuckers.

'No one's going to hit you this afternoon.' I step out onto the pavement beside him as the other kids prepare to draw alongside. Seeing me, they have a change of heart, surprise, surprise, and veer off, looking back venomously but unable to make their move. One of them does a cut-throat motion once he feels he's a safe distance away. I move right into the street and stare him out till he backs off, straight into a puddle, splashing the others and the three of them fall out for a moment, cussing and pushing each other. I look at Adam. For a few moments, we just stand there, laughing.

Foiled. For now, anyway. Adam puts out his hand to me for a high-five. Then we go in for a low-five as well. 'That wasn't so hard, was it?' I say.

He shakes his head. For my part, I'm seriously impressed at how normal I'm feeling just now. I'm standing out here, right out on the street … *and nothing is happening!* That really wasn't so hard. The observation fills me to the brim with a momentary ray of hope.

'Pity I can't take you around with me everywhere I go,' he observes.

'No.' That's truer than he knows.

'What I really need is for you to go talk to the teachers about those bullies for me.' His clear green eyes look into mine for a moment.

'You can't talk to them yourself, Adam? They'd listen to you more than me, surely?'

He shakes his head, looking sad.

'No, Nate. Nobody ever listens to me. And if they do listen, they don't believe me. Those boys don't do that in front of the adults. Believe me, they're not that dumb.'

'It's those teachers of yours who sound pretty dumb.' I frown. 'Why *wouldn't* they spot what was going on?'

He opens his hands.

'Maybe they don't want to know.'

'Why wouldn't they want …?' I stop. The sense of social injustice at what he's going through feels all too familiar, tangling in my belly. Life is frequently very unfair. That's the way it is. It's the kind of thing you shouldn't have to learn at his age, though. 'Someone should *make* them listen, Adam,' I say more gently. 'You shouldn't have to suffer like that. Isn't there anyone, no teacher there at all who …?'

'Maybe it's easier for them not to know.' He's looking sad again. Looking straight at me as if *I* were the father who never wanted to know about him. Jeez. How did I ever get involved in this one? He's not going to want to hear what I have to say to him next, is he?

'You'll go, then? You'll go to the parents evening for me next Monday and tell the teacher?' he pleads.

He really wants *me* to go? I take a tiny step back inside.

'We've got a new lady teaching 4C at the moment, you'd like her, you know, Miss Tierney. She's very pretty,' he pursues.

'Listen, kid. *Adam* ...' I say.

'I think she'd maybe listen to you,' he carries on over me. Those eyes, dammit. Those clear green eyes, so sad and so full of something I recognise but can't put my finger on. Any minute now, he's gonna hold me to ransom with those eyes, I can feel it.

'*Why* would she listen to me?' I ask faintly.

'Because you're a good looking man and she hasn't got a boyfriend any more.'

'Oh, no?' I manage a smile.

'I heard her talking to Mrs Tilbury in the playground about it. He cheated on her in Italy and she left him and she's decided that this time she's really given up on men.' He shoots me a knowing glance here. 'But she hasn't really. She'll change her mind when she sees you.'

Okay. Stop. This has gone far enough already.

'Adam.' I put out my hand and he stops talking. 'Adam. I would really love to read your work.' I indicate the envelope in my hand. 'I *will* read it. And ... and I'll even get in touch with that teacher of yours for you.'

'Will you?'

'Yes. Because somebody needs to make her understand. But the thing is, what your nan told you about me being your dad ...'

He looks away, now. He doesn't want to hear what he knows is going to come next, I think. But no, those sad eyes come directly back up to meet mine.

'She said you'd deny it,' he tells me softly. 'I know that you have to deny it. I understand.'

64

'No.' I pull a pained face at him, 'I don't think you do, little guy. Really, I'm not your …'

'I *understand*,' he growls at me.

'No,' I say softly, 'You don't.'

There's a stand-off for a moment, then, while neither of us speak. Then he says,

'Monday evening, then. Miss Tierney at St Anthony's school, down the road. It's just the parents on Monday. No kids so I can't be there. But *you'll* be there?'

'Yes,' I tell him, even though I don't mean to. *What am I doing, what am I saying?* I'm not his dad! And even if I were his dad, I couldn't go. It's only a mile or less, but I can't get down the road that far. Now this kid who's convinced himself that I'm his father, he wants me to go there on Monday.

'Yes?' He holds out his hand, like a businessman, sealing the deal.

'Okay, yes.' I close my eyes briefly. Maybe I can use this as a spur to get myself out of the flat and take that footage Marcie wants from me? Maybe … having to do this one-off favour for this kid, it'll be one sure-fire way to make certain I go out? When I open my eyes again, he's still smiling, just a little anxiously, at me.

'*Yes*,' I promise him again. 'I'll be there.' I swallow, feeling a deep sense of doom descend. I'm committed now, aren't I?

If I can't bring myself to walk it, maybe I can take a taxi.

Nate

'Hello' she says. This shiny-haired woman with her arms full of report folders, she walks into the classroom and stares at me for a moment. And then she smiles. 'You're in the wrong place. The parents evening was in the hall and it finished half an hour ago.'

'Oh.' I've been a mass of nerves all day, and I've been sitting here for well over an hour already, waiting for her to finish, not being able to face the melee in the hall. That taxi I called never arrived. I waited and waited but in the end, I had to walk it. And walk, lurch, scurry it, I did. Pausing in and out of shop awnings to take in deep breaths, pretending I was sheltering from the rain and then dashing out again for the next few metres. I wasn't happy about it. The pain in my chest was excruciating. I'd wanted nothing more than to run back home but I'd promised that kid, hadn't I? I'd said I'd speak to his teacher, *someone* had to. I'd promised and there was no way I was letting him down. It wasn't till I'd been sitting here for a good twenty minutes that it even dawned on me I'd forgotten to bring the flipping camera along with me to tape my progress.

I make to struggle up out of the small kiddie-sized chair I've been sitting on and the woman's smile deepens.

'That's all right, you can stay there for a moment. We'll need to make another appointment for you, Mr …?'

'Hardman,' I supply. She won't recognise that name from her class, but she's a professional, this one, she doesn't show it. 'But you can call me Nate if you like.'

'Nate.' She puts the folders down on the table, comes and stands in front of me and holds out her hand. 'I'm Miss Tierney but you can call me Jenna if you like.' Her hand in mine is warm and confident. It takes me entirely by surprise because despite what Adam said, she's so not what I was expecting. That boy has good taste. She is ... totally hot. For a split second, I get a glimpse of something I wasn't looking for, didn't even know I was yearning for.

For a second, I even forget to be pissed at myself for neglecting to bring the camera; the missed opportunity to record my journey out, tonight.

'I ... I love what you've done here.' I indicate the classroom around us. While I've been sitting here I've been drinking in the bright and beautiful flavours of the space she has created, from the irreverent cartoons explaining how fractions work, to the huge mosaic made up entirely of spring petals on proud display at the end. I got a glimpse of her already, this teacher.

'Thank you. The children made that collage just this morning.' She beams. 'Um.' Her eyes travel down to her hand, still locked in mine, which I have not yet relinquished. She laughs easily now, takes her hand back.

I cough, slightly embarrassed at myself. Is this only the adrenalin high I'm still experiencing for having made it down here? It must be, I think, but I like it. I like it very much.

'So, Nate.' She pulls up another small chair to come and sit beside me.

'You fit on these petite chairs much better than I do,' I note ruefully. Her eyes come up to meet mine, sparkling.

'There aren't too many strapping, six-foot male teachers at this primary school. It's not a big problem for us.'

She pats the diary in her lap, now. 'We're going to need to rearrange this meeting aren't we?'

Rearrange it? 'Can't we just do it now?' I plead. I can't tell her what it just cost me to get here. I'm still buzzing with it, true. But what if I don't manage it another time? What if I let Adam down?

'Afraid not. They're locking up, now. The times were in the letter, Nate. We have to leave.'

'Ah.' I look at my hands. 'I didn't see the letter.'

'I'm sorry about that.' She sighs, hesitant for a moment. 'Did you have to come very far?'

'I live about a mile up the road, on the High Street,' I confess. In my case, that is a long, long way away. It's a trans-Atlantic haul of a trek. But she wouldn't know that. She shrugs, relieved. No problem, then.

'Which one of my no-shows were you?' Two dimples show on her cheeks as she adds, 'I take it you're here today as somebody's big brother?'

'Actually, I'm here as somebody's dad.' She looks surprised at that but it's truer than she knows. She sits up a little.

'Oh. Well then, let me guess.' Jenna points at my head of dark hair, way too long, way too curly. I know it is, because I haven't seen the inside of a barber's shop in an age. 'You're Chloe Barnsole's father?' She lowers her eyes.

'I'm not.'

'No?' Her eyes meet mine again, curious.

'No. I'm here for Adam.'

'Adam?' She could not look more taken aback if she tried. 'Adam *Boxley*? Really?'

I clear my throat. 'You seem surprised, Jenna?'

'I'm ... quite frankly, I am.' Her eyes are scrutinising mine closely, now, even more closely than before, and I feel a small sweat break out on the back of my neck. Damn, I hate lying. I hate it and I'm no good at it, which is why I never do it. If it weren't for Adam's predicament I wouldn't be here doing this now. I hope he's grateful.

I return her frank stare and at last she turns away.

'May I ask why?' I prompt now. I may baulk at lies but Adam, for all I know, may have no such qualms. If this teacher turns round and tells me that she knows I'm not his dad because she spoke to him at the last parents evening and he's a four-foot midget with ginger hair, I am going to flay that lad alive, I am.

'If you're Adam's father, then I take it you're a very recent introduction in his life?' She puts it delicately. I hope I'm just imagining the sense that her eyes are a little less friendly than they were a moment ago, more distant?

'I ... we've only recently met, that's true.'

'He's nine years old,' she points out. 'He's one of the sweetest, most helpful, compliant children I know. He's also one of the quietest. And the most troubled.' Her voice is trembling slightly and I can tell the lad's got to her. He's worked his way right into her heart the way he got to me.

Good. That's fantastic. I feel my shoulders drop in relief.

She likes him very much. She's going to be a good advocate for him, this woman. When I explain to this teacher what's up I know I'll be leaving his problems in good hands.

'That's what I'm here to talk to you about.' I lean forward eagerly. 'He's troubled, and he's sad. And that ... that concerns me deeply. I don't know if he's ever spoken to you about this, you know what boys are like, but – it seems he's being bullied mercilessly at school.'

Her eyes look tragic.

'May I ask you a question, Nate?'

I lift my shoulders. Fire away.

'Have you lived at your current address for very long?'

I give a slight nod. 'Three years. But about Adam, what I really wanted to talk to you about, was ...'

'Three years,' she cuts across me. 'You have been living here, just down the road, for three years?'

'Yes.' I look at her, perplexed.

'Mr Hardman. You are his father. The child is nine years old. You are telling me you live a bare mile up the road from Adam's school, yet you have never, until only recently, even met him?'

I let out a breath.

'Ah, I should explain ...'

'Perhaps you should. Perhaps you should explain to him, why you haven't been in his life all these years. What you've been doing with yourself all this time, living down the road and never even bothering to once take the trouble to come and introduce yourself?' Her eyes are blazing, suddenly. I swallow, watching as she gets to her feet a little too abruptly.

'You can ring The Office in the morning.' She turns back to her desk. 'For that appointment.'

'This isn't what you think,' I tell her. 'And ... we still need to talk about Adam.'

'We do.' We do, and we both know it but right now, having learned that I live so nearby, she's made up her mind about something, about me at least, about the kind of guy I must be. Even though she has no real idea about me and that makes me sad.

'Can't we at least make an appointment now?'

Her eyes meet mine for an instant.

'I should warn you. You won't find me the same as most other teachers, Nate. There are some things I have my opinions on and if I think you should hear them, you will. I won't be PC about them.' She stops, as if considering for a moment. 'Tell me. Were you *ever* in his life? When he was little, maybe. When he was born – were you there at the birth?'

'I was not,' I admit and I see her chin raise a fraction. I add, my voice thick, 'I wasn't with his mother at the time.' I wasn't with her ever, but I can't tell Adam's teacher that.

'Not even for his birth?' This seems to scandalise her even more than everything else that's been said so far. She turns back to the pile of report files on her desk, starts stuffing them into a bag to take them home. 'Nice one. Good show of solidarity, wouldn't you say?'

'Solidarity?'

'For the woman,' she points out. 'The mother. The woman. You'd presumably had some dealings with her at some point in the not too dim and distant past?'

70

I see what this is about. She thinks I abandoned the lad's mother and him too. Something in her tone gets to me.

'You're assuming that was all down to me, Jenna? What if I had no say in the matter? What if his mother didn't *want* me to see him, had no desire to let me play any role in his life, no matter how small?' My eyes narrow. 'What if I was never allowed to get anywhere near my son because his mother made certain I wasn't allowed to?' I get off the little chair with as much dignity as I can muster and come to stand beside her. 'It is not always the man's fault when a child grows up fatherless, Miss Tierney. Sometimes it is the mother who makes that decision.'

She blinks. Then she comes back; 'Well, I'm assuming she must have had good reason, then.'

'You think?' I spread my arms, affecting hurt. 'You never met her, did you?' *I never met her either*, but right now that feels beside the point.

'No. I heard she died when he was just tiny,' she begins, but I carry on over her.

'You never met her. You've only met me who you think lives so near, just down the road but truly, you don't know anything about me. Not the first thing. You don't know what I had to do to make it here tonight.' A swathe of sadness washes over me, and suddenly, I'm not even acting.

'What did you have to do?' She turns her beautiful eyes on me, green eyes flecked with warm hints of soft brown, the fire in them temporarily doused. She appears open for the moment, curious. But I am not here about me.

'The point is, I'm here now. Just accept that I'm the one who's here for him. I'm the one battling for Adam.'

'All right,' she says at last and I can feel her relenting, coming down off her high horse.

'All right.' She brings out her diary and starts running her finger down the times she can make. 'I'm moving into my new flat tomorrow after school, but how about Wednesday afternoon?'

71

she asks. Wednesday. Today is Monday so that is two days away. Two days and then I can see this woman again.

Why am I even counting?

'Can you make 4.30pm? I realise that early might be difficult with work commitments ...'

'I can make it,' I tell her quickly.

'You can?' Her eyes meet mine and she drinks me in again, drowns me in something so intoxicating I can barely speak.

I nod.

'See you Wednesday then,' she says softly, and at the thought of seeing her again my heart does a painful and unexpected somersault of joy.

It's not till I'm walking out of the school gates that I realise what I've just done. Bloody hell. This is not a date. I've just committed to a second appointment with Adam's teacher, when that had never been my intention at all. This is madness. I'd meant to leave the problem of that lad at her door, today, had I not? I'd meant to bring him to her attention and bow out of that child's life. I have enough troubles of my own.

And yet – the journey home is much swifter and easier than the way up, somehow. And I find myself whistling when I arrive at last at my own front door.

Jenna

'Look – some of the crockery I've brought even matches the colour of your green door!' Mags opens up the box she's brought from her Odds and Sods shop in the High Street. It's chock-full of plates and mugs and dainty, little retro sugar bowls.

I look at her, distracted.

'Your fabulous downstairs door,' she says. 'The one that convinced you to go for this flat even though there's no room to swing a cat in this place.'

'Lucky I don't own a cat then,' I bat back. Though maybe it is not so lucky. For the first time since Sicily, I muse, I'm about to face being on my own. Not just free. *On my own*, in this flat. And I don't know if I'm going to like being on my own.

'I'm going to miss you,' I tell Mags.

'Are you?'

'I am going to miss … having someone to talk to when I get back from work.'

'You've just got back from work at the school two hours ago and I'm here, aren't I?'

'*Today*, you are. Only because you're helping me move in!'

'Besides, I was hardly about last week when you were staying at mine,' she points out. It's true. She's been at some antiques fair, sourcing stock, we've hardly seen each other but that isn't the point.

73

'I know you haven't been about.' We start unwrapping her precious housewarming gifts to me one by one. They are all beautiful, but some of them are definitely going to have to go back. There isn't the room. *How did I come to choose such a tiny flat?* 'You weren't there much. But your things were about. Everywhere I looked, there were signs of another person living there. It's not like ... living alone.'

'No,' she says. 'But that's what happens when you split from your boyfriend of over a year. You've got to feel it at some point. It's not really me you'll be missing.'

'If you think in your wildest dreams I am pining for Alessandro ...' I shoot back, but Mags is now holding up a thick, oblong battery-operated device for me to see. WTF?

'This,' she announces, 'will turn even semi-skimmed milk into froth for your morning cappuccino.'

'My morning cappuccino?'

'I think you'll find it indispensible, my dear.'

'I'm not sure I will. And we're pretty much all out of space here. Thanks for the thought, but that's one thing you will definitely be taking back home with you.' I don't drink coffee. Alessandro is the one who drank coffee.

'Christ, Mags, how did I end up here?' I lean on the counter and stare at it for a bit. 'Two weeks ago today, I was at a christening surrounded by over a hundred of Alessandro's relatives,' I tell her. 'We were drinking champagne and I was exploring the chance of exhibiting some of my paintings at his uncle's art gallery. Then, just days later, I'm booking my ticket to Heathrow, throwing everything I own into whatever bag I can find and just ...' I blink, and an unexpected and unwanted tear drops onto my hand. I turn my face away.

Mags leans forward and pats my elbow. 'Things are all moving very fast for you, aren't they?'

I nod. They're moving fast. Very fast. That's normally good, but today I am not so sure.

'I'm not just feeling the effects of leaving Alessandro, it's about leaving Sicily too.' I look at her regretfully. 'I'd just started getting some good offers of work coming in there, Mags.'

'You wouldn't stay out there, but not with him?'

I shake my head ruefully. I couldn't. 'I've already had texts and phone calls from several of our mutual friends, telling me what a big mistake I'm making.'

'What – they're taking his side, even after you saw him …?'

'I know!' I spread my hands, at a loss to explain it. 'Why does nobody see it from my point of view?'

'Maybe they don't know the full story,' she points out. 'Have you actually spoken to any of them?'

I fold my arms.

'If I haven't even spoken to Alessandro about it, why would I speak to anyone else? I *saw* him in bed with another woman Mags! What's there to say? No, there's no way back from this. I don't want to be in the same town as him anymore. Besides.' I frown, 'I'm already getting the flavour of this. *Nobody* seems to understand why I'm so mad at him – maybe it's a cultural thing? Anyhow – now you see why it has to be this way. A clean break.'

'You'll survive,' she assures me. 'You're young and resilient and I know you, you'll have moved on to the next thing in no time.'

'Sure.' The next thing. I look around me at my brand new, *bijoux* little apartment that I have been dreaming about moving into for the last few days. It's clean. It's newly decorated. The bedroom faces onto a sunny space downstairs that I have no access to, but which is full of flourishing greenery I can at least look at. My few belongings are in place, and with the aid of Magda's linen cupboard I have bedding, enough towels, and even a sweet gingham tablecloth to cover the kitchen table. Homely, I think.

I bring out the potted basil and thyme plants I picked up at the supermarket yesterday as part of my culinary master-plan to produce healthy, delicious soups and stuff, and place them in their new home on the windowsill. Everything's perfect. But I do not feel perfect. I'm feeling inexplicably flat all of a sudden. I watch as she goes and slips the indispensible froth-for-the-cappuccino maker back into the cardboard box. We're both silent for a few minutes, rummaging through a few more plastic bags, sorting out the last of my household needs.

'So tell me,' she pulls out of the air now. 'How's the supply teaching job going?'

I shrug. 'I'm still looking into tattoo and art-related jobs, if that's what you're wondering. Teaching really isn't for me. Not long-term.'

'Shame. You being so good at it, and all.' For once, she's not being facetious.

'Supply teaching isn't like real teaching, Mags. It's more like child-minding with a set of instructions to follow.' I pull a faint smile at her. 'I even did a parent-teacher evening yesterday and I've only been there for, like, three days.'

'Really? You were able to do that?'

'It was basically just handing out the reports the form teacher had already written. It wasn't a problem. St Anthony's is a nice little school in so many ways but ...'

'But?' she prompts.

'The school has a competitive ethos that doesn't always sit well with some of their other stated objectives,' I humour her. 'Conflicted interests, you know the sort of thing.'

'*Politics.*' She rolls her eyes. 'Never been your forte, eh Jenna?'

'It's why I left the profession in the first place, as you know.'

'Learning how to be political is something we all have to get, sooner or later,' she mutters, then adds quickly, 'how about the kids, though?'

I sigh, because this sudden interest in the minutiae of my working life seems a little out of character. I know what she's doing. She's distracting me from thinking about the mess my life's in at the moment, isn't she? I pull out some donated tea towels from a plastic bag and search for a drawer to stow them in. There doesn't appear to be one. I look around, frowning slightly. Are there really no kitchen drawers? I didn't notice that before. No wonder the cutlery has all been artfully stowed in a vase on the worktop.

'Are they a joyous bunch, your form?' she persists.

'Most of them. It's only been a few days.' I look at her, debating for a moment, then I admit, 'There is this one kid in particular.'

'Oh yes?'

'His name is Adam. There's something about his situation that's really sad.'

'Tell me.' She folds her hands sedately in front of her, listening intently.

'Adam's mum is out of the picture,' I tell her. 'He lives with his nan but he seems to be getting bullied horribly.'

'Poor little lad. No father either, I expect?'

'Here's the strange thing. He's got a dad who's just reappeared on the scene and he's – he's a bit of an enigma, too. For starters, he seems way too young to be any nine-year-old's dad.'

Mags smiles. I shake out the tea towels then fold them up deliberately, still wondering where I am going to put them. 'No, I mean it. Way too young, he's like – my age. And he seems too well educated, somehow. I know accidents can happen to anyone, but ...' I shake my head and she picks up on my smile.

'Young,' she notes drily. 'And cute?'

'Kinda cute, but that's *totally* beside the point. No. The point is ... I don't understand how he could have no dealings at all with the child, for the whole of his life, when he lives barely a mile away from the school.'

'Hmmm.' She's sneaking another device out of her box of donated items now, a larger one, this time. 'Maybe he didn't know about Adam till recently?'

'I didn't get that impression. And then again, he managed to turn up only right at the end meaning he missed the entire parent-teacher evening. I had to reschedule his meeting for tomorrow after school.'

'Sounds a little dodgy to me,' she agrees. 'Enough room in the flat for this slow-cooker, d'you think?' Mags points to the latest item she's unearthed.

'Sorry. The flat is tiny.'

'It'd be a waste of space, then. Pity. These things are so handy.' She gives me a pointed look. 'Talking about a waste of space, cute or not, that lad's father doesn't sound very useful I'm afraid.'

'No. But he did seem genuinely concerned about his son. That's what makes it so strange.'

'You're piqued,' she accuses. 'You can't resist a mystery?'

'Nah. I'm just really hoping I can impress upon that guy how much his son needs him before I leave.'

'Well. I am sure if anyone can, it will be you.' Mags rubs her hands together briskly. 'Talking of leaving, it is time for me to be on my way, I am afraid.' I walk down with her. 'You've done well here, Jenna,' she approves. 'It's a dear little place, beautifully appointed. It's just right for you.' When we get to the bottom of the stairs she adds, 'And of course I love, *love*, the downstairs door.'

'I knew you would. Everyone who's seen the picture I posted online, is very envious.' My English friends at any rate. I've unfollowed everyone I knew from Sicily. For now, at least.

'You're going to be very happy here,' she assures me. I smile at her as she's leaving, closing the wondrous, medieval green door behind her, but for some reason I am not smiling inside. It perplexes me that I am not. Because I *should* be happy.

Shouldn't I?

I go upstairs and sit back down in my ultra-tiny kitchen and stare at the potted herbs. 'Just you and me left now, guys. But hey – we're going to do just great here, right?' Plants grow better if you talk to them. That's what I've heard people say. 'I've got a tonne of people who know I'm back,' I add out loud. 'And they've all promised they'll visit just as soon as they can schedule it in.' The plants sit silently in their pots. I get up to rummage in my handbag for a smoke and, not finding any, recall that I don't do that anymore. Instead I turn the potted herbs around so their leaves face outwards towards the daylight, facing their future. Like me.

I don't want to think too much about all the erstwhile London friends who I know probably aren't going to schedule in a visit to my flat anytime too soon because we no longer have enough in common. Michaela and Poppy and Dee were definitely disappointed to learn there was no reconciliation on the cards with 'my Sicilian dude.' I think they'd been looking forward to receiving their invites to the Big Italian wedding. I love my girlfriends, but they've all got partners and leaving Alessandro has put me out of step with them.

All the engaged couples and the wanting-to-be-pregnant couples and the busy-at-work guys and the newly-in-love people who've all got better things to do. I've got so used to being in the thick of things with Alessandro's people in Catania, this feels, frankly, odd to me now. Not having other people around to observe and comment and laugh with; not having people around who notice things, people who care. I wonder if that's what that kid Adam must feel like, at times?

Which brings me to the unwelcome reminder that, after what I believed would be a permanent break from education, I'm suddenly a teacher again! How did that happen? Still, at least the teaching agency were good enough to provide me with a reference so I could get this place.

I sit down and turn my attention to the to-do list I started making on the plane. Now that I have a new permanent address, my list has spilled over two pages with things I need to get on with, get sorted out. I take my pen and cross off number 1 and 2 which were easy – get some chocolate and buy some new tights. I draw a line through number 4 – find a new flat, and then, after a little bit of thought, I cross off number 3 as well. I don't really want to find a new boyfriend. I need to face it. I'm rubbish at relationships. Maybe it's better to be single than to live in the hope of some fantasy that is never going to come true.

In the meantime, I wish I didn't feel so damn lonely.

Nate

My head feels like it's got a ratchet going on inside. I don't want to see anyone, don't want to speak to anyone. If this school receptionist keeps me hanging on any longer while she looks up the appointment I've just rung to cancel, I'm going to have to hang up on her.

'I made the appointment directly with Adam's teacher, so it might not be in the book,' I tell her faintly when she comes back. 'I've only rung up so Miss Tierney doesn't stay behind for nothing.'

And even this is costing me. I need to get off this phone.

'Oh, that's a shame,' she rattles on. 'Would you like to rebook that appointment with Adam's teacher, Mr Hardman?' If the receptionist at St Anthony's is sounding disappointed, it is much, much worse for me. I am gutted.

'No. I can't, just now.'

'Are you sure?' I can hear her down the phone, flicking pages over in the diary. 'I was speaking with Jenna Tierney earlier today and she was very much looking forward to discussing Adam with you.'

Adam. I run my fingers distractedly through my hair. I really had wanted to help that kid, but it's pretty obvious I'm in no place to help anyone.

'I've come down with …' I baulk at an outright lie. 'I'm afraid I haven't been able to get out of the flat since Monday evening.' That much is an understatement. Since my trip out to the school on Monday evening, I haven't been able to *sleep* for the last 48 hours. My body's gone into some kind of hyper-alert mode. I can't function like this and I'm feeling like *hell*. I can't go out again.

'I expect you'll ring us when you're feeling better, then?'

'I'll … I'll let you know.' I won't be ringing anyone back, though. I'm done with this. 'I'm sorry,' I tell her. 'My front doorbell is going now. I have to get that.'

It's not just an excuse. Whoever it is, they've insistently been ringing the bell all the while I've been on the phone to her. I hang up and lean out of my sitting room window. Outside, it is a dank and drizzly Wednesday afternoon, home time from school already. I wonder if my caller is one of those little buggers who were after Adam the other day, and they're back here playing some kind of prank …

'Who's there?' I just want the noise to stop.

No answer, but the bell goes again, drilling right through my head. Am I really going to have to go downstairs now to sort this out? I'm still in my boxers aren't I, haven't yet got dressed today. It's a wonder I even managed to ring the school just now to cancel that meeting. I lean out a little further.

'Whoever that is, *will you please stop ringing the damn bell?* I'm coming.' Several people walking past on the High Street look up on hearing me.

'Nathaniel. *Bon chance!*'

I freeze. Dear God, I know that voice. Can that really be …? I lean precariously far out of my front room window to see.

It's her all right.

The person I both most want and least want to see in the world, right now.

Nate

'*Camille?*' My ex is a vision in a sleek, short dress and heels. Immaculate, beautiful as ever and then there's me standing here in only my smalls. Her amused eyes travel down my semi-naked bod. Not, I see, without some appreciation. She glances up the stairs a little curiously.

'Oh. I am sorry. You already have some company?'

'No …' I choke back my first response. She thinks I'm entertaining a female? 'I don't have company. There's no one here. Camille.' I open my arms. 'What are you doing here?'

In response, she executes a perfect, small curtsey.

'Here to see you, of course.'

'Here to see me.' As if we do this, she and I, just drop by each other, whenever we fancy. We do not. The sight of her fills me with a host of conflicting feelings. We hug. Familiar in my arms now, she smells of flowers and sunshine and I experience a brief moment of peace, nonetheless. 'It's good to see you again. You look … amazing.' She does. There's something else about her too, a new quality. She's looking happier, that's what it is. She's looking more filled out with an inner contentment in a way she never really looked when she and I were an item.

I sigh.

'I mean, *really* lovely.' In response, she laughs, briefly twirling some locks of my hair in her fingers before moving away.

'New look?' she peers at me under long, curved lashes.

'Yeah, it's my caveman look. You like it?'

'Do *you*?'

'Sure I do. I love it. All the girls go crazy for me looking like this.'

She smiles. 'I bet they do. How've you been, *mon chéri*?'

'*Tres bon.*'

'*Je suis tellement contente de te revoir, chéri.*'

'Um. Yeah. You too.' I shoot her a lopsided grin. 'But you've forgotten already? I don't speak frog.'

'As you like.' She shrugs.

Upstairs, she looks around languidly and I hurry to whisk a pot of expensive coloured pencils off the settee, remove a toppling pile of papers, making a space for her to sit down.

'Sorry. You've caught me in the middle of something. I haven't had much time today to …'

'Not at all, it's fine, Nate.' Her hand rests on my shoulder as I bend now, swooping a couple of stray socks off the floor. 'Really.' Her eyes meet mine, coolly amused at the spin I'm in. 'It's *fine*.'

I straighten.

'Give me two minutes.' In the bedroom, struggling into some half-decent jeans and rummaging desperately in my drawer for a clean T-shirt, all I can feel is confused. Camille turning up unexpectedly like this … it's put me out and I don't know why. What I probably *should* be feeling is happy to see her. I should. What red-blooded guy wouldn't be happy to have a beautiful woman like her turn up at their door? Grimacing into the wall mirror, I push back my hair which is way too thick and looks greasy. How *the hell* have I managed not to take a shower in the past two days?

I've not been myself for a while, and she'll know at least some of this from Hal. Just how much, I don't know, but she'll know I wasn't at the awards, she'll be aware of the video-diary. She'll be aware that I never answered their wedding invite. Is that why she's here? To judge for herself what chance there is of me making it? I brace myself to go out and greet her properly. Even now with her sitting here in my living room, I'd prefer for her not to see just how bad things have been. I don't want anyone to see.

'Hey, Camille.'

'Hey.' She looks up from the loose-leaf art folder she's been browsing through. The one I left on the settee. 'Some of these are really good, you know.'

I pull a rueful smile. 'Only some of them?'

'This one, I like.' She holds up the drawing I was sketching out earlier of a medieval-style woman in a long, green flowing robe. 'She's really beautiful.' Camille glances at me a little curiously. 'Who is she, this redhead?'

'No one.'

'No one? One whole year we went together and I never knew you had this in you. And this one ...' She turns over a leaf. A young man with a swaggering black cloak looks proudly out of the page. 'They're real characters, aren't they? It's like you've created a whole other world in here. This is fascinating, Nate.'

I lean forward and gently relieve her of the folder.

'They're just rough sketches I've been doing for an online friend. He writes fantasy games for a living and he was looking for some inspiration.' I feel myself colour a little. 'So. Can I get you anything? A drink? I've still got some of your herbal infusions tucked away somewhere, I think.'

'Still?' She delicately folds one ankle over the other. Gives a small shake of her head. 'No. I won't be staying long, Nate. Actually I just came to ...'

I sit down awkwardly in the chair opposite her. She just came to what?

'To see how you were,' she finishes.

Of course.

'Well, as you see. I'm ... getting there. Been keeping myself busy in here. Very busy, you'd be surprised how much time can get taken up ...' I glance at the sketch folder. 'Man, it's hot in here though. Are you hot?' I get up to put my folder away and I push the sash window up a little higher, take in some air.

'It's not hot.' She takes me in thoughtfully. 'Are you sure you're okay, Nate?'

'I'm sorry?' I turn back. Just seeing her sitting there on the sofa where we used to sit together fills me with a strangely desperate joy.

She indicates with a circling motion around her eyes.

'What?' I force a laugh. 'I don't look right to you? Maybe I just had a bout of flu, Camille. Been under the weather, right?'

'No.' She gives a soft shake of her head. 'This doesn't look like flu.' Then she adds, '*Cheri*, Hal told me the reason why you hadn't answered our wedding invite – all those unopened letters ...'

'I've had ... so much ...' I sit down again, pushing my fingers through my hair, covering my eyes. I dread more than anything to see her pity, but what's the point in trying to hide the true extent of this? I can't hide it! I am so happy to see her but I almost wish she hadn't come here today.

'And Nate.' She puts a hand on my knee, sparing me from digging the hole any deeper. 'Hal also shared with me the reason why you weren't able to be at the awards.'

'Of course he did.'

'Have things been *very* bad for you?' she asks me softly, now.

'Bad enough.' The shame I dread so much is starting to trickle across my chest. She knows. She knows everything, and she wants to talk about it, she doesn't want to pretend, as I do, that none of this is happening. Well then. 'You know. And soon, everyone else will know about it, too.'

'Yes.' She lowers her gaze. 'Hal mentioned about the video-diary they've asked you to make for them.' She tips her head, curious. 'You've agreed to do it?'

'I have no choice,' I tell her thickly. 'But between you and me ...' I stop, remembering who she's marrying, who her pillow talk will be directed at, now. 'Cami. This *is* just between you and me, isn't it?' My ex gives a small nod. I know she'll be discreet.

'Between you and me.' I let out a breath. 'I *hate* the thought.'

'I already guessed that much,' she says softly. She knows well enough what a private person I've always been. Then she adds: 'Hal admires you enormously for taking it on, though.'

'Oh yeah?' I drop my gaze.

'You know what he told me? He said, "If Nate can pull this off, it'll take more balls than the rest of our front line team have got between them."'

'Right,' I give a terse laugh. 'Hal said that?'

'He did.'

Cami gives a little, sad laugh, now. 'You know, you'll think me silly and I hate to admit it, but I was almost relieved when I heard the reason we never got a reply from you.'

My eyes flash up to meet hers.

'You were *relieved?*'

'I'd been thinking maybe you hadn't answered the wedding invite because you were still sore ... about us?'

'Oh God, no!'

'So you're not still feeling any residual disappointment after ...?'

'Look.' I shake my head firmly. 'It's good to see you, Camille. Really good, don't get me wrong but ... it's been a year hasn't it? I'm not sore about us splitting. The hardest bit was the no contact between us like we agreed, but you were right about that, too. So we could each get on with our lives, the way we wanted.'

'And ...' Camille looks up at me through long, curved lashes. 'Have you?'

'You know that I haven't.' I pause. Let's stop pretending, now. 'You have, though, clearly. I mean, a marriage proposal in a year, that's not bad. Hey ...' I lean forward to pat her knee, comradely. 'Don't look so sad, girl. I'm jealous as hell of him, but I'm happy for you both, truly.'

'Thank you,' she says feelingly.

'You're welcome.' I rub at my head for a bit, battling with a host of things. Battling with ... all the decisions I've made in my life, all the chances that I took and those I did not take, that have led me to this point. Rock bottom.

On top of everything else, Camille is getting married and the reality of that, seeing her sitting here in my living room with his ring on her finger, it makes me want to crawl under my duvet and just … disappear. I knew in all honesty we were never getting back together, but the mere possibility of it – that things could go back to how they once were – for a long time, that was still there. Now it is not there. There is no going back. I don't want anything more to do with anyone, today. But here Camille is, still sitting in front of me, saying quietly,

'I know you might think it's too soon to be marrying Hal when we only met a year ago, but I'll be thirty-four, shortly,' she reminds me. 'I've waited long enough.'

I force myself to smile but it feels like my face is going to crack.

'It's what you always dreamed of, isn't it, Camille? You know, right now, sitting here opposite you, I can't for the life of me see why I didn't snap you up, first. When I had the chance.'

She gives a low laugh.

'No, really. I was a fool. Why didn't I do what you asked me to do – quit my dangerous, unpredictable job, sooner? Why didn't I settle down with you and give you that spring wedding and all those babies you were always longing for?' *Why couldn't I just have contented myself with that?*

'Because you needed your job more than you needed me,' she obliges. 'You were born to do this job. You need to do it.'

The irony of it does not escape me.

'I'm not doing it though, am I? I've been stopped in my tracks. I can't. I can't do this work, Camille,' I admit to her at last. 'I feel I've lost something I had, deep inside, that allowed me to do it, and I can't carry on.'

'Perhaps … you need to find that thing you feel you've lost then, before you make any final decisions about your career?'

'Find what?' I throw up my hands.

'*Ton courage.*' She leans forward and lays a gentle hand over my chest before getting up to go.

'My courage.' I wipe at my face desperately. That has upped and gone to hell in a hand basket. I don't tell her all the rest of it: how this isn't just about my job, how it's affecting my whole damned life. I don't tell her how sad I feel about … about everything. How scared I am that I won't be able to deliver on what I have to now, to keep it all together and how I can't – *I won't* – ask either of the two people I once might have asked for help – her or Hal, because it's all just too shaming.

At the downstairs entrance, Camille embraces me again. It's a goodbye hug, I can feel it. A gentle mist is hanging in the air outside as she whispers into my ear, 'Don't give up, Nate. *Écoute ton cour.*'

But my heart, right now, feels broken. 'I don't think I know how to, anymore,' I admit.

In reply, Camille just gives me a long, pensive, look.

'Oh yes,' she says. 'I think you still do.'

Jenna

'Camille?' Adam's dad is sounding rather wistful at the other end of the line. Whoever *Camille* is he'd rather like it to have been her, I'm guessing.

'No.' I put him right. 'This is not Camille. This is Jenna Tierney, your son's teacher.' I glance over at the school receptionist who's pointedly straightening up her desk, clearly eager to pack it in for the day – as am I. It's gone half past five. As Nate Hardman failed to show up, I've resorted to visiting The Office for his phone number.

'I'm still at the school.' Pause. 'We had a meeting arranged for after school today, you remember?'

'I do. I'm sorry, I …' He's sounding a little confused.

'You *did* remember, didn't you?'

'I did.' His voice sounds choked. Well, if he's choked I am not feeling entirely tickety-boo myself. Right at this moment, what I am feeling is tired and stressed.

'*And?*'

'And I … I rung up earlier to cancel it.'

I grip the phone a little tighter. 'You cancelled. When?'

'I spoke to the receptionist about it, Jenna. I'm sorry I couldn't get up there today.' He sounds like he means it too, genuinely upset but I've had the day from hell. Everything that *could* have gone wrong today has gone wrong.

'You rang up earlier to cancel our meeting? Nobody told me. I've been waiting here for over an hour for you.'

'Oh, my goodness!' I turn round to see Mrs Tallyman, the school receptionist, clap her hand over her mouth. 'I am so sorry, I've been so run off my feet, I forgot,' she breathes. 'I took his phone number off the caller's list for you though,' she adds, as if by way of reparation. I stare at her as she scuttles off through the door now, leaving me alone in the office. I'm feeling a little stunned. And angry.

'I am sorry too, Jenna. Could we …' at the other end of the line, I can hear Nate Hardman struggling to get the words out. 'Could we … perhaps speak some other time?'

Some other time. I bite my lip.

'*I'm* just sorry that our second appointment has also proved to be inconvenient for you, Mr Hardman. That's a real shame. I would really have welcomed the opportunity to have told you all about your son's day. He didn't have a good one, I should add.'

'Oh, man.' He sounds genuinely upset.

'I'm not sure *how* much day-to-day contact you have with Adam, Mr Hardman, but …'

'Nate. Please call me Nate.'

'*Nate*,' I give him. 'Your son knew you were coming here tonight and I can tell you it meant a lot to him. More than you can even imagine.'

'I know,' he says faintly. He means it. I can tell he means it and yet he's given no reason for this cancellation. No valid excuse.

'… and it's especially important to him given that there's been this estrangement between you for all this time,' I get in. There's a quiet moment while he seems to consider this. After a while, I venture: 'So. Are you still at work?'

'No, I … I work from home.'

'Oh. You're in Rochester, actually just a few minutes down the road from me?' I make a snap decision, decide to take a chance. 'Look, I'll wait for you. Because this is important. If you can get up here in the next fifteen minutes, we can still have our meeting, okay?'

'Miss Tierney. *Jenna.*' He sighs. 'I really appreciate the offer …'

'I'm really looking forward to meeting with you, too,' I enthuse. 'There's a whole load of things we can talk about; things you could implement if you truly mean to start getting involved in your son's life. And I'll be honest, Adam was *so* disappointed about you missing our meeting on Monday. It's the main reason I waited so long for you to turn up today …'

'I appreciate the offer but …'

But? My spirits take a dive. He's not coming, is he? Son of a gun. 'You're sick?'

There's a strangled sound at the other end of the line. 'Not sick, no. But Jenna,' he says, 'there's something I really need to tell you.'

Tell me what? I give a snort. He's not sick. If he is not sick, then he needs to be here. I don't care what else it is he's got on his mind.

'You're only a few *minutes* away, Nate,' I make one last-ditch attempt to make him see sense. 'If you only knew, if you had the faintest idea how much that child …' I stop suddenly, hearing myself, realising that I have begun pleading. I am not going to beg him.

'I *do* know,' Adam's father comes back to me now. 'And I cannot tell you how sorry I am that we're not meeting today. My one consolation is knowing that he has *you*,' he says thickly. 'At least he has you, right? He's got someone with a strong and powerful voice on his side.'

'He's got *me*?' I almost want to laugh out loud. Is this man for real? And I actually thought he was so cute, such a cool guy. I'd been looking forward to this meeting almost as much for myself as I was on behalf of Adam, it dawns on me now. I'm such a sucker!

'He's got you there for him,' he repeats slowly. 'And I cannot tell you how grateful I am. I have … a confession to make, regarding the relationship between Adam and myself, Jenna. This is going to sound very odd, I know it. This is going to sound …' There's a long pause now, while I listen to my own heartbeat racing, turn my head away from the phone so he won't hear my irregular breathing, how *gutted* I am right now. *Why do I do this, every time? Invest too much hope in people who let me down? Every frickin' time!*

'I am not going to be there for your son,' I apprise him before he can come to any 'confession' of his own. 'Just so you know. Before you legitimise any further excuses why you really don't need to be in Adam's life. I am not going to be there for him, for very much longer. I'm just a supply teacher, at St Anthony's, here for a two-week stint.'

'Jenna,' he says faintly. 'I am not his ...' I hear him swallow. The clock on the reception area wall goes tick-tick-tick in that strangely loud way it has. It sounds even louder now that the building is virtually empty. It's empty and I am still here, waiting. Am I wasting my time? 'What did you just say?' He comes back now. 'You're leaving?'

'Correct. After I leave next week he'll have no one. That's why it was so important that I brought you on board. That's why I waited so long in the hope that you would turn up, today. But I was wasting my time, wasn't I? You haven't been there for this child all his life and you don't intend to be here for him now.' There's an intake of breath at the other end. I realise I've just overstepped the boundaries of politeness but I don't care. This man needs to be told and no one else is going to tell him, are they?

'You must think I'm a real asshole, don't you?'

'What I think is, that it's about time you stepped up to the mark and became a real father to this child. He doesn't have anyone else. And after next week he certainly won't be able to count on me, either.'

'You think I'm an asshole because I can't be bothered to turn up there and meet with you. You think I don't care enough, that's it, isn't it?'

'You've already told me you're not sick,' I put to him.

'Not sick, but unable to come out to you, Jenna. And I do care about that boy.'

'Do you?'

'Yes! Look, I suffer from ...' He sounds strangled now. 'I never said so on Monday, but I suffer from huge anxiety whenever I leave my house. When I came out to see you earlier this week that was the first time I'd left the house in weeks and it … it *cost* me. I'd love to have come to you for that meeting, today, but I haven't been able to physically get myself through the door since.'

'Oh.' I sit back on the edge of the receptionist's desk, feeling a little stunned. And sheepish. This guy is housebound? I'd never have guessed that. But if it's true, that might explain a lot. 'I just jumped to some terribly wrong conclusions there, didn't I?'

'Understandably so,' he allows. 'You were hoping to get some help for Adam. I know why you were so angry.'

'Even so, I shouldn't have …'

'No, my fault. I should have been more upfront with you about my circumstances. The truth is, I haven't really come to terms with it yet.' *Yet? How long has he been like this?* His voice goes very low, now. 'I keep thinking I'm going to wake up one day and it'll all have gone back to normal. That my life will be …' he stops. 'I'm sorry. I didn't mean to burden you with all that.'

'You didn't. You haven't. It's fine.' I rub at my brow, feeling weary, feeling the stress of the hectic school day in the knots in my shoulders. I'd like to visit the gym, now. Or go for a long, energetic run to pep myself up again.

'It probably seems like a lot to ask,' he adds after a bit, 'But is there any chance you'd be willing to come down for half an hour, have our meeting at my house?'

'It is a lot to ask.' I don't know what's going on with this guy. I don't know if I even want to know. He is not what he seems, is he? I take in a breath. 'But I will come if you like,' I agree tentatively. *Why? Why are you doing this, Jenna?* For once, I am not sure of my own motives. There is so much about this guy I instinctively like, and so much that is … odd. Not quite right. Is he telling me the entire truth now? I so want to believe him, but I am not sure that I am doing the right thing.

After a while he says,

'Thank you, Jenna. Thank you for agreeing, it means a lot to me, more than you know.'

93

'That's perfectly all right,' I tell him. 'I'm doing this for Adam.'

'I'll see you in a short while then.' He sounds so relieved. When I visualise him, in my mind's eye his dark eyes are shining, happy. Coming out of school now, I recall how handsome he looks when he's smiling. It makes me smile, too. I'm doing this for Adam, I told him. I'm not sure quite why or how, but in some way I haven't figured out yet, this is important for me, too.

Nate

Now *that*, I did not mean to do.

I jump into the shower, lathering some soap onto my skin, waking myself up to the reality that I've just dug myself a little deeper into this lie. How? I'd been poised there to tell that girl the whole truth: how I am not the lad's father; how I'd just got involved by some strange chance accident when he posted his letter through the wrong door; *how none of any of this is really anything to do with me.* I'd been about to say it, leave all of Adam's troubles on Jenna's capable shoulders, when she dropped the bombshell on me. She let on that she's not staying on at the school, that she isn't going to be around for Adam and in response I ... I bottled out.

Why? Because in the back of my mind there was still that little voice saying: if she's going to be out of the picture, maybe you're the only person standing between that kid and the daily torture he's going through. Maybe keeping up the pretence of being his dad is the only power you have, if you want to get through to anyone on his behalf. Even though it's not right. Even though you don't like it, not one little bit. And besides, that girl – how's she going to take it when you tell her?

Will she really understand why you lied?

For a few moments, the spicy scent of the soap and the warmth of the water running over my skin lull me into a false sense of security. I recall Jenna's friendly laugh, the way her warm, interested,

95

eyes rested on me on Monday. Ah yes, Monday. I close my eyes and the shower runs hot all over my face and my limbs. On Monday, sitting on that little-person chair, pretending to be someone I am not, I still felt more like the old Nate than I have done in months. That's a sad thought. On Monday, I was a man with a life worth living again, some half-decent dude. Someone more akin to how I *was*. I was a man with a purpose and I liked that.

I know she liked what she saw, too.

The guy she *thought* she saw.

I rub the shampoo more vigorously into my scalp, not entirely liking the reminder. My ego's already suffered one blow today, seeing Camille's new-found happiness. And this girl Jenna – I know she's not going to take what I've done, lightly. She isn't, is she? She's that type. All upfront and earnest. She's not the type of girl who's going to appreciate being lied to.

I step into a towel, drying myself off rapidly as the doorbell goes. She's here, and the stark choice before me is clear enough. If I tell her the truth – because I am at heart a man of integrity and lying doesn't sit easily with me – she might just understand, and I'll certainly be doing myself a favour.

But I can't, in all honestly, kid myself that I'll be doing Adam one.

Jenna

'Thank you *so much* for agreeing to come here.' Adam's dad is flustered at the door. His dark hair is shiny and, mysteriously, it's soaking wet as if he's just jumped out of the shower. He pushes it back distractedly with the flat of his hand. 'Please, come on up,' he beckons. 'Can I offer you anything, Jenna? Some tea?'

'It's been a long day,' I admit. 'Some tea would be great.' It's been a very long day, in fact, most of it spent on my feet. My calves are aching. I missed lunch, my stomach is rumbling and I still have thirty-two maths workbooks to mark before tomorrow. I don't mean to stay long – it's nearly six o'clock, but maybe this guy will be more inclined to open up and listen to what his son's needs are over a nice brew?

'Please,' he says, 'take a seat. I won't be long.' While the kettle boils, I check out his place from the comfort of his couch. His flat is on the smallish side like mine, but it's also incredibly cosy and bright. The place is full of books and papers, more homely than untidy, with large poster pictures of faraway exotic places on the walls. Clearly, this man is an adventurer at heart. How incredibly sad that he can barely make it a mile or so up the road to come to the school. How did that come about, I wonder?

While I wait, I bring out some of Adam's workbooks, his English work and his almost non-existent maths. His dad really needs to see these, see how behind the lad's getting with everything. Does he really imagine the nan's been on top of everything? He already knows about the bullying, clearly. We need to get some structures in place so Nate knows what to do to best support his child once I'm gone.

'Hi.' He's back now with a man-sized mug of tea that'll probably take me all year to drink and I don't intend to be here all that long. 'Is that enough milk for you?'

'That's perfect, thank you, Mr ... uh ... *Nate.*' I recall he's already asked me a couple of times to call him by his first name. I pick up my drink, feeling my fingers thaw out. 'It's lovely and warm in here.'

'Is it cold at school?'

'Oh no. Not at all. It's just ...' I look away, a little embarrassed at having brought it up. 'I moved into a new flat yesterday and I haven't figured out how to turn the radiators on, yet.'

'No?'

'I've just moved back here from Sicily,' I add, by way of explanation.

'Nice. Sicily is a magical island. I think I might have been inclined to stay there.' He sets his own mug down on the table between us.

'That's what I thought, once.'

His dark brown, brooding eyes framed by a mass of curly black hair, turn to face me now. Why did I just *say* that? I get a fluttering of butterflies in my stomach, which is ... it's ridiculously unprofessional and most inappropriate. I sit up a little straighter

'I shouldn't complain, though,' I glide on, keen to get us back to the point. 'At Adam's house, his nan doesn't even have any working radiators, does she?'

He blinks. 'You've been there?'

'No, but ...' I open one of his son's workbooks to show him a drawing Adam's done of 'A reiny day.'

'A rainy day?' he says, a little bemused. There isn't much writing to support it, despite this being an English book and it's a scrappy, hastily done picture, but I recognised what it was straight off. Nate needs a little more help, though.

'What is it?'

'It's an old-fashioned clothes horse. See, its load is drying beside a two-bar fire? It is likely,' I explain, 'that they can't afford central heating.'

'Man.' Nate's eyes grow even more sombre. 'He lives in real poverty, doesn't he? I didn't know.' He stares at his hands, pained.

'Look,' I say carefully, 'I don't know what the circumstances were that drove you two apart. I don't know if it was his mum or maybe his nan who never wanted you around your son to begin with, or even if it's something that's come about a result of – your own difficulties ...'

His eyes come directly up to meet mine at that. Then he looks away, lets out a small, hopeless laugh.

'So now you're wondering how come I live in this comfortable, centrally-heated apartment while Adam's nan can barely afford to dry his clothes?' When he looks straight into my eyes I see sorrow, but no guilt. I see a man who still appears to me way too young to be any nine-year-old's dad; I see someone who appears to care, and very much – he isn't putting it on – and yet who's done nothing up till now to make any contact with his child; a well-built, good-looking, well-spoken guy who appears perfectly healthy on the outside but who's told me, in effect, that on the inside he is broken.

And none of it adds up. For a split second, I long to ask why. I'm dying to know *why*. But it is not what I'm here for. It is not any of my business.

'Nate,' I persist. 'You don't have to tell me what happened in the past. I don't need to know. But I *do* need you to know what things are like for your son, right here, right now. I need you to take some action. It isn't just the bullies Adam needs to worry about. It's ... his *whole life* that's shit.'

He opens his mouth as if to say something, but I'm on a roll; 'Living in a house without proper heating, dodging the brats on the way into school every morning and having holes in his socks and shoes that don't fit aren't the worst of his troubles.' I shake my head, emphatically. 'Oh no, things could get far worse for Adam than that.' I pause, aware that this man is not named in any school documents as Adam's guardian and that I shouldn't, in any official capacity, be telling him this.

But if I don't, who will?

'The fact is, there are real concerns being expressed at school about how capable Adam's nan is of looking after him at all. He's more *her* carer, than she is, his – did you know that? We suspect he may be staying off school at times, in order to take her to hospital appointments.'

'Christ.' Nate's staring at me, with his mouth half open, now. 'I didn't know that,' he admits.

'I'm thinking …' I say softly, 'there are a lot of things that you don't know about him. Am I right?'

Nate buries his head in his hands with a soft moan. 'A lot of things. And … there are some things I should have told you at the outset, Jenna. I didn't, and … it doesn't matter now. I can see you want to help him as much as I do but the truth is.' He takes me in, painfully. 'Neither of us are going to be able to do anything for him, are we?'

'Neither of us?' I take a small sip out of the huge mug, feeling perplexed. 'I'm leaving the school, true, but you …?'

'I thought I could do something for him but I can't. What good can I do for anyone, if I can't even leave the flat?' He stands up abruptly. 'Adam's problems,' he says in a low voice, 'they're way too big. They're bigger than I thought when he first came to me.'

'Bigger than you?' I put to him now, feeling my heart sink. He isn't going to commit to doing anything, is he? He turns away, and I take his silence for stubbornness. 'Besides, have you considered the fact that Adam doesn't *have* any problems? It's everybody else's problems that child has been paying the price for, all his life.' I start picking up the exercise books I've brought, dropping them back into my bag and he looks startled.

100

'You're leaving?'

'Your problems, his nan's problems, those nasty little bullies ...' I continue. 'What has *he* ever done to be labelled the one with the problem?' I demand. 'And when's it going to end?'

'What ...' He's pushing his hair back off his brow again, that gesture that he has. 'What exactly do you want me to do?'

'You're the dad,' I remind him, frustrated. 'Do what dads are supposed to do. Start by taking an interest in him. That's mostly all kids ever want.'

'How?' He holds his hands open, genuinely at a loss.

'You could ask to see his schoolwork. Read it, check up on it, praise it, if it's good. Hey – you were a kid once – have you forgotten?'

'I haven't forgotten,' he says in a low voice.

'You could maybe work towards the goal of taking him out places, too. He doesn't go *anywhere*, you know that? There's a school trip to the zoo this Friday afternoon and he won't be going on that, either.'

'The nan couldn't afford it?'

'Oh, there are contingency funds for those who need them. His nan didn't fill in the consent form for it. I imagine she was completely unaware, but nobody chased it up until today when it was too late to be of any use.'

'If we got hold of her now, couldn't he ...?'

'No. The places on the coach filled up so far back, they haven't even got *me* down to go.'

Nate looks really upset.

'I'm sorry he's missing out on so much.'

'Sorry doesn't cut it, Nate. In ten years' time when he's missed out on his childhood, what good will that be to him, then? Just – find a solution to whatever it is that's ailing you.' I stand up, my books safely stowed. No point me staying here if this guy's not willing to see some sense. 'There must *be* a solution. Therapy, or tablets or ... something. You're not the first person this has ever happened to are you?'

'I won't take tablets,' he says through clenched teeth.

'Why not, if it helps?'

'No.'

'Then you should find some other cure.'

'You think it's so easy …?' His lips curl a little, battling sadness, I see. 'You really don't take any prisoners, do you, Jenna?'

'I don't have to, do I? You're already a prisoner here by your own admission.' His jaw drops open and I stop, seeing the unhappiness in his eyes. 'I'm sorry. That was out of order.' I put my bag down. Go over and hand him a tissue to wipe his eyes. *Hell, he's actually crying.*

'I really had no right to say that. It was very unprofessional of me. And cruel. I didn't realise how …'

When I look into his face now he looks mortified. Deeply ashamed.

'And now, to add to the good opinion you already have of me, you think I'm a complete wuss?' He throws me a pained smile.

'It doesn't matter what I think of you, does it? You already believe it yourself. And, no, for the record, I don't think that.' I sit back down again.

'I'm supposed to be making this video-diary,' he says, apropos of nothing. 'As … a way to get some income, as a way of making a recovery. I was supposed to be going out recording; show what happens when I leave the flat, describe it all to camera as it's happening, but …'

I wait.

'But I haven't been able to do it.' His voice is barely audible. 'I couldn't even leave the flat. The first time I did it, my boss at Smart World Productions was on the phone chivvying me along, but on my own … Every time I try and open the door to go out – it feels – like a spell's been cast over me. I can't even describe what that feels like.'

'A spell,' I say, and his eyes come up to meet mine.

'Aren't you leaving, now?' he asks. We both look at my bag, full of all those books, that we haven't really gone over and now we never will. I'm thinking furiously. This man's situation is so much more complex than I'd taken it to be; yet again, I've made assumptions, gone off on one and now I feel like a complete fool. *When am I going to stop doing that?*

'You say you were able to go out with your video-camera when your boss was helping you?' I stand up, now, leaving my bag on the floor where it is. 'How about if I help you? We could try going out of here, you and me. You take your camera with you, and do your recording and you won't be alone. If that's what it takes to fix you so you can help Adam ...'

'What, right now?' He swallows.

It's getting late. I haven't eaten since breakfast and my feet are still hurting. Somehow or other I have been here for well over two hours. Those thirty-two maths books in my bag still need to be marked before tomorrow and my flat, when I finally get home to it, is going to be nowhere near as warm and cosy as this one. But hey.

'No time like the present,' I say.

Nate's silent for a few long minutes, considering this. At last, he nods. 'I'll get my things, then,' he says.

Jenna

By the time we get outside the sun's already going down and it's getting dark outside. There is a chill wind blowing down the High Street and tonight it's pushing through a thin sheet of rain.

'Boy, it's cold.' I laugh, hoisting my bag of school books up higher on my shoulder. 'And these are *heavy*.'

'Please, let me carry those for you. It's the least I can do.'

'No, I'm …' I shake my head, about to refuse when I see he really means it. He's gallant, this one.

'Whoa.' He takes the bag from me. 'It's a good workout, this. Whoever knew teachers needed to be so strong?'

'Anyone who's ever taught. If you're carrying the books, I can help tape you, if you like.'

'Would you?'

I watch as Nate, automatically shielding the camera with his hands, manually adjusts the lens to capture the low-level evening light, the encroaching darkness surrounded by the cheery brightness of street lamps. Maybe it's my imagination but I could swear his hands are trembling.

'Thank you so much for offering to do this,' he says feelingly. 'You have no idea how much it means to me.' I point the video-cam towards him and he takes in a deep, deep breath now, more like someone who's about to jump into a dark icy lake, than someone who's only planning to walk a short distance down the road. The sight takes me aback a little. It's not like there's really anyone or anything out here that is in any way threatening. The streets are practically abandoned at the moment. Is it really *that* hard for him, being out here? I pull a puzzled smile at him and he hesitates,

'Are you sure you want to do this, Jenna?'

'Hell no, it's cold.' I laugh. 'But if it helps you get used to being outside again, that's what all this is about, right?' He's not going to be any use to Adam if he can't get through his front door. I lift my legs up and down a little, trying to get the circulation going in my feet, wishing I had a warmer pair of tights on, wishing I hadn't been quite so enthusiastic as to suggest we come out right now, tonight. It's freezing! Tomorrow would have done as well. Or the weekend. I'm already getting the impression Nate's going to need far more than just one little walk outside to get him going again. What was I thinking? Still, we're here now.

'Shall we walk east, up towards the Chatham end,' I offer, 'or would you prefer to go down towards the river?'

He hesitates and it's perfectly evident to me that what he'd *prefer* is to go straight back indoors. But he's not going back indoors. There's Adam's welfare at stake here, not just his.

'Come on, Nate,' I chivvy. 'You can do this.' For a brief moment, I link my arm in a no-nonsense, business-like way around his, and we push off towards the Guildhall end. 'The more you give in to your fears, the more you feed them, don't you know that?'

'Of course I know that.'

'I am sympathetic, Nate. Please don't think I'm not. But look, if *I* stopped to worry before every action I ever took, I'd be … I'd still be living with my miserable family back in Hull.'

'I never would have guessed you came from a miserable family in Hull,' he says with the ghost of a smile.

'Well, I do. Very damn miserable,' I assure him. 'The only one of them who had any life about him was my dad and as *he* didn't choose to stick around, well …' Nate looks at me in surprise when I say that, and in all honesty, I have no idea myself where that little bit of self-revelatory information just came from. Just as well I caught myself in time and stopped. But hey – maybe it's just what he needs, knowing that other people have their crosses to bear, too?

'My point is, sometimes you've just got to take the bull by the horns, right?'

'Somehow I can't imagine you doing anything else, Jenna.' A brief but gorgeous smile lights up his face for a moment. When he leans in towards me gently, I'm suddenly acutely aware that – no matter what Nate's issues are now – he is still one handsome guy.

One heck of an attractive guy, in fact. I banish the thought and deliberately ignore my first reaction as he places his hand on my arm. Even though it's a very nice feeling.

'Actually,' he says, 'would you mind …?'

What does he want now? I swallow, reminding myself that what we are to each other is just Teacher and Parent. That's all. It stands to reason this guy might be starved of a little company, but – have I misled him about my intentions, somehow? God, I hope not. That could be messy. Should I gently make it clear that I'm here for one reason only?

'Yes, Nate?'

'The camera,' he reminds me. 'You've got to remember to keep it pointed at me as we walk.'

'Oh, sure.' I give a slightly embarrassed laugh. 'Like this?' I point the lens sideways and peer at him through the viewfinder. At least this way he can't see *my* face.

'Hold it this way.' He moves in a little closer, guiding my arm higher.

'Of course. Sorry.'

'Not at all.' He lets my arm go, now. 'How would you know?'

As we walk on further down the High Street, it becomes evident that – even if I have no clue what I'm doing – Nate does know. He's doing a sort of brief running commentary as we go, professional, interesting, and even if he's subdued, in some ways it's almost as if I'm out with a different person altogether. Is this what he does for a living, then? How interesting. He mentioned something about freelancing and earning some income, earlier, I'm sure.

We're doing good, as far as I can tell. We're out. We're moving. He's getting some footage. But as soon as we get to the Cathedral arches, everything changes. Out of nowhere, this look of pained determination comes onto Nate's face and oh! He looks so *earnest*. I stifle the bubble of laughter in my throat, not wanting to ruin what's on the tape but he sees it, anyway.

'What is it?' My companion looks at me, frowning a little deeper now.

'God, I'm sorry, Nate. Please – ignore me. Carry on.'

He stops. '*What?*'

'It's just that you … you look so incredibly *serious*. You remind me of a lad I was watching this morning, trying to stack up a wall of plastic cups and from the look on his face you'd have thought his very life depended upon it. He made me want to crack up.'

'You think it's funny?' he accuses and I feel a rush of guilt at laughing at him, but on the other hand … no matter how he feels, there *is* no real doom about to descend on him, is there? Nothing is going to happen. In his imagination maybe, but not in real life. I blow on my hands now, a little defensively.

'Oh, come on, Nate. You'll think it's funny too, when you see the footage.'

He looks mortified. 'You think people will laugh, when they see what I look like?'

'I don't suppose they'll … what people?' Oh. The people who see the documentary film he's making. Them.

'You think I'm a coward?' he accuses quietly. 'I promise you, before this happened to me, I was never scared of anything, in my life.'

'Nothing?' I look at him curiously.

'Nothing at all.'

'Well then. Why do you even care what I think? Why do you care what *anyone* thinks? You're doing this for your son, remember? If

107

you recover from this, you get him back. More importantly, he gets his dad back. To Adam – what matters more than that?'

Nate looks at his shoes. Then he looks back up at me, slowly pushes his hair back with his hands.

'I know. I remember. When you're a kid his age, nothing matters more than that.' He opens his mouth as if he's about to tell me something else, but then he looks away, up the cobbled street that leads to the dark, protective line of the castle wall. The tower of the keep silhouetted in the distance grabs his attention for a moment and I get the impression there are some things he's still keeping safe in his stronghold. Private things. Things that he doesn't want to share with me. I feel a little disappointed at that, but fair enough.

When he starts up again, he's onto a different tack. 'I agreed to do this video-diary because it's a way back into work for me.' He lets out a deep sigh. 'It's more than that – it's a way back into my life, but I can't begin to tell you how hard it is, Jenna. Not just being out here, but taping it, knowing that ... other people who knew me before will see it, knowing what they'll think when they do.'

'You can't always know what people will think, Nate, and some-times ...' I take a small step closer, 'you just can't afford to care.'

He pulls a rueful smile, looking up as a small, private plane flies overhead. The evening has drawn in swiftly while we've been out together. It's a night of a thousand stars; so many crystal-cut pieces of diamond shining in that huge coal scuttle of the sky, they take my breath away. Nate's been following the line of my gaze.

'It's really something, isn't it? I haven't been out here to look at these properly for such a long time.' He sounds sad. He sounds as if his throat is full of tears and again I get a tiny glimpse into what he must be feeling, what it must be like to be him. How though, how does a strapping, great guy like him come to be in this position? He told me that before, nothing ever frightened him. So he's more like someone who's fallen from a great height, like someone who was once in clutching distance of his heart's desire, before he ... let it all go? Is that how he lost his son?

'Adam's another star-gazer,' I tell him. 'I read in his workbook that he always wishes on the first star out every evening.'

'Does he?' Nate's eyes are on me, intent. 'What does he wish for, I wonder?'

'Who knows? Most kids would be wishing for the latest hand-held console, but in his case ...' I push my one free hand deeper into my pocket as a gust of wind blows an icy and unwelcome slough of rain towards us, leaving the rest of my thought unspoken. I reckon Nate already knows what it is Adam wishes for, anyway – it wouldn't take a genius to work that one out.

My job is to make sure he doesn't forget.

Nate

'So, I think we can both guess what Adam would wish for.' We're standing by the sprawling Catalpa tree outside Rochester Cathedral and Jenna points the camera directly at me, now. 'What about you?' she's asking. 'Apart from the obvious – being able to go out, and all. What else would you wish for?'

'Me …?' I hesitate, and my thoughts go to my visit today from Cami. Would I wish to have had a different outcome from that meeting – maybe have her say something else, say that she misses me, she's made a mistake and she's realised she's marrying the wrong guy? 'Um …' I glance at Jenna.

'You have a magic genie in a lamp,' she's prompting. 'Don't think about it. Quick! First thing that comes into your mind?'

First thing? I blink, reaching back into my mind to the awards ceremony I missed. The opportunity to mingle with powerful TV execs that *might* have been the cake-topper on my potential career, now lying in a heap of crumbs; would it be that? I guess it would be that, but …

'*One thing,*' she urges. 'What is it?'

'I …' What would I wish for? I open my arms, it's hard to pick. 'Only one thing?' I say. We've turned round and started to make our way back into the bottom end of the High Street. I look around us at the deserted streets of Rochester.

'Right here, right now.'

Would I wish for a steady income to pay my bills so I don't get evicted? Christ, I don't know.

Jenna lowers the camera. 'Too late. Genie's popped back in the bottle. Chance gone,' she tells me, clearly a little disappointed.

'Well – what would *you* wish for?'

'Oh, that's easy. Somewhere lovely and warm where I could sit down and enjoy a nice, hot meal.'

Oh, she meant that kind of *right here, right now*. Why didn't she say?

'You want to eat something?'

'I'm ravenous. I didn't make it to lunch today,' she admits. 'I was trying get Adam's nan's permission for this week's school outing, just in case a place became vacant.'

'Ah, yes.' I look at her appreciatively. This girl's got her heart in the right place, that's for sure. 'I don't imagine he can have been too happy to learn he was missing out on the school trip?'

'Kids in Adam's position miss out on a lot of things, Nate.' She doesn't have to tell me. I know that they do.

Jenna pauses now to look through the welcoming window of an old-style Italian restaurant and I stop with her. When we cup our hands on the glass to peer in, it's pretty much empty. They've got little warm tea-lights and a single carnation-stem on every table beckoning us in,

'You want to go in here? You like Italian food?' I hesitate, wanting this girl to accept because – because the man in me wants to be with her a little longer but at the same time I'm apprehensive. This is a more intimate environment. It's bound to elicit more questions, the exchange of more confidences. Under ordinary circumstances I'd have no problem with that, but seeing as we've only been flung together under the pretext of a whopping great lie on my part …

'I *love* Italian food.' She smiles. And somehow the next thing I know, we're inside, ordering food and waiting for our first glass of red wine. In here, in the restaurant, Jenna seems a lot softer, more relaxed.

'I was wrong to say all those things I said to you when we were at your flat, earlier,' she admits now. 'I hope you don't think I'm a pig for saying them.'

'No. Never,' I assure her. I turn my face away and make a little snorting noise, and in response I hear a throaty chuckle.

'Okay, I *was* being a pig ...'

The waiter comes over with a bottle of cabernet sauvignon and we both sit silently while he fills our glasses. After he leaves; 'It's only that ... when you told me that you couldn't help your son, that his problems were too big, I just ...' Her fingers roll up the edge of the linen napkin on the table into a tight tube, which she then proceeds to smooth out.

'I understand.' I stifle a sigh. This is nuts, isn't it? What kind of dystopian universe have I fallen into, that I should be sitting here in a restaurant with this unfairly attractive teacher talking about *my son?* Still, I promised him. Being out tonight is helping me too, I remember. I glance at the camera which is sitting on the table.

'Are we ... are we still taping?' She follows the line of my gaze. I flick the 'Off' switch.

'I'll delete most of this, later,' I tell her. 'And it's okay,' I add softly. 'You didn't say any of it to hurt me, only because you care about Adam, right?'

Her eyelids flicker.

'I do care about my kids. Too much, sometimes.' She leans forward, elbows on the table and her soft, shiny hair falls forward, half covering her face. Then she adds unexpectedly, 'That's why I know this is the wrong profession for me.'

'I'd say it was exactly the right profession for you.' Jenna's shaking her head, but I carry on. 'Adam clearly adores you. I bet the other kids do, too. You don't enjoy teaching?'

'I love it,' she allows quietly.

'You're not tempted to stay on, though?' I take a sip of my drink, trying to make the question sound casual though it is anything but. *Why won't you stay?* If you stay, I can come clean about what my

112

real involvement is, here. If only you say you'll stay on and look out for Adam, I'll be absolved of any further responsibility.

She lets out a long sigh. 'I won't, because I can't bear the thought of being trapped.'

'Trapped?' I look into my wine.

'Schools are institutions that trap you, did you know that? I'd start off doing it for the love of teaching kids and before I know it, twenty years of my life will have flown by and I'll be the same as every other teacher I've ever met.'

I shoot her a puzzled smile and she throws up her hands. 'I mean, can you *imagine* what it's like, never to be able to ... get up and spontaneously lead a class out into the park just because it's been a long winter and the sun's now shining? You can't, you know. You can't take them out without having a dozen permissions signed in triplicate. To have to be stuck there in that one, tiny ...'

'I can imagine it,' I tell her ruefully.

'Oh. Yes. Of course you can. I didn't mean to ...'

'It's okay.' The waiter appears with our spaghetti carbonara and she cheers up visibly. 'Oh, this smells divine. And I am so *hungry* ...'

It does look and smell good. For a little while, as we both tuck in appreciatively, enjoying our meal in this cosy place while the wind lashes cold rain against the glass outside, I can pretend that I am *me* again. The old me, who used to go on dates with pretty girls and enjoy eating out and just being like everyone else.

'You're smiling,' Jenna notes after a bit. 'You're enjoying the food?'

'I'm enjoying being out of my flat,' I admit. 'I'm enjoying being in here with you.'

'Oh.' She laughs. 'Well, good to hear it, Nate, but don't get too used to it. I've already told you I won't be staying at the school for long. I have other plans.'

I look up from my plate.

'Not plans that will take you too far away from here, I hope?'

'Plans that *I* hope will take me somewhere very far away,' she concedes.

113

'And yet ... you've only just arrived here,' I observe. 'From Sicily?'

Jenna shoots me a thoughtful look. Is she wondering if this conversation is steering too close to being personal? 'Not that it's any of my business,' I add quickly. 'I don't mean to pry.'

'No, you're good.' She waves her hand. 'I just ... I never intended to stay here too long. I didn't, in actual fact, *plan* on coming here at all. It's just that a very dear friend lives locally. I've known Magda since art school and when my life changed very drastically recently, I knew she'd help out if she could.' She pauses, running her fingers around the outer edge of her wine glass. 'A thing that seems to happen to me with alarming regularity, in fact.'

'Your life changing drastically?' I shoot her a puzzled smile. 'How'd you manage that?'

'I'm a crap judge of character, Nate, that's how.' She raises her glass to drink and her face is hidden for a moment. 'I always go for the wrong bloke, you see. I never learn.'

'I'm sorry to hear that.' I concentrate on my food for a bit, not really sure how else to answer. I'm no one to dish out relationship advice to anyone else and besides, the memory of a partial conversation I once overheard two girls having in a bar, about how *girls are always happy to share details of their failed relationships with a guy if they believe he's gay*, annoyingly comes back to bug me. Okay, it's paranoia, but – is that why she's sharing?

'You haven't ... come across the wrong bloke in Rochester yet, though?'

'Not yet.' She smiles. 'You know, when I asked you what you'd wish for, earlier on, it was a bit of a trick question, I confess.'

'Oh, yes?' My eyes smile into hers.

'I had a friend at college, once, who was suffering from the same agoraphobic symptoms you do.' She pauses. 'After a while, he began to forget all the things he'd once enjoyed about his life. He couldn't see them anymore. In the end, he stopped hoping for them.'

'Did he recover?'

She doesn't answer that.

'I haven't stopped *hoping* for things, Jenna.' I push the pasta around the plate with my fork for a bit as if I'm going to continue eating it but my stomach's mysteriously closed up. I didn't come out tonight with any intention of talking to Jenna about my troubles. I came out because she offered to come with me and because, I'll own it, I needed that footage.

'You can't give up, Nate. There's a very sad little guy in my class who's still relying on you to come through for him.'

What is this, Guilt Central? I pick up my napkin and wipe my mouth. A chill breeze swoops in as the door opens and another couple, besotted and hand in hand, walk in. We both look towards them but they have no eyes for us. Then her gaze slides back to me. For a moment, my tough-talking redhead looks a little vulnerable.

'Thank you so much for having dinner with me tonight.'

'Thank you for suggesting it.' I look directly at her.

'I'm full of good suggestions, me.' She pulls a rueful smile, her eyes sad. Thoughtful, now, she takes a small sip of her drink. 'In fact, I have another one for you if you're willing to hear it?'

'Go for it.'

'Okay, Nate.' Am I imagining it or is she suddenly choosing her words very carefully? 'I got the impression from Adam's nan earlier on that she was aware of you being back in his life, is that correct?'

I stop playing with my food, feeling more than a little alarmed at this revelation. 'She said that?' *The nan's aware?* Crap. Up to now, all this has only been happening in a little bubble in my mind. The only people who've been involved have been Adam – who *does* know the truth, even if he doesn't admit it to himself – and this teacher. Now suddenly the nan's involved! Things all just got a bit more serious. If Nan already knows about me, the question is – *who exactly* does she think her grandson's been communicating with? I sit up, taking a large gulp of my wine.

God. What's he told her?

Nate

'It's just that …' Jenna runs on, unaware of the anxiety her words have unleashed in me. 'If there are *issues* between you and Mrs Boxley that have remained unresolved over the years, wouldn't now be a good time to deal with them?'

'I guess,' I croak. I look away.

'And … as she told me she's got an ambulance coming for a hospital visit on Friday when the other kids are out on the school trip, I hope you don't mind – I suggested that maybe …'

I push back my chair. *Christ, she's suggested what?*

'I'm not meeting with her,' I let Jenna know straight up.

'I *suggested* that if you were free, she could allow Adam to come and visit you, seeing as he won't be making that school outing with everyone else?'

She wants Adam to have a home visit with me now? How can this be happening, seriously? In this day and age where a teacher can't take her class out to sit on the grass without having permission forms signed in triplicate, a random guy – me – can turn up and be treated as if he were somebody's dad, just because he says he is?

'And she was okay with that?' I thump my fist gently on the table. The old lady's just given her grandson permission to visit a man I'm assuming she hasn't had sight of, for years. If she's ever had sight of him. She's not even going to be present! She doesn't *know* that I am the person she assumes I am, does she?

'Mrs Boxley seemed really delighted at the prospect of Adam coming over to yours.' Jenna pauses. 'I haven't mentioned anything to Adam and I asked her not to mention anything before it was confirmed with you, naturally but … What? Have I overstepped my boundaries? I'm sorry, Nate.'

She *has* overstepped.

'He can't come to mine,' I say tightly.

'Why not? You can help him do his homework. You can … listen to him read. Anything. Just give him the time of day, for Pete's sake.'

'I'd give him the time of day in a heartbeat, Jenna. He's just not coming up to my flat.'

'All right.' A small frown crosses her face. 'Meet him at the library, then. It's not too far from yours. A few minutes' walk. You were fine tonight, you'll be fine another time.'

'Will I be?'

'You have to be. You need to find a way. This isn't just about *you*, anymore, I explained it to you before.' She sounds frustrated, now. 'They've been expressing real concerns about his situation at school and your son's terrified about what it could mean …'

My son.

He is not my son. The rain patters down on the window and for a moment it feels like droplets of sadness and regret beating down on my beleaguered heart. If I'd ever wanted children I'd have made some very different choices in my life. When Cami and I split up, it wasn't just about timing and the demands of my job. If I'd wanted kids – ever – if I'd given her even a smidgeon of hope in that regard, I know Camille would still be with me now.

'I know what it would *mean*, Jenna.' I look towards the door now, a shadow of unease flitting in the back of my heart, wanting to be away from here, needing to get away.

'Do you?' she challenges softly. 'Nate, this isn't just about a little boy with a broken heart. This isn't just about him being bullied. It's worse than that. The harsh truth is, I suspect Nan's no longer properly able to look after him. It won't take much more before

Adam's considered a candidate for Social Care.' She pauses while I take that in,

'He's …?'

She nods. 'He's been off the radar for far too long, don't you think? Look, I could mention the bullying matter formally with senior staff members if you like, but … if we bring the troubles he's having at school into the mix, they might only use that as further evidence that his home life is totally inadequate.'

'God.'

'They could end up sending him to a Home, or to fostering. They might, if they thought that was best for him.' She's quiet for a bit before she adds, 'I don't think it *would* be what's best for him, though.'

I look at her silently. Jeez Nate, just tell the girl the truth. Tell her now before you become any further embroiled in this, *you have to tell her the score.* But there's still some stubborn part of me holding back.

'Does Adam have any other grandparents who could step in – your mum and dad, for example?' she pursues.

'No.' I give a short laugh.

'This isn't funny, Nate.'

Not funny, tragic.

'Seeing as you ask, my own dad disappeared, missing in action – a gunner with the royal engineers – when my brother and I were just ten and eight years old, respectively.'

She pulls a face. 'Oh. They never found him?'

I shake my head. 'No. Mum never got over it. She wasn't able to do a spectacularly good job of coping with me and Mo once Dad was gone, either. Don't get me wrong – I don't blame her, but it was always my dad who wanted the kids, never her. So – no, there are no parents on my side who'd be of use to any child of mine.'

Which Adam is not.

'That's a bummer, Nate I'm sorry. It's going to be down to you then, isn't it?'

It isn't! I wish she wouldn't keep pressing that point and yet, somehow, I cannot let him go. I press my thumbs into my eye sockets, hating this deception more by the minute and then it dawns on me. *She* can't let him go either. This girl Jenna, she really cares about Adam, too. She's come out here to mine, offered to walk out with me; she's even sitting here eating dinner with me this evening, all on his behalf. If I told her the truth now, I wonder – would she judge me?

'Adam's plight has struck a chord with you, hasn't it Jenna?' A slight frown crosses her face but I'm not letting this one pass, I have to know. '*Why*? Why does he matter so much to you?'

'Why?' She stares into her wine for a moment. 'Maybe ... it's just the strength of his belief that he'll find that family he's so desperately looking for.' She sounds sad. 'Every kid should have at least *one* person who's there for them.' Her tone changes slightly now. 'It's why he's been doing his best to cover up his nan's short-comings,' she continues. 'It's the reason why he went in search of *you*. So – what's left? How do we help him, Nate?"

'What's left?' What does she want me to say, what does she expect me to do?

'You're still left,' she reminds me.

I breathe out.

'Okay. I'll meet with him at the library, *fine.*' *What am I doing, what am I promising her?* Why, in fact, am I promising her anything at all? I don't know! This girl, she's ... she's just the soon-to-be ex-teacher of a lad who isn't even my son. And yet I do know this: if they send Adam to a Home, any hope of him escaping torment at the hands of bullies will surely take a nosedive, out of the frying pan into the fire. Her question to me earlier about other grandparents has set up a train of thought in my mind, though. Maybe that's something I can do for him – I can at least find out. And to do that, I am going to need to come clean. I am going to need some more information to work with.

I am going to have to make that visit to see his nan, after all, aren't I? I rub at my face with my hands. Then I pour us both out another full glass of wine.

I don't know if Jenna needs it, but I sure as heck do.

Jenna

'Jenna!' Stella Tilbury, deputy head at St Anthony's Primary joins me now among the troops, her frozen fingers clasping a cup of hot coffee for dear life. 'I wasn't expecting you out here on playground duty with me today – it's Thursday, isn't it?'

'I needed the fresh air,' I tell her. Yeah, like a bullet in the head, after my late night out with Nate yesterday evening, but I have my reasons. I caught the Terrible Trio skulking round the side of the playground, trying to catch Adam on his way to mid-morning break. At least my presence out here is keeping them at bay. For now, Adam's happily joined in with some of the younger kids, kicking a football around.

'Well, it's certainly *fresh*.' Stella's been following my line of gaze. She comes back to me thoughtfully. 'I notice you've formed a particularly good attachment to young Adam, there?'

'Easily done. He's a sweetheart.'

'I'm glad you think so, Jenna. It's a sad story and all the staff here will tell you how desperately he craves attention. Just …' She clears her throat delicately. 'Watch your belongings around him, that's all.'

I stare at her, disbelieving. 'You're saying he steals things?'

'Not exactly. He just – he's very good at *finding* things. Oh – you'll see.' She gives a brief shake of her head, changing tack. 'I heard a rumour his father actually made a show at the parents evening on Monday – could that be true?'

'He did.'

'I'll be blowed.' She makes a soft whistling sound through her teeth. 'None of us have ever had sight of the man in all the time the child's been at school. Then you're in for a couple of weeks as a supply, and he turns up at a parents evening. Wonders will never cease, eh?'

'I guess they never will.'

She blows into her hot drink. 'I heard Patricia Cheska – 4C's regular form teacher – say once, that she thought Adam's father had been very young, a travelling musician of some sort when the child was born?'

'Was he?' I hide a smile. 'We didn't talk about any of that.' *Nate was once a travelling musician? Interesting!*

'… at any rate, it's not the best of circumstances. Some kids don't get a lot of breaks, do they?' she mutters sadly. 'There's not much you can do for them.'

'His dad's a sweetheart too,' I assure her. 'He's gone through some tough times, but as far as I can tell, they're building bridges now. In fact, we even talked about the possibility of the two of them meeting up on Friday when everyone else is on the coach trip.'

'Now *that's* a piece of news our Mrs Ellis will be very happy to hear.' She's nodding.

'Mrs Ellis …?'

'She's our school Social Care coordinator, part of the team who've been keeping an eye on the lad's situation with his nan. She'll be delighted if the father's now back in the boy's life. In fact, she'll probably want a meeting with him, if that can be arranged. Do we have the father's home contact details?'

I look away swiftly, sensing that the school might need to take things a lot slower, if Nate's going to come on board.

'I'm not sure. However, speaking of homes, I've got my own one now.' I steer her off onto a different topic. 'I moved into my flat just this Tuesday.'

'Fabulous, that means you're a local. In fact.' She leans her head in towards me, imparting a confidence. 'It makes you a prime

121

candidate for Miss Cheska's job, if – as is being rumoured – she chooses not to come back after all. Ageing parent issues …' she mutters under her breath. Then she adds, 'your popularity with the children has been noted.'

I look at the ground as a ball rolls up to nudge my foot. A group of kiddies look at me hopefully, Adam among them, smiling. Oh dear. Has he heard what she just said? I send the ball winging back their way again. I *hope* he didn't hear her comment about me staying on because I don't want him getting his hopes up.

'You play your cards right, my dear, and this job may be on permanent offer.'

'Oh, yes?'

'After all these months of supply teachers filling Miss Cheska's place on and off, and just as we believed she was ready to properly come back … it turns out that maybe she isn't returning to St Anthony's after all.'

I smile non-committedly. No point priming her just yet but, while I might keep my Rochester flat on as a base, there is zero chance of me staying on at the school. Not now – especially when I have, this very morning, had some exciting news in!

'A word to the wise, though,' she adds under her breath. 'A whisper has reached The Head that you took 4C out to the Vines to play a spot of Rounders, yesterday?'

'I did. Yesterday was the first bit of sunshine I've seen since I got here. The playground was off limits because of the football training and nobody could concentrate with the site works drilling going on. I thought my class would benefit from a change of scene, they've been so cooped up.'

'Ah. Strictly speaking any off-site trips do need to be agreed in advance with management. On this occasion, no harm done but The Head asked me to mention it. I do appreciate some of the children might be going a bit stir-crazy, we've had an unusual amount of rain for May. Of course, Mr Drummond's all for using sporting activities to help the children let off steam.'

Or for acquiring more trophies for the school sports display cabinet? For once in my life, I don't speak my thoughts out loud. It's too cold to hang about for long, and as soon as Stella walks off, I retrieve the email Jed Miller forwarded to me out of the blue last night. I actually printed it out because I wanted to have a real, physical reminder of it on me. It's from Christiane Finlayson.

Good to hear from you, Jed. Yes, I'm still looking for a PA/tattooist helper for my U.S. tour. I'm excited to see from your email that Jenna comes so highly recommended. She sounds just the person I'm looking for. As I'm in London at the weekend for a joint exhibition at *La Belle Verdin* with one of my former protégées, I suggest she and I should rendezvous. If she's agreeable, this Friday morning would work well for me. Best, Christiane.

I scan once again over the bit where it says 'My U.S. Tour,' and 'just the person I'm looking for', and feel a leap of happiness in my chest, imagining it. In a month's time, I could be headed out of here on that tour with her. Her website indicates that's all kicking off in the sunshine states. Amazing. What better remedy could I have to forget Sicily and all the crap that went down there?

'If you're serious about your tattoo career and willing and able to travel, then this could be the career break most young'uns could only dream of,' Jed Miller has added to the bottom of the email. As if he needed to tell me. It looks as if, after getting his recommendation, Christiane may well have made up her mind that she wants me on tour with her. I got back to them in the affirmative, straight away, naturally. Friday morning, here I come! How lucky, to top it all, that the school don't need me on Friday either, because of the coach trip. Clearly, this was meant to be.

'Is this one *yours*, Miss Tierney?' Adam's at my side suddenly, this time with my mobile in his hand.

I told away Jed's email.

'I think you know that it is, Adam.' Automatically, I feel in my pocket, the place where it no longer is. 'Where did you get it?'

'I found it beside the photocopier, Miss.'

'Did you?' Why would my phone even *be* in The Office, in the first place? I frown slightly. 'What were you doing by the photocopier?'

'Copying a form to say I can stay off school on Friday because I won't be on the coach trip.' A small unhappy shadow crosses his eyes, and I'm immediately aware of how Stella's words earlier – *watch your belongings around him* – have already made me doubt him. *You too?* his look seems to say.

'How strange it should turn up there.' I don't think I've actually even been in The Office this ... Then I recall; he's right, I *did* have my phone out early this morning. I had that email in from Jed, didn't I, and I was in The Office printing it. I give a sigh of relief and another message pops in now. This one's from Nate. Skimming over it, my heart immediately sinks.

Jenna, forgive me, but I have been unable to leave the house again. Don't think I will make that meeting with A on Friday. Have you told him it's definite, yet?

Blast. I haven't mentioned it to Adam, no. But ... Nate promised me! He's not wriggling out of it as easy as this. He *can* make it. He was fine when he went out on that walk and to the restaurant with me last night, wasn't he? He's got to at least give this a go! Adam's still there, taking me in attentively.

'You okay, Miss?'

'I'm ... yes; I was just thinking how clever you were to find this phone for me, because I'd never have thought to look for it there.'

He smiles, now. A sweet, sad smile that makes me want to gather him up in my arms for a big bear hug, but I can't. The whistle goes, and as we start to walk back to class, I do the next best thing:

'Adam, I have some good news for you.' He looks up hopefully. He's not a kid used to hearing much in the way of good news, I know.

'You're not going on the coach trip with the rest of your class, but … there is something else you might be able to do.'

'Come in and help tidy up all the classrooms?'

'No.' I stifle a laugh. 'Not that.' I take in a breath. I'll tell him I've organised a trip to the zoo or into town for some ice creams for the best-behaved children in class, or some such. I need to invent something that will make it up to him for not being able to say what I *want* to say; that his dad is going to be there for him, from now on. But when I open my mouth, that isn't what comes out. This is what comes out, instead,

'I've spoken with your dad, and he's agreed to meet up with you this Friday.'

'He *has?*'

Shit. What have I just promised him?

'Yes. You probably already know that Nate's got a problem with going out places, though?'

Adam gives a rapid shake of his head and I sigh. The kid doesn't know?

'Okay, I'll explain it to you as we walk back to class. But at least Dad wants to meet with you. It's progress, right?'

The look of astonishment and sheer pleasure on Adam's face is worth all the explaining and manoeuvring I'll now have to do to make this happen.

'That makes me the happiest person in the whole world,' he tells me feelingly. As we walk back together, any reservations about whether that was the right thing to say, disappear. Nate *does* want to bond with his son, I know it. He just needs a little help. If it means I have to help the guys out and be present myself, at least for part of their meeting on Friday, then so be it.

It won't be ideal for me, with my other plans. We join the others and I head off the rosy-cheeked chatterboxes in 4C, trooping them back into the warm classroom where they noisily divest themselves of scarves, gloves and coats, everyone diving for the coat pegs outside the classroom – there are never enough. As I bend to pick up the garments that have slid to the floor, a small shadow of unease scurries across my mind. Am I taking on too much? I'm already supposed to be meeting my – *hopefully* – new employer Christiane, in London on Friday morning. She didn't give me much notice, so she won't mind if I put her off till later in the day, surely?

I hope not. As the kids settle down to some work, I text her to let her know there's been a slight change of plan.

In the meantime, I shove any reservations I've got about that, into the same shady corner of my mind where I've put '*Text Nate and tell him he is still on, for tomorrow.*' I've promised Adam now and I'll have to deal with it.

Even though I don't want to deal with it. Any of it.

I sit down at my teacher's desk and watch as the rain begins to batter on the windows outside. While 4C settle to some reading, I get on with dreaming of the time coming soon when I'll be doing art again, in the sunshine.

Nate

I can't believe I agreed to do this.

'The library's only a stone's throw from your flat.' Those were Jenna's precise words in her last text to me. She flat-out refused to let me bail out of my promise. And on one level, I am pleased. *'On a Friday morning it'll be as quiet as you could hope for and no trouble at all for you to get to, especially if the lad walks down with you.'*

Jenna was right about it being quiet, I'll give her that. An old guy came in earlier enquiring after some books on military paraphernalia but apart from that, the place is like the morgue. Jenna also promised me that if I agreed to bring Adam out here this morning, she'd be along, too. I glance towards the door as it opens but it's not her, yet. Where is she?

'Have you ever been up in the air, Nate?' Adam's sitting at the table by the window with an A2-sized relief map of the world which he's busy colouring in. He's using a pot of bright crayons he's brought along with him for the task. Yellow for the desert areas, blue for all the seas, green for the forested places and brown for the mountains.

'Up in the air, like, on a plane, you mean?' I stop what I'm doing on my laptop – scrolling down an eBay list of *plus-size boys' jackets, as new*, to answer him. I still can't quite believe how he turned up at mine this morning. Red-cheeked, frozen hands and nothing warmer on him than the frayed jumper he's wearing now. Turns out he doesn't own a coat. How could it be that the boy doesn't own a coat, in this weather?

A couple of older ladies who've come in together, head straight towards the Mills and Boon section, now. The librarian gives them a crusty look because they're talking too loudly. The military paraphernalia gent stalks up to the desk with a list of books he'd like to reserve. Nothing else happens. The silent clock on the wall moves not an inch, even though it feels to me as if we've been sitting here forever. Yet even in here, the kid's so happy, so – content. He's hunched forward on the chair, colouring in his homework, happy with nothing much more than my company. I check that thought. *Happy because he believes he's in his dad's company.* Not mine.

'Have you been on a plane?' he insists. 'You've got a lot of pictures hanging up on your walls of different places.'

I blink. 'How do you know that?

'I see them from outside, every time I go by.'

'Oh. Right.'

His head lifts now, taking me in. 'But, Miss Tierney says you hardly go out anywhere. She says you've got stuck in there and now you find it hard to go out.'

'Nowadays I do. But, I've been on planes countless times, sure.'

'How many times, exactly?'

'More than I can remember.'

His face turns wistful. 'I can remember the number of times I've been on a plane.' He puts his thumb and index finger together to make an '0' shape. 'A big, fat, zero.'

'Well – neither had I, when I was your age.' I twist round from the screen to look at him properly. 'I always knew I wanted to, though. I knew one day I would.'

'How did you know you would?'

I turn to face him. 'When you're a kid, you dream of whatever you want to dream, right?'

I see a faint smile cross his lips at that.

'I dream that one day I will climb up the Eiffel Tower. I dream one day I'll ride on an elephant's back. But, most of all, I dream that one day I'll visit that burger place in town and order the Burger Super Deluxe. It comes with a special yellow balloon, did you know that?'

'A yellow balloon?'

'A *special* yellow balloon,' he insists. 'You can't get one like it, anywhere else. But Nan won't take me. Says it costs too much. So we can't.'

I let out a small laugh, at that. If he's hinting, he's really good at it, this kid.

'There's always plenty of people to tell you what you *can't* do, tell you what's impossible but nobody can stop you dreaming. Don't you know – when you're a kid there's not a thing in the world that can't be true.' I get up and go to lean over his work. 'I had pictures up on my walls then, too. Not the ones you can see from the street when you go by – those photos I took myself, but other pictures of places I wanted to visit. The pyramids and such.'

'You've been to the *pyramids*?'

'Sure, I have. I didn't get out too much when I was a kid – like you, we had money issues, there were all sorts of reasons but, I told myself, when I was older I'd fly to every location I could think of, on earth. And I have.'

'More times than you can remember,' he echoes. The thought makes him happy, I can see that. 'Does the world look like this, when you get up there?' He makes a circle with his hand, hovering over the map. 'Are the deserts really yellow? Do the mountains reach up into the sky all *brown*?'

'The sea is blue, I can say that much. As for the rest ...' I straighten. 'Nothing in the world is ever quite how you imagine it. You can't know what it'll be like, you can't predict. Not till you see it, smell it, touch it for yourself. Not till you're really *there*, Adam.'

'Do you miss it,' he questions softly, 'the world?'

'More than I can say.'

There's a lull for a few minutes while he continues with his colouring and I check my laptop, venturing a bid on a jacket that I think he might be able to use. I glance at my watch. Ten-fifteen already. Only five minutes before the auction's up, but where's his teacher got to? She sent a text message earlier saying she'd be late because wanted to ask her friend Magda a favour before she came out to us today. I hope Jenna recognises that I'm not happy to take the kid anywhere further without her being there with us. Not just because of the panic attacks, either.

After I win the item – sniping in with my offer at 50p higher than the other bidder with a mere three seconds to go – I turn my attention to the brief email that's just come in from Hal. It's a response to my earlier one, querying if there's been any progress. I stayed up till the early hours Wednesday night cobbling together the footage I took with Jenna. *No feedback from anyone at SWP yet*, he tells me. *But hang on in there.* I close my emails down, feeling a kick of disappointment. No feedback yet. That really sucks. In my experience, that means one of two things: (1) either nobody's looked at it yet, or (2) they hate it. Either way, I'm still waiting for any sign of that advance.

'Nan does that,' Adam informs me without looking up.

'Your nan does what?'

'She sighs like that. Then I have to go and do something for her, like make a cup of tea, or change the TV channel.'

'Well, you're okay with all that. I don't need you to do anything for me, Adam.' I sigh again, only inwardly this time. I still need to get in touch with his nan, don't I? It's been on my mind. The question is, how? I could ask Adam for her number but I don't want to phone her. What I need to tell her isn't something I'd like to say to anyone over the phone, and I don't want to alarm her by simply turning up, either, always assuming I *could* just turn up. Didn't have much luck last time I tried to walk down to Churchfields, did I? Christ, it's complicated.

'I would help you if I could,' he says. 'I like to be helpful. If you want …' He looks about the library, casting around for inspiration.

'I could take the suit you've brought in that bag, down to the dry-cleaners for you. That's what you brought it along for, isn't it?'

Goddamit, he's observant. I did bring this suit out with that intention. But the longer I've sat here, the less inclined I feel.

'Thank you. But I've decided not to bother.'

'Why aren't you going to bother? Doesn't it need cleaning anymore?'

'It does. I'm just not going anywhere where I'd need to wear it.'

'*Why* aren't you going, is it because you're stuck and you don't like going out?' His voice is that little bit high, carries too far, and one of the old ladies turns round to look at us, nudging her friend. I shoot her a knowing smile. *Kids, eh?*

'Yes,' I tell him sotto voice. 'Because I'm stuck and because ... I've also decided I don't want to go there.'

His eyes meet mine curiously. 'Where don't you want to go?'

'What is this, fifty questions?'

He does a brief counting motion on his fingers. 'I don't think we've reached fifty.'

'No, but we will at this rate.'

'Not if you don't answer them.' His head is down, his chubby fingers furiously and industriously working the crayon, colouring in the mountains again, with brown and brown and endless brown. I swallow. Did I just snap at him to shut him up? I didn't mean to. He's only a kid.

'Look, Adam. I'm sorry, okay. Some things about me – they're private, that's all. You don't need to know everything.'

'I don't really know *anything* though, do I?' he points out. That's true enough. Then, 'It's a very nice suit. Were you going to wear it to take Miss Tierney out on a date?'

'No.' I look at him closely, just so he's left in no doubt. 'I wasn't.'

'Well, you should. She likes men who dress smartly. She told us that in class. She said boys should take as much pride in their appearance as girls do.'

'I take plenty of pride in my appearance, thank you very much. If you must know, I won't be needing the suit because I was *going* to wear it to a wedding I've been invited to in a week's time. But I'm not going.'

'Because you hate going out.'

'Yes, that. And also because the bride is someone who used to be my girlfriend before she was the groom's. And because I'm worried it'll kill me to see her walking down the aisle with another guy.' I look directly into his eyes. 'You ever seen a grown man cry, kid?'

He shakes his head, a little worried.

'That's because they try not to do it in public. It … ruins their smart appearance and the ladies don't like it. That's why I'm not going.' I return my attention to my laptop to complete my eBay transaction. Twenty-seven quid. Right now, to me, that's a king's ransom. I hope he appreciates it.

'That's why you should go to that wedding, but take Miss Tierney with you,' he murmurs quietly.

'What did you say?' This kid's going to remain jacket-less if he doesn't watch out.

'I said you should …'

'I heard what you *said*.' I run my fingers through my hair. Oh, man. What have I got myself into, here? 'Listen up, kid. Your teacher's a lovely woman. Pretty, just like you told me, and I'd even …' I let out a breath. 'I even agree that she'll make someone a great girlfriend one of these days when she decides that's what she's after but, you need to get this into your head – she isn't interested in me. She's leaving the school and, pretty soon, she'll be leaving the area too. She's not sticking around kid, so neither you nor me had better get too hung up on that lovely Miss Tierney.'

'She hasn't left the area yet,' he persists, nothing deterred, 'so there's no harm in asking her, is there? What if you asked her and it made her change her mind so she didn't leave?' He's onto the deserts, now, scribbling wide circles with his crayon, acres and acres of hot dusty yellow.

'Adam, there is *no point*. She isn't into me. Even if I took her to that wedding that I really don't want to go to, even if I managed to keep my shit together and not have a panic attack in front of a crowd of the bride's and my mutual friends, *none of whom* really have any clue about what's happened to me, yet … even then – what would be the point?'

'I don't know. Maybe it's like the world. You never know what you'll find until you get there, like you said.'

'Oh, I've been to enough weddings to know what to expect when I get there, believe me. Adam.' I turn the laptop towards him with the jacket I've just purchased. 'You like the look of this one?'

He nods, surprised.

'Good. It was your size so I bought it for you.'

A wide smile comes into his eyes and I need no further thanks.

'Listen.' I go and sit a little nearer him, my voice quieter. 'I know what you're trying to do here, with all your … chivvying me along and your matchmaking. And I appreciate it. I do. You want me to sail off into the sunset with my beautiful princess, right?' I nudge him and he laughs, that deep, gruff laugh of his.

'She might prefer to fly off on a plane, see what the world looks like from up there,' he points out.

'She might. Or maybe *you* might. One day you will, too, kid. You won't always be poor, and … lonely. You won't always be the little guy with no one to turn to, troubled by those bullies in Year Six. But it's *you* who you need to be concentrating on right now, not me. You want to help me out because you think I'm your dad, but …' I pause, deliberating what's the gentlest way I could say it. What's the least cruel way to say the one thing I know he really doesn't want to hear, but there isn't any kind way. 'None of this is going to work. You know that, don't you?'

He turns his attention back to his map. Pulls another colour out of the pot, now. Green, this time. Deep green for the forests of the world.

'Adam, you do know that?' I pull at his elbow, wanting him to hear me because this isn't fair. This can't go on, what we're pretending to be to each other, him and me.

'You do know I'm not really your dad, don't you?'

'I know that one day you'll tell me that you are.' There's not a trace of doubt in his voice.

'I am not your dad, so *how?*' I ask, perplexed. 'How could that ever be true, Adam?'

'I don't know how,' he regards me steadily, his chin up a fraction, defying me to deny it again. '*When you're a kid you dream whatever you want to dream*, right? *There's not a thing in the world that can't be true.* You said it, just now.'

'Yes, but ...' He's right, though. I did say it. I lean back with my arms folded tightly in front of me. I did say it, and ... once, a long time ago, I believed it myself.

Jenna

'Sorry I took so long to join you guys at the library earlier, but you agree … the wait was worth it, yes?'

'Definitely!' Adam chimes. 'And thank you for borrowing your friend's car so you could bring us here, Miss.'

'You're welcome. How about you – you enjoying the seaside, Nate?' I wipe at my eyes, pretending it's down to the mind-numbingly chill wind currently blowing across Folkestone beach but it's not really. It's the look on his face that's bringing me to tears of mirth. Nate looks so glum.

'I love it.' He tucks in his scarf a bit closer round his neck and looks at me resolutely. 'Don't you?' Ahead of us, his son is already running over the wide, even sand with his arms outstretched, practically whooping for joy. Nate rubs his frozen cheeks.

'Looks like he's having a good time, anyway.'

'He is! Hey, cheer up. When I mentioned I had Magda's car for the day, you heard how he practically begged us to come to the coast. Right now that child is experiencing a dream come true.'

Nate nods, throwing me a rueful smile and we keep walking. I see he's got his camera slung over his shoulder – hoping to take some more footage, today? If he's unhappy about being out in this wide, open space, he hasn't said so. At our feet, the sand is wet and grey and smells vaguely fishy. The kind of biting wind that makes you question *what the hell am I doing here* is blowing into my eyes and despite my enthusiastic words it dawns on me that I never actually meant to come out all this way with these two. I was supposed to be in London, today. I push away the small shadow of unease that crosses my mind at the fact that Jed Miller's contact, Christiane hasn't yet replied to any of the texts I've sent postponing our meeting, for a second time. Did she even get them? Is she still going to be expecting me to turn up? She is, after all, my ticket to the life I'm hoping for next, the perfect antidote to Sicily, but somehow I just couldn't let these guys down. I check my phone again but there's nothing.

'Hey, Adam!' Nate's cupping his hands to his lips, calling across the sand. 'Where you going *now*, kid?'

'I need to fetch some more stones,' the answer comes, half lost to the wind.

'More stones?' Nate looks at the plastic bucket already full of small rocks and pebbles that he's been tasked with carrying, then back at me. The look on his face plainly says, '*Why?*'

I think I know why.

'I once made my dad walk up and down Hornsea beach in weather as bad as this for three hours, collecting pebbles,' I confess. 'I told him we had to keep going till I found my special stone.'

'Damn, that must have been one special stone.' Nate blows on his fingers now, rubs his hands together. 'What was it, a diamond?'

'Better.'

'Better?' We've come to the end of the sandy part. Adam's about to clamber over the slimy green boulders at the end of the beach. I sit down on one of the black crusty rocks by the edge of the sea wall and Nate perches down beside me.

'It got me three extra hours with my dad, didn't it?'

'Ah.' Realisation dawns in Nate's eyes.

I reach into my coat pocket to find my gloves. 'My parents had separated by then,' I explain. 'I was only seeing my dad one weekend a month. Those three hours were precious.'

'I bet they were.'

'Dad cottoned on to what I was doing in the end, though.' I laugh. 'He made me pick out *one* pebble, and then he took a felt pen out of his jacket and he wrote on it; "When you find The Stone, stop looking!"'

Nate smiles. 'Sage words of advice from your dad that you've kept emblazoned on your heart, ever since?'

'If they were meant to be that, they were the last he ever gave me.'

'I'm sorry.' He looks mortified. 'Your dad passed away?'

'He *went* away,' I put him right. 'He went away and he never came back. That was it. Adios. Finito.' I put my head down for a minute, pulling out the fingers of the gloves and feeling a sudden and unexpected sadness at the memory. I run on, wanting to change the topic. 'My ex – he found the pebble in a drawer. I have really *no* idea why I even kept it all these years, but he ...'

Nate's eyebrows go up. 'He threw it away?'

'Oh no.' I didn't really mean to open this up with Adam's dad. But now I've begun, he seems to be waiting to hear the rest. 'Alessandro rubbed off the letters "st". Then he presented the thing back to me in a jewel-encrusted box.'

Nate thinks about this for a minute.

'Oh, okay, I get it. When you find ... The One, stop looking?' I nod.

'Clever. And ... did you?' He looks over briefly, checking his child is safe on the boulders. Adam's still for the moment, dipping his net on a long cane stick into the edge of a rock pool. Nate looks back at me. 'Did you stop looking?'

'Oh, yes. I've certainly stopped now, at any rate.' I pick at the loose bits on the fingers of my gloves. 'I was so besotted with Alessandro it took me a year to see just how badly he'd been lying to me. Turns out he *wasn't* The One. But hey.' I shoot him a crooked smile. 'Maybe there isn't such a thing as a soul mate out there for everybody, huh?'

'No.' Nate's voice seems to get caught in his chest at that. He looks away, out to sea and the wind whips up his long dark hair, blows it back and for a moment he looks really forlorn. And way too handsome, dammit.

'How about you?' I put in tentatively, as much to take the focus off me as anything else. 'You ever feel that way about somebody, Nate?'

He did once. I can tell by the way he's avoiding direct eye contact with me, now. He doesn't really want to talk about her, does he? I want to hold back, but I can't resist asking. 'Adam's mum, maybe?'

He makes a strange noise in his throat.

'I mean, young love and all. You guys must have been pretty young when ...'

'Honestly,' he cuts across me, 'I didn't know her at all, Jenna.'

'What ...?' I give a surprised laugh and a host of possible scenarios flitter through my head. A one-night stand after a tipsy night out? A blind date that ended up being a little more? 'You mean you ...?'

'At *all*,' he insists.

'Wow. You hear these stories about musicians, but you never really think ...'

'Musicians?' He gives a soft laugh. 'Do I look like a *musician?*'

'I don't know. Maybe.' I rub at my arms, feeling embarrassed to have brought it up. 'What do musicians look like, anyway?'

'Handsome and hunky, obviously.' That self-depreciating smile again. He has no real idea of the effect he must have on women, does he?

'I'm sorry.' *How much of a chump must I look like, now?* 'A member of staff at school said she thought Adam's dad might have been a musician.'

'Really?' Nate looks interested, suddenly. 'They told you that about him?'

'They told me that about *you*,' I correct. 'At least, the deputy head said she thought ...'

'I'm not a musician.'

'Oh.' As he doesn't elaborate, I go for it. 'What are you, then?'

'I was a war reporter.'

'Really?' I look at him with renewed interest. 'Is that what started off the panic attacks?'

He looks away from me, clearly not too keen to discuss it. 'I'm sorry,' I say. 'Maybe I shouldn't have asked?'

'You're good, Jenna,' he tells me firmly. 'Obviously I'm not doing that anymore. So if you ask "what am I?" – I'm not anything. I'm just … a guy trying to do his best by a kid in your class. Can you believe that?'

'I believe it,' I say. 'But why are you looking so apologetic?'

'Am I?'

'You sure are.' A sudden thought grabs me now and I just can't shake it. This isn't about his profession, is it?

'Nate. You did see Adam's mum again after you – I mean …' I stop, a little taken aback. What if he's only recently been acquainted with his son, not *reacquainted*, but acquainted? If he hardly knew the mum, it's possible he might never have even seen Adam before. It could explain a lot of things, if it were true. Like how – although I detect a real bond between them in the way they interact – in so many ways, he hardly seems to know his son. A second, even more alarming thought occurs now.

'You did actually know about Adam, didn't you?'

Nate looks at his shoes.

'Are you saying that his mum, she … she never told you?'

'I'm not saying that, Jenna.' Is it really just the blustery wind making his face go red or is it what we're talking about?

'What are you saying, then?'

'Nothing,' he comes back a little stronger. 'I didn't have a relationship with his mother, is all I'm saying. If I told you the full truth of it …'

What? *What?*

He turns his head away again as a young voice reaches us from across the rocks.

'Dad! Look at me. *Look at me!*' Adam's waving a tiny crab he's just fished with his net from out of one of the rock pools. 'I've gone fishing.'

'You actually got one?' For a moment, forgetting all about me and my pesky questions, Nate's face creases into a really wide grin.

How *do* men do that? Seriously. How do they cut off so completely from whatever you were talking about and what they were feeling the moment before?

'I've got one! With the net you bought me. Get rid of all those stones out of that bucket, I need to take this home to show Nan.'

Nate obligingly tips the bucket up and a heap of little wet pebbles, all grey and brown and shiny black, appear on the sand at my feet.

'So much for special stones.' The man of mystery winks at me, on his feet in a trice, and the next thing I know, he's clambering over the mossy boulders to join his son. I watch him go, wondering at the timing of it. Our conversation's been abandoned in favour of a little rock crab. Okay Nate, that's cool. I understand we're here so you two can spend some time together, but I've postponed Christiane Finlayson *twice* so I could be here this afternoon for you guys.

Is it too much to ask you what's really going on?

Nate

'It'll die?' Adam's face is a picture of disappointment. He's been carrying that crab around in one inch of water for the last hour at least. It came with us to that burger joint where we stopped for lunch. It's travelled in and out of all the little shops we've visited in the town and later it even had a stopover at the play park.

'Afraid so. It's time your pet-for-the-day went back into its home rock pool, Adam.' When I glance over, hoping for a bit of backup, Jenna's busy stuffing her phone back into her handbag. She's already checked for text messages a few times today, but by her face, I'd say whatever she was hoping for hasn't come through, yet.

'I'm guessing it's also time,' I defer to our driver, 'that we all went back to ours, too?'

'Ready to go home then, Adam?' Jenna shoots a smile at him. 'Do you need to use the bathroom before we ...?'

He shakes his head, keen to hang about with me on the promenade while she heads off to the Ladies.

'I'll *never* be ready.' He admits to me in a quavering voice.

'No? You don't want to go back home?'

'I don't want today to end,' he declares. 'I think today has been the happiest day of my life.'

Wow.

'Well, I'm glad you've had a good time,' I say. 'I've enjoyed being out with you, too.'

'Have you?' Those wide earnest eyes are on me in an instant, seeking out the truth of that statement. This matters to him *so much*. I feel a twist of guilt at the deception we're both playing – at what Jenna doesn't know – but there's no deception in my answer.

'I've had the very best time being out with you today, kid. In fact, I've actually been …' I stare out over the sea wall for a moment, wondering at it. At the absence of … *that*. That feeling of doom that I was expecting to descend when I agreed to leave the relative safety of the library and come out all this way with these two, this morning. It hasn't descended. Not even an echo of it. Today, for no reason that I can explain, I am feeling no anxiety about being outside at all. Not a twinge.

'In fact, *what*?' 'Adam puts down his bucket on the edge of the promenade. He plucks out the crab delicately by one of its claws, holding it up high so we can both get a better look at it.

'In *fact*, I haven't felt better in months.' I stop, feeling something strange go in the pit of my stomach as the realisation dawns on me. Man. I haven't, have I? I've been so engrossed in being out with these two I hadn't realised how unusual it'd become for me to do a thing like this. It felt so … normal. *I* felt normal. Shit. I wipe away the tear that forms, quickly, before he sees it.

'You got something in your eye, Nate?

'Yeah, this wind, it's really …'

'She had a good time too, didn't she?'

She? I bend to peer at the crab he's still holding tenderly aloft. The kid's that lonely, it strikes me now, that desperate for the company of any living thing. It gets me in the gut, to see it. Maybe when I go meet his nan I could bring up the suggestion of getting him a dog, or something?

'Your new-found friend, you mean. Crabby?'

Adam laughs, a deep, mirthful laugh at that. 'My *teacher*, Nate. She had a good time, too.'

Oh.

'You really think she did?' I swing round just in case she's on her way back, but she's nowhere in sight just yet. 'You think Miss Tierney enjoyed herself today?'

'She was laughing a lot,' he observes. 'And she was smiling at you most of the time.' He's smiling to himself too, stroking the little crab's back with the tip of his finger. 'I think that's usually the sign of someone having a good time.' He glances up at me.

'It is, you're right.'

'She got a bit sad when she was telling you that story about her dad, though.'

My mouth drops open. 'You heard that?'

'The wind blew her words straight over,' he informs me.

'Well – perhaps you'd better keep that to yourself. I don't think she realised you were listening to that bit.'

'I know how she feels, though. You understand too. That's why she told you.'

'You think?' I do up the top button on my jacket, feeling thoughtful.

'I do.' There's a small pause, before he adds, 'You know, I saw the dry-cleaning shop was doing a special on suits this week. You might want to get it done now, *just in case* …'

I straighten.

'Just in case you're still thinking of going to your ex's wedding,' he finishes.

'I thought we already went through that one.'

Adam places Crabby down so it can have a little walk.

'We did. But that was before today happened. Now you realise you *can* go out and have a good time and not feel scared. At least, you can if you've got a good friend with you.'

'Miss Tierney isn't a good friend, Adam,' I remind him. 'Sure, she's a good person. And she's being a great teacher to you by coming out here with us, today. But she's here today for *you*, don't forget, not for me.'

'It's the same thing, isn't it?' He nudges the creature with the tip of his finger, when it doesn't seem to want to move. 'The better you get, the better my life will be too. Miss Tierney knows that. That's why she's helping us both.'

'Adam …'

Doesn't he get it? The more I allow her to help him – and me – the closer she gets to both of us, the more danger there is that she'll learn the truth.

And I have no doubt in my mind as to how she'd react to *that*.

'If I let Crabby go,' he frets now, 'how do we know he'll find his way back to his own home?' His rock pool is all the way over there …' He points to the craggy boulders beyond the sea wall. Course it is. That's another ten minutes' walk, there and back, but I'm not falling for that one. Doesn't he feel the cold at all? Maybe that fleece we bought him at the charity shop before coming down here is just too damn cosy. Anyone else would be bawling to be let off home by now.

'Most creatures have a good enough instinct when it comes to finding their way home. He'll be fine.'

He sighs. 'How do I *know* he will be, though?' He prods it again …' He doesn't want to go either. He's not moving.'

Damn, it's not dead is it? It's been in that bucket a while. I rack my brains, trying to remember how crabs breathe. It hasn't got soggy, I hope?

I pick it up now and set it down on a long pole that runs from the top of the wall to the beach. Then we get to our knees to watch as it very slowly decides it wants to move, taking a good, few minutes before – thank God – it finally scuttles off. Adam looks as if he's about to cry. I put my hand on his shoulder.

'He will be fine, believe me. You just have to trust.'

'I have to trust?' We both scramble up and he wipes his nose on the back of his sleeve. I pat his back, not sure what else to do. 'I'll never see him again, will I?'

'No,' I admit. 'I know you want to, but we don't always get as long as we'd like with people and things, that's just how goes.'

'I see. Are you talking about us, now?' he asks quietly. 'Or are you talking about the crab?'

'I was talking about the crab.'

'I thought maybe you were talking about us.'

'I wasn't talking about us.'

'Oh good. If we go home now then – when will I see you again?' He's looking at me a little anxiously. 'You do *want* to, don't you?'

I blink. 'Of course, I want to. I'm just not exactly … entirely …'

'Because if Miss Tierney's not around, I think you might be a bit good at talking yourself out of things,' he mutters. 'Even when you want to do them.'

What is he – my life coach? *My therapist?* I open up my arms. 'What's even the tiniest scrap of evidence you have for that statement, Adam?'

'Well. You want to go to your friend's wedding, I know you do.' He points his finger at me, now.

'I don't want to go.'

'Why don't you just ask Miss Tierney to help you?'

'I've already explained why. Besides, I can't.'

'You would like to go, really, though?'

'All right, I *would* like to go.' There I've said it. Will he let me off, now? 'I'd like to go because it's one of those things, like, getting back on a horse after you've fallen off it.'

'I think you should,' he says. 'Get back on that horse.'

'Maybe,' I muse. We peer over the sea wall at the boulders below but the crab's disappeared. Gone back to where it came from. Gone to join all its mates, doing whatever it is they all do. I'd like to be able to do that, too. Adam might have a point. Then, for no good reason I can think of, I muse out loud, 'I'd like to go to that wedding if I could. Both the bride and groom have been important people to me, in my life. I love them both, really, it's just …'

'That would be a good reason to go,' he encourages. 'That way you can show them that you don't mind about them being together. I bet they'll have a lot of nice food, too and if you made it, you'd prove to yourself that you can live like a normal person again?'

'I suppose I would.'

Now wouldn't that be a thing? I let myself imagine it, as we stand there together watching the grey waves roll in, feeling the patter of another slough of rain on our heads. How it would be, if I went to that wedding and showed my face and found that *I wasn't afraid?* If only this ... irrational fear ... which has been ruling my life for far too long, would just go away, if I could keep hold of how I'm feeling today. I'd get to keep my flat then, too. I wouldn't have to make any more of that blooming video-diary which I never remotely wanted to do, I could do some proper work. I'd get to go travelling again, write my pieces and make the documentaries I always dreamed of.

'I'd like to, Adam. It's part of what needs to happen before I can ...' When Adam sits on his bottom now, his rolled-up trousers displaying his legs sticking out in front of him, I catch the shocking sight of those bruises again. I frown, feeling my heart constrict. Bruises on bruises, they look like, dark blue and black, edged with faded brown. Those will take ... Fuck me; I *know* how long those'll take to heal over. Another day like this one, rainy-grey, shoots straight through on a time capsule, assaulting me now from the forgotten spaces of my heart.

Mo. My brother, Moses. Born before me but always, always, so much younger than me. *Damn it, Mo.* His curly hair sticking up like a black bird's nest, crumpling against the grey of the playground wall, his face wet with tears, he shoots into my mind now.

'Those little bastards been at you again?' The words are out before I can stop them. Adam looks down at his legs, then he gingerly rolls the upturned edges down.

'I told them I was going to tell you about it, this time,' he says quietly.

'Why didn't you tell me?'

'I wasn't sure if you ...' He swallows. 'I told them they would get in trouble but they didn't believe it.'

Inside my pockets, my fists clench.

'This time, they'd better believe it.' There's a moment, then, a mere microsecond slither of time when Adam looks directly at me as if to see how much I mean it. I look right back at him, our eyes locking and something in his face just … collapses in relief.

'All done here?' Jenna's soft voice is a shock, coming from behind us and I turn to find her looking thoughtful. Has she just arrived back? I didn't notice her. Adam scrambles to his feet.

'I think we are.'

'I was going to bring up the bruising with you.' She turns her face away slightly, her comment for my ears only. 'They got to him again yesterday on his way home. It's why I'm desperately worried what's going to happen to him once I'm not in school anymore.' She beckons for me to walk a little further on ahead with her, to make sure we're out of earshot.

'It's why I really need you to make an appointment to see Mrs Ellis next week. Preferably before I leave, if possible.'

'Mrs Ellis?' My eyebrows go up.

'She's the School Care coordinator. If Adam's got his dad back in his life, she's the one who needs to know about it.'

I glance apprehensively at Jenna. 'Does she already know?'

'The staff are aware you came to parents evening, so she'll have an idea. She'll be a key figure in the discussions surrounding his welfare, Nate.' Jenna stops. I sense she wants to say more but she's gauging my reactions, not wanting to overwhelm.

'Mrs Ellis. Right.' Jenna wants me to make myself 'officially known.' Impersonating someone's absent dad sounds like some kind of criminal offence. I'm pretty sure it is, but then … in the back of my mind I always knew that this was potentially coming.

Adam catches up with us now and we wait while he tips the water out of the bucket, now that Crabby's gone.

'Never know when this might come in handy again.' Adam's face takes on a hopeful glint.

I smile.

'We could use it to put fish in, next time?' He suggests.

Next time.

Something about being out here in this wide open space where the water meets the land and the air blows in from frozen places

147

so very far away, it makes me feel that there *could* be a next time. Oh, it's madness, I know. But standing here, on a day like today, the world feels so big, and the possibilities so wide. It feels like it when I'm standing here with these guys, watching the little waves rolling in from far out at sea. I turn my collar up, proof against the gusts of wind, push my face down where it will be hidden, into the warmth of my scarf. I think: I haven't forgotten you, Mo. I never will forget you.

'Your lad has had a good day out today, hasn't he, Nate?'

'I have too.' I pull myself back to Jenna, to answer. Strangely enough, it is true. We make our way back to the car. As Adam skips ahead along the promenade, I can't resist adding,

'I've just *loved* the burning sensation of cold around my nipples and dicing with the danger that my ears might succumb to frostbite any minute, haven't you?'

'Your fault for having sticky-out ears, Mr Hardman. As for my nipples, that's my own affair,' she comes back pertly.

'I'm sorry,' I look away, embarrassed. 'I didn't mean to sound ...'

She bursts into a gale of laughter, slapping her hands over her mouth and for a few minutes, allowing myself to forget the reality of the situation, I laugh along with her. Adam's right. She does laugh a lot when we're together. Maybe she's always like this?

Or maybe she just likes me?

'Now. About this friend's wedding,' she murmurs to me as we reach the car at last. 'Tell me. Would it really help with your situation, if you could find someone to go along with you?'

Jenna

'I'm not sure how much you overheard Adam saying to me just now.' Nate turns to me by the car, a little startled.

'Only that there's a friend's wedding you'd really like to go to but feel you can't and he was trying to persuade you to ask someone to go with you.' I pause. 'Specifically, me.'

I can't see Nate's response to that because he's turned his face away, embarrassed.

'I'm sorry. The lad's got some very strange ideas into his head.'

We both watch for a bit as Adam sits down on a nearby low wall and proceeds to shake every last grain of sand out of his shoes. The child is wrapped up in the moment, oblivious of us, but if I had any doubts about whether I did the right thing or not, coming out here today, the look of happiness on his face dispels them all.

'Adam's been trying to matchmake us ever since you came to teach in his class, hasn't he?' Nate looks apologetic.

'Children do this. Especially kids who long for parents. They get their hopes up. It happens.'

'I keep telling him he mustn't.'

'Please.' I lay my hand on Nate's arm for a brief moment. 'Don't apologise. He's adorable. He's trying to look after both of your best interests in the only way he knows how. Look, Nate.' I pull off my gloves and stuff them in my pocket. 'I know all this is none of my business, but ... why don't you get someone to accompany

149

you to that wedding? You seem to cope beautifully being out, as long as you've got someone with you?'

Nate pulls a pained face.

'Who, though? I've kept such a low profile from my friends for so many weeks, I'd feel ...'

"When you say you've kept a low profile, do you actually mean ...' I stop, looking at him in surprise. 'Bloody hell, Nate – do any of your friends actually *know*?'

He gives the tiniest shake of his head. My, he's a dark horse.

'Barring the two who are getting wed, no. They don't. And I don't want them to know.'

Adam's on his second shoe now, clearly in no hurry for this trip to end. We give him his space.

'Perhaps,' I suggest delicately to his dad. 'Your friends need to know, though? You're feeling vulnerable, I can appreciate that. But that's what friends are for, surely?'

Nate shoves his hands deep into his jacket pockets.

'In my experience, when you're at your most vulnerable that's the worst time to let anyone know how you feel.'

'But not with friends, Nate!' I pause, wondering what's happened to this man, that he feels this way – *when you're at your most vulnerable that's the worst time?* Holy crap.

'Come on, a guy like you must have *loads* of friends?'

'I have.' He pulls a rueful face, 'but I'm not a "wear it on your sleeve" kind of guy.' Then he adds, tellingly, 'The only person I ever let my guard down that much with, is the same woman who's marrying another guy in a week's time.'

'Your ex? She's the one who's getting married?'

'Her name's Camille.'

'Ah. I see.' Camille. How longingly he says that name. He thought it was her on the phone when I called him from school the other day, didn't he? I feel a small, unexpected shot of disappointment at ... what? I have no idea at what. I push back my blown hair behind my ears, and unlock the car door, pondering on it. Maybe

150

this little pang of envy is only because this guy is clearly still so in love with his Camille? Every time he says her name, I feel it.

Look at him, right now he's practically looking *tragic*, at the thought of her marrying someone else. It's cutting him in two. Lucky Camille, that's all I can say. As I climb into the driver's seat out of the cold, I wonder; what must that be like, to have someone love you that much?

Especially him.

I bite my lip, not sure where exactly that thought just came from, and wishing it would go right back. It's not like I'm actually … starting to have *feelings* for him.

No, of course I am not.

I hardly know this guy. He's told me he used to be a war reporter but I don't know if that's related to the reason why he's had no contact with his son up to now. I don't know why he broke up with his girlfriend or a hundred other things people usually get to know about each other. And, let's face it; there is no reason why I should know, why he should tell me any of it. I'm on my way out of their lives. We're just ships that pass in the night, and yet …

I'm twenty-six years old, and of all the boyfriends I've ever had I doubt anyone of them felt this way on breaking up with me. I never felt that way about any of them. Not even Alessandro, when I think about it. The thought shocks me at first. And then it just makes me feel so … sad. Did I never really love *any* of them? Did none of them ever really love me?

'You okay?' Nate leans in through the passenger side, still waiting for Adam.

'Sure, I'm …' I pull down the driver's mirror, mussing up my hair a bit so he can't see my face. I'm not about to go into all of this with him. I'm his son's teacher, that's all, and he's just warned me he's not a 'wear it on your sleeve' type of guy. But somehow I can't stop myself from saying it.

'I'm feeling a little bit jealous, I guess.'

151

'Jealous of whom?' He swings himself into the passenger seat, pulls the door partly closed.

'Jealous of a woman who could inspire such feelings of love and longing that even her ex can't bear the thought of her marrying another guy.'

'Of Camille?' He looks a little puzzled. 'You?'

'You really loved her.' I nudge him gently. 'You're *still* in love with her.'

'Maybe your ex is still in love with you?' he offers.

'Oh, no!' I give a wry laugh. 'That he is not. You know how I can tell? Because he never *was*, that's how.' I stare through the front windscreen for a bit, our breath already misting up the glass. 'Can you believe, I got together with Alessandro after I saw him one day in the park in Catania, how he was with all his little nieces and nephews. Apart from his looks, that's what attracted me most. How he was such a caring, attentive guy, and he'd have clearly killed for any of them! I loved that. I thought it meant something about how he'd be with me, but you know ...'

'He wasn't?'

'Oh, I can't explain it, really.' I'm feeling a little embarrassed, saying it, now. 'When I see you, all the feelings of turmoil you're going through about attending this wedding, I see ... something different going on, deep inside. I see feelings of longing that I could never make anyone ever feel for me. Up to now, anyway.' I shoot him a sad smile.

'You so *could*,' Nate comes back staunchly.

'What?' I look up from the dashboard, where my gaze has come to rest. Is he just trying to make me feel better, or does he really mean that?

'Don't be jealous of her, Jenna.'

'Be honest,' I insist. 'Your reluctance to attend this wedding – it's not just about your fear of having a panic attack in front of your friends, is it?'

'No,' he allows. 'But that's still a huge part of it. It's the largest part of what's stopping me, and that's the truth.'

'Not the thought of seeing her marry someone else?'

'That'll hurt, no doubt about it. But strange as it sounds, I also want ...' His mouth does a strange twisting movement. 'I want them both happy and I know they'll do that for each other. I know she's found the right guy.' He hesitates. 'You will, too, Jenna'.

'Find The One?'

'I have no doubt about that.' He reaches out to draw a heart-shape with his finger on the misted glass. He's a real artist, though. He doesn't just do a plain old heart; he draws the semblance of grapevines down the side of it and the silhouette of a lady with long hair, and a haunting moon and inside it all, he writes:

J + ?

Outside Adam is doing some last stalling tactics, picking up bits of a discarded sandwich and throwing it to the seagulls that've come swooping. I smile.

'How about you, Nate?' I reach out and trace another question mark on the glass. 'Do you think you ever will? If you start getting out and about again, maybe you'll meet someone new.' I draw a second heart on the windscreen beside Nate's one. I leave it blank.

'I don't know.' His voice is thick, full of doubt. 'But I'd like to try. Would you consider ... helping me yet again, by coming with me to that wedding?'

'Me?' I give a small laugh. 'As what? Your son's temporary teacher?'

'As ... as my esteemed friend. As someone who matters.'

'Ah. As someone who matters.' I turn my face away to hide my smile. Is he asking me because he needs to go and he can't make it without me – or is this some prelude to a date; I can't tell?

'I know I'm no match for you right now, Jenna. But I'd be very honoured if you'd agree to come.' Underneath the wariness there's something else in his eyes, too. A brightness, a hope, the sense of some deep affection stirring.

Something I can't quite put my finger on because I don't think I've ever seen it before.

Nate

'I've got a lunch meeting I need to go off to in about an hour, but I thought I'd come round and see you, first, Nate.'

I hand Marcie the vodka and tonic she's just requested, watching warily as she settles herself down on the tidy side of my sofa.

'Ooh,' she says, feeling the covers with the palms of her hands, now. 'This is a bit … *crunchy*.'

'Yes, it is. Sorry.'

Up till half an hour ago when I finally got round to clearing it all away, Adam's plastic bag was sitting where she's sitting. It's been there all weekend, full of sand from Folkestone beach and when I picked it up earlier I noticed it had left a little damp patch on the seat. I'm hoping that doesn't end up staining her suit. How I ended up carrying that bag all the way back home for him is anyone's guess.

But I have more pressing matters on my mind.

'So. All going well your end, Nate?'

'I hope so.' I sit down tentatively on the edge of the seat opposite her. 'I'm just wondering to what I might owe the pleasure of this visit?

'You can't guess?' Typical of Marcie, right now her face is giving nothing away.

I squirm.

'This is about the video-diary, right?'

154

It's been two weeks since Hal asked me to send along a sample of my video-diary. Even though I sent them off something last week, I know that until I went to the beach with the guys on Friday, I simply hadn't managed to take enough footage. I was up till the early hours of Sunday morning with it, scraping the bottom of the barrel, desperate to have something to send them. I push my hands through my hair, now, distracted.

'I'm sorry if it's shite,' I admit to her now. 'I've been struggling with it. I know you can't release any advance to me if it hasn't been approved, so if that's what you're here to tell me ...'

'You've guessed right.'

I stop, feeling a little shocked.

'I'm here about the video-diary. But you're wrong about it being shite. The team I showed it to at SWP on Monday morning *loved* it.' She raises her glass to mine. 'You're a natural at this, you know, Nate. You come over so well. Perfect, in fact.'

I gulp.

'Thank you.'

'We especially loved the beach footage in the piece you sent over at the weekend. That pretty much nailed it for the team, I'd say.'

'It did?' Wonders will never cease.

'It's been approved and I signed off on the advance this morning. The amount should show up in your account anytime now.'

'I didn't expect that,' I say thickly. Funds in the bank at last. I actually want to hug her. 'I wasn't sure how the sound recording would turn out; the wind was blowing a real gale on Friday.'

'Yet all three of you were clearly enjoying yourselves! Including the two others in it with you gave it that much more pathos, somehow.'

'Did it?' The two others.

'Especially the kid.' Marcie takes a slug of her drink, intrigued. 'Who's the young lad, Nate?'

I blink. This isn't about him. He shouldn't be in there. Did Jenna take some footage I didn't notice before I sent it off? She'd taken a lot of the shoreline. I thought she was just taping waves!

'Adam. His name is Adam.'

'And what relation does he bear to you? He's your friend's son I take it? Pretty girl, by the way.'

'No, she's …' I look away. 'She's his teacher. He missed a school trip so she offered to take him – and me – out for the day.'

'We'd have to get his parents' permission to use any footage, then.' She's topping up her drink with a little more tonic.

'He doesn't have any parents.' I take a sip of my own tonic – no vodka in mine, too early – but the way this conversation is sliding, perhaps I'm going to need it?

'He's an orphan?' Marcie's face crumples in sympathy.

'I know his mum's dead. I don't know about his dad.'

'In that case, how sweet of his teacher to take him out. We'd need permission from whoever has parental responsibility then. So …' She smiles now. 'How did *you* get involved, if you don't mind me asking?'

I do mind her asking, but if Adam's on the tape he's on the tape and there's no way I'm lying to her about this too.

'The kid put a letter through my door a few weeks' back.' I look Marcie straight in the eye and say it. 'Absurdly, he's got it into his head that I'm his father.'

Marcie baulks.

'Hal didn't happen to mention about it to you, then? He was the one who suggested I open the letter the kid sent through here for "Dear Dad".'

'You?' Marcie puts her glass down carefully on the floor beside her. 'And … are you? You'd be a bit young for that. He's about – what, 8 or 9, isn't he?'

'It's technically possible.' I pull a small smile, 'But no, I'm not his dad.'

'You sure?'

'One hundred percent, no. The nan who he lives with has made a mistake. I think he knows it too, but he's refusing to come to terms with it.'

'So he wants to believe you're his dad and ... you accompanied him with his teacher out to the beach?' She's frowning, understandably perplexed, trying to work it out. 'How did that come about? Are you using your journalistic skills, helping him to locate his real dad?'

'It's part of the larger plan,' I allow. 'Marcie ...' I confess suddenly. 'I never meant to get involved. I didn't. I kind of got sucked in. It was only after I saw how much he was being bullied that I went to the school. I meant to apprise his teacher, that was all. I wanted to get the school to do something about it ....'

'And they're not?'

I shake my head.

'But ... that teacher of his would be a good advocate, surely?'

'She's leaving,' I tell Marcie. Saying it out loud, I get an unexpected sinking feeling in my stomach. Jenna is leaving. 'She's agreed to accompany me to Hal's wedding, but she won't be around for much longer, after.' The thought of her coming with me has been bolstering me up ever since the weekend, but she's still ... leaving.

'And the nan?' Marcie's mind goes directly to the next obvious port of call. 'You mentioned he lives with her. You've made contact with her, I take it? You've let her know the score?'

I sigh, still with the fact that I'm soon going to be back on my own again.

'Not yet, Marcie.' I already worked out that was something I was going to have to do. 'I've been busy cobbling that footage together for you all weekend. I've been going nuts working out how I'm going to pay my bills. Talking to the nan didn't feel that urgent, even though it's been my intention to do it.'

'Entirely understandable.' Marcie's nodding sympathetically. 'You've had enough on your plate. But what an interesting narrative that would make, eh? A child contacts a young man who he mistakenly believes is his dad and their mutual support ends up benefitting both of them ...'

157

'I wish!'

'But the nan still needs to know *from you* that you aren't who she's told the boy you are. Might that pretty teacher be of any assistance, perhaps?'

I hang my head. I don't want to admit to this but I'm sick of telling lies.

'His teacher doesn't know,' I croak.

Marcie's eyes open a little wider at that.

'His teacher doesn't know ... what?'

'That I'm not the boy's father.' I look directly at her and say it. 'His teacher's been helping me because she thinks I *am* his dad. She's been offering to accompany me out. It's how I've managed any of it at all ...'

'Lordy, but *why?*' Marcie claps her hand over her mouth. 'Why didn't you just tell her, straight off, Nate? The day you first went to the school?'

'Because they wouldn't have listened to me, would they? Who was I?' I growl. I push my hands deep into my pockets, feeling the heat of shame burning on my brow. 'I had no right to be there, had I? Just a guy he sent a letter to, begging for help – who'd have listened to me?'

'If you'd got a reason to think the child was being hurt, they had a duty of care to listen,' she reminds me quietly, 'no matter who that information came from.'

'Maybe,' I allow. 'But then where would it have led? To social services?'

'Perhaps. Probably.'

'I know what it would have led to,' I remind her. 'I've been there, haven't I?'

'Nate ...' She puts her hand out to my arm but I shrug it off.

'I didn't mean to pretend to anyone I was his dad. I meant to go in and make sure his teacher knew and let the school deal with it but they won't. Nobody will. Kids like Adam aren't catered for in the system, Marcie, unless they have someone advocating for them. Don't tell me they do because I know they don't.'

'Nate,' my boss straightens, now. 'I know you've been through a hell of a time. I know you're in a vulnerable place. Lord knows, we've all been there from time to time, but as a friend and a colleague, please, *listen* to me.'

I look at her.

'His teacher needs to know,' she says, her face dead serious. 'Even if she's leaving. You can't bamboozle the school like that.'

'I haven't bamboozled the school. I haven't spoken to anyone else at the school other than her.'

'No one? No ... official staff representatives other than her?'

I shake my head.

'She's a bit of a maverick herself. I doubt anyone other than the nan knows we were out together on Friday, but ... if I tell Jenna now, she'll have a duty to let the school know my real relationship to the boy, surely?'

'And then you'll be unable to speak on his behalf any further?' Marcie looks pensive. 'So ... if this teacher weren't leaving – would you tell her then?'

'If Jenna wasn't *leaving*, I'd never have needed to become involved in this like I have.'

'Ah, I see. Jenna.' Marcie's face takes on a subtly different demeanour. 'You mentioned something earlier on about her agreeing to come along as your "Plus one" to the wedding?'

'She has. It's kind of her, isn't it? She's keen to help me onto my feet so I'll be of use to Adam after she goes ...'

'And ... will you be?' Marcie muses now.

'I might have to now, mightn't I?'

'Wow,' my boss comes back. 'You really are committed, then. And the teacher ...' She looks at me slyly. 'You *like* her, this girl Jenna, don't you,' she accuses now.

'Any man would,' I come back.

'Oh I can see that, but you're not any man, are you? You were always a little more picky when it came to the ladies, as I recall.'

'She's ... she's a very lovely girl it's true.' I add, for good measure, 'and she's kind. Caring, as you say. And ... funny.'

'And sexy?'

Despite myself, I smile. I recall Jenna doing her version of a supermodel's exaggerated wiggle, fully-clothed, walking along behind two coiffured poodles on the sand. I recall the sound of her husky laugh and how ready she always is to take the mick out herself, as much as everyone else; her spontaneity, her boldness, how unafraid she is, of getting it wrong. In my books, a woman who's as prepared as she is, to just be *herself*, can never get it wrong.

'Sexy too, yes. But before you run away with any ideas – she isn't interested in me, Marcie.'

'Oh, no? The girl's got eyes in her head, hasn't she?'

'She isn't interested. She's only recently been through a messy break-up of her own. Apart from all that, she's *leaving*.' I push the point home. 'She's made her intentions plain to me. We're working together for Adam's benefit, and that is all.'

Marcie's chin goes up.

'You need to tell the nan, at the very least then, Nate. You need to tell the nan today that she's made a mistake and you're not the child's father. Tell her and be in the clear, once and for all.'

'How?' I pull my hands out of my pockets, rub at my head delicately. Right now I do not want to think about Adam's nan. All I want to do is to find a way to admit to Adam's teacher that I made a big error of judgement in not trusting her with the truth. She deserves to know it, and talking to Marcie has brought that much home to me. But finding a way to do it, that won't hurt Adam's interests, is about as far away from my grasp as getting on a plane to Paris was, a few weeks ago.

'How can I go down to the nan's.' I turn to Marcie, heartsick to my core. 'Have you forgotten I'm not capable of making any trip out of here by myself?'

Marcie sighs. Then she pulls her phone out of her pocket, types a quick text in to one of her contacts – the person she was due to meet for lunch?

'Okay. I'm now free for the next hour,' she tells me staunchly. 'You have the boy's home address, you say?'

'Sure, I … it was on the original letter.'

'Right, then.'

Can she really be suggesting what I think she's suggesting?

'What are you waiting for?' My boss downs the last of her drink and she's at the door before I can even get my shoes on.

'Let's do this.'

Nate

'So, how are you feeling, being outside today?' Marcie's clipping along the High Street at a fair old pace. She's tall for a woman, almost as tall as I am, and clearly keen to get this over with.

'I'm good.'

She turns to look at me curiously as we cut through the Cathedral arches.

'Really?'

'Being outside, yes. Trying to figure out what I'm going to say to this woman – not so much.' Is the lack of anxiety I'm feeling because Marcie is here, or is it because I've turned a corner with this condition? I hardly dare to hope it, but … since the weekend, I feel like I've turned a corner with *something*, at any rate. This morning the sun is shining through a hazy mist of low cloud. The temperatures are due for a hike a bit later – our first real sign that spring is on its way. My advance is in – I've had a reprieve – and I'm feeling hopeful. Heading uphill towards the castle grounds, we move over to one side now, fishes going against the flow as a line of chattering nine-year olds holding clipboards troop down Boley Hill. Marcie follows my gaze with interest.

'What's that? You see your lad in among that lot?'

'No.' I tuck my head down. 'And he's not *my lad*,' I remind her. 'That's what we're about to break to his nan this morning, right?'

'You are,' she puts back to me. 'I'm not going in with you.'

162

'No?'

'You don't want to make us look like a delegation,' my boss points out. 'Far better you go in to see her by yourself.' We cut across the grass now, headed for the steps down onto The Esplanade. 'So ... have you any idea *why* this lady settled on you as being her grandson's father?'

'She's never seen me, has she?' I admit. 'I have a feeling she simply got the wrong address.'

'Let's hope she doesn't get too much of a shock when you turn up and she sees you're not him, then.' Marcie's got her head down but she can't hide the grin on her face.

'Thank you, Marcie.' That's settled the nerves in my stomach, big-time.

'Do you think maybe the father in question *used* to live at your place?'

'I did put out feelers about that, but no. Turns out two old ladies had the flat before me, and they were there for ten years between them.'

'Oh. And Nan hasn't tried to contact you herself, at all?'

I shake my head. Adam doesn't have my number. Jenna does.

'I'm *assuming* Mrs Boxley's never asked anyone for my number because she's not tried to ring me up to now, at any rate.'

'How strange.' Marcie shrugs. 'Anyway. As long as we get permission from her to use the footage you sent us.'

I shoot her a look.

'... oh, and that you let her know who *you* are, of course,' she adds rapidly.

'I don't even know what she looks like.' I pull a face. 'What if someone else opens the door and I start explaining I'm not the father to the wrong person?'

'Perhaps we should have brought Mr Jeremy Kyle along?'

'Please, Marcie. If you could leave your "light entertainment" head off, just for today, I'd be very grateful.'

We cross over and walk along the flowerbeds by the river, just because I haven't been down here in a while. The tulips are out, bright yellow and red, and here and there purple primroses are pushing up under the trees. The sun shines through a deep blue patch in the sky and now another class of kids appears out of the play area, chattering and laughing and looking for landmarks on their worksheets.

'Kids.' Marcie gives a little shudder, moving sharply out of their way. 'Everywhere you go, eh? And always so boisterous, finding wonder in all they see, so full of ... *life*.' The way she says it, you'd think she was referring to the amoebic kind of life you'd find in a stagnant pond or on the underside of a manhole.

My footsteps slow down, a little.

'I hope his nan doesn't forbid Adam from seeing me again once she finds out,' I mutter out loud.

'You want to see him again?'

'Sure, I ...' I falter. *Do I?* I said that without thinking, but the fact is, I do want to see Adam again. I'm not sure why, or how, but the kid's got under my skin in some inexplicable way. His situation is no more my business now than it was at the start but somehow ... I'm involved, now. I've witnessed his troubles and I've seen his pain but I've also seen how easy it is to make him happy again.

He matters.

'I've kind of liked having him around.'

'And his teacher too?' Marcie offers. *Yes, her too.* But whatever else happens, moving forward, I can't keep them both in my life. I'm already beginning to recognise that. Once Jenna finds out the truth she'll have no reason to see me again. And once I tell the nan, it dawns on me, that may happen much sooner than I've realised. But I can't back out of this now. We've come to the bit where we need to cross over the road.

'Adam knows I'm not really his dad,' I tell Marcie as we climb the steep open area up the hill at Churchfields. 'I've told him enough times. Surely he'd have passed that on to his nan?'

'You'd like to think so, wouldn't you?' My boss stops, and turns round to look at the view over the River Medway from this height.

Far away over to the left, the clean, modern lines of Medway Bridge span the choppy water. The sun throws a handful of glitter, like golden coins, across the river and a line of tethered boats bob up and down, raring to go. Like me, I think. I take in a long, deep breath. Today I feel like a normal human being again.

Will it last?

'The house is … just up there,' I say.

Marcie sits down on a sun-warmed bench, and takes out her phone.

'Off you go, then.' She waves me onwards. 'I'll be here for half an hour, but any longer than that, you'll have to make your own way back, okay? Other than that, let's you and I make contact again in – shall we say, a couple of weeks? Hopefully you'll have some more footage to show me, by then? '

'Okay.' I take in a breath. Then I carry on up to the top of the hill, and turn the corner, looking for the place where Adam's nan lives.

Nate

'It's you, isn't it?' The rotund, slightly stooped woman who comes round from the smallest patch of garden I've seen in my life, seems to know straight off who I am.

'Uh …' I hold out my hand. 'Nate Hardman,' I tell her. 'I'm looking for Adam Boxley's grandmother – would that be you?'

The old lady takes me in with misty eyes now, wiping her damp hands on her apron before taking mine. I see she's been hanging out some clothes – a large-sized boy's jumper which I recognise and a line of black socks among them.

'You'd better come in, Nate Hardman,' she says. 'I've been expecting you.' Revealing my name hasn't given her any pause for thought, it seems. I follow her straight into a cramped lounge stuffed with large, dark brown furniture straight out of the fifties. If she's Adam's nan, I muse, then his mum would have been a good deal older than I was when he was born. I'm thinking, fifteen years, maybe. How they ever got *me* involved in any of it …

'Will you have a brew?'

'Sure, I …'

Mrs Boxley picks up a used cup – there's some undrunk tea still left in the bottom of it – and goes through to the kitchen and plonks a teabag straight into it. Then she fills it with some hot water from the tap.

'Actually, I'm good, thank you.'

'You're what, sorry?' She indicates her ears. 'I'll be needing new batteries, soon, but I have to wait till my money comes through.'

'I'm good. But thanks anyway.'

'You're good?' She comes back through into the lounge. 'What do you mean, *you're good*?' She frowns up at me. 'I didn't say you were bad, did I?'

'No, I mean, the tea. I don't need any.'

'No,' she repeats after me. 'I don't need any. Myra bought me some last week. You saw me take some out of the tin.'

'I'm sorry. I meant, *I don't want any tea* thanks.' My heart sinks. This is not going to be the easiest conversation I've had in a while, is it? And not for the reasons I was afraid of, either … She shoos a mangy cat off her sofa now, so I can sit down. The cat turns round to spit at me before it goes.

'It's not mine,' she assures me. 'It's a stray. It keeps jumping in through that window over there.'

Right now I feel more inclined to jump out of it, but hey. I have a job to do this morning.

'Mrs Boxley.' I clear my throat. 'I'm here about your grandson Adam. You do know that, don't you?'

She turns her misty eyes on me thoughtfully now.

'I can look after him, y'know.'

'I'm sure you can.' At last, an indication that we're on the same page. I'm not sure how much this lady understands, but I need to cut to the chase.

'Look, I'm here to visit you because you told Adam I was his dad.'

The old lady thinks about this for a while, then she says, 'That's right.'

'You gave him my address. And – I hope you don't mind me asking, but you clearly seem to know my name. Do you mind if I ask how?'

'Was in the book,' she tells me.

I bite the inside of my cheek. 'Which book?'

'The telephone book.'

Is she really telling me she got my name and address out of the *telephone directory?*

'Do you mind if I ask *why* then?' I shift my weight to retrieve a lacy cushion out from under me on her sofa. 'Why me? Because … I'm not his dad, you do know that, don't you?'

'His teacher rung me, said you were,' she insists now.

Hang on a minute.

'That's because Adam told her I was. Adam was only repeating what you told him, first.'

'His teacher took him down to the seaside on Friday, with his dad, so she said.'

'No, Mrs Boxley, that was me. She took Adam down to the seaside and I came along too because she's helping me, but I'm not the child's father.'

'Call me Vera, please.' Then, 'that tea'll be brewed now.'

'No, I'm fine. Really. Please don't bother.' But she's already pulled herself up on swollen legs to go and get it for me. Am I honestly going to have to drink that? My stomach curdles. And why won't she just believe me? She genuinely seems to be convinced that I'm related to her grandson. The cat sidles back onto the sofa beside me, its tail swishing as if daring me to do anything about it.

'Mrs Boxley, *Vera,*' I say the minute she gets back with the tepid mug. 'Thank you for the tea.' I put it carefully down on the floor beside me. 'But – you do know I was never with your daughter, don't you?'

'She'd have loved you,' she assures me. 'That beautiful dark hair of yours. She always went for boys with dark hair like that.'

'Adam has blond hair,' I remind her.

'So did she.'

'Maybe. I didn't know her, though.'

'Boys always say that, don't they?'

She points to the TV that's been left on, rumbling quietly in the corner. An overwrought couple are face-pulling and wagging accusatory fingers at each other while the caption underneath reads: **David and Stace are waiting for the results of the DNA test to come back.** Jeremy again.

I blink. Have I actually stumbled into a real-life nightmare version of *The Jeremy Kyle Show*? No. This cannot be happening. I imagined this old lady was going to be horrified when she learned the truth from me, not that she'd actually deny it!

'They *always* say that.'

'No, they don't Mrs Box … Vera. They don't always say it. And sometimes when boys say they don't know a girl, it's because it's true.'

'His teacher told me that you went to the parents meeting, so it must be true.' Her eyes take on a slightly darker hue, now. 'Are you telling me you lied to the school?'

I swallow.

'Yes, I did lie to the school, Mrs Boxley.'

There's a momentary pause as she takes this in. When I first arrived I was a little concerned about her mental state. Now, however, as long as I'm sitting here where she can see my lips, she seems to understand very well what I'm saying to her.

'And are you sure you're not now lying to me?'

'I'm …' I swallow. 'I assure you I am not lying to you. I got involved when it wasn't my place to, I admit that much. I wanted to help your grandson. Because he was so … desperate.'

'The poor lad does get very down, sometimes,' she comes back immediately. 'He's not had much joy in his life, as you probably know.'

I sigh. 'No. I can imagine things have been pretty rough for him. For both of you.'

'Since he's been in contact with you, he's been a changed lad, though.' She cheers up visibly.

'I am happy to have been of help, but, Mrs Boxley.' I lean forward, my hands in prayer position. 'I am not his dad.'

'You are,' she tells me. 'I have a knack for knowing these things.'

I straighten.

'I am not his father and Adam knows I am not. So do you. Even if you're in denial about it, I believe you both know the truth.'

Hell, if I'd expected any reaction at all from her today it would have been anger at me, fear maybe, suspicion of some sort. Not … this.

'And his teacher?' she challenges. 'She told me you went to my grandson's parent-teacher evening. You saying that she's lying too?'

'She isn't lying. She just … doesn't know the truth, yet.' When Jenna finds out the truth, she's going to blow a gasket, I realise. I'll be yet another man who's taken her for a ride, and the thought of that makes me very sad. As sad as the thought of losing Adam from my life.

'*Whose truth though?*' Right on cue, the TV show host comes back and the old lady turns her eyes towards the box in the corner for a moment. '*Everybody has their own version of the truth,*' he's telling his riled-up audience, '*but life is never as simple as that, is it?*'

'Adam's been so happy, a changed lad,' Mrs Boxley mutters. 'Ever since you've been in his life, Nate Hardman. Are you really going to take that away from him, now?'

'I don't want to take anything away from him,' I tell her slowly. 'I just can't pretend to be something I am not.'

'Can't you?' She stares at the telly, engrossed for a bit. She seems to switch on and off. I've never quite seen anything like it. I quietly pour the tea into an ancient potted plant that's standing at the side of the sofa and wonder how long I've been here. Has it been half an hour already? Will Marcie have wandered away from that bench where she was waiting for me? I get a shot of anxiety in my chest at the thought of having to make it home alone. Damn it. Marcie will want to know if I got the parental permission for using the footage taken at the seaside. That's what she walked up here with me for, and I still haven't got it.

I don't know how to get it.

'Well.' Vera's back. 'What *are* you then, young man?'

What am I?

170

I'm a guy who's lost his way, that's what. A sometime reporter and film-maker, a former optimist and traveller of the world. Right now, I'm …

'I'm a … a documentary maker.' The idea comes to me in a flash. 'I'm making a short film at the moment, a sort of video-diary, and I'd very much like your permission for your grandson to be in it.'

'Ah, I see.' Vera puts on some glasses she's taken from her pocket and squints at me as if seeing me for the first time. 'Is it about kids who are being tormented at school?'

'Actually, it's …' I hold out the empty mug, not sure what to say to that and hoping to distract her. She takes it from me, but she isn't distracted.

'You know about that, don't you? You got involved because you wanted to help him, isn't that right, Nate Hardman?'

I look at my shoes. 'I do want to help him.'

'Well then, I will give you permission for Adam to be in it, this documentary. If you think it'll help him, any?'

'I …' Dear God. I fish in my jacket pocket for a pen and the form Marcie shoved into my hands as we walked up here; *you need to get her to sign it.*

'If you could just …' I swallow. 'Over here. That's great. Thank you.'

'Thank you for coming into our lives and coming to the rescue. I have no words …'

'None needed, Vera.'

She hands me back the paper with her name in scratchy writing at the bottom of it. I close my eyes for a split second and I can feel my face colouring. *What now, have I really committed to telling another lie?* Twisted the truth round a bit so she thinks I'm making a documentary about school bullies so I get to keep my advance and my flat and I get to see Adam and help him for a bit longer if I can? This'll all come crashing down sooner or later, I know that. It'll happen as soon as she talks to Jenna Tierney, in fact.

But until she does …

Jenna

'Jenna. You made it.' My trip into London took a little longer than I thought. Christiane Finlayson is already sitting at the window seat of the tasteful, fifties-inspired bistro off the Caledonian Road she's chosen for our rescheduled meeting, gesturing for me to come over and join her.

'Yes, so sorry about cancelling you on Friday.' I smile at her, hopefully hiding the nerves that I'm feeling inside. Of course I made it. She never called me to answer my text till yesterday – Tuesday evening – so I've been a little bit worried she was none too pleased about it.

'From your text, you sounded pretty caught up, where you were?' With a gesture, she's already offered me a glass of the same expensive Merlot she's drinking. I nod gratefully, taking a seat opposite her.

'I was.' But we're not here to talk about that. 'Um. Did you get here early?' I look at my phone, feeling a little out of breath. 'I had to rush out of class at 4 p.m. to catch the train but I was sure I'd be on time, today.'

'You're bang on time, no worries.'

While she pours, I get a chance to check her out, this finely chiselled Nordic beauty with a no-bullshit piercing blue gaze and the most elegant red lacquered nails I've ever seen. Then she adds, 'You know, I wasn't so sure about you when you cancelled

Friday, but the minute you walked in here, I knew I'd made the right decision.'

She's already made a decision?

'You're a confident girl, aren't you, Jenna? And the work of yours that Jed Miller has shared with me is nothing short of exquisite.'

I beam.

'I went and checked out your website too. I haven't seen the like since Rod Taylor teamed up with Little Joe Beany in the eighties. They worked out of New York cafe back-rooms for years till they each made their name among the rock stars, then of course they became iconic figures in their own right practically overnight.' The striking lady in front of me who'd be in her mid-forties takes me in curiously now. 'Would you say you were influenced at all by that movement?'

I shake my head.

'No, I ... I just like fantasy elements. I like using dreamy colours, drawing robes that seem to ripple with the slightest muscle and sinew movements underneath.'

'Using the body as part of the art piece,' she's saying slowly. 'I like that. It should be flowing, organic, become part of the owner. Of course, part of that philosophy means never committing to a tattoo that won't work with the person who'll wear it, correct?'

'Body art isn't like a haircut,' I agree. 'Whoever owns one is going to own it for a very long time. And, for me it isn't just about aesthetics. Whether it's on permanent display or not, it needs to *mean* something, or what's the point?'

'I couldn't agree more.' She's nodding rapidly. She raises her wine and we chink glasses, clicking instantly. I glance at Christiane's sleeve tattoos, Japanese inspired, beautifully illustrated carp. I do a double take. At least, I *think* it's a carp ...

'The dragon koi swims up The Yellow River and transforms into a dragon, overcomer of all adversity,' she explains, catching me looking, now. 'So ... where do you wear yours, if I may ask? It's unusual, isn't it, for a tattoo artist not to have any of their own on display?'

173

'I have none on display, that's true.' I imagine Christiane's going to probe a little further – most people do, but for now, she's content to leave it at that.

'Any favourite motifs?' she puts out.

I shrug. 'The swallow's always a favourite, isn't it? The one who flies far from home but always returns.'

'If you come to work with me you'll be flying far from home,' she assures me. 'I'll be leaving for New York on the first leg of my U.S. tour, two weeks today, exactly. How does that sound?'

My heart skips a beat. She really has made up her mind then, that quickly? Dear God.

'New York in two weeks?' I lean in, my fingers cupping the stem of my glass. Right now I'm feeling so excited I could *dance* on this table. New York, New York! Here I come.

'It sounds … *shamazing!*'

'Does it?' She's looking at me thoughtfully. 'Once we leave here, we won't swing back round to the UK again till Christmas at least.'

I open up my hands. 'Awesome.'

'For anyone who's young and fancy-free, got no commitments, it'll be better than awesome. You'll meet some people and see some sights you'd never do in a million years on your own. I'll also teach you – and hope to learn from you, too.' Those bright blue eyes are scrutinising me like a hawk. 'But you need to be committed, Jenna. You need to be one hundred per cent available. So …' She leans back, watching my reaction.

'I need to ask you this now. Do you have any doting boyfriend tucked away, perchance, that you'd be leaving behind to come away with me?'

'None. I left my *cheating* boyfriend behind in Catania just a few of weeks ago.' I do a throwing off movement with my hand to emphasise that. We're done.

'No … family members who might need to call on you, no children or pets? No long-term no-get-out lease taken out on a flat? Nothing?'

'I haven't been back long enough to settle on anything,' I assure her. As for my family … huh! 'I have just moved into a flat with a six-month lease, true. But I'd keep it on, that's no problem. So, really, there's nothing standing in the way of me going.'

Apart from accompanying Nate to that wedding this coming weekend I don't think I've got anything planned, really. Lucky I'm leaving in two weeks' time then, and the wedding's well before that. I wouldn't want to let him down. Even if he's only just asked me and he's not my boyfriend, or anything. It's not as if he ever could be, either.

The thought gives me a strange, empty feeling inside, I don't know why.

'I'm very glad to hear that.' She picks up her phone as a text pings in, and then puts it away again, not pausing our conversation. She already warned me when we spoke yesterday that she had another meeting booked in for today. I was only getting fifteen minutes. I had a feeling that might mean I didn't have much of a chance, but …

'You know, I've interviewed over twenty young people for this job over the last month, practically all of whom would have given their eye-teeth for the opportunity. One of them had to commute from Wales, and one of them took the coach down from Edinburgh to see me.'

'I'm not surprised. I checked out your profile online,' I admit. 'You're the business, Christiane.'

'Thank you.' She pauses. 'They were all eager, available and talented. None of them had your talent, granted, but enthusiasm counts for a lot and probably anyone of them would do. You should know.' Her eyes narrow, now. 'I very nearly didn't ring you back,' she adds, 'after you cancelled our meeting on Friday.'

I gulp. 'I'm really sorry about that. What happened was …'

She puts up a hand to stop me.

'It's okay. I don't need to know what happened. You had your reasons Jenna and I don't care. What I *do* need to know is this; if

175

I take you on, you agree to commit to me, and whatever the job requires, before anything else.'

'You needn't worry. I am completely available to commit to you.'

'I'm glad to hear that. So you're sure you want it?'

'I am so, *totally*, one hundred per cent sure.'

'The job's yours, then.' We chink glasses and finish our wine. Oh, my! She's just offered to take me to New York! She has contacts and experience beyond my imagination.

'Jed mentioned something about you working at a school temporarily?' She smiles at me now.

'I've been working at St Anthony's as a supply teacher but that finishes this week.' I blink. My excitement at her offer subsides, but only the tiniest notch. Of course I'm going to be a little bit sad to leave the children so soon, it's always a wrench, moving on, but this is what I've wanted for ... forever. It's the kind of opportunity I was dreaming of before I somehow got caught up with Alessandro and his life. I sit up a little straighter, recalling how I arrived at Rochester in the rain just a few short weeks ago, all in a faff. This is me getting back on track, nothing short of it.

'You seem a little sad at the thought of leaving the school?' Christiane puts to me now.

'I am a little sad.' God. Does this woman miss nothing? 'But I'm also thrilled at what you're offering.'

She's already looking around, checking out the joint for whoever's coming next. I put down my glass. An older dude, more her own age, comes through the doors now. My new boss holds out her hand to me for a brief handshake. Then she stands up, waving to her friend. I stand up, too. 'My PA will send the details of our contract through to you via email, and I guess ... we'll meet at Heathrow in a couple of weeks' time?'

'I'll see you there, then.' Is that really it, we're done? This has been so ... easy.

I walk out of the bistro gliding on air, in my mind, the colourful lights of New York are already beckoning me, and after that, all the rest of it, her U.S. tour … I couldn't have asked for anything more. I'm on cloud nine, all the way home, but when I get back to Rochester, back to my ever-so-tiny-flat with the medieval green door, Nate's had a little posy of pink and yellow spring flowers delivered to my doorstep.

'To the best teacher. Thank you for Friday and for opening up my world again.'

Aw. It's a lovely gesture. So thoughtful of him. They make me think of sunshine and honey and warm and lovely moments. They make me think of how stunningly handsome Nate looks when he gives one of his rare and beautiful smiles. The memory makes me feel full and happy. I pick them up, and hold them to my face. They smell so sweet.

And then suddenly, I feel sad and strangely upset, for no reason I can think of, at all.

Jenna

'Are you really leaving tomorrow, Miss?' It's Thursday afternoon and Adam's pushed all the chairs away neatly under the tables for me. The stray bits of shredded paper that 4C have been working with all afternoon – brown and straw-coloured, perfect for bird's nests – have been swept away, and I've counted up the children's decorated hen's eggs for the third time. They've been waiting to do these since Easter. They didn't have a regular teacher in then, so I promised them we'd get to it before I left. There is one egg missing, though. I still count only thirty-one.

'One egg is missing,' I tell him, ignoring the question because we both know the answer to that one. 'If we don't find it, some kid in my class is going home for the half term without any hen's egg in their paper nest.'

For once, my Finder Extraordinaire does not jump to the task. 'Are you *leaving*?' he insists.

'I am leaving,' I tell him quietly. It's 4 p.m., all the other pupils left half an hour ago but young Boxley's been hanging around desperately, holding onto every little helpful task he can think of doing, just not to have to go home. I put down the box of painted eggs.

'Is everything all right, Adam?'

'You know it's not.' Unusually, he won't give me eye contact, seems close to tears, today. Jeez, this is hard. I hate this. I've been

178

here just over two weeks, it shouldn't be this hard. I wasn't expecting any tears until tomorrow. It's usually the girls. Seeing a boy cry is so much harder, somehow.

'Sweetie,' I bite my lip. 'I have to leave. You always knew I was leaving. You all knew it from the start.'

'You don't have to leave, now,' he mutters mutinously. 'I heard Mr Drummond telling the deputy head that they'd be happy for you to stay on till the end of the Summer term, seeing as Miss Cheska's not coming back.'

Shit. Why don't these senior teachers realise that their raised, made-to-carry voices can be heard by little inquisitive birds all over the school? Why don't they ever think to exercise a little *discretion?*

'When did you hear that?'

'I heard it yesterday.' Eyes down, he's playing unhappily with some little pieces of something in his hand. 'I heard it when I was waiting by the chairs outside The Head's office.'

'Oh yes?' I've been noticing he's been a little 'off' ever since yesterday lunchtime. 'So,' I pause. 'What were you doing, waiting outside The Head's office?'

'Nuthin.' His head hangs a little lower. 'Doesn't matter now, anyway.'

'No, really. What happened?'

'Mr Drummond wanted to speak to me. One of the parents of those kids in Year Six put in a complaint about me, that's all.'

I straighten, feeling my brow furrow a little. 'They complained about *you*? Why?'

'One of them's out of the next lot of football fixtures because he hurt his foot when I ...' Adam's mouth twists perilously. 'When I pushed him.' His eyes come up to meet mine now. 'Nate told me, if they tried anything on, to push them back, Miss.'

Nate did? I stand up now, my arms folded, and take a better look at the child.

'Your dad told you to push them back?' I bite my lip. That's not *official* policy of course, but if I had a kid I know what I'd advise him.

'The Head told me I was a nasty little bully and I've let the school down because the boy was one of our star players and now I should be ashamed of myself.'

I feel a rush of blood to my face at that.

'And did you explain to Mr Drummond what's been happening all this time? Did you show him *your* bruises?'

'No.'

'Why not?'

'Because he wouldn't care, Miss. I don't count, do I?' He squeezes his fists, crushing the item in his hands into even smaller pieces.

'Of course you count.'

'He wouldn't care,' he insists. 'Apart from Nan, the only people who cared were you and Nate, and Nan can't *do* anything.'

Cared. Past tense. He's feeling abandoned, isn't he? I pull out the chair beside him and sit down on it with a sigh.

'Nate still can though, can't he? He's going to be your champion now, Adam.'

'Maybe.' The boy's face is closed, but underneath he feels hurt and angry. I know exactly how he feels. God, I hate this about teaching. I hate it even more than staffroom politics and wrangling over who gets what cupboard space where and who's got to do the early morning playground rotas, and more than having to mark thirty-odd worksheets at nine o'clock on a Sunday evening when you haven't actually had a moment to yourself all weekend and you just want to collapse into bed. I hate that I have to see *this*: children with messed-up home lives, children hurting, in deep distress and pain who you are powerless to do anything to help.

I hate that.

'*Maybe?*' I echo softly. Is he worried that his dad's not up to the job? That he's never going to fully recover from his agoraphobic condition enough to take on the lad's care when the nan no longer can?

Adam points his face away from me, towards the door.

'Or maybe as soon as you go, Nate's going to leave, just like you are?'

Ah, I see. He grimaces, opening up his hand now and I can see all the remnant shards of a crushed shell in his palm. So that's where painted eggshell number thirty-two went. He found it, after all?

'It was my one,' he tells me, seeing my face. 'But I didn't like it.'

'That's a shame, Adam. We won't be able to put it with all the other children's class display of eggs now, will we?'

'I don't care.' He shakes his head. 'What're eggs for, anyway? What's the point of them?'

'What's the point of them?' Nobody's ever asked me that, before.

'Why *eggs*?' He insists.

'Eggs are ... they're a symbol of something, that's all. They herald the start of spring.' I shoot him a significant look. 'They're about new beginnings, Adam.'

'Huh! Then they're the wrong symbol. You're not starting anything, Miss Tierney. You're *ending*,' he accuses.

'I'm ending here because I'm starting somewhere else,' I point out. I pause, and then I decide to tell him. 'I've got a new job as a tattoo artist.'

His mouth drops open in surprise.

'When I leave here, I'll be doing what you like doing best.' I give him a small smile. 'Colouring in.'

Then he pulls a disgruntled face.

'You want to do colouring in on *people*?'

I nod.

'*Why*? Why do they even want pictures painted on their skin? Why can't they have ... pictures on their walls, like everyone else?'

I imagine that could have come straight out of the mouth of his nan. I laugh, despite his dead serious face.

'Some people like art on their body because the pictures are of things that have a special meaning to them. They aren't just there for decorative purposes.'

'Tattoos have *meanings*?' He frowns in surprise now. 'Like, Easter eggs in the spring, you mean? New beginnings and things like that?'

'Sure. But they're personal meanings. To remind people of what's precious.'

That one sets him thinking. He cocks his head to one side. Then he goes and rubs all the little bits of broken shell off his palms, into the bin.

'I liked your picture,' I say sadly. While other children had painted flowers on their eggs shells, Adam had painstakingly drawn a picture of a cartoon horse, if I recall correctly. He shakes his head. It's gone.

'Do you have any tattoos, Miss?' He's still sad. I can see the hurt raging in his eyes, but he looks at me curiously now. 'To remind you of what's precious?'

I can feel my mouth twist.

'Absolutely everyone asks me that.'

And I've never told anyone the answer to it, have I?

'*Do* you?' he insists.

'No,' I say tautly now. 'I do not.'

'Because you don't need reminding?'

'Because I …' I stop, feeling my throat close up. It isn't because I don't need reminding. I turn away from the child, my arms crossed over my chest and feeling the sudden, urgent need to escape. When I look up at the classroom clock hanging by the door, it's already four-forty-five.

'Isn't your nan going to wonder where you are if you don't get home, soon?' I put to him gently.

'She never minds what time I come home, Miss Tierney.'

His eyes look straight into mine. In that one sentence, I read a whole series of things that he doesn't need to say. Not that his nan doesn't care, but that this is a kid who's left to wander around freely, maybe a little too freely, left to his own devices when he's at that stage in his life when he still needs someone to be looking out for him. And she can't. No fault of her own, but she can't do it.

I sigh.

'Why are you so sure your dad won't see you anymore once I go away?' This is at the real heart of what's troubling him so much this afternoon, isn't it?

'Why am I sure?' Adam pulls a rueful smile, reminding me of Nate. 'He only does things like that when you tell him to. Like … going to the beach with us, and going to see my nan.'

I lean in a little closer, pleasantly surprised.

'He went to see your nan then?' Oh, well done Nate!

'She told me that he did.'

'And …?' I open up my hands. *What happened?*

'I wasn't there. I was here when he came home.' Those wise green eyes in that soft round face are on me again. 'She said … he was a lovely young man,' Adam admits reluctantly. Why isn't he happier than this? I'd have thought he'd be over the moon!

'It sounds as if they made good contact,' I encourage. 'Don't you see – it means they'll want to keep in contact, from now on. It means you'll see more of your dad, once I'm gone.' I'm going to talk to Nate when I see him for the wedding on Saturday, push the point home.

'No, I don't think so. Actually, Miss …' A soft knock on the door makes us both look up, now. *Damn.* The deputy head scooches round the door without waiting for me to answer.

'Ooh, in trouble and kept behind again, young man?'

Adam shakes his head resignedly. 'No.'

'Run along, then, there's a good lad.' As he closes the door quietly behind him, she says. 'I just needed to drop this paperwork off to you before you made final tracks tomorrow. That's a *lovely* display of Springtime Joys 4C have made, by the way – even if they are a little late.'

'Thank you.' My voice sounds dry in my throat. I look at the papers she's just handed me. All admin stuff. Nothing of any significance. Is this going to be all my legacy from my stint at this school?

'All well, here?' Her hand goes to the doorknob, poised to leave, herself. Then, seeing my face, 'He was in a bit of a scuffle yesterday,

I heard? Head not best pleased and Adam's banned from attending tomorrow's half-term treasure hunt, did he tell you?'

'No. He didn't tell me.'

She shrugs, a little sad, but it's par for the course.

'He's going to miss you, Jenna. We all will.' She takes her leave now but what she's just said has left my head in a spin.

So Adam won't be allowed to take part in tomorrow's treasure hunt? He's probably one of the few kids in the school who doesn't get showered with presents throughout the year, too. I can't imagine his nan can afford it. That's so unfair, it really makes my blood boil! It makes me want to go out and buy him a present, myself. It makes me want to go and give that headmaster a piece of my mind. Maybe I will, too, before I leave.

Every room you walk into in this school, every corridor you walk down, there's some reminder of that ubiquitous phrase 'Every Child Matters.' Looks good on the posters, yes. Not so easy to implement when you've got a Head hell-bent on his own agendas and *the child* only matters when he brings in some accolade for the school, more sporting scalps to put around Mr Drummond's 'outstanding achievements' belt.

I put my hand to my head, easing out the throbbing that's starting up in my temples, telling myself that I've got to stop thinking like this. That I've got to just … let it go. Be grown up about this and move on gracefully instead of running away in anger like I always do. I want to stop doing that.

I don't want to do that anymore.

Soon, very soon, all I'll have to worry about is Christiane's U.S. tour. I drag my eyes away from the classroom door. Adam's gone and, soon, very soon, I will be, too.

Jenna

Standing in my heels outside Nate's flat, I'm feeling strangely *nervous* this morning and I can't account for it whatsoever. This wedding we're going to, today – it's nothing to me, Nate's the one who I expect is going to be feeling nervous. They're all his people, aren't they? His former girlfriend is marrying his good mate, and no doubt a load of his former work colleagues will be there who he's keen not to show himself up with. That's where I come in. I'm about moral support today, that is all. I won't know anyone and I don't have any expectations. Other than what Nate's told me – that it's being held at a private rural location in Surrey, and that it'll all be very well heeled, I have no idea what today's going to bring.

A shiver goes through me as I reach up to press the buzzer, and again, I wonder *why?* It's not cold today. Quite warm, in fact. At last. Hooray! A perfect day for a wedding.

'Hello, Jenna.' Nate's head appears at the window above me – so rapidly, you'd think he'd been sitting there just waiting for me to buzz. I smile up at him. For a moment, he says nothing. Just stands there looking down at me, his mouth slightly open.

'You scrub up well,' I tell him. Actually, Adam's dad scrubs up *bloody well.* Not that he looked like a sack of old potatoes when I saw him last. That was just over a week ago, our time at the beach with Adam. But Nate's always got this air of … somewhat startled abandon about him. A sort of Heathcliff, but how he'd be if he refused to go out onto the heaths, I imagine. That kind of look. But, there must be something about that suit Nate's wearing this morning, because it makes him look … quite … I turn my face away, rubbing at my arms because the hairs have all just stood up on the back of them.

'Thank you. You don't scrub up too badly yourself,' he comes back softly.

I push some material down over my hips. 'I've had better compliments for this dress.'

'I'm sorry. I didn't mean …' He looks crestfallen. 'I didn't mean to suggest you looked anything other than … perfectly beautiful.'

Hmm. I did go to a *little* bit of effort on his behalf this morning.

'If I'm going to pretend to be your girlfriend for the day, we might as well make your friends a little jealous, right?'

I see him blink, taking that in.

'They'll be jealous all right, but … hang on.' He disappears from view for what feels like a few seconds. Then he's down there with me, only looking like the handsomest geezer I've laid eyes on in the past few months and that includes *all past boyfriends who I especially don't want to think about today on the day of somebody else's wedding,* too. When Nate opens up the door this morning, I can actually feel my heart rate going up, and that hasn't happened in a while. *What is wrong with me today?* This guy is still someone's dad and I need to remember I'm only here on a mercy mission to help him get with his son.

'Let me get this straight. You're going to pretend to be my girlfriend, for this event?' Nate's eyes open a little wider.

'Yes,' I tell him confidently. 'A new one. I've been thinking about this on the way over here. I'll be … someone you don't know intimately, but who you'd like to. It's the best strategy to adopt, so no one will suspect anything,' I assure him. 'That way, nobody will wonder why we don't know too much about each other once the conversations get going.'

'Because they won't expect us to …?' Nate steps out cautiously onto the street beside me. For a moment I let him have his space, testing how it feels. And it strikes me forcibly, how incongruous this all seems, that a guy like him, physically and in so many ways mentally strong, should find himself experiencing this difficulty.

'Think about it,' I say after a while, wanting to distract him from his thoughts. 'If we're not already good buddies and we're not a couple at least hoping to be an item, then they might wonder why I am accompanying you otherwise, mightn't they?'

'And ... you don't mind?' His eyes narrow. 'Telling a ... a white lie, so to speak?'

'In this instance no,' I assure him. 'Needs must, and all that. Why?' I point him towards the car park down the High Street where Mags told me she's left her car, generously offered for our use once more today. Nate carefully closes the front door behind him. He turns to me, looking strangely relieved and a little bit wary all at the same time.

'Why? Well ... I thought you might be the kind of girl who insisted on sticking to the complete and utter truth.' He opens out his hands. 'Being a primary school teacher, and all.'

I laugh.

'You have me there.' I lower my eyes. 'I normally *am* a stickler for the truth. In this case, however, our story might come undone and there's a greater good at stake.'

'You have no idea,' Nate says to me, 'how *glad* I am you feel that way about it. The greater good being at stake, as you say. I just didn't want to put you in the position of having to lie to people.'

'It won't be lying, as such,' I assure him. 'Look at it more as ... role playing. We won't tell them what I am to you, but we'll let people assume what they will.'

'They'll have a live band playing today.' He's smiling faintly. 'It does mean you might be expected to get up on the floor and dance with me, you realise?'

'I *love* dancing.'

'I'm the worst dancer in the world,' he warns. 'Worse than two left feet, but it'll be expected, I'm afraid. I apologise in advance for any crunched toes.'

187

I am not thinking about crunched toes. The thought bubbles quietly, an unchecked, runaway sensation of *frisson* under my skin, *that I might have to stand up close to this man and actually touch him, today, put my cheek up against his cheek and* ... Boy, the sacrifices I make for people!

'I'm prepared to do that for you,' I tell him quietly. What would it feel like, dancing with him, I wonder, even if we're only role playing, even if we are only *pretending*, for his and everyone's benefit?

'But hey,' I point out. 'If you're actually able to dance in front of everyone else today, that'll be mega. It means we'll have got you past quite a few milestones, doesn't it?'

He swallows, hard. Stops walking, suddenly.

'Jenna, what if I can't go through with this?'

'You're not the guy actually getting married.' I give him a soft nudge. 'He's the one traditionally supposed to be having all the reservations.'

Nate pulls a pained grimace. 'I don't know if I can show my face. I've been up since 5 a.m. getting myself ready ...'

'That's supposed to be the bride.' We've reached the car and I obligingly open the passenger door for him. 'She's the one who'll have all eyes on her today. Nobody minds what *you* look like.'

Nate suddenly looks panic-stricken.

'Seriously, Jen! I don't know if I ...'

Jen. He just called me Jen. Something in my chest does a flip – was that my heart?

'I'm so scared of ...' His voice goes very low now. 'So scared of letting everyone see how *damn scared* I am! I used to be a war reporter, and we don't ... we don't do scared.'

'I know.'

'I was one of those annoyingly alpha males that all the other guys wanted to be; fearless, professional, with a reputation for getting the job done and now I can't even ...'

I wait quietly, letting him say what he needs to say.

'If I slip up and they see it, I'll feel so ashamed, I don't know if I can go through with seeing all these people who know me today. If I

188

can keep pretending I'm still the guy I used to be. I don't know if I can stand in a room that's got so many other people in it and stop myself from running out of it. Or if I can sit in that church long enough. Or if I can even bear the thought of seeing her marrying someone else.' His face crumples, now. 'I don't know if I can do *anything*, Jen.'

I slip my hand into his just for a few seconds. His fingers in mine feel warm, not cold, as they tighten around mine. Then I take my hand back.

'Yes, you do,' I say softly. 'You do know this much, at least; you know that you can sit in the car beside me while I drive you there for the next hour. You know that you can make conversation with me and we can listen to music. Any music you want to – I'll let the choice be yours for the day. You know that you can take your jacket off and fold it away in the back so the sun warms your skin but you won't feel too hot and if by chance you do, we'll roll the windows down. You know that we can even take the top of this car right off if it gets warm enough, and when we get to the venue we'll find a cool, shady place to park outside somewhere on the grass and we'll hang out there, drinking lemonade and watching the people go by for as long as you like, for the whole entire event if you like, just you and me, until you decide you want to do anything more. You know we're just going to take it one baby step at a time,' I coax. 'One, teeny, little tiny step at a time. Like children do. You don't have to get anywhere. You don't have to promise anyone anything, you just have to be prepared to trust me to look after you. Just for today. You know you can do *that*, don't you?'

'I guess I do,' he concedes. After a while, he adds, 'you're really quite something, aren't you, Miss Tierney? One of these days you're going to set the world on fire.'

He shoots me a shy smile now, dark brown eyes looking out at me from under curved lashes so long they have no business at all being on a bloke.

'You make me wish I'd met you years ago. Even – just one year ago, before I …' He shakes his head, stopping the words. What's gone is gone, and done. Then he adds, 'You've given me something to aim for, at least. You've given me more than I can say.'

'Attaboy, Nate,' I say. 'You're going to make your boy Adam proud of you today. You're going to make *me* proud of you. And one day, when you're ready to let everyone know just how much this trip cost you, all your friends will be real proud of you, too.'

When he finally makes a move to get into the passenger seat, he's got water in his eyes. Careful not to let him know that I've seen that, I make my way round to the driver's side, feeling a whole host of strange things that I don't want to feel right now, myself. In my ignorance, I imagined this was going to be something straightforward. I thought – Nate's a guy that's got stuck, he just needs a little helpful nudge, a little push and he'll be on his way, but in truth, seeing him like this …

I'm leaving this country in just over a week's time but his problems are going to take a hell of a lot longer than that, to shift. I don't know if I'm going to be able to do what I wanted to do for Adam. If I can do what I wanted to do, for Nate.

I don't honestly know if this guy's going to make it.

Nate

It's taken us just an hour and a half to get here, the tiny village of Little Summersfield tucked away on the edge of deepest Surrey where Camille's people hail from, and every turn since the motorway has been raking up memories. Bittersweet ones. Ones I'd so much rather not have.

'Wow.' Jenna makes a low whistling sound as we drive gently across the old stone bridge. 'This place is *stunning*.'

'I always loved it here. It felt like a place I'd maybe one day like to call home.' Makes my throat feel tight, just thinking about it. The girl beside me turns to look at me and I nod at the one-hundred-year old cherry tree laden with blossom on the other side of the river. It sways gently in the breeze, stirring echoes of the past.

'I remember walking under that tree with Cami, one particular time.'

'Do you?'

'She came away that day with her hair full of all these ... pale pink petals.'

'I bet she looked pretty.'

'She did.'

'If you were walking beside her ...' Jenna's got an innocent grin on her face. 'I bet you got your hair full of pretty pink petals, too?'

My eyes slide over to hers.

'With all that beautiful dark hair of yours …' Jenna's hand leaves the steering wheel for a fraction of a second, touches my own, 'I bet you looked even prettier than she did, Nathan?'

'I don't know about that.' I feel an embarrassed smile cross my lips. 'And … my name's Nathaniel, actually.'

'Nath*aniel*?' Jenna splutters on the laughter that comes out now. The car wobbles precariously to the left – we're still on the little stone bridge, watch out, girl! I put my own hand on the wheel to steady it. 'Seriously, *Nathaniel*?'

'Seriously. What's wrong with that?'

'Nothing, it's … lovely,' she grins. 'Nathaniel. It sounds so – biblical. Like Adam, I guess. What does it even mean?'

'It means "God has given,"' I tell her. *As in, God has just given us a reprieve from ending up in the river.* I take my hand back from the wheel.

'Does it? God has given.' She sits up in the driver's seat, a little more interested. 'You know about these things? Okay then. What does "Adam" mean?'

'It means; "of the red earth".'

'Of the red … Oh. Wow. And … my name, do you know that one?'

'Little bird.'

'No way!' Jenna laughs, delighted. 'My name means Little *Bird*? I love that!'

'I thought you might.'

'Though "Little Bird" does sound a tad Native American. A bit like …' She casts around for inspiration as we come over the bridge, sighting some walkers with their chocolate lab at one end of the village green, 'like, Running Dog.'

'Running Dog.' I hide a grin. 'You're definitely more of a little bird than a running dog.'

She's still giving it some thought.

'And it also sounds like the name of an ever-so-sweet type, don't you think?' She crinkles up her nose a little. 'It also sounds like someone who's kind of young and vulnerable, too.'

'It suits you.'

'Really?'

'Really. You're sweet and ... and kind, aren't you?' I've hit a feminist nerve. I can tell from the glint forming in her eye.

'Is that how you see me? Young and gullible? Because I'm no pushover, you know.'

'I didn't take you for one.' *Gullible, where did gullible come in? I thought she said vulnerable?* 'And anyway ... I didn't give you your name, Jenna.'

'You sure you're not just making these up?' She shoots me a slightly suspicious look, now. 'How come you even know these things?'

'I know them because I'm a word-geek.' I sigh apologetically. 'I was a reporter and a journalist. Words have always been my stock-in-trade. I enjoy looking up meanings and word roots, all that kind of stuff.'

'Word roots. Really?' In the five seconds it's taken for me to tell her that, the storm has passed. Her wide eyes look seriously impressed. 'That's kind of *clever*, Nate.'

'Thank you.'

'... because, too many people don't think about meanings enough, do they? I come across this, doing tattoos, all the time. They never think to look what's behind a word or a symbol, they just take everything at face value.'

I stare at her. 'You do *tattoos* for people?'

She laughs. 'It's what I've been doing for a while. The teaching job's only temporary, remember?'

'I didn't know.' It figures, though. I can imagine her doing them. She leans back in the driver's seat, a slightly dreamy look coming over her.

'There's something seriously sexy, I always think, about an intelligent man.'

'Do you?'

'Absolutely. I *love* that you showed such an early interest in learning. I think maybe – speaking with my teacher's hat on – you'd have been my dream pupil.'

'I think … maybe you'd have been my dream teacher.'

Her eyes widen slightly.

'Nate …' Then she looks away, lowers her lovely lashes regretfully so I feel obliged to run on rapidly.

'I also learned all that stuff because …' I look at my hands. 'I discovered early on that girls just *love* it when you can tell them things like that.' She laughs out loud and I nod my head. 'It's true. I spent one whole long summer in my youth devouring a book on baby names,' I confess, 'just so I could impress the girls. The name meanings have stuck, I guess.'

'I can't imagine,' she tells me, quite sincerely, 'That there was *ever* a time when you had to work too hard to impress the ladies, Nathaniel.'

'I was a very shy lad, believe me.'

'Not *too* shy.' Her eyes are firmly fixed on the cobbled road ahead of us, now.

'I was,' I insist. 'Women always terrified me. To be honest, sometimes they still do.' I open my hands, wondering why she's making such a point of it. Do I come across as such a Lothario-type to her? Honestly?

'What?' I throw her a puzzled look.

'You're such a … a *liar!*' She laughs.

'I swear.' I cross my hands over my heart. 'You women scare the hell out of me. I love women, don't get me wrong, always hoped I'd get with the right girl, always wanted to find her, but …'

'But …?'

'It took me a good while to get my act together in that department.' I push my hair back, leaning out of the window now and wondering how we got onto *that* topic. 'Let's just leave it at that.'

'Come on, Nate,' she nudges. 'You couldn't have been too much of a late developer *in that department.*'

'Why would you assume that?'

'Well,' she reminds me. 'You couldn't have been more than – what – eighteen, when Adam was born?'

I bite the inside of my cheek, silent at that. Eighteen; I guess I couldn't have been more than that when he was born. Not that I had anything to do with it, but what she'll conclude from that couldn't be further from the truth.

'Jenna, if you …' I swallow. 'If you could avoid bringing that up today …?'

'Course I will,' she assures me cheerfully. 'I won't go round reminding everyone of the indiscretions of your youth, never fear.'

'No, I mean.' I clear my throat, feeling a faint sheen of sweat on my forehead; why did I not foresee that this might be coming? Nobody here will ever have heard of *my son*. 'Just, please … don't bring Adam up today,' I beg. And then for good measure, I add, 'Don't mention him *at all*, Jenna.'

'I won't. I already told you. Oh, look … Shall we park it here?' Helpfully distracted now, Jenna pulls into a grassy lay-by sign-posted 'Wedding Guests'.

'Let's hope there's only one wedding going on here today.'

'There will be,' I assure her. The nerves in my stomach are already beginning to jangle at the thought of it. Only one wedding, but many, many people.

'Everything all right?'

'Everything's perfect.' I look at the long line of cars parked alongside ours, the sheer scale of it beginning to dawn on me.

'There are going to be a lot of people here today, aren't there?' she notes.

'Every single person in the village and every single person who's ever played a significant role in their lives will be here, from Cami's preschool ballet teacher upwards.' Let her be under no illusion about that one. 'It'll be like something out of a BBC sitcom, nothing like real life.'

'No drunken singing on the lawn in the early hours, then? No catfights and flower-girls in tears or arguments over wedding presents?' She laughs.

'Absolutely none of that. Camille's people are very civilised.'

She turns off the engine. 'You want to go say hi to some of these civilised people, then?'

I freeze. Get out of the car, she means? 'What, now?'

'We could stay here a little longer if you like.'

But, as it turns out, we can't.

'My *God*,' a sharp tap on the window is followed by an all-too familiar, slightly supercilious voice, directed at me, now. 'You made it after all, Hardman?'

The sight of my once-upon-a-time nemesis Wallis Strong does nothing to improve my confidence, but it does kick-start me out of the car. If this argumentative, brown-nosing little runt is here, it'll be because he imagines there's some career advantage to be had in it. No other reason.

'And you?' I step out onto the grass and he offers me a quick hand-shake.

'Of course *I* came. You weren't at Daley's stag do, though, so I assumed …' He doesn't look best pleased. He assumed I was out of favour. He assumed I wouldn't have the heart to show my face, let the world see my reaction as Cami marries another man? Just because I didn't make it to the awards …

'Always dangerous to assume, Wallis.' I'll be damned if I let Wallis see me, sinking. I walk round and open the door on Jenna's side. She steps out, looking like a million dollars and I feel an undeserved shot of pride, seeing his reaction.

'Would it also be dangerous to assume that she's with you?' He waves his champagne glass at her. 'Or – as it's understandable you might feel the need to get a little *drunk*, today – is this little beauty just your designated driver?'

Jenna threads her arm carefully through mine. She looks delectable, true, but I can feel her bristling even from here. 'Jenna Tierney,' I introduce them reluctantly. 'This is a … a colleague of mine, Wallis Strong.' *Wally Wallis.*

She tips a brief nod towards him by way of acknowledgement. Nothing more.

'I hope I'm a bit more to you than just your designated driver,' she says to me demurely.

'Just a little bit,' I allow.

'Pity,' Wallis says.

'Not for me, I promise you,' Jenna throws back. As we move away, her eyebrows raise. 'That one of the more *civilised* people you are expecting to encounter, today?'

'One of the least.' I close my eyes for a second, regretting that we had to come across Wallis of all people, him first of all. 'He doesn't like me very much. I had ...' I hesitate. Do I really want to drag her into the murky waters of what the politics of my job can be like? 'I *once* had everything that guy longed for in the world. Not so long ago, I did and then I ...'

'And then you lost it all?'

I nod.

'And do you regret that, very much?'

'Some of it,' I allow. 'My work was important to me.' I enjoyed it, the excitement of it and the adventure. The esteem of my colleagues and commanding a halfway decent income, that was all important to me. 'Some of it used to make me very happy, but ... not all of it, Jenna.'

Now I think about it, there are some things that have come into my life of late, trickled in, almost without my noticing them, that have made me very happy, too. As we move away from Wallis, Jenna carefully unlinks her arm from around mine. The gesture was purely for his benefit only, I know that, but it was comforting while it lasted.

'Are you going to be expected to say hello to a whole lot of people, today?' She's looking over to the group of gaily decked-out people already gathering by the shady yew trees in front of the medieval church where the nuptials will take place. 'Would you prefer to do that now, get it over with right at the start, or work your way in?'

What would I prefer?

I turn to look at Jenna. The sun's picking up glints of copper and ancient gold in her hair. Her eyes are the colour of the little river we've just crossed over, green and flecked with molten brown, the colours of the early spring, *the colours life is making anew, what the world's becoming,* I think.

I'd prefer us to take off our dress shoes and just run off down that little narrow lane and spend the afternoon in a quiet corner of the village pub, just you and me, Jenna Tierney. I'd like to spend the next few hours getting to know you, enjoying the companionship and the newness and the unexpected excitement of having someone like you walking into my broken life. That's what I'd prefer to do because the more time I spend with you, the more I am starting to feel whole again. The more I start to feel like me. But I don't say it.

She smiles at me, waiting patiently for my answer, not pushing me, just waiting, as if she knows how hard this all is for me, this girl Jenna Tierney who's landed so suddenly in my life, this fierce warrior woman, Little Bird.

Jenna

'So ... that didn't go too badly, did it?' I've been sitting beside Nate in a dark corner at the very far end of this hushed medieval church for over an hour and in all that time he's not said a word or turned to look at me *once*.

'Hey.' I lean over to shake his arm gently. Nate's eyes come up to meet mine, slightly startled.

'It's over,' I tell him.

'The church part is over,' he grants, looking about us at the empty pews. Had he even realised that everyone else filed out of here about five minutes ago?

'You survived it.'

'True.' I get that rueful smile, now. 'It's over and I didn't disgrace myself by having to rush out.' When he links his hands and stretches out his arms in front, I can almost feel the relief flooding through him. 'That's pretty much a triumph, in my book.'

'It is.' I pick up our hymn sheets and place them carefully on the ledge behind the pew in front. 'I'm so glad you didn't miss it. It was a beautiful ceremony, Nate.'

'I barely took in a word of the ceremony.' He admits. 'I, er ... wasn't actually listening.'

'No?' I keep my eyes demurely on my hands clasped in front of me but I can't say I'm surprised. Could've been him up there, right? I'm really glad it wasn't, though. I push down that

199

unexpected and totally inappropriate thought and clear my throat.

'This was never going to be easy for you was it, seeing the two of them get wed?'

'I didn't actually get to see much of it, either,' he confesses. 'I was …'

I know. He was looking at his shoes most of the time. I take a small bottle of water out of my handbag and take a sip, letting him take his time.

'I was concentrating real hard on *breathing in and breathing out* and staying in my seat.' He pushes back his hair distractedly. 'Christ. Maybe this wasn't such a triumph after all? I was here but to all intents and purposes … I missed it, didn't I?'

'The main thing is, you were here. You did great,' I rally. 'Really great. Only, another time.' I shoot him a small smile. 'It might be an idea not to wait till the organ music changes to announce the bride's arrival before you choose to rush in.' Nate hadn't wanted to make a move while everyone else was going in, he'd kept on seeing people he knew so we'd held back till the very last moment.

'Uh, yeah. I'm sorry about that.' We both look towards the back of the church. The last person going out has left the door open for us, but neither of us make a move. He turns back to me. 'That was … a bit awkward, wasn't it?'

'We got a few looks. I think some of the guests suspected we were gate-crashing for a while there.' I hide a smile. 'And I thought the whole plan was to keep a low profile?'

'It was.'

'A few seconds later, and we'd have been a lot more conspicuous.'

'True. We'd have become part of the bridal party.' His mouth twitches. 'Oh, God.' A laugh catches in his throat as it dawns on him. 'A moment later and we'd have had to actually follow them all up the aisle!'

'You'd have had to pick up the trailing hem of her gown, pretend you were actually *doing* something.'

He blinks. Then he realises I'm teasing him.

'And I suppose *you* could have nicked one of those cute flower-girl baskets and scattered rose petals in her wake all the way up …?' He stops. At least he's now smiling again.

'Do you think we could have blagged it?'

'Me – not so much, but I reckon *you* could have.' For a split second, his eyes gaze into mine appreciatively. 'You're looking every bit as pretty as any of those flower maidens or whatever they're called that Camille had with her.'

'Thank you.' I hide the ridiculous flush of pleasure I feel at his compliment. Because I don't want to feel it. I don't want to feel anything about this guy. No, really. 'And I think … those would have been maids of honour.'

'I think you would have made a wonderful maid of honour,' he comes back earnestly.

'Bridesmaid.' I take in a long, slow breath, willing my heart-beat to stop racing. Because he's going to *see* it: this silly, heady, Jenna-turned-to-jelly schoolgirl effect he's starting to have on me. Why and when and how exactly I don't know, but I recognise the symptoms.

I need to get a grip, here.

'I'd have been a bridesmaid. You can only be a maid of honour if you're already married,' I explain.

The puzzlement on his face is a picture.

'It's more complicated than I realised, this business of getting wed.'

'It is.' I drag my gaze away from him. 'We both dodged that bullet, didn't we?'

He gives a small chuckle, now.

'It's almost a pity we didn't follow them up the aisle. Can you *imagine* what would have gone through the bride's mind when she got to the altar and finally turned round and saw us?' At last, he's seeing that this is a lot funnier than it is tragic.

'Would she have minded very much, do you think?'

'She'd have had a heart attack, Jenna!'

I grin. 'And Hal?'

201

'He might have fallen off the altar steps in shock but then ... he'd have been happy to see me.'

The thought cheers him up a little.

'You're starting to feel glad you came, then?'

'I felt it the moment I looked out of the window this morning.' He doesn't add *'and saw you,'* but it's pretty plain that is his meaning. My heart skips a beat. Again. This won't do. It really won't. I turn my body away from him and make a show of picking up my handbag from the floor where it's been stowed.

'I heard some of the other guests commenting that the reception venue was walking distance from here. That is ... if you feel ready for it?'

He thinks about it for a bit. The sunlight filtering through the coloured glass of the windows makes a bright halo on the chancel floor. The organist upstairs, believing the church to be empty, starts playing, appropriately enough, a rendition of 'A whiter shade of pale.' As we sit listening to it, a small smile comes to Nate's lips. The colour floods back into his own face. This cool, shady nook in the corner of the little church of St Athelstan has been like a sanctuary to him this morning – but, does he want to make tracks now? I'm totally up for it, if he does. Nate gives a tiny nod.

'I'm ready.'

I lean over and fasten the pink rose in his buttonhole a little more securely. It's just an excuse, really, because I want to be nearer to him and I have no valid reason to be. While I fix his buttonhole, Nate becomes very, very still, and I'm acutely aware of it. I'm aware of his eyes, so gently on me and how my fingers feel so strangely slippery and fumbling that I fear I'm not going to be able to put the darn thing back in place. Is he feeling what I'm feeling? Even the tiniest hint of it? He's nervous, sure – but is that because of me, or is that his situation? And – more to the point – *why am I even going there?* I'm leaving. Soon! I'll be out of his life before you can say one, two, three.

'Adam would be very proud of you.' My voice sticks in my throat a little. '*You* should be proud of you.'

'I am proud.'

'Good.'

'I'm especially proud because ... you're here with me,' he admits unexpectedly. 'I bet a lot of the looks you noticed earlier were aimed at you as much as me. They're curious about you, Jenna.' His hand touches mine tentatively. 'They'll all be wondering who my new girlfriend, is.'

'Your *brand new* girlfriend.' I give a little laugh, stifling a sigh of regret that none of this is true. That none of it can be, because we've both got other plans. And I need to remember my plans! This is my one lesson in life, what I need to learn. Not to be so impetuous. Not to fall in love at the drop of a hat every time a guy comes along who I think is the one I'm going to want to be with, not to *do* all that cycle again because I've done it enough times before and I need to ... I need to just change my ways.

I swallow, moving back a little out of his space because it's way too intoxicating, being there. I'm not safe.

'The brand new girlfriend who I hardly know anything about, and who hardly knows anything about me,' he reminds me softly. 'And ... we don't, really, do we?'

I take in a breath, going into executive mode, because I've got to save myself from this. I've got to, for the sake of my future and my career and my sanity.

'Perhaps we should do a bit of conferring before we go on to the reception then, get our stories straight?'

'Conferring.' He blinks, recognising that my choice of words – conferring – puts us back on a safer track. We're partners in the same cause, here with a job to do. That is all.

'We could,' he agrees.

'Okay. If you're not keen to bring Adam into the picture ... then, where did we even meet?'

We both pause to think about this for a bit.

'Maybe ... we met in the local tattoo parlour?' I put out. 'We could say you went in for a consultation and I was there?'

'Perfect,' he agrees.

And then I ask it. The one question I shouldn't ask, because it's not a conferring type of question, it's an intimate one. A personal one.

'I've just realised ... I don't even know if you *have* any tattoos?'

His dark brown eyes take me in, teasingly. 'Maybe ...' he ventures, 'you don't know me well enough to have found that one out, yet.'

Yet?

Is this guy still in role play, practising for what we'll tell the others or is he – actually – flirting with me? I have no idea right now.

Jenna

'What an entirely unexpected pleasure to meet you.' The bride's grandfather has cornered me coming out of the dessert marquee. The whole reception's taking place in his sumptuous, walled, medieval garden and the setting couldn't be more perfect. He extends a formal hand, brigadier-like. 'You're Nathaniel's new squeeze, I'm told?'

I immediately swallow the sugared almond in my mouth. *Squeeze?* Is that some sort of World War Two euphemism for lover, I wonder?

'I'm Jenna Tierney and … we're … fairly newly acquainted,' I tell him.

'Tierney.' He inspects me slightly more closely. 'Would that be the Dublin branch or the Cork branch of the O'Tierneys?'

'The Hull branch. And we dropped the "O".'

In, like, the seventeenth century or something, I imagine. Maybe we never even had an 'O'?

'Hull branch? Can't say I've heard of them, but listen here, Jenna. You and Nathaniel are newly acquainted, you say?'

'That's right.'

'How newly, if you'll forgive me for asking?' He leans in, a mischievous twinkle coming into his eyes. 'I used to be in reconnaissance in the war, you see. Camille's cousin Lucinda and her mother Cassiopeia have sent me over to you on a recce.'

'Have they?' I follow his surreptitious '*look over my shoulder*' signal and, sure enough, there are two women in fancy hats hovering just

205

out of earshot, peering a little anxiously in our direction. They turn away casually the moment they see me looking. 'That's them?'

He gives an almost imperceptible nod.

'They've been watching you since luncheon, but they daren't approach. Turns out my other granddaughter has long had something of a secret crush on young Nathaniel.'

'On Nate? Really?' That could have been a bit awkward. *Nathaniel* went off to visit the little boys' room, twenty minutes ago, and I've not had sight of him since. I take a sip of my rose-flavoured water.

'She only confessed it once Camille and he had split, naturally. The boy's got an impeccable pedigree, so I won't lie, the family would be happy to have him back in the fold.' He leans in, imparting a confidence. 'He's from a proud military tradition y'know. One of the Dorset Hardmans.'

'Seriously? Nate was in the military?' He's a dark horse, for sure, but … I look at the old guy in surprise.

'His family were, for generations. I believe the only thing he himself ever shot in a war-zone was *photos*, but still …'

I look around a little nervously, not entirely sure where this is going.

'I've been asked to find out if this is simply, shall we say, *un amour de rencontre* or if the young man's taken.'

'I see.' My French teacher didn't cover this phrase but I'm getting the gist. They're interested in whether I'm more than just a … what was it he said? A squeeze.

Is he asking me to confirm or deny this? I can't. I cast around with a glazed smile on my face, wishing that Nate would resurface. Hopefully, he's coping beautifully, enjoying himself somewhere. I don't really mind being abandoned – fair dos, we're not really 'together' – but I hadn't bargained on the sheer curiosity of these people.

'Don't feel too bad about it.' I give a polite laugh. 'I've already been asked the same question by ten different people in ten different guises.' These folk all know each other, and I'm the stranger in their midst, let's face it. The two women have finally given up waiting on granddad's spying skills. They're at his elbow, now, politely sidling in with their arms outstretched to make my acquaintance.

'So charmed to meet you.' Camille's aunt, Cassiopeia, says. 'So – forgive me for being curious, but Nate's been out of circulation for a while. Where did you two actually meet?'

'I'm a tattooist.' I tell her the same story I've already told the others. 'Nate came along one day, interested in exploring the idea of having one and ...'

'Oh, *how fascinating*.' I see the mother and daughter exchange glances. Lucinda – who looks all of seventeen – has got a pout on her face. Shall I put her out of her misery and explain that she needn't worry – I'll be out of the picture and the field will be clear for her soon? I don't feel very inclined to.

'Does Nate have a tattoo?'

'Did you draw it?'

They both speak at once.

'What's that?' The Brigadier interrupts. 'What's that, this girl draws tattoos? Like the marines have?'

'That's right, Pappy.'

'Whatever for?' 'He's looking genuinely puzzled.

Lucinda shrugs. 'It's fashion, isn't it?'

'It's not fashion. Fashion is something you women discard after every season,' he blusters. Then he turns to me. 'Ask my wife.'

'What tattoo did Nate have done?' The older woman wants to know. 'Do tell.'

'And where?' Lucinda is definitely more interested in *where*, I can just tell. I look about at the milling crowd of guests, wishing the guy at the centre of all this interest would show up, already. We didn't discuss this. What am I supposed to do now – make something up? I think fast. If I locate Nate's tattoo in a place neither of these ladies is ever likely to go, I guess there's less chance of ever being caught out.

'It's … um … somewhere discreet,' I tell them. Best leave the rest to their imaginations.

'Really?' The mother's eyebrows go up. 'Men have it done … *there?*'

Where? What's she even thinking?

'Oh, I can't tell you where, precisely.' I take a sip of my water. 'Client confidentiality and all that.'

'Amazing,' she says.

Cousin Lucinda looks even unhappier than before.

'Darlings, you're all looking so *gorge*.' The cheerful lady who joins us now comes in like a whirlwind, dispensing kisses and hugs till she gets to me. 'And you, of course, are Nate's guest? I saw you two earlier doing your last minute dash into the church.'

'I think everybody saw that,' Lucinda mutters.

'Uh, yes.' I put my hand to my mouth. If I had a penny for every time that had been brought up … 'That was …'

'Marcie Phillips,' the newcomer shoots out a hand. 'Very pleased to meet you.'

'I'm Jenna Tierney. Of the Hull Tierney's,' I add for good measure. *Who's Marcie, now?*

'I've worked with Nate on many projects for Smart World Productions,' she supplies. 'Don't worry – we don't expect you to know who we all are, my dear. My, what a fabulous day for the wedding though, eh?' She turns to the assembled group. 'It's been so damn cold, I didn't know what I was wearing till this very morning, I swear. Didn't Camille look radiant, though?'

'Absolutely radiant. Most women would be too, in her situation, I daresay. Hal's a real catch isn't he?' Camille's aunt Cassiopeia turns to me now. 'She has a talent in that department, I'm sure you'll agree.'

Back to Nate again? I look at my hands demurely.

'Her dress was beautiful,' I say. And, like most bridal dresses, not designed for inclement weather. 'I'm sure she's happy the sun came out.'

'Just in time for the May hols, eh?' Marcie looks pointedly at me.

'Oh, you have a child who's already at school?' the aunt enquires. *Nate's new girlfriend has got a kiddie* she'll be telling everyone in a minute.

'No, I don't.'

'I was *referring* to the fact that you schoolteachers will all be off on your half-term holidays already,' Marcie smiles.

Teachers? I feel my heart sink. Is she talking to me? I look at the other two hopefully, but from their expressions it appears that, yes, she is still referencing me. So Nate's already mentioned me to Marcie? And told her I was a schoolteacher?

When did that happen?

'Yes, the weather's turned beautiful with perfect timing,' I croak.

'So ...' Aunt Cassiopeia smiles pleasantly but she's not to be distracted. 'You work at a school?'

What else has Nate told Marcie? I can feel my face getting a little hot, here. Has Nate told her I'm *his son's* schoolteacher? He was so keen for us not to mention Adam, and I didn't question it. I assumed his young 'dad' status might be one of those skeletons in the closet that everybody knows about and nobody talks of, but ... this is starting to get a little complicated. Who actually knows what, here? What am I not supposed to say? I look around desperately, still hoping to spot him.

'So – are you a tattoo artist or a teacher?' Lucinda's looking at me suspiciously.

'Both.'

'Both?'

'I do the tattoos in my spare time.'

'None of the teachers I know ever seem to have any spare time,' the aunt puts in now.

'Do you really?' Marcie's all ears. 'You do *tattoos?*'

I sigh, wanting to escape but not sure where exactly I can escape *to*. I already ducked grandpa a few times, coming out of the bathroom. I can't pretend I need to go back in there again.

209

Hell's bells. Where are you Hardman of the Dorset Hardmans? You've really abandoned your post, here, haven't you?

'She did one for Nate too, didn't you, Jenna?'

'You did a tattoo for Nate?' Marcie's more than interested now. 'When? And where?'

'She won't tell us where.'

'I expect you'll have to ask him yourself, won't you?' the Brigadier pipes up, indicating behind us, and there Nate is, standing by the drinks tent with some people, looking around. For me?

'Is he coming over here?' Lucinda breathes. She's looking at Nate with such unrequited longing I almost feel sorry for the girl. He's looking good, admittedly. Pleased and relaxed and … just for the moment, without the worry at his back, so different to how I've ever seen him before. He's navigated the lunch and the speeches and all the people who've come up to say hi, and he's still smiling. None of his fears about today have come true, have they? I am so happy for him.

'I doubt it,' Marcie tells the girl. 'Some of our SWP people have got hold of him now. They were keen to have a word, so it's unlikely he'll be coming our way, for a bit.' She's right. When Nate turns and smiles apologetically in our direction, I can practically hear Lucinda's yearning heartbeat thumping from here.

Right now, I'm only hoping that no one can hear mine.

Nate

'Not so *fast*, young man.' The lean, muscular arm slipped neatly through mine turns me round on a dime. 'Come over here. You've barely said hello, yet.'

'Hal!' I've just slipped away from the Smart World Productions team but there's no way I'm getting away from this guy.

'Nate.' Our handshake, as usual, turns into an affectionate bear hug. 'I know, I know.' The bridegroom leans his head in towards mine for a second, 'you were heading back to your date, but she's fine where she is for the moment. Coping magnificently, I'm sure you'll agree?' We both cast a glance over to where Jenna is chatting happily to some of the other guests. I'm all too aware I've left her on her own for too long already – *some date I am* – but it's true, she still seems to be smiling.

'You have a talent, it seems, for picking the loveliest ladies.'

'As do you.'

'True.' He lowers his eyes for a moment. A passing waiter stops and I allow him to press another champagne flute into my hand, feeling a shiver of sadness inside and also, strangely, some relief. I raise my glass to the bridegroom.

'Congratulations, Hal. I mean it.'

'Thank you, my friend.' He adds, 'and thank you for making the effort, I know that it's cost you.' He pauses for a bit, while we both acknowledge the truth of that. 'I was so happy when Marcie

211

mentioned at work that you planned to make the nuptials. She said you had a companion who'd volunteered to help you through it. Some … teacher friend, she said.'

'Marcie told you that?' Bang goes the tattoo story I've been telling people during lunch.

'Kids are all lucky bastards these days, I'll say that much.' He looks over towards Jenna again, impressed. 'I never had any teachers who looked like that when I was at school – did you?'

I feel a smile creasing my face. 'Not really. My schoolmasters were all balding, bearded blokes wearing suits that might have fitted them once, ten years previously.'

'Balding and sweaty, with names like Mr Montgomery and wearing wristwatches that they checked every two minutes and crumpled trousers that looked like they'd been slept in …'

'True,' I grin. 'Pretty young lady teachers were a bit thin on the ground in my time.'

'Mine too. I have to hand it to you. How does a bloke who can't even go out get to meet a beauty such as her, Nate?'

It's an innocent enough question. He's merely making conversation now, but I'm not sure how to answer. I've fenced that one with everyone else by using the 'tattoo' story, but if Marcie's already been talking to Hal … I stall for a second, looking at the ground as I feel the worry rise – what else might she have told him?

'You okay?' He picks up on my change in ease, instantly.

'Yeah, I'm …' I take a swig from the flute and the champagne in my mouth threatens to go down the wrong way.

'All getting a bit too much?' he supplies gently. 'There's a quiet conservatory area inside the house if you need a bit of space …'

'I'm good, Hal. I just …' I look around to make sure there's still only us two in this conversation. 'I just spent ten minutes in there.'

'You took some time out?'

'After lunch,' I admit. 'I needed some space.'

'You're okay now?' He's all sympathy. 'We don't have to stay out here if you …'

212

'I've been indoors a couple of times already,' I tell him reluctantly. Hopefully, no one has noticed, even Jenna. I've been discreet about it. 'I don't want to go back in.'

'What do you do?' He looks at me curiously. 'When you go inside?'

I stare at him, sticking my hands deep into my pockets. 'What do you mean, what do I *do*? I go in there and just, like ... breathe.'

'You breathe?' He cocks his head to one side, smiling faintly. 'I breathe all the time, myself. I find it generally most conducive to life.'

I dig into his ribs with my elbow.

'*Ouch!*'

'Wanker.'

'Okay, sorry. I'm just trying to understand.' He rubs at his side remorsefully. 'How does it help?'

'It stops me thinking, that's how.' I lower my voice as some other guests make towards us. 'It helps stop my imagination running away to some God-awful place where it shouldn't be running to. It's like a ... a physiological response to a fight-or-flight stimulus that's been set on a hair-trigger.'

Hal does an almost imperceptible motion with his hand now, I see it out of the corner of my eye, and the friends of his who were approaching suddenly stop, sidle off to another group.

'And that's what causes the panic?'

'Yeah.' I hate this, even *talking* about this. I look away from my friend, feeling a host of feelings rise, chief among them, regret that I've even brought this up. *This is his wedding day.* I down the rest of the champagne in my glass in one swallow. *What the hell am I doing, opening all this up with him, now? For fuck's sake.*

'But ... let's talk about something else, eh?'

'For sure.'

He holds out his own champagne glass to me now.

'No, I don't want ...'

'Take it,' he counsels. 'It'll do you some good.'

He watches as I knock it back.

'You've coped well, coming out today, I'll say that much.'

213

'Having Jenna here has helped enormously. She makes me feel …' I examine the empty glass in my hand, 'as if nothing can go wrong.'

Saying it out loud, I at once recognise the truth of this statement. That was how I always used to feel before, I recall. As if I were charmed, perfectly protected. As if nothing in my life could ever go wrong. That was before I lost the girl who, today, has become Hal's wife: six months before I went into Afghanistan with Jim Nolan and the rest of my world got turned inside out.

'Nothing *will* go wrong,' Hal's assuring me. 'And as for that pretty girlfriend of yours, I'd say you're onto a winner there.'

'Not really.' I take in a long breath. 'She's off, soon. In about ten days' time, in fact.'

His eyebrows furrow sympathetically.

'Pity. Every time we looked over at your table, she wasn't able to take her eyes off you. Even Camille commented on it.'

'Did she now?'

'She did.' He adds, tentatively, 'she'd like to talk to you, too. You mustn't ignore her.'

'No. I won't.' I look away from him, feeling sick.

'So.' Hal takes me in curiously. 'You and Jen. Have you two actually …? '

'*What?*' I frown, colouring a little. If he's asking me if I've taken her to bed yet …

'Have you two planned to meet again, after today?'

Ah. I shake my head.

'No? Really?' He seems surprised.

'She'll have plans to make, Hal. Once she leaves, Jenna's on a long-term contract, away for months at a time if I've understood her correctly. No. I'm grateful she's helped me out today, but …'

'Jenna's still around for another ten days though, isn't she?'

I shrug. 'What of it?' I let my gaze slide away from his.

She hasn't left the area yet Adam's voice echoes back to me now. *What if you asked her and it made her change her mind so she didn't leave?*

214

I swallow. 'I won't be able to change her mind, if that's what you're thinking, Hal.'

'That wasn't my thinking, as it happens.'

My eyes come back to meet his.

'Ten days with a woman who's clearly as good for you as she is, is still ten days.' He gives me a significant look. 'That's all some people ever get.'

I give a short laugh.

'Nothing could come of it, Hal.'

'Maybe some short-term good could come of it?'

'Date her till she leaves – is that what you're suggesting?' I pull a disparaging face, but the idea, crazy as it is, is growing on me. I don't want to give Jenna up, just yet. In truth, I don't want to give her up at all.

'Why not? She's leaving, so no strings attached. Treat it like a holiday romance, maybe? Enjoy meals out, walks in the bluebell woods, ice-creams on the beach. Do anything,' he says, 'just enjoy the time you have with her. Be ... *happy*.'

Hal's looking a little sad.

'You still feeling guilty about marrying my ex?' I shoot him a rueful smile.

'Hey, man ...'

'You needn't be.' I slap my old friend on the back. 'You really needn't. You are far more right for Camille than I ever was.' He is, too. The thought he's just put in my mind is still reverberating round, though. Ten days. I never thought of it, but he's right. Jen and I could still have those days – like a holiday romance, he says, no strings attached. If that's what she wants. I laugh again, for no good reason feeling at my ease suddenly, feeling *happy*. Would she go for it? Agree to see me again? The thought lifts my spirits immeasurably.

'It's good to see you more like your old self,' he observes. 'The difference having a woman in your life can make, eh?'

'I feel it.' We both turn to look at her.

215

Jenna's still with Marcie and the Brigadier. Camille's joined them and my date's looking strangely winsome now, a little lost and I feel this sudden urge to take her in my arms, sweep her way somewhere safe like some old-fashioned knight on a horse. I smile inside, at the thought of how she'd take that, too. Even if she's looking a little vulnerable to me, she's not the helpless type, is she, Jenna? As much as she seems lost at this moment, she's still managing to look even hotter than she did before.

From somewhere down the bottom of the garden I can hear the live dance band starting up and I remember: I promised her one dance. I hand him back his glass.

'I need to go catch up with my date, Hal.' I've been away too long already. I know Jenna can hold her own, but I know Cami, too.

She's got a way of worming things out of people.

Jenna

'Here she comes!' We all turn to look and the Brigadier holds out his hands as Camille glides over. Her bespoke ivory dress is covered in tiny pearls that are shimmering softly in the sunlight. At her neck 'something borrowed'; a family heirloom of pearls and emeralds that set off her honey-coloured hair to perfection. The cooing sounds from all the women around her are both admiration and envy.

'Never known you to look more beautiful, my dear. You've outdone yourself.'

'Oh, Granddad.' Camille's smile under those beautifully curved lashes is genuine enough. This girl is one happy bunny today, no regrets about *the one that got away*, I see. Not so sure if Nate feels the same way. I spied him gazing over at her on the top table earlier, and so poignantly, it did make me wonder. He was pretty cut up on our way back from the beach when the subject of his ex's wedding came up, I recall. *You're still in love with her*, I challenged him, and he never denied it. *Maybe your ex is still in love with you?* is all he came back with. But he's wrong there. Alessandro's given up even trying to get any reply from me.

I stand a little to one side as Camille greets her relatives, embracing them one by one.

'He's right, darling,' the aunt Cassiopeia puts in now. 'And I'm *so* glad your father went with the Tiffany-blue Daimlers for the bridal party. I suggested they'd work well with the girls' dresses, didn't I?'

'You did. And you were right.' Camille smiles sweetly. She's got the air of a girl who's used to this, I think; emeralds and pearls and Tiffany-coloured Daimlers from Daddy and … and blokes that just can't get over her, even when she's marrying someone else.

I take a long, cool, sip of my water, as much to hide my face as anything else. Right now I've got a strange, spiralling feeling in my stomach, like something's being ripped away from me but I have no idea what it is.

'Your mother even got them to match the men's buttonholes with those cars,' someone says and there's a round of appreciative laughter.

I study the grass for a bit, standing back while the family shower their congratulations. Details of the forthcoming honeymoon in the Maldives are shared, and of the apartment in Wimbledon which the happy couple will be loaning from a willing relative whilst waiting for their house purchase in Kensington to go through. There is so much affluence and family support, here. The lovely Camille takes it all in her stride.

A few other people come over and the Brigadier starts telling jokes and I stop listening now, wishing I could get away. In the time I've been standing here waiting for Nate to come over, at least three others have joined us. He was talking to the groom and looked as if he was coming over to join us a moment ago but they've started chatting again. I give an inward sigh. No worries really, that's what he's here for after all, to get with his friends, start getting his confidence back, but … I'm kind of starting to miss him.

'Oh, I'm sorry!' Camille's gaze comes to rest on me, at last. 'We haven't been introduced yet have we? You must be …?'

'Jenna Tierney.' I put out my hand to take hers.

'Of course you are.' Why do I get the impression she knows exactly who I am, she was just working her way up to me? 'You came with Nate, didn't you?'

'I did.'

She looks me over curiously. Then she smiles, glancing over the heads of the assembled group as if she's spotted some other people she needs to speak to.

'I need to circulate. Please, excuse me, everyone.' Her soft hand plucks my sleeve, pulling me a little away from the group. 'Walk with me. I want to know all about how Nate's doing. I can't believe when we last spoke, he never even *mentioned* he had a new girl in his life.'

I lower my eyes.

'Maybe when you last spoke to him, he didn't.'

'You've only met him recently then, I take it?'

'Very recently.'

'I never knew he went for redheads.' She's still smiling sweetly.

'I'm sure when he was with you, he'd never have looked at another woman, so how would you?'

She laughs, taking the compliment.

'We were placing bets on the top table, you know, as to how long Nate had been with his new girl. The way you two couldn't keep your eyes off each other the entire meal, it was quite sweet.'

'I'm surprised you even noticed.' I can feel my face going hot. 'And I'm sure it wasn't quite like that.'

Of course it wasn't. I did notice him looking over at me quite a lot but I figured that was just for reassurance. Or effect. Well, he knows that and I know that but I suppose it's logical some of the guests might have imagined it was something else. We stop, as a passing waiter pauses to offer us champagne.

'No.' I shake my head at him.

And then I change my mind and take one off the tray. Camille smiles softly. I've been teetotal up to now in case we needed to make a quick getaway but it's perfectly plain Nate's coping just fine. Maybe he's even in his element. And I can imagine this reception is going to go on for *hours*, yet.

'So ...' There's an infinitesimally small pause before she asks, 'How's Nate been?'

'Good.' I nod my head, in a non-committal, encouraging kind of way. Once again, I feel myself floundering a little bit. Just how much of *how Nate's been* would a very recent girlfriend be expected to know, that's the question? If he's been keeping his problems from his friends – How much does his ex even know? I take a sip from my flute and the champagne glides deliciously over my tongue. Expensive champagne. Sublime, probably stupidly expensive, *free* champagne. Look what I've been missing all afternoon.

'He wasn't in a terribly good place when I popped round a few weeks ago,' she murmurs now.

'I'm sorry to hear that.' I keep my face pointed straight ahead as we walk across the soft grass of her granddaddy's lawn. On a raised area above the grass, a quartet are playing chamber music. Young waiters and waitresses weave more drinks, dessert canapés and cocktails in amongst the guests and everywhere, the sun is smiling gently, brightening up faces and moods and the floral displays that have been tastefully positioned in every nook and cranny. It's all very lovely and I want to suck it up, just bathe in it all, enjoy the ambience while I'm here.

But it's no good. I can't distract myself from being curious about this elegant woman, Nate's ex, who's walking along beside me.

And I can't, it seems, distract her either.

'So – where did you two meet, exactly?' she tries again.

'I met Nate in Rochester.' I keep it neutral. Between the teaching and the tattooing stories I'm getting a little lost. 'Where we both happen to live. How about you?'

'Oh.' She waves her hand airily. 'I've known Nate for about a thousand years. It was he who introduced me to the groom, as it happens.' We glance over to where Nate's standing beside her new husband, both of them still deep in conversation. 'Hal's very fond of him. He always has been.'

She stops, now, suddenly pensive. 'You do know …' She looks at me a little unsurely, uncertain whether or not to continue.

'That you and Nate were once really close?'

'Practically engaged, but I wondered if he'd mention that.' She gives a small smile, now. 'He's a private kind of guy, like that.'

'He told me you were the only person he's ever felt comfortable enough to open up, with.'

'I was.'

'And … you both seem like you two were pretty fond of each other, one time?'

'We were!' She's playing with the satiny pearl bracelet around her arm. People smile at us as they go by and we start walking again so they won't stop. 'He's a … an extraordinary guy, Jenna. Not only is he caring, he's soulful and creative. Quite apart.' She gives a soft laugh. 'From being a hunk. But I guess you're already starting to discover that for yourself?'

'I am.' I look away from her now, feeling a little envious at the good fortune she's had. Nate's not my boyfriend like she thinks. He never will be. In just over a week's time I'll be leaving this country and I'll be gone so long, I'll probably never see him again. But there's still something inside me wishing and wondering.

'He was the first man I ever loved with all my heart and there's a little piece of it that will always be his.' She sounds a little sad, now. Not *gutted*, the way Nate sounded when he first brought the wedding up, but sad, nonetheless. And I feel a burning curiosity bubbling up inside me, unable to help myself;

'So, do you mind if I ask, why did you two ever …?'

'I want him to be happy, Jenna.'

We've both spoken at once.

'I want him to be happy, too.' I rub at my arms, feeling a little chilly even though it's far from cold. I take another sip of my drink. I want him to be happy, and that's what he'll be once he's reconciled with his son. That's why I'm here. That's the *only* reason why I'm here.

'Do you think … you'll be with him for a while?' She's asked it like she knows – she really knows – how hard Nate's been finding everything. I take this on board. He's doing that video-diary, I

221

recall. And her new husband Hal had something to do with that, I'm sure Nate mentioned it in the car on the way down.

I shrug, smiling demurely in response to her question of how long I'll be with him. *I don't know.*

Only, of course, I *do* know, don't I?

'I hope I'm not speaking out of turn, but, you two do look very good together.'

I sigh. She still cares about him, this woman. She cares about him at least enough to want to go off on her fabulous honeymoon to the Maldives with her hunky new husband knowing poor old Nate's being taken care of, is that what it is?

'Thank you. I bet you two did once, too,' I put it to her. 'Your granddad's been telling me all about how very fond your family are of Nate.'

Her eyes lock onto mine.

'They are. They adore him.'

'Especially seeing as he's one of the *Dorset Hardmans*?' I mimic the Brigadier's gruff voice now and Camille claps her hand over her mouth, her eyes crinkling in amusement.

'Who told you that?' she gets out.

'Who do you think?' I indicate over my shoulder.

'Granddad told you Nate was a ...?'

'From a grand old military tradition.'

'He isn't though,' she tells me in a very low voice now. 'Nate didn't have the privileged background I've had. Things were much tougher for him ...' She stops, changes tack suddenly. 'His dad was in the military, yes, but not from Dorset. We let Granddad believe what he wanted to believe so he'd give Nate a chance, that's all.'

My eyes widen.

'You let your grandpa believe that, so Nate would be accepted?'

'So he'd get to *know him*. And it worked.' She smiles casually into her glass, takes a tiny sip. 'Grandpa still doesn't know any better. And now that it doesn't matter anymore ...'

I guess it doesn't.

222

Which leads me back to the question I tried to broach earlier …

'If you don't mind me asking,' I put it to her delicately. 'I'm just curious. What *happened*? I mean, given how in love you guys were and all – why did you and Nate ever split?'

Her fingers tighten around the little pearly bracelet now.

'Jenna, he's …' She stops walking. 'Nate's not spoken to you about that yet, then, I take it?'

I shake my head slowly.

'And you've been together how long?'

'Not very.'

'Not very.' She takes me in thoughtfully. 'That's probably why.'

'So … will you tell me now?'

'No. I'll leave Nate to tell you that one himself, if he wants to.' A dark fierceness, like an unresolved anger, flashes over her beautiful face, warning me. It disappears as soon as it came. This is, after all, her wedding day. But I know what I just saw. And it's left me feeling a little shocked. And confused. *What is she talking about?* Whatever it was, she's never moved past it, that's for sure.

And then it hits me – how could I not have seen it before? I know what it is!

It's his illegitimate son, isn't it? It's got to be that. She split up with him over Adam, I can't think of anything else. How very sad.

Camille shakes her head, opening her dainty little handbag and then closing it again, *click, click.* 'Now I really do need to go and circulate,' she says. This time I keep my mouth shut.

I watch as she gathers up her composure, along with the hem of her dress, waving to her mum, who's just left Nate and Hal. She and some other people who've decided we've had long enough are making their way towards us now across the luscious grass.

'Hello, you darling things,' she calls out and my time with Camille is at an end. I look over to where Nate and Hal are back to their tête-à-tête and I wonder what it is they're talking so earnestly about. Old times, probably. Work matters. Football fixtures. Cars. *Stuff.* Men-stuff. I won't disturb them.

223

And once again, I am on my own, with no one to talk to. I'm just the stranger at the wedding. I'd go and hook up with some other little group, but the conversation I've just had with Camille has left me feeling … weird. Reflective. It's left me feeling sad. Could that lonely little boy of Nate's really have been the bone of contention that drove these two apart?

Really?

I've never seen myself as anyone's mum, never imagined my life would spin that way. But if I'd ever found myself in Camille's situation, I can't help but think … I'd have made some very different choices to the ones she made. But that, of course, was the path that was once before her.

It is not the path currently before me.

Jenna

Finally – Nate Hardman, the most mysterious and sexiest non-date I've ever had, is walking over to join me.

'Hey.' He holds out his hands to me, apologetic. 'I'm sorry, Jen. I've abandoned you for too long, haven't I?'

'Not at all.' I give a quiet shake of my head. 'We came here precisely for this: so you could show your face and catch up with all your friends.' He comes in to hug me and to the rest of the world, we are just like any 'newly dating couple' greeting each other affectionately. Up close, I get a drift of the spicy aftershave I've been catching every time he's near. I don't know what it is, but it's got to be the best scent anyone's ever invented. Maybe I'll even buy some when I get to the U.S. just so I can remember ... remember today. Nate's head leans in towards mine and for one, slightly intoxicating moment, I wonder if he's going to kiss my cheek. *Just in case anyone's watching,* I think. Sadly, the moment of danger passes.

'I'm done with doing what we came here to do,' he tells me in a low voice.

'Oh, yes?'

Nate's taken my arm and we're walking very fast, in the opposite direction to everyone else, across the lawn and away towards the clump of trees in the distance.

'You'd rather make yourself scarce?' I look at him surreptitiously. I don't like to mention the words *panic attack*. 'You've been doing

225

brilliantly all day, so if you're starting to feel a bit wobbly now …'

'No, it's not that.'

'No?'

My date is looking unexpectedly sheepish.

'I'm done with talking to other people. I just realised …' He's quiet for a bit before he comes out and says it. 'I realised I'd *rather* be spending more time with you.'

'With me?' My heart does a ridiculously happy leap and I keep my eyes down, trying to quash it. Trying to quash everything, in fact, that I've been starting to feel in the last few hours. Nate and I have each been doing our own thing ever since lunch ended. He's done what he needed to do. I know I was only ever here as backup but, if I'm honest, every moment I have spent with all these strangers at this wedding, watching him from afar, I have missed being with Nate.

And that is wrong. That is never what either of us intended. That is not why I came.

'With *you*, Jenna Tierney.' His face creases into one of those beautiful, rare smiles. 'I've just been reminded I've got the prettiest girl here as my date, and I've been ignoring her.'

'You're forgiven. But only because I'm not a *real* date,' I remind him. Nate looks a little crestfallen. He indicates over his shoulder, now.

'I see you just met the bride?'

I nod. 'I see you just missed her.'

'I'm sure she and I will catch up at some point, Jenna.' His words are clipped.

'Well, she and I have had a lovely long talk.' I give a little laugh, teasing him because he's looking so serious again. 'Don't worry. She said only the best things about you.'

'I'm not worried.'

'You shouldn't be.'

'I'm not.'

Oh, God. Why are we even talking about *Camille?*

'If you're planning on taking me for that dance now.' I slow down, change the subject, 'we're headed in totally the wrong direction.'

I see his face crease.

'Not yet.'

'You're not trying to wriggle out of your promise to dance with me, are you Mr Hardman?'

'I'm not trying to get out of it. There's something I wanted to show you first,' he entices. 'It's down here, in a clearing amongst the trees but you'd never guess.'

'Down *here?*' Wherever we're headed, it's well away from everyone else. We come to it a few minutes later, his special place. It's a little ornamental water fountain with water tumbling from the mouth of an ancient goldfish.

'Oh, my. How pretty.' I perch on the edge of the stone rim, trailing my fingers in the cool water, trying to forget whose house this is. Who he'd have experienced this place with, first. 'I love places like this. It reminds me of Italy.' It's very tucked away. Very peaceful. All around us, acacia trees sigh gently, moved by the breeze. The water gurgles and bubbles from the fountain spout and a few green leaves drift lazily on the surface. I look up at him happily.

'It's the kind of place you stumble across and you imagine no one else in the world has ever been there before you.'

'It's the kind of place where you hope no one else *will* find you, once you've discovered it.'

I shoot him a sad smile. 'Are you hoping no one else will discover us, now?'

'I am. But not because I'm scared of them, Jenna. Not anymore.' He stretches his arms out, opening up his chest, and there's a feeling of lightness and joy about him that I've not seen before. 'I wanted a bit of space away from them all, so I could thank you properly. For being here. For all that you've done for me. For ... helping me remember who I am, again.'

'It's been my pleasure helping you.'

'You didn't have to come out all this way with me, give up your whole day,' he says feelingly, 'but you did.'

227

'Hey, I've been the envy of every woman here.' I bat away the unexpected and unwanted feelings of longing and sadness that are coming up.

'Because you were here, today I feel one hundred per cent more like the man I was, before.'

'The man Camille fell for,' I point out softly.

'Long time ago.' That hit home. Nate turns away so I can't see his face. Damn it. *Why did I bring it up?* I couldn't stop myself. She matters to him, doesn't she? Still.

And I'm hating that I care so much.

'… the man *a lot* of the women here seem to have fallen for, judging by the grilling many of them have given me.' My comment is intended as a light throwaway, but somehow it doesn't come out quite like that.

'I never cared for any of them, Jenna.'

'Only her?'

He bows his head.

'I cared for her, once.'

'Not now?'

'Not now! Not *that* way, no …' He clears his throat. 'Why do you ask me that?'

'No reason.' My eyes go down now, watching the eddies my fingers are making in the water, dark green and silver, little ripples that skim out and out and out, concentrating very hard on them because I don't trust myself to give him eye contact. *Why did I just mention her again, am I mad?* I daren't let him see all these feelings coming up that I'm not supposed to be feeling. And I am not going to ask him – *I am not going to ask* – why they split. Not today. Not now.

'Your ex was very interested to know all about you and me,' I distract now.

'And did you tell her all … about us?'

I smile. 'I told her practically nothing.' I feel him relax almost instantly. Then I add, 'Camille thinks we'd make a lovely couple, apparently.'

Nate lets out a breath. Then he says,

'Camille could be right.'

My eyes go straight up to meet his. 'What are you saying, Mr Hardman?'

'Maybe we would,' he suggests quietly, '… make a lovely couple?' He moves in a little closer now, as if he's just noticed something. 'You all right, Jenna?'

I swallow, nodding my head even as a few, stupid, uncalled-for tears spill onto my cheeks.

'I'm … perfectly all right.' I wipe them away furiously.

Nate sits down beside me, so close that the length of his thigh is touching mine. *Doesn't he know what that does to me inside?* I turn away so he won't see it on my face, but the growing yearning I've felt all afternoon to be close to this man, like a physical ache, is growing stronger.

'Hey,' he says. He leans in a little closer, now, looking mortified. 'I'm sorry, if what I just said upset you ….'

'It didn't. It isn't that, I promise you. It's … something else.'

He waits.

A few long, horrible moments go by while I take stock of the confession that's just come tumbling out of my mouth. About how *not okay* everything is, for me. Today wasn't meant to be about me, was it? I came here for him. And yet the tears … they keep on coming. They tumble down like the waterfall behind us without ceasing, falling like they never fell when I left home for the first time; falling like they never did when I left Alessandro behind in Sicily. *Oh hell, what is he going to think? Why is this happening to me now and why can't I stop it?* I don't *do* tears.

'Do you want to tell me?'

God, no.

'I'm so sorry, Nate. I didn't mean to go all girly waterworks on you.' I scrabble for a tissue in my handbag, trying to give an embarrassed laugh, shrug it off, but I can't. The truth is I'm feeling too sad.

'Sometimes girly waterworks can work wonders.' He smiles softly.

'It's just that … this place, this wedding, it's all been so beautiful.' I realise how lame this must sound, but – what else am I going to tell him? That I'm falling in love with him? And this … *thing* that happens to me when I fall in love, that's so out of my control, it's happening again. How it makes me feel crazy things, like, how I just want to be with him. And how I'm starting not to be able to concentrate on anything else when he's near and that makes me feel gauche and awkward and so not like myself. And that's … so unfair, because it shouldn't happen now when the circumstances couldn't be worse and we're both only pretending, for God's sake. And … and I *promised* myself I would never do this again because it never works out, does it?

Did he … did he really just tell me he thinks we'd make a lovely couple?

Did he mean it?

'Weddings seem to have that effect on females,' Nate's still answering my last comment. Then he nudges me wickedly. 'Especially the unmarried ones.'

I gulp. 'I'm not on the shelf *quite* yet, Nathaniel.' He's teasing. I know he's teasing, but I can't resist adding: 'And … and even if I were, the shelf is where a lot of young women want to be these days, you know. We're empowered enough to know that …'

'And yet even in these empowered days, women still cry at weddings,' he notes.

I stare at him, feeling unusually at a loss for words. I wasn't feeling sad about the wedding, as such. Not really.

'Today's celebration has been what every girl dreams of. I don't just mean all the costly accoutrements, I mean …' I look up at Nate uncomfortably. 'All the *other* things. Like, how happy the bride looked when she came into the church on her dad's arm. The way her family were all so proud of her.'

'I'm sure your family will be equally proud of you when your day comes?'

'Ha!' Best not go there, probably. 'My family aren't like that. They're … they're often mean-spirited and petty and divisive. My family have never pulled together. They're generally a lot happier when they're pulling each other apart.'

I stop, and the sadness that I felt before rises up like a wave to wash over me.

'I'm so sorry, Jen.' I close my eyes as Nate's mouth brushes the top of my head. So soft, I can't tell – was that a kiss? *Did Nate just kiss me?*

He tilts my face up towards his and answers that now with another kiss. First, he kisses away the tears in the corner of my eyes. I hold my breath and it is as though the world around us quietens and stills. The rustling leaves on the trees stop sighing. The cheerful strains of the band, the waterfall behind us, I don't know where they all go because all there is in the world at this moment is me and this man and all my sorrow has mysteriously lifted like a mist. In its place, there's … something else. Something I want so much more than I should want. Nate pulls me towards him. His next kiss is on my mouth, tentative and sweet and hungry all at the same time.

And then I kiss him back. Oh, God.

Are we really doing this?

Nate

Adam is still pestering me to learn more about my weekend.

'So you and my teacher had a slow-dance together ...' He's just caught the football he was supposed to kick back to me. He stands there squarely, looking impressed. 'Down in the woods by the goldfish fountain, and she told you ...'

'You know, when you turned up at mine this morning with that football in your hand, I kind of *assumed*, it was because you wanted to get in a little bit of footie practice, not to talk about my love life?'

When he turned up bright and early and unannounced at my door this morning, telling me his nan had sent him over, I assumed that's what she'd intended for him. A bit of a run around for the kid, a little bit of exercise. And after the weekend I've just had – thanks, in large part to Adam – I was in the best mood. I was feeling solid, good about myself and glad of the chance to go outside to play footie with him. If I'm honest, I was also keen to see if my new-found courage was holding up.

The lad frowns. 'But I thought she told you ...'

Kick it over this way, I indicate, waving wildly as much to shut him up as anything else. Does he have to speak so loud? It's not as if we're all alone. There are a few other dads out here having a kick-about with their kids on this sunny, start-of-the-half-term Monday morning. But Adam isn't taking the hint.

232

'Miss Tierney told you she'd never met a man with a bigger ...'

One of the fathers shoots me a shocked look that borders on impressed, at that.

'Heart,' I finish for him rapidly. 'She said she'd never met a man with a bigger *heart*.' I open out my hands and the other dad smiles wearily. *Kids, what can you do with them, eh?*

Sheesh. I sidle up to Adam.

'Sorry.' He places the football on the grass, lining it up ever so precisely. 'I've never been to a wedding, you see. I was excited to hear about it.'

'I know, but ... I'd prefer to keep at least a few of the intimate details about my weekend private,' I hiss.

'If I talk lower,' he puts on a gruff, *sotto voce* now, 'can we still talk about it?'

I ignore that question, jogging backwards to my former position. 'Come on, kid. Over to me.'

'Can we talk about the food, at least?'

I'm back at my post, waiting for him to kick it over. Behind me, his well-used plastic water bottle and the jacket I bought for him on eBay have been laid out on the grass to mark out the goal area and he hasn't got one past me, yet.

'Food. You want to talk about food?'

'I *like* food,' Adam smiles. 'Especially party food. Did they have jelly? Cakes and crisps, fizz?'

'No jelly or crisps.' I jump up and down, limbering up. Then I open my arms out wide, encouraging him to take the shot but he's still waiting for the rest of my answer. 'Fizz, yes. Champagne. Lots of very good champagne.'

'Champagne.' He rolls the word around his tongue, thoughtfully. 'Is that like ... expensive, very tasty fizz?'

'It is.' I give a happy inward groan, remembering just how tasty. I'm normally more of a lager man. Still, I'm not complaining about the effect that expensive fizz had on either Jenna or me, after we made the decision to stay on and not travel back Saturday night after all ...

233

I'm still slightly in shock – a very happy, delighted shock – that she agreed to that. Oh, man, *so* happy. We drove back late yesterday afternoon.

'Come on Adam. You gonna kick that over to me, or what?'

He shoots, and the ball goes wide, sails up and over and hits the back of a little black dog that's trotting past.

'Oops. Sorry.' His hands are covering his face, but the dog's owner jogs along with her earphones in place, unaware and unperturbed. The only time she looks up is when I cut in front of her to retrieve the ball. She smiles coyly at me as I boot the thing back.

Adam catches the ball. *Again.*

'You need to concentrate, kid.'

'I am concentrating. I'm concentrating on learning what the wedding was like.'

I stop jumping up and down. Stand facing him for a moment, hands akimbo.

'Do you actually want to play, or not?'

'I did want to play football. I do.' He's lining the ball up again, frowning slightly. 'We can still talk while we play, though, can't we?'

'Fine. But remember, it's *foot*ball. You kick it, don't catch it.'

'You *kick* it,' he says, with relish.

'*Oof!*' I clutch at my solar plexus, doubling up. 'Jeez Louise, where did that cannonball come from?'

He laughs.

'You're meant to aim it at the goal, Adam Boxley, not the bloody goalkeeper!'

'I *was* aiming it at the goal. You were just standing in the way.'

'What? No! You're …' I let myself drop to the grass, winded.

'You're unfit,' he accuses.

'I've had a very active weekend, thank you very much.' The memory brings a happy smile back to my lips. I'm not as unfit as he thinks.

'While you're getting your breath back.' He comes over and throws himself heavily down on the grass beside me. 'Let's talk about the cakes.'

The cakes. I peer up at him through the pain.

234

'You haven't told me anything yet about the cakes at this wedding?'

'Okay,' I give in. He wants details. Let's give him some details. 'They had a whole tent dedicated to the desserts. Inside, there was this big display of berry tarts, and pastel-coloured macarons and dark chocolate mousse cups and ... something lemony with pretty little ...' I do a circular motion with my fingers, 'little flowers or something.'

The lad is practically drooling.

'I've never tried any of those things.' Then, after a slight hesitation, he enquires tentatively. 'Did you bring me anything back?'

'I'm sorry?'

'Did you bring me anything back?' He wants to know. 'Nan went to a wedding one time and she brought me back cake. Two bits of cake. Very tasty.'

'No, I ...' I shake my head. 'I didn't bring anything back with me, other than a lot of happy memories.' And a hangover, but we won't go into that.

'Tell me about the dancing, then.' He rolls over onto his tummy, head propped in his hands. 'Tell me what Miss Tierney said to you, again. That bit about how much she liked you and how she'd be very happy to spend some more time with you before she has to go away, even though,' he reminds me earnestly, 'you stepped on her toes.'

I cringe. Perhaps I shouldn't have filled Adam in on quite so much when he came in wanting to know all about it this morning. I wouldn't have, but the kid's got a way of wheedling things out of me.

'Did you have to bring up the crunched toes?'

'I *told* you she liked you.' He sighs happily.

'She likes me,' I agree. 'But you mustn't run away with any ideas about where this is going, kid.'

'I'm not running away with anything.' He plucks at a tiny daisy that's growing on the ground. One white petal, two white petals, three ... fall onto the soft grass. *She loves me ...* 'I'm taking it one step at a time, like you two are.'

'You are, are you?' I shoot the kid a wide grin, lying back on the warm ground and enjoying the feeling as the wind subsides and the sun hits my belly. He mimics my movement and we lie there for a bit, companionably. A big puff of cloud, like a comfortable white pillow, floats by. Then it turns into a dragon. Adam's staring at it too.

'That looked like a lump of mashed potato a minute ago,' he murmurs. 'But now it's turned into a big stick of candyfloss.' His gaze returns to me. 'What are you thinking, Nate?'

'I'm thinking that … this is a very pleasurable thing to be doing, lying here. It's a … a very comfortable, simple, but extraordinarily good feeling, just to be lying on the grass.'

'It is.' He sighs.

'I was wondering why people don't do things like this more often. Why I don't do things like this more often.'

'Were you?'

'Yeah. I've been up this way to play football countless times in the past. Why is it I've never before thought to just come and lay down on the grass and squint up into that blue, blue sky and feel the earth trembling beneath me?'

'Perhaps you haven't,' he suggests sagely, 'because you're not normally out with a kid? I see other parents do it, sometimes.'

'Is that right?' I turn sideways to face him. 'Other parents do it?'

'Parents get to do lots of things that normal people don't do. Like … sometimes you see them sneaking a turn on the swings when it's quiet.'

'Do they?'

'And … they'll ride their kids' scooters back from the school, pretending it's just quicker. They'll buy *huge* ice-creams for their tiny kids when they know who'll end up eating them. And they get to sit and watch cartoons. And *also*,' he's on a roll, now, 'they buy cool toys they'd really love to play with. Like, there's this really cool train set I've seen …'

'Whoa.' I laugh. 'I get the picture.'

'Do you like being a parent, Nate?' He's plucked another daisy, and now he's divesting that one of its petals too.

'What are you trying to prove, with that?' I ask softly. He doesn't answer.

I let out a sigh.

'I love you, kid. But I'm not your parent.'

'You're just … telling everyone that you're my parent?'

I roll over, and up into a sitting position.

'You *know* how that came about, Adam.'

He looks at me silently and there's a stand-off for a while until a couple of girls about his own age come by. One of them mutters 'hi' and the other says nothing while Adam looks straight ahead, distinctly uncomfortable.

'They some of your friends?' I nudge his arm.

'Hello,' he says reluctantly. A look I can't quite place passes between the girls, now

'Girlfriends?' I moot the possibility. Adam shakes his head fiercely, doesn't take up my smile. '*Classmates*, then?'

'Classmates when I'm *in* class,' he mutters dully. 'Which I won't be, for two days, when we get back.'

I have no idea what he is talking about.

'You won't be going back to school?'

The kid's head drops and a few tears spill onto his cheek. What, he's crying too? I push back my hair. I seem to be having this effect on people, recently.

'So … why will you be missing school for two days – what, your nan needs you to take her somewhere, is that it?'

Adam shakes his head, silently. He sits up and pulls a letter out of his pocket, now.

'This came from Mr Drummond, on Saturday. He sent it to Nan and she told me to bring it round to you. So I came.'

Mr Drummond. That's the headmaster at his school, isn't it? Jenna was talking about him in the car on the way home, yesterday afternoon. She also mentioned a Mrs Ellis, again, the woman she touched on briefly the day we all went to the beach. Is Adam in some sort of trouble? Why have I got this sinking feeling I've just stumbled on the *real* reason his nan sent him round to mine this morning?

I take the note from him and skim-read it. Then my eyes go back to one particular line.

'... After investigating the parent's complaint, I must remind you that bullying tactics of this nature are totally unacceptable in a school such as St Anthony's. I hope you will be able to impress this upon Adam and he returns to school two days after the half-term break with a different attitude.'

'It's a ... notification that you're being excluded from attending school for two days after the half-term break?' I frown unhappily, holding it out to him. 'What's all this about, Adam?'

'Some parent's complained,' he says in a small voice. 'After I pushed one of those bullies back and he fell.'

'He fell, *and* ...?' I feel a twist in my stomach and a long ago morning, a grey playground in the yard of a school that's since been bulldozed to dust, echoes dully. *Walk away and leave them, Mo. Don't even look at them, don't give them any excuse. And then my shorter, weaker, older brother who never did learn how to stay out of trouble, dragging me into yet another scrum. Because how could I walk away and not defend him; he was my brother, older and stupider maybe, but he was my blood? And in that playground, as all the boys eventually came to learn, nobody could beat me.*

'And now,' Adam's telling me. 'That child can't play for the school team because when he fell, he twisted his ankle.'

'I see.' I come back to my young companion now with an unhappy shudder. 'And are these are the same boys I saw, harassing you, the day you first came to my door?'

He swallows. 'Nan says you've got to deal with it,' he whispers. 'She says she can't.'

'Let me get this completely straight. The same kids have been harassing you for months. Your legs are covered in bruises, and you didn't point this fact out to – whatshisname – Mr Drummond?'

'I tried to, but,' he nods, crushed. 'I don't think he believed me.'

'So how does he – or any of the staff at school, for that matter – *think* you got those bruises on your legs?'

Adam's shoulders lift.

'They don't think. They don't care. I'm not in the school team and I don't have any parents going in making complaints, do I?'

'I went in,' I remind him. 'I told Miss Tierney.'

'You told her, and she's protected me while she's been there, but …'

But now she's left.

He's right. I feel the injustice of it rising in my bones. Nobody is paying attention to what's happening to him. And when he finds the courage to defend himself, he's suddenly the one getting excluded.

'So – with no prior offence, no warning, and for an incident that occurred as you were defending yourself, they think they're going to lay this one on you?'

He nods, and a few more tears drip onto his nose.

'They're calling me a bully who's let the school down and needs to be made an example of. He's saying he wants to see you with Mrs Ellis, the Social Care lady, present.'

Fucking hell.

'Fatherhood isn't just about finishing off those ice-creams and gazing up at the clouds, is it?' I shake my head, sadly. 'Well. You tell your nan she can leave Mr Drummond and Mrs Ellis to me, Adam.'

Bang goes any niggling thought I've been harbouring over the weekend that maybe I should come clean to Jenna. I've had moments when I wanted to, sure, but that was just me wanting to make more of our relationship than it could ever be. Jenna's been honest with me, been very clear on one thing: we can enjoy the next week or so together, we can relish every last delicious moment while she's still around, but when she's gone, she's gone.

I rise slowly to my feet.

I can't put Jenna in the ethical position of needing to tell the school the truth.

And I can't – *I won't* – put this kid in the position of not having anyone on his side, either.

239

Nate

'I win!

When I come through from the kitchen area holding the starters, Jenna's practically dangling out of my living room window, her face turned upwards towards the sky. Well, *something's* just captured her interest more than the dinner I've been lovingly preparing for us. I put our plates down on the table.

'The only thing you're angling to win from that position is a piece of pavement pie ...' I move in smartly behind her to catch hold of her about the waist.

'Oh,' she half-twists round, a grin spreading across her face. 'That's *snug*, Nate.'

'Safety first.' I tell her. 'Besides, I am not insured for any incidents befalling young ladies who might lean too far out of my flat window.'

'Look at that.' She puts her hands over mine, gazing up at the sky again and I recall the game we were playing on the way back from our walk this afternoon. We were trying to see which of us could spot the largest cloud formation that actually looked like something.

'Where is it?'

'Over there.' She points it out, triumphant; three unrelated lumps of cloud, just floating along, bearing no resemblance to any identifiable thing.

240

'What's that supposed to be?' I bend my face towards the back of her head, hiding my smile and her hair smells of flowers and honey. She hasn't won. 'Three camels … with no humps … and no legs?'

'You know very well it's a train with three carriages,' she scorns. 'Look, you can even see the driver, waving at you, if you squint.'

'Squinting doesn't count in this game.' I tighten my hold on her waist. This feels good. Very good.

'Why wouldn't it count? I *think*,' Jenna turns, pouting a little now, 'you can see it perfectly well, Nathaniel Hardman. You're just cheating.'

'I'm not cheating.' In my arms, she feels soft and smells sweet, no matter that the words coming out of her mouth are so fierce. She *isn't* fierce, not one little bit, not really. 'But I'll give you the train, if you're so determined.'

'I win?' She turns right round in my arms to face me now, slides properly back into the room. 'You sure?' She frowns ever so slightly, suddenly in earnest. 'You *can* see it, can't you, Nate?'

I nod, giving in to her, and her mood is immediately mollified, like a prowling kitten who's just captured her piece of string.

'Good, then. I win. That means you're the one who has to do a forfeit.' Jenna taps me on the chest, delighted with herself.

Damn.

'I'd forgotten we'd said about a forfeit. What is it then?' I roll my eyes. 'What do you want me to do?'

She leans in towards me a little, considering what must be my forfeit and I kiss the top of her head.

'Be lenient, please, Miss.'

'Of course I'll be lenient.'

'I've already cooked us our dinner.'

'You have. And you'll also do the washing up?'

'I will do the washing up,' I say cautiously. I have a feeling that won't be the sum of it.

'… wearing the vinyl apron I bought you as a dinner-party gift?' Her eyes flicker up at me, suddenly mischievous.

'The one with the body of the dude?' I sigh.

'The one with the body of a hunky naked waiter on the front, wearing nothing but a bow-tie and a *rather large* fig leaf.'

'I put it more succinctly.'

'You left out all the good bits.'

'So – you want me to promise to do the washing up later on wearing *that*? Okay,' I give in. 'I'll wear that for you. Satisfied?'

She hasn't finished yet, though.

'That and nothing else,' she presses.

'What, *no!* I feel my face colour slightly. 'You've got to be kidding me. In this day and age of instant mobile uploads? Not likely.'

'You have to.' Jenna smiles sweetly. 'It's your forfeit.'

'You're really that keen to see my naked butt, girl?'

A gurgle of delighted laughter is all that comes back in reply.

'You have to do it,' she says when she recovers her composure. 'Otherwise you'll have to spend all of eternity in limbo, waiting for the chance to come along to redeem yourself.'

'I'm not a Catholic,' I tell her. 'I don't believe in limbo. And the only thing I know for sure that lasts for eternity is hilarious naked butt photos posted by friends on social media.'

'Who said anything about photos?' She pulls a solicitous face. 'Okay. No *pictures*,' she promises. 'I'll give you my mobile phone so you can hide it away and know for sure, okay?'

I consider this proposition for a bit.

'I guess it could have been worse,' I acquiesce.

'You agree, then? *Really?*'

'I agree.'

She doubles up with laughter, now. She laughs so much that her giggling becomes contagious and we both end up on the settee, barely able to hold ourselves up.

'God. It's been a while since I've done that. A *long* while.' I look at her admiringly, trying not to make it too obvious that I'm gawking at the long white limbs now crossed over mine on the sofa. 'What … I mean, *what* are we even laughing about?' I get out at last.

242

'You. Your face.' She stops, sucking in her lips so she won't laugh anymore.

'I'm laughing at my own face, now?'

'I wasn't actually going to hold you to it, you know. The *naked washing up.*'

'Oh, don't you worry, I'm a man of my word.' I fold my arms, resolute.

'The thing is …' She grins wickedly, 'that cloud didn't really look anything like a train with three carriages, did it?'

My jaw drops open. Then I snap it shut.

'No, actually. In all truth, it really didn't.'

'But you were sweet enough to let me have it, anyway.'

I open out my arms.

'You're my date, and you seemed like you really wanted to win. It felt like the gallant thing to do,' I admit.

'You know, I really *love* that about you,' she says. Then her arms snake up around my neck for an instant, drawing my mouth towards hers for a kiss and all thoughts of sitting down to eat fly out of the window. Who cares about forfeits and food just now, anyway? This girl's lips taste so good.

At this rate, there might not even be any washing up.

Jenna

The first thing I notice when I blink my eyes open this morning, is that the light is coming from the wrong place. The window and curtains are on the opposite side of the room. I swivel round.

'Oh, my.'

'Good morning, Gorgeous.' Nate's lying alongside me, propped up on one elbow, beaming. He's clearly been awake for a little while, waiting for me, even if he's still wearing little more than his boxers. I stare at him for a moment.

'Nate, did we …?' My voice is croaky. I put my hand to my head, wishing I hadn't drunk quite so much Prosecco last night.

'I'm sorry, no.' He's shaking his head.

No? Why is he apologising? *And why are we both lying in this bed together – his bed – if we didn't …?*

'The washing up,' He traces the length of my arm with his fingertip, 'did *not* get done last night.'

'The … *what?*' I lean over and smack his arm lightly. He lets out a laugh. The night is returning to me in a delicious rush now. Oh, boy. 'And what's this?' I pluck at the T-shirt I seem to be wearing … the *only* thing I seem to be wearing.

'My Simpsons T-shirt.'

'Simpsons? God.' I groan, gently easing myself up onto my elbows, then turn to grin at him. 'So I've spent the night with a guy who wears a Simpsons T-shirt?'

'I've never worn it,' he admits easily. 'That's why I lent it to you.'

I look down at it, then back up at him, still grinning. The night is coming back to me now, and what a night …

'There's no answer to that, is there?'

'If you don't like it, you can always take it off.'

'You *wish!*'

'I do wish.' He tugs at the bottom of the T-shirt.

'What about the washing up?' I remind him, laughing.

'Such a shame about that.'

'Oh, so now I've spent the night with a guy who owns a Simpson's T-shirt *and* leaves dirty dishes to fester in the sink after a party?' I give him an arch look. 'I am not getting the best impression here, Nathaniel Hardman.'

'My secrets are out. I'm sorry.' He leans in a little closer. 'Let me make it up to you,' he suggests.

'Hmm … I'm not sure. Is that all of them, though?' I turn to him, snuggling back down because he feels so familiar and so … so very *comfortable*. As if I've known him all my life.

And then some.

'All of what, beautiful girl?' He kisses the top of my head. Then my face.

I lift my chin.

'All of your secrets?' I tease. 'Do I have all of them, now?' I stroke the top of his chest, enjoying the feel of his skin beneath my fingertips and Nate leans back. I see his tongue goes to his cheek, now.

'*What?*' I laugh, 'I saw that!' I push myself away, pretending to want a better look at his face, but more to make him squirm a little than anything else. 'You've got another secret,' I accuse, grinning. He has, too. My poor, handsome hunk Nate has got the strangest expression on his face.

'Men and their little quirks,' I tease gently. 'You're looking absolutely mortified, now.'

'I am not.'

'You so are! What is it?'

'Nothing.'

'You leave the toilet seat up?'

'You're safe there,' he says wryly. 'That one's been trained out of me already.'

'Worse, then.' I half-close my eyes, thinking hard. 'You wear polo necks?'

'I do not!'

'You own some of those little elastic things that men wear to hold up their socks?'

He laughs.

'Can I take the Fifth Amendment?'

'It's the sock things?' I pull an astonished face.

'It isn't, but ...'

My eyes look deep into his, laughing.

'I wouldn't want to admit to anything that might, shall we say, ruin the moment,' he finishes.

'A girl should be allowed to know what she's getting herself into, though?'

'You know what you're getting yourself into,' he reminds me softly, pulling me closer to him. 'We did it last night. We're just continuing here where we ...'

His next kiss is long and deep and takes a long, long while. Long enough for me to realise that kissing other men was never as good as this, ever. No; all the other men I have kissed in my life, including Alessandro who I thought I would marry, did not have this effect on me when we kissed.

'I feel ... so *different* with you, Nate,' I admit when we come up for air.

'I feel different when I'm with you, too.'

'I mean, you make me feel – almost like a different person.'

'What kind of a person?' He leans back easily now, in no rush, his hands pushing back my hair. I shake my head a little. 'Not like you to be at a loss for words, Jen?' He smiles.

246

'Men don't do that to me, normally. Make me feel ... oh, I don't know,' I give a short laugh. 'Like someone I left behind, a long time back.'

'Regressed?' His turn to tease. I punch him softly on the arm, but the sweet smell of his skin, up so close, is intoxicating.

'Not regressed, you buffoon, just ...' I swallow. 'More relaxed. More like I can let my guard down, just be *me*, you know.'

'Watch out, you're going to share some of your own secrets with me any minute, I can feel them coming.'

'Can you now?'

'If it's that you wear those little elastic things women wear to hold up their stockings ...' His hand reaches round to softly cup my bare backside.

It's distracting, to say the least.

'Suspenders,' I provide. 'And no, I don't. Who wears those things unless they're into burlesque?'

From his expression, I'm guessing maybe his last girlfriend did.

'Anyway,' I continue, 'I was trying to be *serious*, here. Just for one minute.'

'Of course you were.' His hand is still on my butt. At least he's stopped moving it.

'What I was trying to say, was ...'

Nate twists his head round a little, intent, his eyes still smiling.

'What I was trying to say ...' I swallow. Suddenly, I can't remember what I was trying to say, or why I was trying to say it. I lower my eyes. 'Oh, it doesn't matter,' I tell him quietly.

'What you were trying to say was, that you're falling madly in love with me, even though you didn't mean to?'

'Oh, really!' I have to gasp at his sheer audacity. 'I've fallen for you, hook, line and sinker, have I?'

'Pretty much,' he assures me, eyes twinkling. 'You've realised that you can't imagine your life anymore, without me, and you wanted to ask me if I felt the same way.'

'Argh!' I flop my head down on his chest. 'The sheer and utter arrogance of men.'

'It's a genetic propensity,' he agrees.

I let out a deep breath.

'So ...' I venture after a bit. 'Do you? Feel the same way, I mean?'

'Absolutely,' he answers in a heartbeat.

I look up.

'Ha! *Really?*' I give a little laugh. Then I add, 'It's just the sex talking, isn't it?'

Nate bites his lip.

'I mean, yeah, we're pretty good together, *that way,*' I admit. 'Mind-blowing sex always makes you think you're in love, right? Makes you feel you'd never want anyone else quite so much, ever again?' I'm watching his eyes closely. My heart is beating so fast right now I can feel it, thump-thump-thumping right through my breast. Lying here, on his chest, I can hear his heart thumping, too. *Why am I even saying all this stuff to him?*

'I'm getting the impression I might not have had as much experience of that as you have,' he admits softly.

'You think I've had more lovers?' I look up sharply, 'because if you're implying that I ...'

'I'm not implying.' He leans up, and flops me right over so I'm lying on my back again. 'I'm *telling* you, that I've never had such good sex with anyone, as I had with you last night.'

'Oh.'

'And, for my part, at least, it isn't just the sex that's making me feel the way I do about you.'

'No?' I swallow.

'No.' He kisses me again, more tenderly this time. 'It's much more than that, isn't it? I know you feel it too.'

'I don't know what I feel,' I say helplessly.

'I think you do.'

'I *don't,* Nate! I'm just ...' I flounder. 'We had the best evening together last night and ... maybe I'm a bit confused right now?'

He gives a small nod.

'We don't have to do it again,' he says easily. 'Maybe you'd prefer it if I brought you some breakfast, instead?'

Is this the part where I say that I wouldn't prefer breakfast? That what I would *prefer* is for us to stay exactly where we are? Make love again, only this time sober, both of us totally present. Oh God, I want to tell him that. And I *would*, normally I would, but … this is not normally, is it? With Nate, nothing feels normal. Everything feels different and I'm not sure how to navigate this.

'A morning cup of tea?' he offers now. Nate moves away slightly, allowing me my space. If I gave him just the slightest indication, we both know where this would lead. But for me, this is no longer *just sex*, he got that much right. My date pulls himself up now, taking my silence as an expressed preference for some tea.

'I've enjoyed this time with you so much,' I tell him regretfully.

'I know. Me too.' He plants a soft kiss on my forehead before he goes to make us that drink.

'Nate,' I add, as he gets to the door. 'I'm sorry. I … I wasn't even meant to stay over, last night, was I?' He isn't sulky and cross, like I know some other dates might be. He isn't reproachful, either. He just seems happy after our time together, and … *grateful*. 'I never stay over with blokes, after …' I trail off limply. Even when we went together after Camille and Hal's wedding we spent the rest of the night in our own rooms. 'How did that even happen?'

'I already told you *how*,' he smiles softly. 'You just don't believe me.'

Jenna

'Need a helping hand out here?' When I pop my head around the open door at the back of Magda's shop, she's sitting out in the sunny courtyard at the rear, unpacking crockery from a tea chest.

'Hello, stranger.' Mags pats the stone bench she's sitting on, inviting me over.

'Hardly a stranger.' I help myself to a handful of the grapes from the art deco bowl by the door. 'And anyway, I've been really *busy*.'

'I haven't heard a peep from you since you dropped my car back round Sunday evening and that was practically a week ago!'

'Sorry. This half-term holiday has just spun by.'

'Most of it spent sorting out your plans and expediting the paperwork for your sojourn in the U.S. I expect?'

Most of it spent with Nate, as it happens. I step over the rug that's covered with bric-a-brac to join her.

She laughs. 'You've had a good week, anyway. I can tell that just by looking at your glowing face.'

'I have! I'm in the best place ever, Mags.' I hug my arms happily. 'To think – just a few short weeks ago, I couldn't imagine I would ever feel like this again, and now here I am ...'

'... here you are, about to fly off to a foreign country leaving everyone behind and start up all over.'

Why did she have to remind me? My stomach does a flip, now. And then it takes a strange dive.

'You okay?'

'Sure, I am.' I swallow. The sun dips out of sight for a moment, casting a deep shade over the high enclosing walls at the back of her shop and making my arms feel cold. 'I just ... haven't been focussing *too* much on the leaving part,' I admit.

'More on the "getting there" bit?' she offers.

Yeah. Of course.

'The "getting there" bit is what it's all about, correct? Living the dream,' she reminds me.

'That's ... exactly right,' I tell her. My mind's still with her previous comment that I'm going to be *leaving everyone behind*. Dammit. I don't want to be reminded about that bit. I haven't been thinking about it at all. I stretch out my arms, pretending to examine the state of my nails. 'I've been waiting for an opportunity like this one that Christiane's offered me, all my life.'

'You have.'

'It's not just the chance to travel widely or to learn from a master, or ... or draw the creatively new and daring tattoos I've been longing to do for years,' I enthuse. 'It's so much more than that.'

'I know it is.'

'It's like ...' I'm looking at her earnestly, but I can't for the life of me read the expression on Magda's face right now. 'It's the culmination of a dream. You know – like, the reason why climbers scale Everest. They do it because they feel this deep, internal *need* to do it.'

'I know.'

'And then when they get to the top, they feel as if they've accomplished something. Because they've reached out further than they thought they could. I imagine once they've battled their way to the summit they must feel like they're touching a little bit of heaven.'

'I imagine they must.'

She puts her hand on top of mine and there's this strange silence between us for a while. A silence that bounces back and forth between my happiness at going and the regret I have not, up to this point, wanted to feel at leaving, making me feel all weird inside. Mags gingerly places a dinner plate she's been holding in her lap, down on the rug. She pulls out another one.

'And you've sorted out your visa, yes?'

'I did the visa thing yesterday. It took me a few hours at the embassy, but I got it all done in the end.'

'Needs must.'

'I guess. It felt like such a waste of time though,' I admit. 'All I kept thinking was: those were hours I could have been spending with … with the people I wanted to spend time with, instead of wasting them waiting in a queue.'

'Indeed. Speaking of people you've been spending time with – how are the young lad and his father?'

'Adam's well but he was pretty sad about me leaving.' I pull a face. 'Managed to get himself into trouble right at the end of term and now Nate's got to go in after the half-term to contest it.'

'Oh dear.'

'It's all codswallop, really.' I sigh. 'He pushed back one of the kids who've been harassing him for months and now *he's* the one who's in trouble.'

'Sounds as if his dad means to rescue the day, though?' Mags cocks her head to one side. 'As for what's been going on with you and Nate – I know my brother came in and interrupted us just as you were about to fill me in on the details of the weekend – but then you never rang me, afterwards?'

'Ah, yes. The weekend.' I give a happy sigh. Last weekend feels like an awfully long time ago, now, all the days of this last week seem to have rolled into one. 'There wasn't all that much left of it by the time we'd finished. We went to that wedding, remember?'

'Naturally, I remember.' Her eyes are twinkling. 'You went to the wedding with that handsome and mysterious young man. *And* …?'

'And what?' I give a small laugh.

'You danced with him?'

'Oh, yes.' I cast my eyes downwards. 'We danced!'

'*And.*' She smiles slowly. '*Was he a good dancer?*'

'Not to start with. But by the end of the evening I can safely say that he was. Very good.'

Mags is beaming broadly.

'I imagine he had a good teacher. It sounds as if you both enjoyed each other's company?'

'Immensely. Now that I've got to know him better, Nate is ... he's funny and sexy and sweet. Better than ... than ...' *What is Mags looking at me like that, for?* Oh, all right. I know what she's thinking.

'You've fallen in love with him, haven't you?' she accuses. 'After that one date?'

'It's been more than one date,' I admit. 'We've been seeing each other every day since, all week.'

'Uh-oh!' She shoots me a warning look. 'This is starting to sound a little familiar, isn't it Jen?'

'What d'you *mean*?' I can feel my face reddening even as she says it.

'You fall madly in love with a guy. It hits you like a thunderbolt and you become convinced there's nobody like him, there never will be. You alter all your plans ...'

'I'm not altering any of my plans!'

'You sure?'

'Nate and I both know it's only temporary, Mags. You needn't worry that we haven't thought it through.'

'Are you sure it's going to be so easy to say goodbye and walk away from each other this coming Wednesday? Is it ... *wise?*'

'I won't be changing any of my plans for him, Mags. I'm only too aware, this dream job with Christiane is never going to come my way again. And you're right,' I admit. 'I've always been way too impetuous. I know this has always been my pattern but ... I've changed.'

'You have?' she challenges. 'How? What's changed you?'

I stare at my friend for a few moments, not sure I can answer that one.

'Well?'

'I don't know. All I know is, I *feel* different this time.' How can I explain it to her? 'I feel more grown up. More … steady, somehow. I went into this knowing it would be a brief romance and that's all it is.'

My friend has been scrutinising me carefully. Now she turns away, back to unwrapping a beautiful Royal Windsor dinner plate on her lap.

'Well, given your imminent departure date, it could never really have been anything else, could it?'

'No.' I examine my nails. It couldn't.

'And the ex?' Mags enquires curiously now. 'What was she like?'

I watch as she divests the dinner plate of the last of its tissue paper, positioning it carefully on the rug. Then she places a separate item in my lap. I did offer to give her a hand. I tug obligingly at the sticky tape holding the whole bubble-wrapped thing together.

'Camille was … very beautiful. And she was nice. They seemed to be avoiding each other a bit,' I add hesitantly and I see Mags smile.

'Maybe that much was to be expected?'

'Was it?'

Mags shrugs. 'Residual feelings about the one that got away, and so on. You'd feel the same if you were ever to be invited to Alessandro's wedding, I'm guessing?'

'I wouldn't, though.' I give a definite shake of my head.

'You sure about that?'

'Absolutely sure.' I pull at a long length of sticky tape, unravelling the packaging from the plate on my lap. 'But, she and Nate did both seem a little awkward together.' I pause now, recalling how Nate had left it till the very last moment before approaching Camille, and even then, their contact had felt stilted, reluctant. I add with a small sigh,

'I reckon he still loves her a little bit.'

'Perhaps. But thanks to your help and encouragement, that'll all change once he engages with someone new?' Mags suggests briskly. 'And now that he's practically on the road to recovery, I doubt it will take too long before he finds her.'

Someone new?

'Once I'm gone, you mean?'

Perhaps she's right. He's starting to spread his wings already, isn't he?

'He's already going out without me. I know he's been to the green playing footie with his son a couple of times. He's got to go down to the school to sort out the suspension issue too, of course.'

'Well done him. Maybe your work with Adam's dad really is done, then?'

'I guess.'

'And most importantly,' she reminds me gently, 'it sounds as if Nate will be able to manage in the long term, with taking on Adam's care etc, once you've left?'

'I hope so,' I tell her absently. I tuck my hands under my legs, feeling suddenly reticent. Feeling *sad*. Again.

'Hey,' she pats my knee. 'You're off to conquer the world shortly, don't forget. As soon as you've departed from Rochester, Nate will be a distant memory. Just like,' she murmurs quietly, 'Alessandro already seems to have become.'

'He won't.'

'Begging to differ, but he will.'

'No, Mags.' I shake my head resolutely. 'Not this man. He won't, because as I explained to you, I've *changed*.'

'There is only one thing I know that can honestly change a person from inside out and top to bottom. Only *one* thing makes it possible to throw out the rule book you've lived your entire life by and never look back,' Mags tells me now. 'And that is when a gal truly gives her heart away. Not lust. Not infatuation. But true love.'

'True love,' I echo. I've believed myself to be in love so many times and yet it's always eluded me, evaporated like the mist off a mountainside, shimmered and shimmied and then disappeared like the heat evaporating off the long, dusty road of my life, always

255

ahead of me or behind me or above me, but never in the place where I am. 'When I look back on it now, I don't think I've ever been in love, before. How can you ever know?' I throw open my arms. 'How can you know when you're in love for sure?'

'Ah, that.' Mags gives an enigmatic smile. 'Well, here's a little secret. *Whoever* your man is, he won't always seem so wonderful to you. He'll let you down, because he's human. You'll wonder what you ever saw in him, how you could ever have imagined he was so smart or sexy or funny, because there'll be times when he isn't any of those things. There'll be days when you're convinced hooking up with that guy was the worst mistake of your life, and you want to run.'

'Tell me about it.' I sigh. 'Been there, done that.'

'Haven't you just? Well, the day you finally fall in love, you'll know it's for real because you won't run.'

'I won't?'

'You'll want to. You'll be sorely tempted to, but you won't. Because for the first time in your life, you'll be caught fast. Captured, by true love. And even in your angriest moments you'll remember: there's still that other side to him, and that you have many sides to you, too, good and not so good and downright bad. Because you too, are human. And you won't run.' Mags moves in smartly, catching the precious, unwrapped plate that's about to slip from my lap.

'And that is how you'll know.'

Nate

'Did you know, Nate – the very first bridge across the River Medway at Rochester was built by the Romans?'

'The Romans, eh?' I'm trying not to let him see it, but today I just can't concentrate too well on Adam's chatter. 'You're a veritable mine of information, aren't you, kid?'

'Am I?'

'You've been supplying me with historical and engineering facts for the last twenty minutes,' I point out, hoping he'll take the hint. I can't in all honesty say I've been listening. It's the first day back after the half-term break. When I phoned his school earlier on I wasn't expecting they'd offer me to meet me and *my son* at midday, but there it is. Adam and I have had a little nerve-calming walk into Strood but right now, we're on our way over to St Anthony's. He's unperturbed, but my mind's been on little else since I picked him up.

'Veritable.' We stop on the footpath part of the bridge while Adam opens up the small notebook he's got in his backpack, to write that down. 'That's a good word. Veritable. What does it mean?'

'From the Latin, *veritas*, meaning truth.'

'Truth! I like it. I like words,' he enthuses. Then he looks up at me a little shyly. 'Same as you, Nate?'

I sigh. 'Same as me.'

Though the *truth* is, if that is so, it's purely a coincidence. It's not something he's inherited from me – how could he? And yet here I am, *in loco parentis*. About to go in to speak to the authorities as if I were his actual dad because I can't see what options are left and the *truth* is, right now I'm not feeling too chipper myself. No. I'm definitely out of sorts. There's a line of sweat forming on my brow, I can feel it, cooling, as the breeze blows across us on the bridge. Is this because I'm outside? The old symptoms returning again?

Somehow, I think not.

'The Romans built, like, columns out of stone,' my young companion prattles on with the history lesson. 'We had to learn this last summer for our Year Three project. Anyway, they put oak beams on top and then laid wooden planks across them to make a roadway, did you know that?'

'I did not know that.'

'And, Nate, did you know that ...'

I shake my head a little, warningly, as he's about to start up on a new topic and he quietens down. Instead, we both stare at the bubbling brown water for a bit. The river's moving fast today, urgent, as though it's on a mission. Like me: only, I do not want this mission, I think. I do not want it, I never asked for it, and the thought of going in to talk to these people on this lad's behalf this morning is cramping my stomach into knots. School authorities and me: never been a good combination, isn't that the truth?

'Did you know that the river gets really shallow, really fast, once you're past the bridge?' Adam informs me.

'I did not know that, either.'

'It's true. Boats have to watch out when the tide is low, like today. Sometimes there isn't enough water under the keel and they get caught out.'

'That sounds ... unfortunate.' I, also, need to watch out. I do not want to get caught out, today, either. I frown; turning my head away from him, wondering how all this is going to go because there are certain unknowns that are troubling me. When I walk into St Anthony's this morning – are the school going to ask to see my credentials, at all? Would they do that? Ask to be shown proof that I am indeed the child's father, and ascertain that I have the right to be there? I can't imagine they would, but then again ... does that mean just anyone can go in and claim to be a child's father? Honestly? How do these things *work*? I scratch my head, wishing Jen could be there this morning, a friendly face to support us, wishing this meeting could just be over with.

To the left of us, bright green spikes of waterweed poke up from the freshly uncovered riverbed which is dark mud and silt.

'Shall we move on?' I urge gently. I'd rather be there early, give myself time to settle down but the lad seems in no hurry.

'My legs hurt,' he tells me now. I turn to him, more frustrated than concerned. Is it the bruises? He's never complained about them before, but now I think about it, he was shuffling a bit strangely as we came over the bridge.

They're not going to like it, are they, that headmaster and Mrs Ellis, when I tell them what's been going on? When we uncover the lad's legs and we show them? From the conversations I've had with Jen about this, chances are, they'll have been in denial about the bullying for a long time. Chances are, they'll try and put it all back on the kid, make out like he's the perpetrator and they won't even have *seen* what's been going on right under their noses ...

'When the tide is low like this, the chances of a person surviving the fall if they were to jump from this height are very much reduced,' Adam tells me now.

I frown at him, suddenly paying attention.

'I'm sorry, *what?*'

'There isn't enough depth of water to break their fall,' he tells me, matter-of-fact.

I take that in.

'You're not telling me that's one of the topics you covered in your *Year Three project?*'

'No.' He puts his notebook away carefully. 'I learned that fact by myself.'

'Oh, yes?'

'Yes.'

'Why?'

'I looked it up. Because I was curious. After I read about a guy in the paper.'

'You were *curious?*' I frown.

'He jumped, but he survived. He told the paper: "if you want to make sure you end it all when you come off this bridge, you've got to make sure you find the right time to do it."'

I stare at him.

'That's pretty ... morbid, isn't it, Bud?'

'What's that?' Out comes the notebook again.

'Morbid: an unhealthy interest in a not-very-nice topic.'

'That's a new one. Thanks, Nate,' he says quietly.

I lean in a little closer to him and nudge his arm, sensing a definite change in mood.

'*Why?*'

'I like collecting new words.'

'I know. But why the interest in the bridge?'

'Oh, that.' For once, he doesn't give me eye contact. 'No reason.'

'Adam, you've never ...?' The new thought now forming in my mind shocks me deeply. I can't even bring myself to say it. 'I mean ...' I indicate the river below us with my head.

'What?' he says in a strangled voice.

'You've never actually thought of ...?'

He gives a short, not entirely convincing, laugh. 'Of course I haven't thought about doing *that*, Nate!'

'You certain?'

He nods rapidly.

'I'm not like that guy in the paper, am I? He had given up hope. Besides,' he adds, almost as an afterthought. 'What would my nan do?'

'I'm very glad to hear it. *Very*.' I punch his arm lightly, feeling an incredible relief flood through me, now. 'If anything ever happened to you, I'd be ... I'd ...' I trail off. I'd be completely and utterly *gutted*, that's what I'd be. More than a random guy like me with no real relationship to a kid like him, should be. Except, I'm realising slowly, maybe we're more to each other than that, now? He's growing on me, that's what it is. He's growing on me, becoming significant in my life in a personal way and I hadn't noticed just how much.

'If anything ever happened to you, I don't know what I'd do,' I finish softly. I want to hug him, but I can't, because … maybe it's not appropriate and all that. But I really want to. 'You matter to me, Buddy.' I say it, even though my throat is hurting and my heart is hurting. 'You just gave me a shock, saying a thing like that.'

'I'm sorry.' Adam looks down at his notebook, where he's written *Moorbid*, then back up at me.

'It's only got one "o".' I swallow the frog in my throat.

'Morbid.' He looks at me thoughtfully. 'They're powerful things, aren't they, words?'

I nod.

'I heard once that the pen is mightier than the sword.'

'I heard that, too.' I pull a small smile.

'It means that a weaker person can defeat a stronger or more powerful person, right? They can if they know the right things to say?'

'True.'

'You believe it?' His eyes are cast downwards now towards the shallow, fast-flowing river. 'You're a journalist and a reporter, aren't you?'

'Words can be powerful, Adam.' I pause. 'They've been known to make or break kings. They can elect or topple governments. Make or break marriages. Take, or save, lives.'

'Take or save,' he echoes. A white seagull soars straight past us, taking advantage of the thermals on the bridge and Adam's eyes come up to meet mine, intent, now.

'What's the most powerful thing you've ever done with words, Nate?'

261

'Me?' I give a laugh. What shall I tell this lad? That a piece of mine once helped forestall a coup in a minor African state, saving dozens, possibly hundreds, of lives? What would he *care* about?

That my first published article was part of a campaign piece to install a lollipop lady in a known hotspot for accidents involving kids?

I size him up, now.

'How about you tell me, Adam? What's the most powerful thing *you've* ever done with words?'

'That's easy. That would be the letter I wrote to you.' The lad's voice has gone uncharacteristically quiet all of a sudden. 'You see.' He twists his thumbs together, screwing up his eyes and gazing into the far distance. 'The day I wrote you that letter, I hadn't had a very good week. Everything had gone wrong at school. Nan's test results hadn't come back too good ...' Adam dips his head now to peer over the metal railings where we're standing. The water below us surges past, choppy and cold, wild and uncaring. He shivers and I get hold of the lad by the shoulders, give him a firm shake. *Don't go there, kid. Don't ever.*

'... so I went back home and I wrote that letter and you came to be in my life.' His clear green eyes come up to meet mine. 'That's the most powerful thing *I've* ever done. How about you?'

'Me?' I wrap my arm warmly about his shoulder. We walk on now, off the bridge and into the top end of Rochester and the sun is shining brightly off the pavement ahead of us. 'The most powerful thing? Hmm ... I'll have to see.' The more I think about it, the more I'm wondering if that's what today is really all about? I smile at him, feeling for all the world like this kid is my own, even if he isn't. Feeling that I'd do anything for him, like a true father would, because he matters to me and I think he knows, like I do, deep in my heart, that my most powerful moment ...

That's the one that's yet to come.

Nate

'I'm Mrs Ellis.' The smart, middle-aged woman with the purple-framed glasses is friendly enough, greeting us at reception.

'Hello Adam.' She smiles at him.

'Hello, Mrs Ellis.'

Then, proffering her hand to shake mine, she says: 'I do appreciate your coming in, Mr Boxley.'

'That's ... Mr Hardman, actually.' I take my hand back.

'Oh, my gosh! Of course you are.' She gives a short laugh. 'I do apologise. Families are a little more complicated these days than they used to be.'

'I suppose they are.'

'If you'll just follow me, we can talk in here ...' Round a corner, she pushes a door open for us but Adam hangs back.

'That's the Headmaster's Office,' he points out.

'So it is.' She pauses, deliberating for a moment. 'Would you be a good lad and go and sit in the Reading Area by the big windows? I want to talk to your dad for a bit, Adam, but we'll call you in, soon.'

He shrugs, throws me a *watch out for them* warning glance before he shuffles off. Interesting how his entire mood altered the moment we entered the school premises. Was it the sight of his own form trooping out to play Rounders in the sunshine; the fact that it wasn't Jenna heading the class out – or the thought of this meeting?

'Please, do take a seat.' Mrs Ellis takes her own pew on the opposite side of a large, well-organised desk, alongside an obviously empty chair. 'Oh. Head said he'd pop by in a while,' she answers my unasked question, casually. 'He was very keen to meet you, actually.'

'I'm keen to meet him.'

That careful smile again, sizing me up.

'It's always nice to make contact with parents, wherever possible.' She pauses, then adds; 'Especially in cases like your son's, where his home situation has been ... shall we say, a little unsettled for a while, now.'

'Of course.'

'Also, I should tell you, that as Adam's *nan* is his actual appointed guardian, I took the liberty of telephoning her this morning.' She hesitates again, a little apologetic. 'I hope you understand. We just needed to make sure we weren't stepping on anybody's toes, having this meeting with you, but she was perfectly happy about it.'

I let out a silent breath, and a whole avalanche of worry immediately falls straight off my shoulders. No grilling about *How do we know you're really who you say you are, then?* Thank you so much, Adam's nan!

'She's not in much of a position to make these meetings,' I agree.

'No.' Mrs Ellis clasps her hands together on the desktop. 'So – did you have to travel very far this morning, Mr B ... Mr Hardman?'

I shake my head and Mrs Ellis screws up her eyes in what I take for a sympathetic look.

'It is my understanding that you and Adam have only recently been reunited, though?'

'Only recently, correct.' If she's hoping I'm going to launch into the complete tale of our back-story here, my estrangement from *my son*, she's in for a disappointment. 'Mrs Ellis,' I bring their letter out and place it on the desk in front of us. 'There are some things we really need to discuss. It says in here that Adam's been excluded from school for two days ...'

264

'Indeed. That decision was taken.' She leans back, now, nodding sorrowfully. 'Of course, our *preferred* route is to work closely with the parents/guardians as soon as a problem's been identified, in order to de-escalate. That just wasn't possible in this case. But it makes me doubly glad to see you here, and hopefully working with us on this one.'

'I'll be glad to work with you.'

She relaxes a little.

'The fact is, there's been a situation of ongoing hostility between some of the older boys, and unfortunately Adam's been identified as the one who's all too often at the centre of it.'

'I'm well aware,' I say.

'You'll understand that we're really keen to put this situation to bed, now. Given that there's been an actual injury and a complaint to the governing body, I think you'll agree this has gone far enough.'

I nod, not entirely sure who's made the complaint. Still, I'm heartened that she already seems to be familiar with the situation: a fact that can only make my task today easier.

'With your backing, and his nan's too, we'd like to see Adam learn more appropriate means of dispute resolution, perhaps take on some anger management techniques?' she continues. 'He needs to understand that it's completely unacceptable to take his aggression out on ...'

'Mrs Ellis,' I stop her dead. 'If Adam's been at the *centre* of the troubles, you need to appreciate, that is only because he's the one they've been picking on.'

She blinks.

'I'm sorry? Who has?'

'The group of lads involved in this ongoing hostility you just referred to. Them.'

She frowns, now.

'I have witnessed them doing it, myself,' I assure her. 'I've seen them after school, intimidating him and I know they've been pushing him around ...'

She gives a small, choked laugh, now, as if this was entirely *not* what she was expecting me to say. Then she opens up a folder she's got on the desk, labelled 'Adam Boxley', and takes a cursory look through it. Finally, she snaps it shut.

'I'm afraid I've heard no such reports, Mr Hardman.'

There's a momentary silence, while we each acknowledge the stand-off.

'That is unfortunate. Because Adam tells me he's tried to get staff to listen to his troubles in the past, and nobody was interested.'

'He might have told you this,' she says evenly, 'but if we have no record of it, there is no way anyone could have been expected to act.'

'Oh, there is a record,' I tell her. 'In a moment I will ask him to come in so you can take a look at his shins.'

She sits back, definitely a little more uneasy now.

'I can assure you, children will often come up with things to try and mitigate their own situations. It's human nature.'

'He didn't self-administer those bruises, I can assure you.'

'I have *no record* of any other child's involvement … I asked you in this morning so we could focus on Adam's part in his own exclusion. I think, it's what we really need to be concentrating on …' She looks up, relieved, as the door is opened now without anyone bothering to knock and the Headmaster lets himself in. He frowns, seeing us. Has he forgotten how *keen* he was to meet with me today?

'Mr Drummond, this is Adam Boxley's father, Nate Hardman,' she tells him breathlessly.

'Ah. Yes.' The Head offers me an unsmiling, peremptory shake of the hand that signals his clear intention: *I'm a busy man. This meeting can't take up too much of my attention, so let's get it over with.*

'Mr Hardman seems to be under the impression that Adam has previously put in complaints himself, about some of the other lads …' she trails off. The Head turns to face me, his frown deepening.

'Is this true?' He picks up the folder, as she has already done before him. He glances through it. Then he puts it down. Opens up his hands – *where's the evidence?*

'Even his supply teacher Miss Tierney was aware that he was being picked on, mercilessly,' I look him straight in the eye. 'She spoke to me about it during the parents evening.'

'Unfortunately Miss Tierney has now left us, so I can't call her in for any corroboration of that.' The Head sits, swivelling his chair round to face Mrs Ellis.

'I understood this meeting was to be about the way forward for young Boxley, but I take it from the father's response that he's *actually* here because he's not happy about the lad's exclusion?'

'I'm not,' I answer for her.

'I see. Well, neither am I,' he comes straight back. 'You're within your rights to challenge a fixed period exclusion, naturally. However, let me assure you, Mr Hardman, exclusion isn't a step we take lightly at St Anthony's. I'm pleased to tell you it isn't one we need to take too often, either. In your son's case, as detailed in the letter sent home to the child's grandmother, as he had injured another child – we felt it was entirely warranted.'

'Adam is punished because he lashed out at a child who was part of a group who were systematically and sadistically injuring *him?*' I put it back to them. I'm aware of a small tic starting to go in my jaw.

'A fact which, sadly, no one here seems to have been aware of.'

'I'm apprising you of it, now.'

'An accusation is not proof, though, Mr Hardman.' Mr Drummond rubs his fingers gingerly along the edge of his temples now, as if my presence is giving him a headache.

'With the greatest respect,' he says slowly. 'I have been teaching boys for over twenty-five years. I have known your own lad, coming to my school, for the last five. I know you've recently re-entered his life, and I salute you for that. Family life is a complicated matter these days, but one thing my experience tells me, is that boys in particular benefit from having fathers in their lives. Boys benefit from discipline. Boys benefit from boundaries. All of these things I hope you're going to be able to help us instil in him, and it's the reason why here at St Anthony's we're so keen on the sporting route. Boxley's a good lad at heart, I know that. But he's no sportsman. He probably looks on some of these other kids as being more … privileged than him, you agree?'

I don't answer that, so he carries on.

'That boy he injured was one of our star football players, did you know that? Our A team at St Anthony's wins trophies countywide and beyond. The child your son injured is a large part of that.'

He's angry at this, it's obvious. Angrier at this, perhaps, than the fact that some child has been injured and a parent has complained?

'Are you saying that if the injured child hadn't been so important to your *football team* – if he'd been someone a little clumsier, a little overweight, say, like Adam is … then nobody might have been excluded for it?' Saying it out loud, I get an immediate, sharp, shooting pain in my chest.

'Not at all,' The Head comes back, indignant. 'I treat all of them equally.'

'Doesn't sound like it.'

He stares at me for a moment. Then he leans in a little, his thick, bullish neck reminding me of a sports teacher I had back in my own school days. That guy used to make his form start every morning with twenty press-ups and those who couldn't easily manage twenty were made to do another five before their day began.

'It may not sound like it to *you*,' he tells me slowly, 'But the harsh fact is, that sometimes boys need to learn hard lessons. Some people might think it a little grandiose, but in some small way, all these children in my school are like my own kids, to me. I care about them, Mr Hardman. *Every child matters.*'

So it says on all those posters he's got scattered around the school. I take in a long, silent, breath.

'Some of the children matter more than others though, it seems? Adam gets injured, nobody takes note, nobody wants to know, no action is taken. This football star of yours gets hurt, it's another matter?'

He leans back, now. He looks bored. He looks like a man who believes himself to be fair and just and *in the right*, but who's got a lot more important things to do than sit around arguing with the likes of me.

'Let's see the extent of your son's injuries, then, Mr Hardman. Could you call the boy in please, Mrs Ellis?'

While she scuttles off to get him, neither the Head nor I say a word. The atmosphere in the room grows thick as smog. And the overwhelming urge to just run out of here, go home, is playing havoc with my intention to see this through. I'll be damned if I let Adam down, though. I'm not going anywhere.

They're back.

'Let's see your bruises then, Adam.'

The kid leans down and rolls up his trousers. Mrs Ellis winces at the sight. The Head does something with his mouth.

'Did you *fall*, Adam?' Mr Drummond asks sternly, now. 'Be honest, now, lad.'

'I didn't fall.' The kid looks him straight in the eye. He speaks so clearly and firmly I could hug him, I'm that proud of him. 'They kick me, like I said before. They kick me every single day.'

The Headmaster and Mrs Ellis look at each other silently.

'Very well,' Mr Drummond says at last. 'Seeing as we have no proof either way, and you clearly have sustained injuries of some sort. I'm prepared to lift the exclusion on this occasion. But I want an undertaking from you that you'll steer well clear of the others you've been *involved* with.'

'How can I do that, when they come after me?'

'I'm sorry?' The Head looks weary. This is his lunchtime, I imagine, slipping away, and we're only the first day back after the break. He wants us to go away, now. Quietly. And increasingly, as this meeting has gone on, I've become aware of how much I would like to do just that. How it's returning, the desperate desire to just … get out.

'How can I stay away from boys who look for me, everywhere I go?'

The Head looks stumped.

'What do you want me to say, Adam?'

'I want you to say the same things to them that you said to me, when I pushed that boy back. I want you to tell them that you won't tolerate bullying of any sort in your school, and send their parents home a letter like you did for my nan ...'

The Head's eyes look as if they might be about to pop out of his head.

'Maybe you'd better just report to your classroom for now, young Boxley?'

I push back my chair and it makes a loud, scraping noise along the floor.

'Maybe he'd better not.'

Adam looks at me in surprise.

'We've got an appointment at the GP for him to take a look at those bruises, this afternoon,' I make up. 'He'll be back in school tomorrow, though.'

The Head and Mrs Ellis look distinctly uncomfortable.

'If that's what you feel you need to do, Mr Hardman,' the Head says stiffly. He stands up. Beneath the formality of our parting handshake, his anger is still simmering. I just hope he hasn't noticed how badly my own hands have started trembling.

'Given the severity of the *accusations* you have brought to my attention, I'll be following up with the other lads, please be in no doubt about that.' His eyes come to rest on Adam, but there is little hint of friendliness or reassurance in his tone.

'I won't tolerate troublemakers in my classrooms.'

I stand, too, my legs damnably weak.

'I didn't expect to hear anything different, Mr Drummond.' I motion to Adam. We're done here. Let's go. *God, let's just go.* My heart is starting to beat much faster, much louder. I rub at my chest surreptitiously. Damn it. It is happening again. The symptoms, they've come back and I need to get out of here, like, *now.*

270

It's all I can do not to run off the premises.

'Thank you, Nate.'

We must have walked out of the school grounds and away into the sunshine now because Adam has stopped to give me a hug. I can feel him, his arms wrapped around my body, his head squashed up so tight against my chest.

'You're the best dad I ever could have hoped for,' I can hear him saying. I lean my face in and his voice sounds as if it's coming down some ancient phone line, coming from a long, long way away. 'Thank you for helping me,' he is saying.

But right now I do not feel like the best dad anyone could ever have hoped for. I do not want to be the best dad or anyone's dad. Right now I feel as if I can barely take care of myself.

'You okay?' Adam is standing back a little. I can feel him, looking at me strangely. Behind him the sun is glancing off car windows, bright light zinging around and my head feels light. Very light. Jeez. How far away am I from the flat? How long will it take me to get back?

'Yes. I just … need to go back home,' I get the words out with difficulty. I look at him now, my face creased with pain as my chest constricts again, my body doubling over. 'I'm not feeling too good, that's all.'

'You having a panic attack, Nate?'

My eyes come up to meet his in surprise. *He knows?* My head drops down in assent.

'Yeah. I get these …' my finger does a circling motion in the air, filling in for words. These. Whatever they are. These horrible moments. But they pass.

'Nan used to get that all the time.'

'She did?' Why the helpless laugh that's coming through my lips, now? 'You've sure got some great people on your team, kid.'

'I do,' he asserts, and there is no irony in his voice. 'Nan found a way to get over them, though.'

'How?' I puff.

271

'She stopped going out,' he says simply.

Great. That's really … helpful.

'Adam, I need you to help me get back home,' I croak. I have no idea how he's going to do that. But he's going to have to help me.

'I know.'

'If we start walking back, very slowly, together …'

'I've got a better idea.' He steps off the pavement a little bit, out onto the road and my heart sinks because I need him to stay. What's he doing? *Where's he going now?*

'Adam …' I raise my head just as the sound of a car swinging close by us – far too close by – takes the corner. It reverses, fast. Then halts right in front of us. I look at it, feeling shocked, feeling like I very nearly got run over by some careless motorist but Adam opens the car door and scrambles inside.

'Come *on*, Nate.' And then it dawns on me.

He's only gone and hailed a taxi for us, my buddy, my little lad, this *genius* kid.

Jenna

It's the first Monday in June: two days to D-Day. Just two days to go till I fly off to my new life in the States.

'Perfect day to take delivery of these.' The postwoman is pleasant, waiting patiently as I sign for the package I had completely forgotten I'd ordered. 'You planning on putting these out today?'

'Uh-uh.' I take the parcel from her with a rueful smile. It's from the 'Plants through the Post' website; some little peony bushes I ordered in the determined fit of home-making, the *I'm definitely laying down some roots here* mindset I was in, when I first arrived here, early in May. God, that seems a long way back, now.

'Not planting, I'm afraid, *packing*.' Packing is what I got up this morning determined to start tackling. There's only forty-eight hours to go before my flight but I've been putting it off desperately. 'I'm leaving here.'

'Oh! Shame. I do love peonies.'

'I do too. When I first came here I was looking forward to those champagne pink peonies ...' I remember thinking how splendid they'd look, flourishing in a pot outside my amazing, green, front door.

'Going anywhere exciting?' she asks carefully. Most people probably stay in a place a little longer than a few weeks, let's face it.

'*Very* exciting.' I infuse my answer with all the happiness I was expecting to feel at this point. The fact that I'm not actually feeling it is beside the point. 'I've been offered my dream job in the States,' I enthuse.

My absolutely, most coveted, wonderful dream job. I need to keep reminding myself of that.

'Ooh.' The postwoman looks suitably impressed.

'So I won't be needing these peonies.' In fact – what the heck you can keep them if you want to.'

'Me?'

'They'd only go to waste …' I plonk the parcel back in her hands before she can protest, but the instant I've done it, instead of feeling lighter – one thing less to have to find a home for – I feel even heavier than I did before. Why do I want the blooming peonies? I do not need the peonies. I do not need anything that ties me to this place, or anything that I cannot pack into a suitcase that will be of use to me in the months ahead, so why do I feel like I just punched myself in the stomach?

Today is not making any sense, really it is not.

'Well, I probably shouldn't, really, but … thank you!' She's clearly over the moon with her unexpected gift. 'Um. Is that for you?' My postie indicates with her head, up the stairs.

'I'm sorry?' I come back to her with some difficulty. I'm finding it so damn hard to concentrate this morning. Maybe I didn't sleep so well, that could be what it is. Maybe I got woken up too early by the schoolkids – first day back today after their half-term break – bowling down the alleyway out the back. I got up at just gone seven – it was grey and a little squally outside at that point – and checked out of the window in case any of those children were some of my kids from 4C. They weren't, and I felt a little disappointed. I felt weirdly … redundant … actually caught myself *missing* the thought of lining up the troops in the playground, this morning.

Which is totally crazy.

I could've snuggled back down under the duvet at that point. Over this last week or so, I've got used to lazy mornings, getting up

274

later. But that's not been in my own bed. Lazy lie-ins are definitely a more fun thing to do with a partner, I decide.

'That phone going upstairs, is that yours?'

'I'm sorry, *what*?' Crap. A zap of urgency goes right through my body. That's probably Christiane. She said she'd ring me today to check the ticket info came through all right and that I was all set to go.

'It's been ringing for a little while,' the postie informs me, just as it stops ringing. How did I not hear that? I pause, listening intently and it goes to answer-phone.

'I should be hounding up the stairs,' I tell her. But after she's gone, taking my flower bushes with her, I do not hound up the stairs. I take them slowly, one step at a time all the way to the top, waiting and listening for the female voice at the other end to stop talking. I do not want to pick up the phone and talk to Christiane. I cannot explain why, but I do not. The e-tickets arrived through all fine last night. I saw them when I got back from *maybe my last dinner* with Nate. I could not fathom what they meant, just then. I put them out of my mind.

Last night, not staying over at Nate's for the first time in a week, felt ... odd. It felt wrong, somehow. When I woke up in my own place this morning I realised straight away that this was not where I wanted to be. I pick up some plastic bags that are littering the upstairs hall, telling myself that if I'm already missing him this much, then it's a bloody good call that we decided not to meet up first thing. I'll do my packing and sort out papers and flat stuff and I'll wait till tonight before going to see him.

I go into my tiny living space where my phone is,

'So please, if you're there, ring back *urgently*, we'd really like to hear from you ...' the woman's voice is finishing.

Urgently?

Her voice sounded vaguely familiar, too, which is strange. I press the playback button.

'Hi Jenna! It's Mrs Tallyman from St Anthony's Primary School.' I pause. *Mrs Tallyman?* I take my bearings, as she runs on. 'I know this is

275

a very long shot, but I'm just ringing you in case it so happens you're going to be around at all from now until the end of the school year.'

Ha! I think, my heart racing, she knows full well I am not.

'Our immediate plans to replace you have just fallen through,' the message goes on, 'and before I get hold of the agency to draft in another temporary body, we wondered if you'd like to pop round to discuss a more enduring arrangement? So, please, if you're there …' I press the stop button.

Oh dear, her ringing me really *is* a long shot. They must be desperate. It's that time of year when the schools find it hard to nab anyone who's interested in a longer term placement, so it'll be 'musical teachers' from now till the end of July and they know it. Poor 4C. I'd do it for you guys in a heartbeat if I were sticking around, but patently, I am not.

No, I am not. I need to be looking forward, now.

Last night's email from Christiane was full of supplementary information about our itinerary; from New York, we're flying to Austin, Texas, to do the rodeo circuit, tattooing at every stop. Then on to the West Coast, the golden beaches of sunny California, and in the fall heading up North to attend our final expo in her home town of Toronto. Six months, all told. Yippee. Well, *sort of* Yippee. That's a hell of a lot of time.

I pick up my suitcase and lug it onto the settee, unzipping it as I go. In six months' time, all my form – including Adam – will have moved on to Year Five, heading for the 'Big Class' a year later when the scramble to get into the best secondary schools begins. Life-changing months for all of them, months when the stability of a permanent teacher would have been a blessing but – it can't be me. It's nice to have been asked, but …

I'll call Mrs Tallyman in a bit and tell her I can't do it.

I have to follow my instincts, follow my heart's desire. I've known what that is for a long time now, and I've known what it isn't.

I go to the little box under the kitchen table where I've kept all of my stuff that I have no other place to stow, and pull out my tattoo portfolio. Apart from a bit of work I did at Jed Miller's one quiet Sunday, I haven't done any tattoo jobs in a little while. I'm sure there must be a latent part of me that's raring to go, by now? My book is full of wondrous designs. Did I really draw all of those? Flipping over the pages, I'm impressed with myself, feel a flutter of pleasure at my own cleverness. No wonder Christiane picked me! Seriously. This is something that I was born to do, and all of these drawings *mean* something, that's the best bit. Every single one of the tattoos I've drawn on people has had some special significance to the client having it done. That what makes it worthwhile doing, surely? The rest is just art.

And art, I think ruefully, I could do on the back of an envelope. I could draw it on a paper serviette, like the pictures Nate and I have been drawing for each other every night, like the little swallow he drew in blue ink above my navel while I slept because *a swallow always returns* and *I've got to stop thinking about him, dammit.*

I've got to stop worrying that without him my life's going to feel completely and utterly empty and my heart's going to be broken. He is … just a man.

Okay, Jenna baby, get a grip now. Concentrate on what you're doing and you'll be just fine. I will be fine.

I am.

When the phone goes again, it's trilling so loud it almost drills a hole right through my brain.

'Yes?' I pick up a little sharply. Mrs Tallyman? 'I'm sorry,' I moderate my voice. 'Jenna Tierney here.'

'Jenna,' the smooth North American voice at the other end is definitely not Mrs Tallyman.

'Christiane?'

'Indeed, It's me. How're you?' I can virtually see her smiling, friendly face, down the phone.

I swallow.

'All good, Christiane. I got your email through last night.'

277

'Wonderful. All packed up, now, or nearly there?' she asks politely. 'I ask because it always catches me by surprise, every time I have to leave. You think you've got ages, and then …'

I stare at the virtually empty suitcase on my settee.

'I've got my suitcase out,' I tell her.

'That's good. Pack more than you think you'll need. We'll be visiting states in every season – in some, you'll be wanting to peel your skin off. In others, you'll need every stitch you own to keep you warm.'

'I figured.'

I bite my lip. Over the last, amazing week, I've had *better than clothing* keeping me warm at night. I've had more sunshine in the core of me than any Sunshine State could ever bring. Quietly, I put the phone on speaker and put it down, now. As she speaks, I fold away some paired shoes into the plastic bags I've just rescued from the hall, preparatory to putting them in the suitcase. I've laid them all out, the ones I really want to take; the walking boots and the comfortable-but-stylish working flatties and the pretty sandals Nate admired so much and the really high killer heels that I can't bear to leave behind. It's a lot of shoes, and I've never considered myself an Imelda but … it's *six months*, it hits me again, now. Six.

'You feeling excited to go then?'

'Super-excited,' I say in the flattest voice but I can't help it.

'It's a lot more of a commitment than most people realise. It's not just *you* who's going to come back changed. All your friends will have changed, too, you never think it, but everyone … just … moves on, you know.'

I stare at the phone. What is this woman, a psychic? And why is she telling me all this?

'Six months,' she repeats gaily, 'is a very long time. But you will love every single minute of it, I promise you. A young person like yourself, who's keen to get away and explore and *find what's out there* … you're going to have a real blast.'

The longer she keeps talking, the more my desire is slipping away by the second. What's happening to me? This can't be right. It can't be. I want to go. I really, *really* want … But suddenly, I'm not so sure. What am I really leaving for? *When you find the stone*, Dad said, or even 'The One', as Alessandro amended it to, *Stop looking*.

I rub at the top of my arms, which are feeling chilly even though the weather's cleared again and it's a hot spring day that I need to make the most of, and I wonder where Nate is, and what he's doing today. And then I allow myself to wonder where he will be with his life in six months' time? Maybe he'll even be living with Adam by then. Maybe the nan will be happy in sheltered accommodation being looked after by trained adults and Adam and his dad will be living a new life, all exactly as I'd hoped for them?

I hope that will be how it is. One thing I do know for sure; Nate won't be stuck in his house anymore, kicking his heels. No way. He'll be … he'll be out making documentaries again, I have no doubt about that. He'll be rolling around in that spacious bed of his with some other woman – maybe it'll even be the kind of woman who wears suspenders at the top of her stockings, and who can cook as well as he can instead of burning everything like I did when I tried to cook for him a couple of days ago?

'Christiane,' I cut through her, my voice so high it hardly sounds like my voice but the words are coming from my core. 'I'm not coming.'

Her voice stops dead.

'I can't,' I apologise. 'Something's changed.' Something I could not even begin to explain to her, even if I thought she'd understand. The minute the words are out, I feel so … *released*. I feel all the excitement I thought I should be feeling at my trip to the States and never really did.

Oh, God. What I really, *really* want, is to stay here with Nate. I want that more than anything. I can't wait to see his face when I see him next, see the joy in his eyes when he realises that I've chosen to stay here because of my feelings for him.

'Are you *sure*, Jenna?' She sounds dumbfounded, shocked.

'I am so sorry. I know that I have let you down.'

'... because the chances are, no career offer quite as good as this one will come your way too quickly, again?'

'I'm sure.' Because it's the right thing for me. Because I want Nate more than I want this opportunity of a lifetime Christiane is offering, even if I can't know that another chance like it will come my way, ever again.

Even, I realise now, if I knew for certain that it never would.

Jenna

I thought I saw Nate's blinds move up there just now. I'm *sure* he's in. So why's he not answering his doorbell? I stand back from the door a little, dialling his mobile and feeling perplexed. He isn't expecting me, true. In the interests of 'laying off the intensity' we weren't due to meet up till this evening but to hell with that. I'm not going anywhere now, so we are free to meet as often as we like, *be* together. I almost can't believe what I've just done. Christiane was gutted and I felt so shite about that, but I have made absolutely the right decision, I know it. Nate's the best thing that's ever happened to me. I had to come straight down to tell him, face to face. Oh, yes! He's just picked up.

'Hey, it's me.' Can he feel the huge, cheesy grin on my lips from here? Then, 'Why aren't you answering your doorbell Nathaniel, I've been ringing on it for two minutes?'

There's a strangled noise at the other end of the line. I look up at his window. I can definitely see movement going on up there.

'You are *in*, aren't you?'

'Um …' I can hear a lot of sounds going on in the background, as if he's shuffling around.

'Nate.' I laugh. 'What are you *doing?*'

His face appears at the window.

'I was putting some clothes on,' he admits, his voice sounding strange.

I step back, smiling, indicate the door with my hand. 'Aren't you going to open up then?'

He hesitates for a fraction of a second while I hang my head to one side, wondering what's up. Nate wasn't expecting me to appear just now, true, but I might have hoped for a slightly warmer response than *this*. He disappears from view, only to appear at his door partially dressed a few moments later. The change in this dude's demeanour from the last time I saw him, is almost shocking.

'Hey, girl.' His voice is very quiet.

'My gosh.' I step inside, and close the door. 'What's *happened* to you, Nate?'

He gives a small shake of his head.

'What?' I follow him up the stairs. 'I thought maybe you were in the shower, hadn't heard the doorbell going …?'

'I was sleeping,' he admits.

'Oh.' I give a little laugh. That could explain a lot. 'I had a flat-mate who used to feel like death whenever she woke up after a nap taken in the middle of the day. She said it ruined her REM cycle.'

Nate stands at the top of the stairs, pushing back his hair, looking distracted.

'… or something like that,' I finish, leaning in to kiss him softly. I feel a small pang of disappointment at the lack of reciprocation in his kiss, but maybe he's not fully awake?

'Is that what's happened to you?'

I watch a little regretfully as Nate reaches for a T-shirt that's hanging over the back of a chair. He might look hot but he's evidently not in the mood right now.

'I'm not sure,' he tells me. 'Maybe.'

The guy I've just given up my dream job for sits down on the easy chair now – the single one, not the sofa where we could have snuggled up together – and rubs his face with his hands.

'I'm sorry, Jen. I wasn't expecting you.'

'No.' I perch on the edge of his sofa. Clearly not.

282

'I thought you weren't coming till this evening.' Boy, he really is in a stupor. He seems to be dredging his words up from some faraway place. *By the sounds of it* – the unwanted thought creeps in – *he would have been quite happy not to see me until later on, too.* But, no. That can't be true. I look around, clasping my hands together now and stretching out my arms in front of me, not sure what to say.

'Would some coffee help?' I offer. This feels so *odd*. 'Or if I've come round at a horrible time, I could always ...' I indicate towards the door.'

'No.' He rubs his hands together briskly as if he's trying to summon up the energy to be polite to me. What's going on, here? We're like ... two polite people who barely know each other, again. 'Please don't go. I want you to stay.'

'You sure?'

He nods.

'So um ... has something *happened*, Nate?'

'I went out earlier on,' he tells me. Then he stops talking, examining his clenched hands. He admits tightly, 'the panic attacks came back.'

'Oh. I'm sorry.' I let myself ease back onto the cushions, feeling relief. That's not great, but *thank God it's just that.* 'I was beginning to think you weren't very pleased to see me.'

'*How* could I ever not be pleased to see you?' He pulls a pained grimace.

'I don't know.' I shrug. 'Maybe you'd resigned yourself to the thought that we couldn't be together and had sort of ... disconnected?'

'I haven't disconnected from you.'

He looks as if he's disconnected.

And not just from *me*, either. The fizzle of excitement I've walked all the way down the street with is starting to ebb away somewhat.

'I nearly phoned you, earlier,' he's telling me now. 'But ... I knew you had to get on with your leaving arrangements and I didn't want to crowd you, wanted to leave you your space.'

'I wouldn't have minded, Nate.'

283

'No?' He pauses. He seems to be making a monumental effort to stay with me, now. 'I suppose you've been running around all day, doing your packing and stuff?'

'Not really.' I hide a smile. Shall I tell him? He's clearly not had a great day, but maybe my news will cheer him up? I delve into my handbag for the bottle of bubbly I purchased on the way down. Then I place it carefully on the table between us. He looks at it, frowning softly.

'You have something you want to celebrate?' he asks in a quiet voice.

'I do.' I feel a frisson of excitement, aware that he has *no clue* what I'm about to tell him. I look up at him, feeling strangely shy and ... unusually vulnerable. 'I was hoping you'd want to celebrate it with me, too.'

'Of course.' He looks at me through parted fingers. 'Forgive me, Jen. I know you're excited about your trip to the States. I *am* happy for you, truly.'

'This isn't about the new job.' My eyes lock onto his. 'Are you really happy, though?'

'For you, of course.'

I swallow. If he's that happy that I'm leaving, there is always the possibility he might not be quite so delighted as I thought, at my change of plans? And why's he sitting in that stupid single chair instead of here on the sofa with me? I get up and fetch some wine glasses for us. When I come back I deliberately place both of them near my end of the coffee table. If he wants some bubbly he's going to have to come and sit over here, and that's that.

Finally, Nate takes the hint. He gets up to sit beside me and now I'm so nervous I can barely twist the cork off the damn bottle. He has to take over but he's finding it a struggle as well. What is up with us, today? Finally:

'Okay, so ... I've got some wonderful news.' I take in a deep breath, chinking glasses with him. 'I know you're probably wondering why I haven't told you earlier, but ...'

'I was out with Adam earlier today,' he comes back unexpectedly.

I stare at him. He's clearly not that bothered to hear *my news*. Okay. Stall that, then. I lean back on the sofa again, fold my arms.

'We went to the school, to see that headmaster and Mrs Ellis.'

'You did?' I take a glug of the bubbly, re-orienting what we're talking about. 'Oh, of course you did.' I've been running around so much I forgot they had their meeting today!

This explains *a lot*. It's not good and I shouldn't be relieved, but from my point of view Nate's forlorn mood is now beginning to make some sense. No wonder he's not in the best state of mind, if he was down at St Anthony's earlier on tackling that Head …

'So …' I venture, watching his face carefully. 'How did it go?'

He looks at his hands.

'I went in with Adam and we managed to get the suspension overturned.'

'You *did*?' I allow my free hand to fall onto his knee. 'My hero! That's amazing. So we actually have *two* things to celebrate, then? And I haven't even told you the first one, yet.'

He pulls a pained smile.

'Only.' I feel my stomach constrict in regret, 'you are really not in any mood for celebrating, are you?'

Nate gives a small shake of his head.

'Why?' I ask softly. 'Is it because of me? Is it because you think I'm leaving?'

There. I've as good as *told* him now, haven't I? It's there in that sentence, for anyone who was keen enough to pick up on it. The fact that I am not going anywhere. But he does not pick up on it, pounce on it with both hands and ask *what do you mean, think? I think you're leaving? Are you not, then?*

Nate doesn't say anything for a few long moments.

'I realised today that I have not come anywhere near as far as I thought I had come.' His eyes close tight for a moment. 'I'm so sorry, Jen.'

'Why are you apologising?'

'Because this is me,' he says in a strangled voice. 'What you're seeing now. It's me.'

'I don't understand.'

'I nearly had a full-blown panic attack sitting in that Headmaster's office today. I wasn't the cool and collected hero dude that you imagine me to be. I wanted to run.'

'I don't care,' I tell him. 'I don't need you to be a *hero dude*, Nate. I like you fine just as you are.'

'You think so?'

'I do.' I take in a deep breath. And then I say it. 'I like you so much, in fact, that I've just turned down that job with Christiane.'

'No! You've done what, Jen? *Why?*' He stares at me, looking horrified. Not just surprised, not just a little shocked at the suddenness of it, but *horrified*.

'That wasn't … exactly the response I was expecting from you, Nate.' I feel my heart plummet right down to the floor. 'You'd rather I went?' I say stiffly.

'I didn't say that.'

'You'd rather I didn't *stay*, that much seems to be clear.' I struggle to my feet, my heart pounding, and the strange way he's been behaving towards me ever since I arrived here suddenly falls into place. 'I'm sorry.' I plonk the wine glass down, a little too hard, on the table. 'This has all been one horrible mistake, hasn't it?'

'No,' I can hear him saying faintly, but I'm not listening anymore. Why should I listen to anything he says when he's clearly so disappointed to learn that I'm not leaving? I've deluded myself. I was a temporary fling to him, nothing more!

Nate

'Please, don't leave like this.' I stand up after Jenna. 'I'm sorry about my reaction just now, but – that wasn't what you think it was about.'

'I think it's pretty *clear* what it was all about.' She dives under the settee to retrieve the shoes she kicked off when she arrived.

'It isn't.'

'Oh, don't worry about it Nate!' she growls. 'We had an agreement – short-term only, no strings attached because I was leaving and if I imagined I meant anything more to you than that, it was all my own mistake, I read the signals wrong.' Jenna scrambles up but now I'm in her way, grabbing hold of her by the elbows, even though I know this might be risking a slap.

'You didn't.'

'I *did.*'

'You didn't, Jen.' I'm shaking my head rapidly. 'You didn't misread anything at all. Not with regards to how I feel about you, anyway. Of course I want you to stay.' I give a small, helpless laugh as it's starting to sink in. My dream woman has given up everything to be with me. I can hardly credit this. Can it be true?

'Please believe it. I want you to stay more than anything. I just wasn't expecting you to …'

'Don't.' She regards me through hurt, glittering eyes. 'Don't apologise anymore, there's no need. Besides, this is the norm, for me.' She's cramming her feet into her shoes, preparing

287

for a rapid exit. 'Didn't I tell you? I'm shit at relationships.'

'You're not *shit* at relationships, Jenna.'

'How would you know?' she throws at me, her face looking redder by the second. 'You're shit at them, too.'

I blink.

'If I've not been very good with you, then I'm sorry.' I'm a bit taken aback at that one. I thought Jenna liked me? If she doesn't like me, then why has she just …?

'Let's face it.' She looks up at me suddenly. 'Your last girl didn't stick around either, did she?'

I swallow, feeling the kick behind that one.

'She didn't.' I frown softly. 'But that wasn't because she was unhappy with our relationship.'

'No?' Her chin raises a fraction. 'Why, then? Why didn't the lovely Camille want to stay with you, Nate?'

'Because …' I stare at her, perplexed. Jenna's got her shoes on now, her handbag at the ready in her hand and yet she's still here, taunting me about Camille?

'Oh, come on, it's obvious. You're a commitment-phobe, and she realised that.'

'I'm sorry?'

'It was all because of Adam, wasn't it?' Jen puts in.

What? I sink back onto the settee. I have no idea where Jenna's going with this, now.

'You two spoke about him?' I ask faintly.

'No,' Jenna says scornfully. 'Of course not. You asked me not to, didn't you? I imagine he might have been a bit of an embarrassment to them all, that poor kid you'd fathered when you were barely more than a kid yourself?'

I make a noise in my throat at that but no words want to come out. Jenna's on a roll, though. She feels she's just been rejected by me, I can see that. And hell hath no fury …

'I imagine that experience might have put you off wanting to commit. And then there was the question of how a girl like Camille would have taken to the idea of bringing up someone else's lad? Not too eagerly, I imagine?' she puts to me, now. 'Maybe he was the bone of contention between you, that ruined your chance with her?'

'Maybe *you've* been doing too much imagining, Jen?' I sit up straighter on the settee. If she's got a bee in her bonnet about Cami and me and why we split, she needs to stop. 'Maybe you should have just asked me for the information if you'd wanted it?'

'Well?'

I feel my face redden.

'Why are we even talking about this?'

'Because I think you're full of bullshit, that's why. You're like every man I've ever met who made out he wanted a relationship with me but was only after one thing …'

That's hardly fair given that any relationship we had was clearly outlined at the beginning, was never meant to be more than the short time we had, and yet … is this the real reason why she's mad at me? She thinks my previous relationship failed because of *my son*.

'You're wrong,' I tell her quietly. 'Our split was never about Adam, Jenna. It was never anything to do with him.' If she thinks that, then I can see why she's made the huge leap that she has. Why it is that I'm suddenly as unreliable as *every other man* she's been with, to date?

'Oh, come on! I saw Camille's face when I asked her why you two didn't last …' Jenna stops, looking a little sheepish as she realises what she's just admitted.

'You asked her that?' The lump in my throat grows bigger. 'When? *Why?*'

'I asked her. At the wedding.' Her eyes are still glittering, wild with hurt. 'Maybe I shouldn't have, but I did. And I figured out from her reaction that it must have been because there was Adam. That's the truth, isn't it?'

'No.' I swallow. 'It is not. Cami wanted children, Jenna. She split with me when I told her that I never did.' It's not a thing I'm proud of. 'Most men do, I know. But my job wasn't the best fit for being a family man. And from some of the experiences I had when I was a kid, I guess I …'

Jenna forgets to be mad at me for one moment.

'Oh.' She clasps her hands together tightly, now. 'You two split because you didn't *want* a family?'

'That's the reason, Jen. I believe we still had feelings for each other for a long while after. It wasn't for any other nefarious reason that I've been keeping from you.'

Jenna thinks about this for a bit, knitting things together in her mind.

'But … you already had a child, didn't you?'

Shit.

Okay. That is the one thing I *have* been keeping from her. The illegitimate child that I do not have.

I bite my lip and she picks up on my increased discomfort in a heartbeat.

'What about Adam?' Jenna's sounding incredulous. 'Camille wouldn't have simply accepted you didn't want a family if she knew you already had a child, surely?'

'It wasn't as simple as that. I told you. Adam didn't … he didn't come into the picture.'

'What do you mean – she couldn't have not known about Adam?'

'She didn't.'

There's a strangled gasp from her, now.

'You *kept* that from your girlfriend? How could you …?' Rather than walk out as she'd plainly been intending, Jen sits down heavily beside me, now, as if the shock of this is all too much. 'I've just given up my job for you, Nate Hardman. But I don't … I don't really know you at all, do I?'

'It's true. There are some things you don't know.' She has deserved better than this, for sure. *But there have been reasons* …' And I didn't keep anything from her, Jen,' I add quietly. And then I say it.

'It's you. You're the one who I've been keeping things from.'

She stares at me, uncomprehending. 'What do you mean? What things?'

290

'There are some things I didn't tell you because I thought you were leaving,' I get out faintly. She's still leaving, isn't she? I thought she was mad at me? I don't know why she still even cares. My voice catches in my throat. 'Please, don't think I ever meant to lie to you on purpose.'

'You've been *lying*?' Her eyes open wide, and Jenna looks stunned, now. Really stunned. And disappointed. 'To me?'

I swallow.

'Jen, the truth is, Adam's not really my son.'

She almost jumps backwards on the settee.

'*Now* you're really lying! Why would you even say such a horrible thing?'

'Because it's true. He and his nan have got it into their heads that he's mine, but I only met him a few days after you did.'

'*No*, Nate.' She stares at me, furious and still disbelieving. 'How in heaven's name can that be true?'

'It is the truth. I'd never seen him before in my life. I never knew his mother. Adam put a letter through my door begging me to help him out, and I could see he had no one else ...'

She's got her hands over her ears, shaking her head, not wanting to hear it, not wanting to believe it but I can't stop now.

'You've been lying to me, *all along*? That can't be ...'

'When I went to school and met you that first time, I only made out I was his dad because I knew it was the only way anyone would pay any attention to me. Oh, I know how it sounds,' I say breathlessly. 'I know how bad this sounds. And I never intended for it to carry on, but once I got trapped in that lie, I couldn't tell anyone.'

Her eyes narrow, at that. *Couldn't you?*

'I swear to you that is the whole truth. I wanted to get the lad some help, that was all.'

Jenna doesn't say another word, now. She looks directly at me, her eyes suddenly drowning in a sadness that I cannot bear to see. At last, she gets up, unsteadily.

And then, without even a glance back at me, she walks very quickly out through the door.

291

Jenna

This isn't happening. No. This really can't be happening. I'm through Nate's door. Already out onto the street and the sky's greyed over, starting to spit and there's a chill in the air that wasn't there before. I can't think where it is I should be going. All I know is that I have to get away from here, fast. It can't be fast enough. Something's gone very wrong and I can't understand it, can't get my head around it. I just want to be somewhere else, far away, where I can pretend none of this ever happened. Nate. *How could you have done this to me, Nate?* But Nate is not here. Maybe the real Nate never was?

I have just made the biggest mistake of my life.

Why? How? So many questions hammering in my brain. Nothing makes sense and yet it all feels so horribly familiar. Another guy I've fallen for. Another commitment-phobe who's told me a pack of lies, and wow – kudos to you, Nate, you really get the prize because nobody's ever told me a whopper like *this* before. Nobody's ever gone to these lengths to rope me into their deceit. Even now, I'm struggling to believe it. I don't understand it. It can't be true. There's only one thing I know for certain to be true; just when I thought I'd found true love, everything's gone wrong. Again.

The crazy-busy junction at the bottom of Star Hill looms in front of me now, a middle-aged man tugging sharply on my elbow when I try to cross. I look at him, shocked, but the lights are still green, the traffic's streaming down the hill, I can't cross.

'You all right?' he says. I don't thank him and I don't answer. I fold my arms and wait. Where am I headed now? I don't even know. I don't know anything, anymore. Nate's words keep coming back to me and everything that I thought I knew, was wrong. Nate is not Adam's dad: he only said so because he wanted to help the kid. He never intended to lie to me but once he'd started, he couldn't tell anyone the truth. Really?

Really?

Well, you've told me now, haven't you Nate Hardman, even if you never intended to, and what am I supposed to do with this lie of yours? Forget it? Swallow it? Walk away from this city and from you and Adam and just pretend that you and I – and whatever it is you're up to, telling everyone all these whoppers – that none of it ever happened?

I can't do that.

The traffic coming down the hill screeches to a halt. All the pedestrians start streaming over the junction but not me. I stay put. The middle-aged man turns to look at me questioningly, but then he shrugs, doesn't say anything, moves on and doesn't get involved. It doesn't matter. I'm not going that way now, anyway. I'm going somewhere else. I turn right, now, my footsteps headed towards St Anthony's.

If you're honestly not Adam's dad, Nate, then who the hell are you? What kind of bloke goes round pretending to be someone else's dad anyway, was it all some kind of sick joke? Adam doesn't even seem to be aware, if you aren't who you've been purporting to be. Neither does his nan. And now you've even been down and spoken to The Head, oh Jeez.

I can't ... I can't stomach this, I still can't believe it. I thought you were an honest, decent, guy. Someone who had problems, sure, but who was set on doing the right thing. Why else would I have spent the time with you that I did? I thought I was helping Adam's father and you knew that. I thought that was the best way I had to help Adam, that's why I opted in. Drove you both down to the beach. Took you guys out to all those places we visited with Adam over this half-term. Took you to your former lover's wedding, and stood listening to all her relatives blabbing on for hours about … whatever they were blabbing about – while you were somewhere else, doing whatever you were doing. Getting better, I thought. I clench my fists deep in my pockets, remembering now. I thought I was helping the sweetest, most tender guy I've known, to be a loving father to his estranged son, and there's a part of me that still can't believe that isn't what you truly are. Because if you aren't, where does that leave him? Where does it leave *me*?

Maybe that only shows how gullible I am? I put my head down, hastening my footsteps because it feels better to be walking fast, so much better to be almost running blindly. If I go fast enough, will I ever get away from these thoughts?

I really don't know anymore. What I believe, or what I'm going to do, or where I go from here. And now somehow, without too many minutes going past, I'm already standing outside St Anthony's Primary School. Did I really mean to come here? When I peer warily into the playground, there's Mrs Tallyman the receptionist, walking out front with a pile of folders in her hand.

'Coooeee …' She's spotted me. My stomach does a flip. I don't want to talk to her. I don't want to see anyone I know right now. But Mrs Tallyman is waving, hurrying across the playground as if she can sense I'm about to up and fly away. Damn. I've got to get out of here. I don't know what madness turned my footsteps this way, but I'm not ready and this place, I realise … it's just another place where I would rather not be.

'Did you get my message, Jenna? The one I left earlier on your answer-machine?' she's calling out gaily.

What message?

'The message about the post that's still vacant,' she fills in and *earlier* – about a thousand years ago now, when my whole future was a very different prospect from what it is currently – drifts back. I freeze. Try and make out like I haven't heard her but she knows that I have.

'Are you okay, dear?' She's already up against the other side of the secure wire fencing, taking me in curiously. 'You're looking a little …'

'I'm all right.' I nod. And then I shake my head, and her face creases in sympathy, even though I'm holding the tears back, holding everything back.

'You sure?' Her eyes narrow. 'This isn't about the new job, is it?'

'No, no …' I'm not going into the whole story of that. Not with her. Not now. 'It's just … boyfriend troubles.' I force a little laugh.

'Oh, dear. Sorry to hear that.' Then she adds, comradely, 'I had the same problems in my younger days.'

'You did?' I don't care about her younger days. They're gone. My own are ebbing away and I want what I thought I had with Nate, *back*.

'I blame this.' She does a circling motion around her own greying head and gives a small laugh. 'Believe it or not, I was once a redhead, myself, y'know, Jenna.'

'Really?' I stick my hands in my pockets.

'I was the envy of my friends. I had boyfriends galore, but it turned out none of them were ever interested in the long term. Not till I met my Ted, anyways.'

'Oh, yeah?' I peer at her through the fence and the truth of what she's saying dawns on me: that no guy, no matter how sweet they were on me, ever seemed to want to stick around for the long haul. That's always been my pattern. That thought hits me like a club, right between the eyes.

Is it me? Is it because I'm a redhead? Adventurous, exciting, spontaneous. *Redheads are such fun in bed.* But what about the rest of me, what about my life, the *rest* of my life? Why can't you have been the one, Nate? My fury subsides, and again I feel a sob catching in my throat.

Why did you have to be like all the rest?

'Nobody ever lasts,' I admit. 'No one. And I can't stop them from either lying to me so I leave, or walking out, themselves.'

'What is wrong with young men these days, anyway?' she commiserates.

'Even my own blooming *dad* never stayed,' I blurt out. 'He lied, too. Said he was going off to work as a truck driver. Said he'd be away several months but promised me he'd be coming back. He never did.'

She's nodding sympathetically.

'I'm sad to hear it,' she says. The bell goes now, waking us both up.

'Sorry.' I look at her, feeling a little uncomfortable when I realise I've just been standing here pouring my heart out to the school receptionist. 'I didn't mean to …'

'Don't fret. You'll find someone else soon enough, lovely young thing like you.'

'I guess.' I force a smile. 'I need to make tracks,' I say, before she brings up *the vacant post at the school* again.

'And … maybe you'll even sort it out with that nice young man we've all been seeing you out and about everywhere, with?'

Oh. We've been seen?

'Adam Boxley's dad?' she prompts.

'He's not … He's …'

My thoughts are pounding like a hammer warning in my head, *not yet. Don't say anything, yet. You need to get away from here, Jenna.*

'I really must go,' I rasp. I need to give myself time to think about the best way to put it before I land Nate in it, tell the school everything. I wish I didn't have to. I wish now he'd never told me. *Maybe that's even the reason why he never told me!*

Because I will have to inform them now, there's no question about that.

296

Nate

No, no, no. I did not mean for that to happen. I did not mean to make Jen so sad. Now she's gone and she knows the truth and I won't be getting her back. I come away from the window. Again, I try her number but she's not picking up. In vain, I check for any voice messages. That's over a dozen missed calls she will have showing from me but she does not want to reply. I can't blame her. I should have known this would be her reaction ...

I did know it, too. I pace the flat one more time, a bear prowling up and down in his pit, head getting progressively sorer by the minute, trying to work it out. One thing I am not, anymore, is in that shocked, mind-numbed place I was in when Jenna arrived. Not still battered from that encounter with The Head, not groggy from sleep. I've woken up properly now, adrenalin coursing through me. All I can think is: how am I going to make this thing right? All the lies I've told. Not just to her, but to the school, too. It can't go on, I know this. I'm bound to be found out, sooner or later ... maybe sooner, now that Jenna knows, because maybe if she's *not* leaving she'll be going back to teach at St Anthony's after all? Maybe she'll even be the one to tell them, and then I'm scuppered, well and truly, from every direction.

And then so will Adam be. And I will be just another person in the very long line of people throughout his life to have let him down.

The ache in my head grows worse.

I do not want to let him down. Even despite my remorse, a fire courses through my blood when I think of him, because I never got into any of this for my own gain, did I? I did it for Adam. Only for him, because he didn't have anyone else. Like me, when I was his age. Like my brother, who had only me. I let out a deep groan into my hands. I didn't lie to Jenna because I wanted to. I'm not like all those other men she's dated who've let her down. No matter what she thinks, that's just not true. And we'd have been so good together. We *were* so good together.

The sound of the doorbell pierces that thought, coming so unexpectedly now, it fires up all my deepest hopes. *She's back?*

I've never got down those stairs so fast. I fling the front door wide open, prepared to lay my soul bare, prepared to do whatever it takes if she'll only stay long enough to listen to me. And then I stop short.

'Hey, Nate.'

I poke my head out of the door, but it's only him there. No one else. Not her.

'What are you … what are you doing here, Adam?' I glance at my watch. It's four o'clock. Only four. This day is going so slowly. It's going on forever and ever and right now it feels like it's never going to end. I pinch the skin between my eyebrows together between forefinger and thumb. What's the kid doing here now? Give me a break!

'The doctor's,' he reminds me. 'You told The Head we were going to the doctors so she could check out my bruises, remember?'

I blink. I did say that. Hours ago, in the heat of the moment, with The Head. I'd meant it, too, at the time. But I'd forgotten.

'I'm sorry,' I tell him. 'We don't have an appointment.'

'I had to make one for the end of surgery,' he carries on over me. 'They were full but I told them it was urgent and you really wanted them to see me.' He stops, now. 'You do, don't you, Nate?'

I open my mouth. Then I give a short nod.

'Don't worry, I've left plenty of time,' he's saying now. 'Seeing as I knew it might take you a while to walk. Or if you can't walk, we can always take another taxi?'

I put my hand on his arm now, stopping him.

'I can't take you to the surgery, Adam. Not really. I said that to The Head so he'd know we were taking your injuries seriously and he'd have to, too. But I'm not your ...' I take in a deep breath. 'It has to be your guardian who takes you along to things like that. You'll need to tell your nan. Can she do it?'

Adam's shaking his head firmly.

'Nan doesn't go out,' he reminds me. 'Only to the garden. That's why when we have to go for the hospital appointments it's such a kerfuffle. She's like you, only worse.'

It's such a kerfuffle.

His nan can barely make it to her own appointments. No wonder the child's getting overlooked, every which way. No wonder it's easier for no one to notice anything, no one to say anything, because that way, *he is not in anybody's damn file* and nothing needs to be done about it. But today, I am going to do something about it.

'Well then,' I say at last. 'If Mohammed cannot go to the mountain ...'

He looks at me in surprise.

'I didn't know you were a Muslim, Nate?'

'I'm not.'

'And my Nan's not that big,' he defends. 'She's big-boned, like me. A small hill-size, maybe. But she's not really as big as a ...'

'That isn't what I meant.'

'What did you mean?'

'I meant; wait here a sec while I go upstairs and get my things and then we're going round to see your nan, you and me. There are some things we need to do for you, and some things that ... she and I need both to get straight.'

'Righto, Mohammed.' Adam throws me a big, cheerful smile. Like today's been one of the best days of his life. I shoot up the stairs for my keys and my shoes, aware that the reason he's so happy is because someone's stood up for him for once and maybe he imagines it'll all be a walk in the park from here on in.

I wish, *I only wish*, that were the truth of it. It won't be. Not for him, and not for me either.

Nate

'*Nan*, look who it is!' Adam shoves their house key back under a nearby flowerpot and beckons me to follow him in. 'Look. I've brought my dad back.'

Vera Boxley is sitting on a sofa in a darkened room when we walk in.

'Hello, you,' she says to him. She doesn't look at me. The whole house is dark today apart from a glow in the corner where she's got the telly on, volume low, and I notice Adam doesn't switch on any of the lights when we come in. There is no sign of the cat. There is, however, a peculiar smell in the air, like boiled vegetables.

'Nan,' he says, more quietly, 'look who's here.'

'Hello, Vera. It's … Nate Hardman,' I remind her. From her expression as she turns to me now, I can't tell if she knows me.

'Are you the new doctor?'

'She forgets things, Nate,' Adam reminds me gruffly.

'You look like the new doctor.'

'It's a little dark in here,' I note. 'So maybe you can't see me properly. I came to visit you two weeks' ago and we talked about the video-diary I was making, remember?'

Vera doesn't answer that.

'When I visited then,' I persevere, 'you and I spoke about your grandson, do you recall?'

She looks blank.

300

'You were watching *The Jeremy Kyle Show*, and we talked about how you …' I lower my voice a little as Adam fiddles about with the telly volume, not really wanting him to hear me, 'how you've both been under the impression I might be Adam's father?'

She doesn't respond to that either, so I jog her memory a little further.

'We discussed how I'd recently been along to the school to see his teacher?'

'You walked here, today?' Vera takes me in curiously. I sit myself down gingerly on the far end of her sofa. Has she even heard a single word I've just said?

'Yes. We walked.'

'I used to like going out walking,' she tells me wistfully. 'I used to walk out every day. Good for you, isn't it, doctor?'

'He's not the doctor, Nan.' Adam goes to sit by her. Taking her hand gently in his own, he leans in to say it again into her ear. 'He's not the doctor. He's Nate. *Nate*, remember? I told you.'

'I am not the doctor,' I agree. 'Vera, I have no wish to alarm you, but I'm here because we need to discuss something very important.' I cough, recalling how she'd not been prepared to hear the truth from me last time I came, and I'd let her get away with that. I'd needed her signature for Marcie's purposes. And she'd been determined to believe what she wanted to believe. The cough turns into a prolonged bout.

'Nasty cough you've got there, young man.'

'Shall I get you a glass of water, Nate?' her grandson offers helpfully, jumping up.

'Please.'

'You should see a doctor about that cough,' she notes as soon as he's gone.

'Talking about doctors,' I get in when my throat clears. 'Adam needs to see one.' Is she even aware he's made an appointment?

'You walked up?' she asks again.

'Yes. Vera …'

301

'I used to like going out walking, myself.'

'About the matter of seeing a doctor …' I persist.

'I can't walk out much now, though. Like you.'

Like me? I blink. Adam's mentioned my problems to her, perhaps?

'I am sorry.' I study my hands. 'It must be very hard for you, I know. *Especially*, Vera, when you need to take the lad out for something like a doctor's appointment?'

'I used to,' she says.

'But not now? And Adam can't attend a medical appointment unaccompanied, can he?'

'I used to go out everywhere.' She's not catching my drift. 'Even after my daughter died soon after the litt'lun was born. And then one day, I'll never forget it.' Her eyes go misty, 'I had him in the pram, down by the Co-op, and this woman walks in. Spitting image of his mother, she was, down to her blonde pony-tail …' She looks at me, stricken. 'Thought I was looking at a ghost, I did.'

'That must have been a shock,' I agree, patiently. 'A nasty shock.'

'I went mental,' she admits. 'I ran out, calling after her. I was so sure it was her, I left him sitting there in his pram, I did. I thought maybe she needed me. Without me, she'd have been all alone, you see.'

What does she mean, all alone?

'You see, when they put her in the ground all I could think was how *alone* she was. She was always so unsure of herself, never a confident one, my Leah. I thought maybe she still needed me to look after her …'

I stare at her, frowning softly.

'You've been like this since Adam was in his pram?' And I thought I had problems! How in heaven's name have they both coped?

'Couldn't find her outside anywhere, could I?' Vera continues. 'She'd walked into the crowds and I couldn't see, but after that I kept thinking, you know, what if it was *her*?' The old lady's head seems to be trembling at the thought.

'How could it have been her, Mrs Boxley?'

Vera gives me a strange look.

'It wasn't her. Rest assured.' I tell her.

'I can't go out. What if I see her again? I couldn't bear the thought of it, doctor.'

'Vera, I'm not a doctor. I'm ...'

'Some days I'm fine, but not at the moment. I can't go out. I come over all strange even at the thought of leaving the house.' She folds her hands in her lap. There's a noise at the door and I think it's Adam back with the water but from the noises he's making – '*Shoo, scat!*' he appears to be occupied chasing the stray cat out of the house.

'Most folk don't understand it, I know.' Mrs Boxley pulls a strange, twisted mouth at me. 'They think I'm soft in the head.'

'Far from it.'

'They think I'm just a doolally old lady, making it all up.'

'Not me. I don't think that, at all, Vera. Seeing your daughter's double must have ... re-opened up the wound of losing her, that's all.'

'Yes.' She nods rapidly. 'I worry that I might see her again. I worry that maybe she's alone somewhere and she still needs me only now she's in a place where I can't help her anymore.'

I hunch up my shoulders and a cold draught blows down the house through the open front door.

'You can't,' I say. *How have we got onto this topic?* 'But that girl you're worried you might see, that isn't her. And you have to trust that your girl's okay.'

The old lady's eyes widen now.

'You too, Nate?'

'I'm sorry?'

'I can see it in your eyes. Once you've cared for someone, that habit of worrying about them never quite goes away, does it?'

The echo of another time, a memory of my brother, resurfaces. Mo climbs over the fence I have made for him in my mind and stands there, hands akimbo as if challenging me to deny it.

'No. It never does.' I give a small shiver. 'I used to have a brother, once,' I tell her now, not entirely sure how or why this revelation is slipping out. 'He had a bad habit of winding people up, getting into trouble. I was always bailing him out, trying to stop the other kids from hurting him, but ...'

'You couldn't,' she finishes. 'What happened to him?'

Never mind him.

'What happened to *me*, is maybe what's more relevant here, Mrs Boxley.' I shake my head, not wanting to talk about Mo. 'I got sick of fighting his battles for him, that's what happened. I got sick of being the one who had to stand in the firing line, picking up the pieces after someone else messed up time and again.'

She's nodding, softly.

I'm sorry,' I tell her. 'I didn't come here today to tell you all that. I came here today for your grandson. He urgently needs to be seen by someone, Vera.'

'I know.'

'He needs someone to properly pay attention to what's going on for him.'

'It's true. They've warned me they'll take Adam away, if I can't cope,' she mutters quietly now.

I lean in.

'You don't want him to end up in a Children's Home,' I tell her. 'He wouldn't like it.'

'No.' The old lady turns to give me full eye contact. 'You didn't very much, did you?'

'Excuse me? *Do I know you?*'

'I'm Adam's Nan.'

'No, I meant ... do I know you from any other place?' Had she been there all those years ago, when I was a kid?

'I don't think so,' she says. 'Apart from you being his dad.'

'I am not his dad! Look, you're right about me having gone into a Children's Home. They sent me and my brother there when Mum couldn't manage anymore. But he wasn't very bright, my

304

brother. He wasn't very wise. He never had anyone else to look out for him but me and in the end, even I got sick of that. Why d'you think I made the decision long ago that I'd never have any kids of my own?'

I stop, feeling a little shocked. It's the truth but till the words came out of my mouth just this minute I've never known it so clearly.

'You don't want that to happen to Adam, believe me.'

'None of us do.' she comes straight back to me. 'That's why he found you.'

I'm stumped for a moment. We've come full circle, haven't we?

'Vera,' I say gently. 'I don't make a habit of going round rescuing other people anymore. Adam's a wonderful kid and I've come to care about him very much,' I admit, 'but he's not my responsibility. He's yours. And now you need to take him to see the doctor this afternoon so we'll have a record at school of the damage being inflicted on his legs ...'

Vera looks at me askance.

'What about that teacher of his, she knows doesn't she? The one you were sweet on,' she adds, so I know that she knows.

'Miss Tierney and I are through.' I look away.

'You're through? Why – what's happened?' Adam's back, looking worried.

'You always knew she was leaving, Adam ...' I don't need to tell him all the rest of it. Why hurt him any more than necessary?'

'Oh.' He hands me the water, unusually quiet. He's the type of kid who would hang about outside listening, isn't he? I wonder how much he's heard.

I turn to the nan.

'And Adam still needs to go to that appointment with his GP, today.'

'I can't go out, can I? You have my permission to take him, though.' Vera's suddenly with me.

'No.'

'No?'

305

'We'll go together,' I decide. 'We'll take a taxi if you like, but we'll all go. I can support you to be there but you're his guardian so you're the one who needs to show.'

'What if I see *her?*' Adam's nan pulls a distressed face. Her daughter, she means. Or the woman who looks like her.

What if the panic I was feeling earlier on today comes back to haunt me? What if I try and make it down to the surgery and I can't tolerate being out and I'm too far away from home to easily get back?

What if I never get over the pain of knowing I've blown it with the, kindest, sexiest, most lovely girl I've ever known?

'We're all the walking wounded, aren't we?' I give a long sigh. 'But your daughter doesn't need you anymore, Vera.' Mo doesn't need me, either.

'We have to stop looking backwards. It's Adam who needs us both now. This is about him.'

Jenna

The train jolts, pulling us out of Rochester station. A woman sits down opposite me and I pull my bag onto my lap. I was okay but I just saw a man with curly dark hair walk by. He looked a little bit like Nate and he made it all so much more difficult to pretend. I am leaving here but I am not feeling any relief. I am feeling like the wide gaping space inside a mouth when a tooth's just been pulled. Sore and bereft. Bewildered. It shouldn't be like this. I looked for the least busy carriage, walked right down to the end of the platform to get on this one, trying to be brave. When I got on, there was no one sitting nearby but now she's come.

I close my eyes.

'I didn't talk to her.' The woman opposite me is using a low, confidential tone, talking into her mobile. 'I know that I should. But you *know* what she'd have said.'

I tighten my eyelids shut, a little. Move my back to settle more comfortably in the seat and Magda's face comes into my mind. Just for a second. I didn't tell her about how things have turned out. No, I know I didn't. I know what she'd have said. It doesn't matter. She'd have wanted to speak about things, delayed me, and I don't want to talk. Not to her, not to anyone.

The train stops, jolting me alert, and some kids peer into our carriage from a small, back garden. The grass on their lawn is yellow and short and patchy. I lived in a house with a garden like that, once.

In the winter the grass always grew too long. It flopped over on itself like an overgrown fringe. In the spring and summer it'd be like this. Dried-out and bald-patchy. Ours smelled of dog wee. Next door, they grew roses. Cream ones and lavender ones and peach. They blossom into view again, in my memory. Everyone down the road laughed at Next Door. Thought they were a little bit up themselves, so hoity-toity, growing roses, but I used to stand on a chair with my drawing pad and pencils and I knew that they weren't. I told everyone; one day I'll have a garden just like Next Doors'. They laughed at me, too.

The train starts up again and the children wave. Their arms are flapping like little flags on a pole but I can't wave back because I am feeling too full, somehow. Too full and too empty. The washing hanging on the line behind them flutters helplessly. Nate doesn't have kids. He never wanted any kids. Did he ever really want a girlfriend after Camille left?

Did he ever really want me?

My mind tiptoes over the sore places again, tenderly, Nate saying, of Adam; *'It is the truth. I'd never seen him before in my life.'* But my head feels too full of thoughts I cannot think.

'It's stopped,' the woman says. 'And then it's started again. Yes. No. I expect so.'

I bring out my water.

'Nooooo …' The woman opposite me chortles suddenly into her phone. She has a strident voice, now. Very loud. It echoes round the empty carriage, piercing right into my head. 'I'm not going. I'm off to Sheffield for a weekend on the razz, Chuck.'

Oh, God. I settle back again, lids closed to block her out, making sure she hears my loud sigh. This carriage was empty. It was quiet. Why did she have to come in here and disturb my peace?

'Rough night?' she enquires. I open my eyes a slit, but she's not talking to me. 'That happens. Yeah. No. You can't. That's men all over for you, isn't it?'

'Could you …' I do a lowering motion with my hands. 'Just *keep it down*, a bit? Please.'

She looks surprised.

'Sorry,' she says. 'No,' she speaks into the phone, a little more considerately, now. 'I wasn't talking to you. But anyway, have you *told* anyone about this?'

There's a long, long silence now. The even sounds of the train chugging along lull me into a comfortable, exhausted, place.

'Sometimes you've just got to talk to someone neutral, know what I mean?' I can hear her murmuring. 'Old friends are always the best, especially if they haven't actually met him.'

She's right about this. I've got to do this, too. I've got a couple of friends who live in Islington. Another girl I know has just moved to Haggerston. I feel my head rolling to one side, jolt it up again. Lots of old friends. No one knows I'm coming. I decided on the spur of the moment, walking past the station. I didn't bring any clothes and I didn't bring my phone – I couldn't find it *anywhere* in the flat – but never mind …

'So was he an absolute hunk?' The woman's voice goes lower. 'How did I know? He's pretty much broken your heart, hasn't he, Hon? It's usually the hunks. They're the worst bastards. Aren't they?'

Are they? Nate was a hunk. No denying that. But would I say he was a bastard?

'Course they are,' she's countering whatever her friend is telling her, 'it's because they can. Because they're beautiful and they know it.' Her voice is creeping up and I open my eyes a slit. She's got her make-up bag out and she's waving her eyelash wand around emphatically. '*That's why we have to fight back.*'

I have to fight back. I guess I will. I'll have to come back fighting, just like I always do. Right now, I don't want to fight, though. I want to sleep. I turn my body round towards the window, curling up like a ball. The whooshing sound of the train against the tracks is restful, peaceful. For a moment my mind is numb, even if my body is a little cold.

'He kept *that* quiet, didn't he?' The woman with the phone is murmuring sympathetically now. I'm hearing, not listening to her, and her voice is coming through to me in waves. 'He isn't who you thought he was, is he? The guys with the secrets,' she mutters. 'They're the *worst*.'

Tell me about it. I move in a little closer to the window, wishing I could nod off but now the glass feels too hard against my forehead.

'They're the ones with the wives and girlfriends tucked away that you'll never know anything about till the day comes when you try and push for some commitment.'

I sigh, stretching out my legs. *Nate didn't have any girlfriend tucked away. Someone else married his girlfriend.*

'They're fine as long as you're just in it for a little fun. Try getting them to commit to anything more long-term and just watch them squirm. The incredible excuses they'll come up with, then!'

I open my eyes and rub them, uneasily.

'What you want to do is get your own back, before he realises that you've found out.' The woman opposite is in full swing. 'You can't let the opposite sex get one over on you girl, not if you want to keep your self-esteem intact.'

Her words of advice sound very familiar. They sound a lot like the kind of thing my girlfriends, the people I'm heading for, now, would say.

'You can't let him win.'

I sit up. No point making any further pretence that I'm getting any rest, here.

'Come on out with us next weekend?' she's telling her friend. 'Us girls will help you put it all in perspective. Put you back on track with what really matters, right?'

I stare at her now, transfixed by a little glyph I keep catching sight of, on her wrist. A tattoo. I'm hoping my own friends will be able to do what she's suggesting; put me in touch with what really matters. What I've lost sight of, in the flurry of the last few weeks, thinking myself to be so in love; the chance I threw away this morning. Outside, smearing against the glass, the smattering of rain against the carriage windows looks angry, defiant and I

310

want to hold onto that. Nate tricked me. He lied to me. I've been duped. When I stare through the glass at the blue-grey sky it doesn't feel like fury, though. It feels like tears.

The woman opposite puts the phone down now, looks up to smile at me.

'Sorry if I woke you up. That was an actual emergency.'

I shake my head. No point being sore at her. It's not her I'm mad at. I'm not even mad, am I?

'May I see?' I indicate her wrist. 'I'm a tattooist, myself.'

'Are you?' She's immediately impressed and sticks out her arm proudly. 'Had that one done by an Arabic guy in Camden Town last year and he did it for a song. He told me it meant *finder of wisdom*.'

'Did he?'

'Yes. It's sort of thoughtful and deep, don't you think? Makes me *look* deep, anyways, and the guy I was with at the time was soulful like that.'

He obviously couldn't read any Arabic, though, like her. Neither do I, really, but I've seen that symbol done at the parlour, before. One guy I knew used to do it all the time, for a joke. Roughly (and kindly) translated, it means; *only a fool listens to a fool*.

Is that what I'm being, now?

I sit back in my seat, folding my arms, and suddenly I don't feel like seeing my friends in London, anymore. I've gone off the boil with all of that, the thought of seeing them makes me heavy and tired. What're they going to say to me, anyway? Only the same old things she's just said to her friend. And none of it feels right. Not with regards to Nate, anyway. Maybe I should have stayed and spoken to Magda but it's too late for that now, and besides, I couldn't stay in Rochester. I *couldn't*.

Now what? I've never been one to run to ground to lick my wounds but I feel so sad, I feel so *strange*. And the memory of that patch of scrubby garden, next door's roses – it won't go away.

One hour later, following a strange and inexplicable urge that I haven't felt in a very long time, I find myself on the next train going up to Hull. I am going back home.

Nate

'*Hello*, there.' The young lady doctor seems a little surprised when three of us troop in, instead of the usual two. She's clearly familiar enough with my companions. Vera's looking puffed out and stressed, but to be frank, the effort of getting her into the taxi and down here has kept my own mind pretty focussed. The panic attacks from earlier have all but subsided. I wish I could say the same about my memories of Jenna's visit. We were sitting in the waiting room for half an hour and I've had a chance for it to sink in; the fact that Jenna actually turned down that job for me. I can't figure out if that makes our situation better or worse. Maybe both.

'Not often that we see you in here for yourself, Adam. It's usually your nan we're looking at, isn't it? And who's this?' The doctor extends her hand to me, politely curious, as we sit down.

'Doctor, this is Adam's dad.' Vera introduces me before I can get a word in.

'Oh, how lovely to meet you.' The woman casts her eyes cursorily over me and I can tell what she's thinking. She'd only be about my age, herself.

'Actually, I ...'

'You're visiting? That's fabulous.' She turns to Adam before I can finish. 'Bet you're glad to have your dad along with you this time, eh, Adam?'

'Very glad,' he agrees, gruffly.

The doctor looks pleased. Taps something into her screen.

'What can I do for you today? *Ah!*' The doctor pulls a deeply sympathetic face as the lad pulls up his trouser legs. 'So how did this happen, young man? Skateboarding? Trampoline?'

'School.' Adam winces as she touches his shins.

'School sports, eh? Oh, dear. You're going to have to lay off the games lessons for a little while, I'm afraid.'

Adam looks towards me.

'It's not the games, I'm afraid, doctor. He's being kicked by some other pupils.'

'How terrible.' She sits up, frowning a little. 'Does the school know about this?'

'They do now. We wanted you to see it, too. Not just for treatment. For proof. It's been going on for a while and they've been turning a blind eye to it. Now it's got to stop.'

'Too right,' she agrees wholeheartedly. 'These bruises are not very pretty, are they?' Her question is levelled at him, but she shoots a curious glance at me, even as she notes the extent of them.

'Do you mind if I take a record of these, just so we can see how well they clear up, after a week or so?'

'Please do.'

'He's got bruises on bruises, here. Pity you didn't bring him in a little earlier,' she mutters.

'Nate didn't know anything about this, earlier,' Adam tells her gruffly. 'He didn't know anything about me, either. I only found him recently.'

'You found him?' She pulls a small smile. 'And how did you manage that?'

'Nan told me where he lived and I sent him a letter. *Ouch!*'

'Sorry, sorry,' she says softly. 'Nearly done, here. All photographed. Do you happen to have any arnica in your medicine cabinet, Mrs Boxley? Mrs *Boxley?*'

'What's that noise?' Vera's looking around, spooked. The buzz of a drill coming from an adjacent room seems to be bothering her.

'That's just the workmen doing some work on the new extension we're having put in at the practice. Nothing to worry about, dear.' The GP pats Vera's hand, shoots me a meaningful look, now.

'Just as well Adam found *you*, eh? I have a feeling these two guys could do with a capable man about the place.'

'What's that?' Vera looks up sharply.

The doc raises her voice. 'I was saying, Vera, I have a feeling this young man's dad has turned up in your lives at just the right time for you and Adam?'

'Yes?'

'Your grandson deserves to have someone around who can properly pay attention to what's going on for him,' the doctor continues, quite slowly and loudly. I get the distinct impression her words are aimed as much at me as at the nan.

'I've been worried that they'll take Adam away from me, if I can't cope,' Vera mutters again.

'Who has said so?' The doctor is half smiling, half frowning, now. She looks to me for verification. 'Is that true, is it what's being said?'

'I believe it might be. I don't know.'

'I see.' The smile is fading slowly. The kindly doctor is clearly perplexed.

I lean in, quietly.

'Would it be possible for us to talk *in private*, do you think?'

'Of course.' She cottons on straight away. 'Could you come along with me, Dad? We've got some ointment samples in the nurse's room that you might find helpful.'

'Listen,' I tell her as soon as we're in the empty room next door, out of earshot. 'You need to be aware that I'm not the kid's father.'

'Are you not?'

Rather than being astonished, as I was expecting, why do I get the impression this woman doesn't believe me? She probably thinks I'm just denying the truth! Trying to duck my responsibilities.

'Look, I'm just here to help them out. The nan's agoraphobic. The lad's clearly struggling, desperate for some adult input. He sent me a letter, and ...'

'I see,' she says. 'So – you're a friend of the family?'

'Not really.'

'Just someone who got involved after Adam sent you a letter, *mistaking* you for his dad?'

'I know how this sounds, but ... yes,' I tell her tightly. 'That's exactly what happened.'

'Just off the record,' she says carefully, 'I do doubt very much that Adam's nan is the sort of person who'd come after you looking for child maintenance you know, Mr ... um ...?.' She folds her arms.

'It's Hardman. Nate Hardman. And I'm not worried about child maintenance. I'm just not his dad.'

'He seems to think so.'

'Of course he does.' I roll my eyes. 'It's what she's told him and he wants to believe it. So does his nan.'

'Of course, if she's correct that there are possibly moves afoot to remove him from his grandma's care, then if his father *were* to come onto the scene, I'm sure that'd be a great relief for all concerned.'

'Be that as it may ...'

'I can also see that you're not much older than myself,' she commiserates. 'You'd have been very young at the time when he was born. Maybe you never even knew anything about him? I see enough young, pregnant girls here at the clinic to know how it goes.' She opens a wall cupboard and starts rummaging around now – presumably for that ointment sample she mentioned earlier?

'Doctor, you're not listening to me.'

'The trouble is, if Adam doesn't have any other willing relative who can take him, it really is beginning to look as if he'll end up in care,' she cuts right over me. 'And believe me, that isn't an outcome I'd wish on any child of mine.'

'Nor me,' I assure her rapidly. 'Look, Adam's a wonderful kid and I've come to care about him very much,' I admit, 'but he's

315

not my responsibility. He's hers. He's … his real father's, whoever he is.'

She's found what she was looking for, hands me a sample pot of arnica. 'This is supposed to work wonders. Let me know if it works and if you'd like some more for him.' The doctor returns to my previous comment now. 'Couldn't you try and find out who his real dad is? Ask Vera for some clues, maybe?'

'All her clues seem to have led her to me, doctor. But she's wrong.'

There's a slight pause while she gets her head around the next thing she seems to want to say to me.

'This isn't any of my business, Mr Hardman. And please understand that everything I say is strictly off the record, but, from what I've seen, it wouldn't take too much now, for the nan to be considered unfit to look after the child. As someone who clearly cares very much about him, a family friend, at least, have you and Vera ever considered the possibility of you applying for legal guardianship of the boy, yourself?'

I'm stumped for a moment, following her back into the corridor.

'We're all done here. Thanks for bringing Adam in to see me today.' She pops her head round the door to her room. 'If his biological dad is, as I suspect, nowhere to be found, then it doesn't matter if you think you're the dad or not,' she tells me quietly as Adam helps his nan to get up from her chair. 'He's clearly devoted to you. And you seem to have his best interests at heart. If things get too hard for Vera, she could always sign his care over to you.'

'Could she?'

'Wouldn't be the first time I've heard of it. Please – think about it, at least.'

'Okay,' I say.

I must be crazy because when we walk out of that surgery door, I *am* thinking about it. Despite all the problems and difficulties it might entail. Despite all the troubles I have of my own.

Jenna might not want to know me anymore, but I know she'd at least be proud of me for that.

Nate

'Something got your goat, Adam?'

'Maybe,' he admits, and I feel a small pang of frustration. From the doctors, we've come down into Chatham. I promised him and his nan I'd bring them to this burger joint for their tea and we've just finished off with an ice-cream. He should be happy, shouldn't he? Today, I have spoken to the Headmaster for him. I have spoken to his nan. I have accompanied them both to the doctors so someone could look at his bruises. Vera has come alive, cheering up immensely, but Adam doesn't look anywhere near as pleased as I'd imagined he'd be. He ordered the super-supreme double chocolate flake whip, but he's toying with it now, doing that thing kids do with their food when they're not content. I look at him out of the corner of my eye.

'When you spoke to my nan earlier,' he's musing, 'you mentioned that you and Jenna were *through*, Nate?'

'I did.' I turn away to stare out of the window and it's raining. *Let's not go there, Kid.*

'You didn't just mean because she was leaving, did you?'

I let out a sigh.

'You *didn't*,' he insists, 'did you? You two had a fight, Nate?'

'If we did,' I say quietly. 'That would be none of your concern.' I'm gutted myself, today, but I still came good for him, didn't I? I've done every single thing, under the circumstances, I possibly could do. What father could have done more?

317

'If you had a fight just before she left, that's really bad.'

'You don't need to fret about it, Adam.' I take a slug of my coffee that's gone cold while we've been sitting here, waiting patiently for his nan to finish her chips. 'Please, let's just drop it.'

'Why are you and Miss Tierney fighting, though? You love each other. If you didn't fight with her, she'd have come back, I know she would.'

I turn to stare at him.

'She wouldn't have come back.'

'Why wouldn't she? People have fights all the time. They come back.'

'Not this time.' I bite the inside of my lip.

'She would,' he insists. 'She'd make it up with you but … maybe you're being stubborn?'

I don't answer.

'Maybe you're being stubborn because you like being miserable and being alone and finding it hard to get out of that flat?'

'Why on earth would I do that?'

'Maybe you're like my nan, stuck in the past and you'd rather stay inside?'

'No.'

'Maybe it's better than going out and facing what you don't want to see, Nate?'

'It isn't.' I baulk at the injustice of this. 'I do want to go out. I *am* doing what I can, to recover. You've helped me, in that. I've done it to help you but it's helped me, too. Jenna just … doesn't want to be with me anymore, Adam. And she's not coming back. Even if she hadn't cancelled that trip to the States …'

Adam stops what he's been doing, pushing his finger into the chocolate flake, making a mess on the table.

'What? What do you mean she's *cancelled* it?'

'Ignore what I just said.' I down the rest of the coffee with a grimace. 'Time I got you two home. You all done with those fries, Vera?'

'Takes me longer without me teeth.' She smiles at me.

'What do you mean, Miss Tierney cancelled the trip?' Her grandson's still staring at me. 'If she's not going away, then … then …'

318

His eyes light up, and it's obvious where he's going with this.

'Then *nothing*, I'm afraid.'

His eyes gaze into mine, deflated again.

'Why? Is it because you don't love her enough?'

'I love her enough.'

'Is it because you think she doesn't love you?'

'I think,' I tell him quietly, 'she does.'

'What then?'

What then?

'Look. Things don't always work out the way we'd like them to, that's all. Life isn't like a fairy tale, Adam. It doesn't always have fairy tale endings.'

'It could do,' he's muttering defiantly. 'You always used to believe your dreams could come true, when you were a kid.'

'I'm sorry?' I rub at my head.

'"*When you're a kid, you can dream whatever you want to dream There's not a thing in the world that can't be true.*" You told me that when we were both in the library, waiting for Miss Tierney.' He's wrapping the string from the yellow balloon that came with his meal, round and round his wrist.

'Did I? That doesn't mean ...' I look at him, perplexed. 'It doesn't mean she's coming back.'

'Why?' he insists. '*Why* can't you two get back together again if you love each other enough and she's not going anywhere, now?'

'Because,' my throat closes, even as I'm saying the words, but he might as well know it. 'I told her the truth about you and me.'

'What've *I* got to do with any of it?' He looks distraught.

'I told her the truth, Adam. I told her how we came to know each other. How you wrote me that letter and I ... I took pity on you because I know what it's like to be where you are. How I've tried my best to help you, how I've even come to care for you, but ... *the truth*. I'm not your dad.'

His eyes change, now. That painful look I see in there – is it hurt, disbelief, *betrayal*?

'You told her that? *Why?* Why would you say that to her, Nate?'

'Because I am not.'

Adam's clenched fist smashes into the table, now. What remains of the chocolate flake is crushed to smithereens. He stands up, almost knocking the chair over behind him in his haste and the balloon bobs up with him. It looks odd, on a child of his age. I look to his nan for support but she's staring out of the window, in a world of her own, still chewing doggedly on those fries.

'Adam, I didn't mean …' I jump to my feet after him, but he's surprisingly nimble for his weight, and nearer to the door than me. 'Don't.'

'Young man,' his nan says sweetly, and I turn back to her in dismay. 'Do you think you could …?'

'He's upset,' I begin. 'I'll go after him, Vera. Don't you worry.'

'Young man. Do you think you could be kind enough to take me to the loo?'

My eyes track her grandson, hot-footing it out of the door. I need to get after him, damn it. I don't want him running around, feeling so upset like this.

But by the strange look of concentration that's come into his nan's eyes now, I get the feeling Vera isn't going to wait.

Nate

'I couldn't find him,' I tell Vera. I got the duty manager at the burger joint to take her to the Ladies in the end. I ran out into the High Street, all the way down as far as the Old Post Office on Railway Street. It was the direction I thought I'd seen Adam go, but he'd had a good few minutes head start on me. He wasn't anywhere to be found, so I ran back here again: to his grandma Vera, who's suddenly become my charge. In the minutes since I left, it's begun raining hard and it's getting pretty dark. The manager who's been waiting by the door with Vera seems relieved to see me arrive back.

'Oh look,' she tells the old lady. 'Here's your Carer come back for you at last.'

'I'm not her Carer.'

'She's *been*,' the manager informs me. 'So you should be alright to go home. Won't you, Vera?'

'Where's Adam?' Vera asks.

'I have a feeling the lad might have doubled back and gone home. Shall we go there, now?' It's the third time today I've forked out for a taxi but the thought of Adam, running around in the rain, distraught, angry, it makes me feel anxious. It makes my chest feel tight. Of course he'll have gone home. Where else could he have got to?

'He's a good lad,' Vera's telling me, all the way to their house. 'He never gives me any trouble at all.'

'I know he doesn't.'

'He'll be all right, won't he?'

'I'm hoping so, Vera. Kids run off sometimes. They do that. He's a clever lad and I'm sure he knows his way back.' I'm thinking fast. Deep in my gut, something's telling me Adam won't be there when we get to the nan's house. 'Does your grandson have any friends you know of, who he confides in?' I ask now. 'Is there anyone he might have tried to contact, if he was mad at ...' I can't say *his parents* – 'his home situation?'

His nan looks stumped.

'Why would he be mad at me?' she asks in a small voice. 'I just bought him a burger that came with a yellow balloon. I bought him an ice-cream, didn't I?'

She didn't buy them. I bought them, but I let that go.

'You aren't taking him away from me, are you?' Her face is troubled. 'His dad's back now, you know.'

'*Is he*, Vera?' I turn to her so she can see me, full on, and she smiles.

'Oh, there you are. I thought you'd gone to look for Adam?'

'I did. I think he's gone back home.' I sit back in the seat, feeling suddenly exhausted.

'Why is he angry at me?'

'Look, it's me he's mad at, Vera. Because Miss Tierney and I have parted ways.' I have no idea why I'm telling her this. I feel compelled to. Maybe it's the nerves. I've got to tell someone. 'I think your grandson had the mistaken idea that she and I would be staying together.'

'You will be staying together,' she comes back straight away.

'No, we won't.' My voice sounds cracked.

'I saw you and the nice teacher, living together.' Vera does a circling motion with her hand.

'Where? What do you mean?'

'I saw you in my head,' she says, smiling. 'Just like I saw you, being Adam's dad.'

The taxi driver inclines his head casually to the right, doing that thing they do when they're listening in. He's not even trying to disguise the fact.

'I'd listen to her premonitions if I were you,' he counsels gravely. 'She sounds as if she knows what she's talking about.'

'She doesn't!' *What kind of twilight zone have I wandered into, today?* 'The main thing is,' I tell them both, 'we need to make sure that Adam's all right. Has he ever run off like that, before, Vera?'

'Your young lad run off, then?' the taxi driver chips in from the front. 'How old?'

'Nine. And he's not my …'

'He's angry with his dad,' Vera informs him.

The guy adjusts his mirror to peer backwards at me.

'Kids. What are they like? I saw a boy of about that age, on my way down here. Heading full pelt over the bridge into Strood, he was. Only noticed him because of that yellow balloon you just mentioned. Saw him stop running when he got to the middle of the bridge, though, so you might catch up.'

'What do you mean, he *stopped*?' I sit up, straight, my heart going ten to the dozen. It's taken a good forty minutes to walk Vera with her poorly legs to the taxi stand so it could well be Adam he saw, he'd have had the time to get there. He could still be there, thinking thoughts he shouldn't be thinking. Or worse. I don't need this stress in my life. I don't want this. Having to worry about someone, like this. Having to keep them in your mind, all the time. Where they might be, what they might be up to. *Shit.*

'He stopped. He was looking down. I thought maybe he'd dropped something into the water.'

'In that case,' I breathe, 'can we please drive over the bridge, before going to the address I gave you?'

By the time the taxi rolls to a stop on the corner of The Esplanade, there is no one on the bridge. Nor is there anything that looks like a crowd of curious onlookers. The tide is high tonight. Thank God.

'Adam's not there anymore,' I tell them both. 'If it was him, he must have gone home.'

'It's likely, isn't it? You want me to take you back to the house, then?' The taxi driver nods sympathetically.

'Please.'

When we get back to her house, it's almost pitch black. A cold wind is blowing off the river, and there is no sign of her grandson at their house, either.

No sign of him at all.

'Are you sure that Adam has no friends, around here, Vera? He must know *some* people apart from you, surely?' If he doesn't, God help him. How is the lad even still sane? I am feeling frustrated. Worn out. Today has been the longest day of my life, and it's not over, yet.

'There's his dad, of course.' We're sitting in Vera's cold kitchen and she turns to me now with such assuredness in her eyes, I get the sense that she's actually 'with me' again. Until she says, 'His name is Nate Hardman. He lives along the High Street. I think you'll find him, there.'

'Adam cannot be there, Vera, because I am Nate Hardman. And I am here.'

Then it hits me. Could there actually be another guy with my name living down the same street as me? *Blow me, why did I never think of that, before?* I grab Vera's telephone directory off the shelf and scroll down the pages, my eyes stinging with tiredness. Am I actually about to discover Adam's real dad? Was it really always that simple? I know I did a bit of research when the lad first made contact, but I was always looking for a dude with his surname – Boxley. I hit my forehead with an open hand. Call myself a journalist! I feel ashamed that this obvious solution has only just occurred to me. The guy Adam's been longing to make contact with could have been living here, under our noses, all along.

His real dad.

'Did you ever know him, Vera?' I ask her now, 'Did you ever have contact with Adam's dad in the early days, after he was born?'

324

She stares at me blankly.

'Vera,' I say, frustrated. 'Did you ever … oh, forget it!'

I've never given the father much thought up to now, but as I go through the directory, I picture the kind of man he'd be. What kind of bloke abandons his son, anyway? Only one who doesn't care, I imagine. One who isn't interested in his kid or who wouldn't be interested in doing all the things a dad should do for his son, even if I did find him. Because who could live down the road from his kid and never make contact? Then I recall that this is exactly what Jenna presupposed of me when she first met me, and I realise that the truth is … maybe we will never know.

I have come to the end of the Hardmans, and double-check with a Google search on my phone now, just to be sure. But there is no one else who lives around here with that name, only me. Maybe he was here and he's moved? Maybe the nan is as touched as I suspect she is, and really did pick my name out of the telephone directory at random? I snap the book shut and the disappointment I expected to feel at this dead end is tinged with a huge and unexpected sense of relief.

Because Adam deserves better than this. He deserves to have someone there at his Sports Day, cheering him on. He deserves to have someone notice when he's in the house or when he isn't. And right now, by my reckoning, he's been gone for a couple of hours, at least.

Should I get his nan to phone the police? Two hours might not be long enough for them to get involved, especially if the lad went off in a huff. He's a nine-year-old lad who's had his hopes dashed and he'll still be cooling down, they'll say. No. Not yet. I've got to go out looking for him, myself. Adam must know at least *one* other friendly face in this town, surely?

And then it hits me. He does.

But I'm pretty sure I'm the last person she wants to see right now.

Jenna

'Bloody Nora!' Steph's already hauled her buggy halfway up the steps outside the house before we catch sight of each other. It's dark. And *late*. As I left my phone behind, I have no idea what time it is. All I know is that no one was here to answer the door. No lights were on in the house and I didn't want to trouble the neighbours. I've been curled up in a ball on the top step for ages, waiting for a member of the family to get back.

My sister peers at me a little closer as if she thinks she might be seeing a ghost. 'Is it really you?'

'It's really me.'

'You're back?'

'Not permanently.' I get up off my backside, everything feeling stiff and we hug each other awkwardly. The babby in the buggy dangling precariously off one step is mercifully asleep.

'Is this Keanu?'

'Keanu One,' my sister says proudly. In the lamplight outside the door, the nephew I have only ever seen in photos looks peaceful, angelic.

'Keanu *One*?'

'Kev, my new partner, has a child by his former girlfriend who's also called Keanu.'

I blink. O-*kay*.

'He's beautiful. How old is he now?'

'He'll be fourteen months, this week.'

'Wow. Times flies, eh?' It's been five years since I visited last. I feel an unexpected pang of nostalgia and regret. All the things I don't ever feel. And *cold*. I rub at my bare arms. I must have been sitting out here for a good hour.

'You'll be all right sleeping on the couch, I take it?' My sis is already hauling the buggy up the last few steps, opening the front door.

'Better than the front step.'

I hear her give a dry laugh, and she disappears upstairs for a bit – settling Keanu into his cot? When she returns she's got an old duvet in her hands, no pillow.

'There's a cushion on the couch,' she tells me without ceremony. Typical of my family, she asks no questions about how I've been or where I've been or even *why am I now here?*

It's left to me to enquire.

'Where is everyone, Steph?'

'Mum and Des have flown out to Marbella for a couple of weeks. First holiday they've had in six years,' she adds, almost defensively.

'Oh.' That pulls me up short. I hadn't been expecting that, somehow. I'd been expecting them to *be here*.

My sister looks weary.

'You don't need any tea or anything, do you? It's late. If you need a brew, you already know where everything is …'

I shake my head, rapidly.

'I don't need tea.'

'I guess, I'll see you in the morning, then?' There's a question in her voice. As if even that may not be a given.

If I had not just come in on the last train from Leeds, it might not have been. I hunker down on the couch which is covered in dog hairs and my whole body feels out of sorts. Damn, but this place sucks. I remember now why I left! Why did I come back? Mum and Des aren't even here. Fine, I'm not in touch often, but in my mind, this is the place where they should be. Even if I don't come back and visit, this is the location I have them at. I don't even know why I wanted to see them, but now I am here, it feels wrong that they should be somewhere else.

Coming as it does, at the end of this shittiest day of my life, where nothing has turned out like I thought it should, it seems appropriate, somehow.

Nate

I need to go home. Jenna's not answering her doorbell. This is the third time I've been back here, trying. In the dark, her beloved green door appears ghoulish to me, unfriendly. I get the feeling there's no one who lives in the flat above that door who'd want to see me. The night is nearly over; it's past 5 a.m. Either Jenna's asleep, or she's gone. Either way, as she's still not picking up her phone, I cannot reach her. I want to go home, but I cannot. How can I, when I don't know if Adam's home and safe, yet? Is he with her and they're both asleep? I'd like to think so but I know she'd have taken him back home if she'd seen him. So he isn't here. How can I rest, when I don't know what's happened to him? When I left her, his nan seemed unperturbed '*He's coming, he's coming*,' she said. Then: '*Leave them alone, and they will come home, dragging their tails behind them.*' Quoting nursery rhymes, she made me want to weep. I could not leave it alone. How could I? I caved in and phoned the police at midnight and they asked me who was calling in – a family friend, I told them, a guy who he looks on as his dad.

Standing outside Jenna's silent door in the small hours, the truth of that has been echoing round in my head for a while. He looks on me as his dad. I never knew his mother. I never knew he existed till a few weeks ago and yet Adam's grown on me, grown all over me, like the shadowy ivy blanketing the wall behind me, till I can barely imagine my life without him being here.

Like her. I want her to *be* here. In my life again, and in his. But she is not, and she will not be. My head knows too well what my heart won't yet accept and I don't know how to bring together the two. I don't know how to make it all right again. And I cannot find him.

What are the police doing? My heart constricts, feeling sore. Feeling helpless to intervene.

From the last communication I had with them, they've put a 'misper' out, a missing person alert, the operator told me. It was 2 a.m. by then. They felt he'd still be likely to make contact, but took it seriously enough. Children do this, sometimes, the friendly liaison officer told me, reassuring me just like I reassured his nan, but she can't know how that boy feels, what he's really going through. I do, though. I think I do.

There's no point staying here. Jenna can't help, and I need to keep moving, I've got this itchiness in my feet to keep moving, cover more ground. Find him. In my mind, that's all that matters, that I find him. I won't rest until I know he's safe. Rochester is quiet at this hour, but not deserted. Dark, but there are plenty who can find their way about happily in the darkness. On the benches along the green space of The Vines, a few homeless men are already sleeping, others sitting drinking. The atmosphere is close as I approach, fairly intimidating. This sunny place where the mothers come and sit by day belongs to others at night, no place for children. Is my lad hiding out here? I can't see him, but I can feel their eyes following my back as I walk by. Is it strange that I'm feeling no fear for myself whatsoever at this point? No palpitations. No tightening of the chest. Maybe caring for Adam has cured me – but what have I managed to do for him?

'Hey, you.'

I spin round, and unusually, one of the homeless guys is addressing me. It's got to be me. Apart from his mates, there is only us here.

'Yes, *you.*' When he stands up, he's a good six foot tall and built like a navvy, wearing a bandanna. I stare back at him. I know his type. What's he after? It'll either be money or a smoke. Or a fight. My eyes swivel towards the gate at the exit. I've been in enough close shaves in my life to know the crucial distance needed to escape from a confrontation but I'm heart-sore, tonight, in no mood to run and in even less mood for a fight. I need to find Adam.

'What do you want?' I turn to square up to him.

'You don't *know* me, do you?'

'Should I?' An echo of something is tugging at the back of my mind, earlier days I'd rather leave behind me. Fuck him. 'I'm looking for a young lad, about nine.' I turn my head, addressing the lot of them. If Adam's been running about here tonight, he might have passed through this place. One of them might have seen him.

'Your lad?' A little closer to me, and he smells pungent. He smells of unwashed flesh and clothes, rough living on the streets and booze. A memory trails in on the cloud of his scent and I want to be sick.

'Not mine. Someone I'm looking out for.'

'Nothing much changes then, does it?'

'Pardon me?' I look him straight in the eye and straight away there's something familiar there, something I can't shake off.

'Don't remember me, do you?' When he grins, half his front teeth are missing. 'I remember you, though.' He leans in and slaps me on the shoulder. 'Hard not to. That bloody brother of yours never stopped talking about you, did he?'

'You mean Mo?' I swallow.

'You used to come and pick him up from around here, right? When he'd get bladdered. When he'd had a little bit too much ...' He does a pushing motion with his hand on his arm, 'you know.'

No. I'm not going there. Not now.

'I stopped looking after my older brother a long time ago,' I tell him and my voice is croaky.

'He was proud of you, though. Never stopped boasting about how his brother had made good. A reporter, he said, on the TV. You still doing that?'

I blink. Behind him, some of his mates are gathering in, curious. All these down-and-outs – did they used to know Mo, too? *He was proud of me?* Who ever knew?

331

'Yes,' I breathe.

'Didn't see you at the funeral,' one of the blokes behind him says quietly, now.

'I didn't go.'

There's a murmur among them at that. Let them think what they like. Mo died. He jumped off that bridge at low tide and broke his neck. I didn't go. Because I was still mad at him for having died the way he did. For having lived the way he did.

'I couldn't save him,' I tell the guy with the bandanna. The stinging behind my eyes is not for him, I tell myself. That stinging is for everything else. For me. For Adam. For the girl who I've lost.

'He didn't want saving, Brother-Of-Mo, that's why.'

'He didn't,' I agree.

'And this little lad you're looking out for,' the guy laughs, now. An open, deep-bellied laugh. 'Does *he* want saving?'

'He wrote me a letter,' I tell him, 'which is more than Mo ever did.' In the distance, the sound of a police siren – or is it an ambulance? – going past, gives me a shot of urgency in the chest. Is it Adam? Have they found him?

Is he all right?

The hour is later than I thought it was, the moon sinking down deep into the sky which is getting lighter, already getting lighter. I asked Vera to phone me on my mobile if she heard anything, if he wandered back home, but would she? Will she? Should I go back there now, or would that simply be disturbing her, an old lady, frightening her in the night? Should I phone the police again?

'Was that lad of yours carrying a yellow balloon, earlier?' one of the men asks me and my heart leaps.

'He was. You've seen him?' I spin round, but the tramp isn't looking at me. He's clutching a can of beer to his chest, his face upturned, and in the clearing sky of the dawn I see it plainly now, drifting upwards like a spectre, coming from the direction of the river and the bridge: that special yellow balloon.

332

Jenna

'They were gettin' on my nerves, like.' Steph's just come in with a brew which she places down on the carpet, beside me. 'Kev came in with his two early on but you were sleeping in here so I sent them all off packing, to the park.'

I rub at my eyes, wondering for a few seconds how I got here. *Back home.* My heart sinks and it's as if all the recurring nightmares I've ever had where I've found myself back here, have come true.

'Told Kev not to bring the sprogs back till lunchtime at the earliest.'

It's all drifting back. Mum and my stepdad are in Marbella. I sit up, puzzled and feeling vaguely horrified. They are not here. I am. I look out of the window.

'It's raining,' I tell her.

'Is it?' My sister flicks her fag end into an ashtray, her fierce blue eyes suddenly alert. 'Fuckkit. Gerrup, girl, we need to bring the washing in.'

I swing my legs round and the newspapers my feet have been brushing into all night, fall onto the floor. I slept right through on that uncomfortable sofa but I'm feeling exhausted, heart weary. Two nights' ago, I was in Nate's bed. We were still together. Two nights' ago, was as good as things had got, so far, in my life. I push my trainers on, reluctantly following Steph into the patch out back. It's even smaller than I remembered it to be. It's even crappier!

Next Door's garden is all taken up by a kiddies' trampoline with safety net. The one rose bush Dad had ever planted in ours – in response to constant nagging from me – is missing.

'If you're still looking for the roses, they're gone.' Steph follows my line of gaze, laughing scornfully. You were always loopy about them flowers, weren't you?'

'Only because they brought a bit of colour to the place.'

'Haven't the space for *colour* here though, have we? With all that colour, how'd I get my laundry dry?'

'I don't know,' I mutter. The rain is dripping onto my nose and onto the one and only T-shirt I have with me, the one on my back. I'm feeling very cold. My old home feels so gloomy and all so dreary and *empty*. Just like it always did.

'Without a little beauty, what's the point of it all, anyway?'

'What is the point?' She seems puzzled by the question.

We pull at the pegs, releasing Steph's towels and duvet covers from the line, and some of her pillowcases fall into the mud. She curses softly and in the bright light of morning I can see all the harsh creases beginning to settle under my sister's eyes. I can see the resignation that must have set in years ago and I don't envy her, her life.

I turn to her. 'God. Don't you ever just wish … you could get away from it all, Steph?'

'Get away from what?'

'All *this*.' I indicate with my hands around the garden, the house, but I'm trying to encompass much more than that. I mean everything. All that she's settled for. She was a pretty girl, my sister. And clever, in her own way. Good at numbers. She could have done so much better for herself.

'Nah.' She's still plucking at pegs, nimble and quick, onto the little paired socks now. 'Why would I want to get away?'

'To find something better, of course.'

'Like you?' Her eyes flicker up, slightly defiant, a little hostile even. 'We're not all like you, Jenna.'

'What d'you mean?'

'It's what you left home for, isn't it? Sweet sixteen. So besotted with that big-shot artist guy from the college, you followed him all the way to Paris. What happened to him, anyway?'

'Don't know.' I shrug. Don't care, either. I watch as she lights up a ciggie, that desperate for one, even in the driving rain. The socks she's put into the basket are soaking up the water, her sheets are flung over her shoulders, momentarily forgotten.

'Then there was that biker guy,' she's recalling. 'The tattooed one you spent the summer with? What happened to him?'

I shrug.

'I learned how to tattoo, then I left him.'

'He cheated on you?'

'Not me. Someone else. I found out he already had a girl, back in York.'

'Too many like him, around.' She looks up curiously. 'You were in Sicily, last I heard?'

'Another liar.'

'It's the story of us Tierney women's lives.' She sighs. 'It's how it is.' Steph folds her arms for a minute and I stop, too, my arms full of tea cloths. 'It's a fact. Like the rain. One day you're a little girl wearing princess dresses, waiting for Prince Charming, and the next thing you know you're up the duff and all you can see in front of you is a ballroom full of frogs.' Her face creases in resigned mirth.

'I guess.'

She gives me a sharp nudge with her elbow.

'You stopped looking for that handsome prince yet, Jenna? Because you will, you know.'

'Will I?' I don't feel like smiling back. My sister's never met Nate. She's never met anyone like him, and before now, neither had I.

'Oh, yes. You will.' My sister's eyes are narrowed, a little triumphant even, back at tackling the laundry again. She throws another pile of smalls into the basket. 'Don't think for one minute that we don't all know what's been happening with you, all these years.'

I frown slightly.

'What d'you mean, *you know what's been happening with me?*'

'These … dreams and big plans you've always had. You've always been like it, haven't you? Always such a romantic. With your …' She waves her hand airily, 'wanting rose bushes and … art, and the like. But none of that ever comes to owt, does it? Prince Charming leads to one thing only …' She indicates the line of nappies getting softly wet in the dank morning.

'You're wrong,' I say.

'I'm not wrong. All these … amazing love affairs you have that never go anywhere,' she points out. 'Me and Mum always said that sooner or later, you'd be back.'

Despite the rain, I can feel my face going hot.

'I'm not back, though.'

'Aren't you?' Steph looks at me askance. 'Am I looking at a ghost then, and not my own sister? You are back. Face it. I thought when I saw you sitting on the doorstep last night, you were done for.'

'I'd had a rough day …'

'We've all done it,' she says matter-of-factly. 'When the going gets tough, sometimes all a girl can do to save herself is scarper. Once you know it's over.' She shoots me a knowing look. 'What's to stick around for and who can blame you?'

'I guess.'

'Another bloke who turned out of be a wrong 'un, eh?' My sister's observation is not without some sympathy. 'Got a name, this one?'

'He … his name is Nate.' My gaze drops to the muddy ground. For some reason I'm acutely aware of the drops of rain sluicing down onto the yellowed, battered blades of grass at my feet. Maybe in a few days' time this lawn will bounce back, green and lush, I'm thinking. Maybe all it needs is a spot of rain?

'*Nathan*,' she's saying, 'How posh.'

'Nathaniel, actually.'

'Even posher.' Steph looks impressed. 'And yet – even he is history, now.'

336

I give a small nod.

'Did he know you were leaving him?' My sister goes into practical mode. 'You didn't tell him you were coming up here, did you? Generally best just to get out of it and never look back, I always found. Don't contact them. Don't answer calls. They get the message soon enough.'

'I left my phone behind,' I say in a small voice. 'If he's tried to contact me, I wouldn't know.'

'All the better, then. Once you're out of it, you don't go back,' she warns. 'He'll suck you back in and before you know it you'll be giving him another chance and he won't deserve it. He'll only cheat on you again …'

'This one didn't cheat,' I stop her. 'Shall we go back inside?'

'What did he do, then, this fella Nate?' We lug the washing back in and she's all ears now, eager for the gossip. She'll be on the phone to our mum with it before the morning's out, I know that much.

'He pretended to be a young lad's dad, when he wasn't.'

'Oh.' She pulls a dour face. 'Benefit cheat?'

'No!' I look at her, crossly. 'Nate didn't get any benefit at all, out of the pretence, as far as I can see. Not at all. He did it all on the lad's behalf – a boy in my class – he wanted to help him out, that's all.'

'That's never all,' she mutters darkly. 'Men like that don't put themselves out like that for no reason.'

'This one did. And what do you mean, *men like that?* You don't even know him.'

'I know he's the first man to have you running so scared that you've finally turned up home after five years …'

'I didn't run home because I was scared of him, Steph. He never threatened me in any way.' I frown at her, wishing we had a more similar take on men but I know her experiences have been somewhat different to mine. 'Nate's not that kind of guy.'

'Why have you run back then?' She looks at me archly. 'I'm happy to see you back, make no mistake. I left a few frogs in the lurch mesself before I found Kev. He's no prince, mind, but he'll

337

do. There's no shame in coming back to the place where you belong, Jen.'

'No,' I say uncomfortably. She's trying hard to be kind but the only shame I'm feeling right now is this overwhelming sense that *I don't* belong here.

'There's plenty of teaching jobs going if you don't mind mucking in at the rougher end,' she's rattling on happily. 'And that Darren Tolby from the newsagent's who was always sweet on you was asking after you again the other day. He's separated now, you know,' she informs me cheerfully. 'Might be a keeper, that one. So you never know your luck.'

'God, Steph, stop it! I'm not staying here,' I get out. 'I only came back here because I thought … I thought Nate really was the one and when he lied to me that hurt so bad I didn't know where else to come.'

'He lied to you.' My sister folds her arms. 'Why?'

'I imagine he thought if I knew the truth I'd have to inform the school and then he wouldn't be able to help the lad anymore.'

Her eyebrows arch.

'Sounds like a pretty kosher lie to me, pet.'

'What do you mean?' I stare at her, feeling all the hurt come tumbling back. 'Nate lied to me, *he lied!* Don't you see – I had to leave him and I didn't really want to leave him but what else could I do?'

'What's lying got to do with leaving?' She laughs drily, getting back to her laundry. 'Everybody lies sometimes. Little white lies, convenient lies. You must do it too, no doubt? It's not the end of the world.'

'I don't,' I come straight back. But the memory of Camille's wedding, the day I pretended to everyone that I was Nate's girl-friend, sneaks traitorously in. 'Well, okay. Sometimes, I do. If it's really necessary. It's the gratuitous lies that I hate,' I defend. 'Like, when people promise you things they have no intention of making good on.'

My sister's separating out the clothes now, the smalls from the shirts that'll need ironing.

'That's people for you.'

'Even our Dad lied,' I throw at her under my breath.

'Say again?'

'He lied. To me. To you. Said he was going off on that job and he never came back, did he?'

My sister's eyes are a wide 'O' of surprise.

'Once people who matter, lie to you ...' I remind her, 'how d'you ever know you can trust them again? You might give them your whole heart, love them completely. But how do you know you can rely on them to stay?'

Steph blinks.

'Let us hope none of your exes were ever relying on *you* to stay, then,' she mutters under her breath.

'What?'

'Well, you never stuck around with any of them did you?'

'Are you calling me a hypocrite?' She didn't, but I'm starting to feel like one.

'... not even this paragon of virtue, Nate, who doesn't seem to have done anything too wrong, from what you yourself have said?'

I rub at my face with my hands.

'You're confusing me now, Steph,' I accuse.

'Lies aren't always for the wrong reason,' she points out. I look away, feeling more confused than ever. 'And if you're not back to stay, then why did you really come back here, Jen? What are you after?'

'I don't know,' I tell her in a small voice, but as I push away from the kitchen cupboards, for the first time, I am starting to feel the strength returning to my legs. All those things she's been saying to me, some of them are starting to hit home. Like little missing pieces of a giant jigsaw, the pattern of my life, flying back into the picture after all this time, *making sense*. Dad lied, and he left. Does that mean every other guy who tells me a lie in my

339

life will also abandon me? It does not! And yet it's how I've been living my life, running away from every relationship before the guy could leave me.

My sister turns to the table where we've dumped the wet washing and shakes out one of the sheets vigorously.

'Perhaps better face it, then. Whatever it is you're looking for, you're never going to find it, are you, sis?' she notes briskly. 'You certainly aren't going to find it here.'

I join her in folding the wet clothes, very aware that I'm feeling sad and relieved and all sorts of conflicting things at one and the same time. When I give her a quick hug she pushes me off rapidly, 'Gerraway with you,' but underneath I can tell that she's pleased.

'It may be way too late,' I tell her. 'But I think maybe … maybe I just did.'

Nate

'*Adam. Don't do it!*'

My heart just skipped a beat. By the time I've caught up with him, Adam's already perched quite comfortably on the edge of the metal railings on the pedestrian path across Rochester Bridge, peering out over the water. I look down at the drop. The water's hurried today, brown and bubbling beneath the surface, disturbed. There's a cool, dawn breeze just licking my skin as I approach and his young face is strained, red about the eyes. It's obvious that he's been crying. I slow down my pace instinctively, my relief palpable but it's not over, yet.

'Don't do what?' he growls at me.

'Anything.' I open out my hands in front of me as I draw nearer. 'Just don't ... do anything.'

He turns his gaze from the water for just long enough to come back to me.

'Like ... *what?* What is it you think I'm going to do?'

I don't want to answer that directly.

'Just stop and think for a bit, Adam.' I nod my head over to the breaking dawn in the East. 'I know yesterday wasn't great. But today's a whole, brand new day.'

'Every day is a brand new day,' he observes wearily. 'All the days bring the same old things, Nate.'

'Not always.' I inch a little closer. From here, I can see he is not as comfortable as I first thought. He's got his hands clasped in

341

front of him, the tips of his fingers bouncing together in a tiny, almost imperceptible motion. His eyes narrow at me now.

'You lied, Nate.'

I give a small shake of my head. That's unfair.

'I never lied to you. To her, yes, so that I could help you. But never to you.'

'You *lied*,' he insists. 'You told me that when you're a kid there's not a thing in the world that can't be true.'

Oh. I stare at him.

'With time,' I say helplessly. 'I didn't mean we could snap our fingers and make like a genie, Buddy. Life doesn't work like that.'

'You told me when you were a kid, you dreamed of travelling all over ...'

'And I did it!'

'You did. And then you got stuck in your room and the world became smaller again. The good changes never last, do they? You never told me that bit.' He turns away from me, the hope dying in his voice.

'The bad ones never do, either,' I get out. 'Please believe me, Adam.' The breeze over the bridge turns colder, now. I'm aware that my hands and my arms are frozen. And him – he's been sitting up here on these railings for heaven knows how long – he'll be frozen, too.

'I'm out of my flat again now, aren't I? Largely thanks to meeting you, if I'm honest.'

His wide clear eyes come up to meet mine for a second.

'Thanks to me, *how?*'

My throat feels tight.

'You gave me a reason to want to come out and meet the world again. I can't tell you the huge difference you've made in my life, Bud.' He looks pensive for a moment, and, I think, *I hope*, a little pleased. 'Won't you come down, now?' I plead.

He shakes his head.

'Do you want to know what I dreamed of, Nate?'

342

I close my eyes for a second; just wishing I knew what words I should say to get him down off these damn railings. What words. I'm a wordsmith, aren't I? Last time we were here, right in this same space, Adam asked me what was the most powerful thing I'd ever done with words? An image of my brother swims before me, and I recall why I never answered the kid. I'd failed, that's why. In the most important endeavour of my life, all of my words had failed.

And yet, I recall, this kid wrote me a letter, asking for my help. Something Mo never did.

'You don't know, do you?' Adam accuses.

'You dreamed of ... ordering the super deluxe burger that comes with the special yellow balloon?' I furrow my eyebrows, recalling it. I bought him one of those, already. Adam had the balloon. He let it go. *What more does he want?*

'A mum and dad of my own, that's what.' Adam's voice has gone very quiet. 'And I dreamed it would be you and Miss Tierney.'

My mouth has gone very dry.

'I wish that could be true, Buddy.' I say. 'I really do.'

'Do you?' He lifts his shoulders as if shrugging me off. 'Don't know why I ever wanted you, really,' he adds in a gruff voice. 'You don't understand me. You're not my dad. You're nothing like me, really, are you?'

I ease myself up onto the railings to perch down beside him. If Mohammed cannot go to the mountain ...

'I am, so. I'm good at finding things, aren't I?'

'Like what?'

'I found you, didn't I?' I shiver, blowing hot breath into cupped hands. 'Might have taken me all night, but I found you, in the end.' I shoot him a shivery smile.

'Don't know what for,' he counters.

'Because I care about what happens to you, that's what for! I was going out of my mind with worry.'

'And now you've found me.' Adam looks at me cautiously. 'What difference is it going to make?'

343

What difference? I feel a twist of sadness in my gut when he asks that, because the events of tonight are going to have had some impact, whether we want them to, or not. Up to now, it's just been me and him and his nan and Jenna. Up to now, we've been playing with the issues, but it's all about to get much more serious.

'I'm so sorry, Adam. You're right. Things are going to be different,' I admit gently. 'The police have been out looking for you, tonight.'

'Why?' He looks surprised. 'I come here often, when I can't sleep. I always get back before nan wakes up, and they've never come looking for me, before.'

I stare at him. He's done this before? Blow me! And I need to get onto the fuzz in a minute, when I've got him down, let them know the lad's okay.

'They're looking for you because I called them. Kids your age can't go wandering around all over the place at night, Adam. It's not safe. When we saw your GP yesterday she also became alerted to how neglected you've been. Now your case has been highlighted, things can't just go back to how they were. Your nan, too … she really needs to be looked after properly, in a home, doesn't she?'

Adam's head sinks lower, all the puff gone out of him. He's silent for a while, sniffing, wiping away the tears that are dripping down onto his nose.

'If Nan goes into a home, then I will too.' He looks up suddenly, stricken. 'I *will*, won't I?'

I am not going to lie to him.

'I wish I could tell you that weren't true, Adam. I really do.'

'If that happens … I won't see you again, will I?'

The truth? I let out a long, breath.

'Maybe they won't let me. Maybe once people find out I've been pretending to be your dad, they'll want to lock me up.' I smile at him ruefully. 'At the very least, they might want to keep me well away from you.'

'Is that what *you* want, Nate?' He shuffles in a little, almost imperceptibly closer to me, pushing his shoulder next to mine.

My fingers close around his own chubby ones, and I'm surprised at how large his hands are. Warm and capable. He's going to be a big, strong, geezer when he gets older. One of these days, he's going to go out and make a big impact in the world.

'What do you think, you daft bugger?'

He gives me a ghost of a smile. He's very sad, I can tell. But there is part of him that's relieved at the same time.

'Shall we climb down off here, now?' I suggest.

'We can if you like.'

But for a little while, neither of us move. We sit, at peace, watching the sunrise. The clouds to the east sail by, brave ships sailing in on a dawn of orange and pink. Then they turn into a kaleidoscope of other shapes, and we name them as they blow across the sky: a boat, then an elephant, then a star. Adam points out a white puff that he says looks like a couple holding hands.

'I think that's you and Miss Tierney.' He nudges me.

'Even though you and I both know that she is gone?'

He shrugs.

'What's it look like to you, then?'

'I think that smaller one is you,' I play along. 'That guy next to you is the person who's going to be there for you, all of your life. Someone good. He's someone kind, and worthy of the privilege of being a dad to you. He's coming. You have to keep wishing for him.'

'Really?' He's not sure whether I'm being serious or not, anymore, I can tell.

'For sure.'

'In that case, Nate, I have one last request of you.' He sits up a little taller. 'Will you come and see me at my Sports Day on Friday afternoon this week?'

'Sports Day?' I consider that for a bit. Sports Day at St Anthony's, where the competitive ethic is so strong, and he's still covered in bruises? 'I thought the doctor recommended that you shouldn't do sports for a bit?'

'I'll be careful.'

'Added to which, I'm not your headmaster's most favourite person in the world,' I reflect. By Friday, the whole lie about me being his dad could well be out, I think uneasily. If I turn up for his Sports Day, how's that going to go down? I told that doctor I was not his dad, didn't I, and she's seen how confused the nan can be. How easily a person who was up to no good might deceive her. I've told Jenna the truth, and I can't believe she'd have kept quiet about it, either.

Jenna. My lover. And now my enemy. My heart still feels sore at that. All this rushing about all night to save the kid, maybe I was also trying to save myself the heartache of remembering how she and I parted? I want to go back home, and lock the door and go to bed for a week. I don't want to show my face out there, at his school. I did my best for him, but I don't want to keep this pretence up, anymore.

'You *sure* you want to take part in it this year, Adam?' Best thing would be if I could dissuade him.

'I do if you'll be there.'

I rub at my face, feeling weary. By the time Friday comes around, they'll all know I've been posing as this child's parent and the way the world is these days, God knows what they'll all think. Maybe I'll be suspected of being some pervy weirdo who did it all for his own reasons? Maybe I'll even get arrested? The police sergeant who took down my details when I reported him missing earlier, seemed a bit put out to learn that the kid believed me to be his dad, even though I wasn't.

'*Why*, Adam?' I lower myself down off the railings and stretch out my arms to him. 'Why do you still want to take part, so much?'

'To let them see. To let them see that I am not afraid.' He jumps down, holding onto me, but he's surprisingly as lithe as a cat.

'And to show them that I am not alone.'

Nate

That noise is my phone going.

I swing my legs off the sofa, still feeling groggy. I was dreaming of chasing a yellow balloon that turned into Jenna and sailed off into the spreading dawn. I was dreaming the police had come to knock my door down, with batons and a battering ram. When I went to them I couldn't see their faces, everything was dark and nobody spoke but I knew why they were there. 'Where is your brother?' They silently wanted to know. 'What have you allowed to happen to Mo?' *Nothing*, I told them. *Nothing.*

But that phone's still going.

When I go scramble for it, still half-thinking it'll be the police – *I was the one who alerted them about Adam last night, will they now be curious about me?* – my legs are shaking.

It's Marcie, though.

'Nate! It's Tuesday,' she chides. 'We were going to make contact after two weeks, remember?'

I don't remember. I close my eyes and the only thing that's in my head right now is a deep and throbbing pain.

'About your video-diary,' she prompts. 'The producers are loving it, but the feeling is, the premise would be even stronger if we came at this from the angle of your relationship with Adam ...'

'*My relationship with Adam,*' I croak, 'is what's about to land me in some deep shit.'

'Say again?'

'He ran away last night and I had to alert the authorities. I was up till the small hours till I found him myself on Rochester Bridge.'

I can practically hear her intake of breath.

'He ran away?'

'He's terrified he's going to be sent into care, Marcie. The nan's no longer able to cope at home so he can't stay. They've got no one else.'

'No one?' Her voice is sorrowful.

I stumble over to the window to pull it up for some air. He's got no one. It's 11.15 a.m. on a glorious June day in Rochester. All the people on the street are cheerful today, greeting each other; the mums with their precious kids and the elderly folk with their cute little dogs, all greeting each other and smiling as if all is right with the world, but Adam – where's he, at home, at school? He's still got no one, and I can't help him. I can see the spire of the Cathedral from here and I can hear the bells going. A memory flutters past, of the day they buried my fellow reporter Jim Nolan. I couldn't help him, either. The little clouds Adam and I were counting on the bridge this morning, have gone. Dreams, that's all they were. Dreams and wishes, but in the light and heat of day they've all vanished into thin air.

'I took the lad down to see his GP yesterday, Marcie, for his bruises. She was horrified, and rightly so. The neglect issues surrounding this child go way beyond the bullying at school,' my voice breaks.

'Hey, Nate,' I can hear Marcie murmuring. 'It's all right.'

'It *isn't* though,' I growl softly. It isn't all right. 'They'll take him into care and I *know* what that'll be like for him.'

'I know you do.'

I give a small, dark, laugh now.

'Hey – that doc didn't even *believe* me when I told her I wasn't the father, can you believe that? Thought I was trying to duck my responsibilities, I guess.' It's almost exquisitely ironic. 'She suggested I should try and get the nan to sign Adam's care over to me!'

There's a silence at the other end of the phone, now.

'Marcie?' I grip the handset a little tighter. Hasn't she been listening? She phoned about the video-diary, I know, and she's a busy woman. Maybe I've gone on too long.

'I'm here,' she tells me. 'I'm just thinking.'

'If you're thinking we can incorporate all this into the VD somehow – a classic "triumph over tragedy" story, then forget it,' I tell her thickly. 'I'm done.'

'I wasn't thinking that. I was mulling over what the GP suggested to you. You've amply demonstrated how much you care about the lad, Nate, that's why she did it,' my boss points out. 'But Adam's GP can hardly appreciate the complexities; why you wouldn't think about taking on another man's child, when you don't have any partner to share the task, your job as a freelance journalist takes you away most of the time, and, not to mention, you haven't been able to work for the past few months because of debilitating panic attacks …'

Those attacks have abated since I met him, though. He's become my saviour, instead of me becoming his.

I'm silent for a moment. Then I admit,

'I *did* consider it for all of an hour or so before Adam ran off and I spent most of the night out looking for him.'

'Did you?'

'I spent an hour or two researching things after I got back home in the early hours, too. How kids who have no one else can sometimes get taken in by family and friends. I sent out a couple of email enquiries to contacts …' I stop.

'You're serious about it, then? What have you managed to find out?'

I let out a heavy sigh.

'It's a real minefield, Marcie. And …' I push back my hair, feeling tragic inside. 'I think Adam's about to fall foul of it, which is partly my doing.'

349

'*Your* doing? How so?'

'I alerted the police last night, didn't I? I told them I'd got him back, but now they know he's run away they'll have a duty to at least alert the social workers. Add that to the alarm I saw in his GP's eyes, I have a hunch she'll have done the same. They're going to be coming for him.'

'To take him into local authority care, you think?'

'What else? Who else *is* there? ' Then, as the silence stretches out long enough to make it clear what she's thinking, I add, '*I'm not his dad*, Marcie!'

'If he goes into local authority care, it still won't be his parents looking after him,' she points out. 'He ostensibly doesn't have any, so either way, that's a moot point.'

'I thought about it, long and hard, last night, believe me. But – how could it happen, seriously?

'Exactly how, I'm not sure.' Marcie sounds thoughtful, now. 'But I've just come out of a three-month collaboration project on social care, as it happens.'

'You have?'

'SWP "People Division" have only this week completed a fly-on-the-wall training video to show the procedures followed by social workers placed in precisely the kind of scenario we've been talking about.'

'Uh-huh.'

I've moved into the kitchen as we speak, filling up the cafetière, putting it on the hob. I need a kick-up-the-arse shot of caffeine. I don't know what Marcie's going on about, clutching at straws if you ask me. Only a few hours ago, I'd have been all ears. Now I'm worn out and upset and I'm only still listening because she's my boss and I owe her the courtesy of hearing her out.

'The video was looking at what happens when a child's own family care has broken down – what are the options the Children and Families Team need to look at, before considering making him a LAC – a "Looked After Child". Sounds like your scenario, yes?'

350

'So,' I say cautiously, 'how does it work?'

'They'd send someone around to undertake an initial assessment of him, to see if he's at immediate risk and to determine if a Section 47 Child Protection Assessment is in order.'

'Oh, yeah?' I pour some sugar into my coffee cup, warily. Been there. Done that. Maybe they called it something else in my day, but I know what it all entails. 'Section 47. That all sounds pretty heavy, doesn't it?'

'It is. They're pretty thorough. It'd involve looking at any comments his doctor might have on the matter, what his school think about him, etc.'

I give a derisive snort.

'Right, *them*. They'd be very helpful, I am sure.'

'That'd only come into play if the child was deemed to be at risk ... which Adam is, if his nan's being taken out of the house, obviously.'

'Yep.'

'I still reckon,' Marcie says faintly, 'that they'd take any proposal for you to take over Adam's care into careful consideration.'

'*Do you*, Marcie?' I position the cafetière more securely over the hob, wishing it wouldn't take so long. Everything is taking too long. Even this conversation, which I don't want to have. There is no point. 'You've just highlighted my circumstances, yourself. Even if everything in my life was hunky-dory, wouldn't I have to ... prove I was related to him or some such? They wouldn't just allow the child to be handed over to *any* old ...' my voice catches. 'I'm no one to him, Marcie. I'm just a random guy who stopped to help, that's all. And don't forget, I pretended to people that I was his father. That's not going to look too good to anyone taking the trouble to enquire about it, is it? Be honest.'

'If you want honesty,' she says carefully, 'then my honest opinion is that it wouldn't count against you.'

But Marcie was never brought up in Social Care. I was.

And what does she really know?

Jenna

I spent the day yesterday with Steph and her family. I enjoyed being with them, more than I could have expected. I didn't want to spend too long there, but I didn't want to run away, either. When I got back home to Rochester this lunchtime to find this letter from Adam, I rang Mags straight away.

> Dear Miss,
>
> I don't know if you will get this now. Nate told me you had gone and you are not coming back but I hope somebody will give it to you.
>
> I wanted to say Thank You.
>
> Thank You for noticing me.
>
> Thank You for stopping those boys from hurting me when you were tiching us.
>
> Thank You for helping Nate to help me, even if you di-cided you do not love him.
>
> Thank You for showing him he is brave enuf and he does not need to run home. I think he is very brave and I love him very much too.
>
> From,
> Adam xx

'Hang on a minute.' Mags is confused. And understandably. She thought I was ringing up to hear her say 'Good Luck and Bon voyage' – only to discover that I'm now not going anywhere.

'It's a great little letter, isn't it?' Reading it out loud to her over the phone, it's got me quite choked up. 'That kid Adam, he's one of those who really gets under your skin.'

'It's a lovely letter. But I really have no idea what's going on! When you rang me just now you told me you'd just got back from Hull of all places. I assumed you'd gone up to see your family before leaving for the States but now you tell me you're no longer going?'

'I'm not.'

'You changed your mind because of the child?' Mags sounds a little incredulous.

'I changed my mind because of Nate,' I confess. 'But then I found out he'd been lying to me and I got mad at him, only …'

'Stop! Nate was lying to you about *what?*' My poor friend is still trying to piece the bits together but my life has turned into such a maelstrom in the last few days, no wonder she's confused.

'He's not Adam's father,' I breathe. 'He made out he was because the lad was desperate for a dad, that's all.'

There's a stunned silence for a moment.

'If he's not, then who is?'

'Who knows? I don't think anybody knows. Maybe the mother once knew but she's long dead, that's not the point. The point is … it's not Nate, trust me.'

'So … if you're estranged from Nate, are you changing your mind about *not* going to the States? I mean, can you still go?'

'I can't. After the way I let her down, I doubt Christiane's still holding out much faith in me. Besides …' I catch my breath. 'I don't want to go there.'

'You don't?' I can hear Mags taking a quick gulp of her tea or coffee at the other end of the line. Mags is used to me and my life. The way I change my mind like the wind, turn like a weathervane this way and that, but I think this time I've managed to stun even her.

'I don't want to go because I realise all I'd be doing is the same thing I've always done – running away. Don't you see?'

She gives an affirmative grunt at the other end of the line.

'Well, now I've seen it for myself. It's the issue I've been trying to help Nate with all this time, and yet … I'm not so different to him, in an opposite kind of way.' The kid got it in a nutshell. *'Thank you for showing him he is brave enuf and he does not need to run home.'* 'Nate runs back home. I've been running away from whatever place I make my home.'

'Been telling you that for years, my love.'

'We've both just … got to stop running.'

'So now,' she ventures, 'you're going to go and tell Nate all this?'

'Lord no! I can't do that.'

'Why?'

'I'm back,' I tell her testily. 'That's quite enough for me, right now.' I can't tell her how it churns me up inside, even the *thought* of going back to Nate again. I know Steph pointed out that sometimes lies can be well intentioned, but I'm scared. What if there were even more lies behind the ones he told me? What if he said a lot of things merely to impress, knowing he'd never have to back them up because we were never destined to be an item?

'Adam's enamoured of this guy who's been his hero, but what if Nate really does turn out to have feet of clay?' I point out to her. 'I'd rather not risk it.'

'And *going back* to someone once you've left them is not something you've got any experience in doing,' she helpfully points out.

'I can't,' I tell her. My throat is feeling so full and sore. I can't go back. I just went up to Hull, and what did that prove, really? That everything was all as I'd always thought it was. There was nothing better for me there. I'm the kind of person who's got to move on and never go back. Doesn't she get this?

'This hero Nate, he doesn't have feet of clay, you know.'

'*How can you know that?*' I breathe. 'I always pick the wrong man! Surely you haven't forgotten, Mags – you're usually only too fond of reminding me?'

'I know it,' she comes back patiently, 'because I too, am a man. A fact that *you* are usually only too fond of reminding *me.*'

Touché.

'How about Adam?' she asks softly. 'Will you see him again? Are you planning on going back to work in the school?'

'I'm not going back to St Anthony's,' I tell her. 'So I don't imagine I'll see Adam again, either.'

'Oh,' Mags says. 'I am sorry to hear that.'

After we ring off, I pick up Adam's letter meaning to put it away somewhere, but I read it again, instead.

Thank you for noticing me, Adam says. *Thank you for showing Nate he is brave enuf.* Lord, why does this kid tug at my heart-strings, so? I fold the letter away in my handbag, and then, without thinking, I slip on my shoes again.

I'm back, and I need to pop out and get some bread and milk and while I'm out maybe I'll mosey on down to the nan's house and find out how the kid's doing, not for any specific reason, just to pop in and say hi. And then I will move on.

Jenna

'Miss!' When my favourite pupil opens the door, his eyes light up, so happy is he to see me. 'You're *back?*'

'Just for a little while.' I laugh. 'I came by to say thank you for your lovely letter.'

'My letter. I knew it!' He rushes out and throws his arms about my waist, gives me a hug like he'll never let me go. '*The power of words,*' he murmurs, squashed up tight against me.

'Who's that? Who's there?' The elderly lady's voice coming from inside sounds frightened, wary. 'Adam! Who's that at the door?'

I see the child's face drop immediately. Underneath his happiness at seeing me, the true strain he's under is beginning to show.

'It's all right, Nan,' he calls out. 'It's only Miss Tierney.'

'Only who?' I can hear her shuffling over to see who's come. 'Who's there? Who is it? Tell them to go away!'

'My teacher,' he calls back. 'Don't worry, Nan, it's okay.' To me, he says. 'Are you coming in?'

'Mrs Boxley,' I call out, stepping inside into the dark. 'Oh, are your light switches not working?' I turn to Adam.

'They're working,' he puffs. 'We just don't use them. Too much electric, costs too much.'

'Oh.'

'Who is it?' His nan has reached us. She looks spooked. 'Who're you?' You're not the doctor? He's a man, now.'

356

'The doctor *is* a woman, Nan,' Adam reminds her wearily. Even in this half-light I can see the child's got dark rings under his eyes. 'And this isn't her. This is my *teacher*.'

'Not that woman with the frizzy hair who's come asking if they can take you away?' Mrs Boxley turns to me now, distraught. 'You're not with her?'

'I'm the teacher,' I tell her softly. 'I'm not with her.'

'The woman from the Social, came,' Adam informs me quietly. 'Nate took me to see the doctor and then *she* got in touch with school and then this person came home to see us. She said she had come to look into our home situation.' He goes very quiet all of a sudden.

'Your home situation?' I look from one of them to the other. The house is dark and feels strangely musty. It smells faintly of cat pee. The nan is looking at me very intently, as if she's capable of sussing me out.

'I'll put the kettle on, then,' Mrs Boxley says, suddenly cheerful. 'If you're not from the Social.'

'I'm not.'

'All right then.'

Adam leads me to sit down on the lumpy sofa and I look around, taking it all in.

'You know,' I tell him. 'I've just come back from the place where I grew up, in Hull. My family all live in that same house and it reminds me of this one.'

'Pretty crap then?' he comes straight back.

'Pretty crap,' I agree.

He smiles, unexpectedly. 'You survived, though?'

'Just about.'

He looks around him, taking in his surroundings.

'You never had to go into care, then, Miss?'

I shake my head.

'You were lucky,' he tells me.

I baulk at that. I never saw it that way, but it's true that there are always those who're worse off.

'Is that what they're telling you must happen to you, Adam?'

'To both of us.' He nods towards the kitchen where his nan's just gone to make us tea. 'Her too.' He sounds so sad, he takes my breath away.

'Nan needs to be looked after properly, and they're telling me I must think of her. If I can't do it properly, I must let her go. I've been trying my best, Miss, but ...' His eyes fill with tears.

'What about ...' I get out, barely able to say the words, 'What about ...?'

'Nate?' The child looks directly into my eyes. 'He's not really my dad, Miss. Didn't you know?'

'I ...'

'You do know. That's the reason you got mad at him, isn't it? Because he lied.'

'It's ... complicated, Adam. Maybe one day you'll see it,' I try and explain. 'But if I know one thing, it's that no good relationship can ever be built on a lie.'

'I understand.' He's picking at the loose thread around the bottom of his school jumper, pulling it out further and further. *In a moment*, I think, *he's going to unpick the whole thing.*

'I don't suppose you do.'

'In one way, Miss, Nate wasn't lying at all though, was he?'

'No?'

'He's been everything the best dad could ever be, to me.'

'I suppose he was.'

'What's a dad, really Miss, if not the person who looks out for you, cares for you, *does all the things a dad is supposed to do?*' Adam puffs himself up a little, now, tells me earnestly: 'I know people in my class who'd be envious to have a dad as good as I had in him, even if it was just for a little while.'

'You know, that is actually true.' I smile.

'Nate went to the school after you left, even though he had a panic attack doing it. He went in with me and spoke to The Head and got my suspension lifted,' Adam rushes on. 'Nate told

The Head what's really been happening with those bullies. He made him listen.'

'Did he?' I lean in a little closer. Nate told me this already, but hearing it all again from Adam's viewpoint only reminds me how impressive an act it was. 'So … Nate spoke to The Head on your behalf?'

'Yes. And now The Head's called those boys in and he's spoken to them.'

'I'm frankly … amazed.'

There's a loud crashing sound that comes from the kitchen now and Adam jumps up.

'Don't worry Miss, it's only the tea-tin. I recognise the sound, she keeps doing that, I don't know why. Hold on.' He disappears from view for a while. Longer than I'd have expected him to, but when he comes back, he says,

'Nan didn't boil the kettle. I forgot I took the cord away this morning because I was worried she might burn herself, so she made our tea with cold water. Do you still want some?'

I shake my head.

'Never mind the tea, Adam. Come sit down and finish the story.'

'I've put her to bed, now. It's the tablets, they make her tired, even in the daytime.' He closes the door carefully and comes and sits down beside me.

'You were telling me about The Headmaster,' I say softly, still wondering at how things seemed to have turned around in such a short time. 'So did he tell you himself, he's actually had words with those bully boys? That's reassuring.'

'No.' Adam hangs his head, closing up again.

'No, *what?*' I have to lean in and touch his knee, prompting him to continue.

'The Head didn't tell me he'd had words with the boys. When I went back into school this morning they were there, waiting for me before break had finished. *They* told me about it. And they were very angry.'

359

I stare at him, feeling fear stir in my stomach for the first time. 'Adam, they didn't touch you, did they?'

'No,' he mutters. 'They said they'd be careful not to leave bruises in future, not to leave traces so I couldn't tell tales.' He looks up. 'They were angry that The Head called them in. He called their parents too, after the woman from the Social dropped by to talk to him. He's told them he's had to put everything down in a file, about what's been happening. None of them were happy about it and they've promised they'll get me back at the Sports Day, Miss. Said they'd make it look like an accident, but they were going to teach me, good.'

'Don't go, then!' I look at him, horrified. 'Don't put yourself through that, Adam.'

'I have to go.'

'What for? What'll you prove?'

'That I can face them, Miss. That they're not going to ruin my life using fear. Nate faced his fears for me. He's the only man who's been anything like a dad to me and I still want to make him proud.'

'God, but ...' I blink back the tear that's come into my eyes. I won't be there, doesn't he realise this? I can't support him if they try anything, and I know how tricksy some kids can be. 'You say Nate's going to be there?' I get out.

'He'll be there, Miss. He says he's going to still support me, however he can,' Adam says proudly. The he adds,

'As long as they don't put him in prison, first.'

Nate

Damn it, the woman from the Child Care team – *Children's Services*, I think she called it – is early. I thought she said she'd be here for 4 p.m. not 3 p.m.? The flat's been spruced up for her and I'm all ready for our meeting, but still …

I roll up my cuffs an inch, feeling a sprinkling of nerves in my stomach as I head downstairs. This woman – Susan Gregory – rang me yesterday after I found Adam on the bridge. I thought she was ringing about that, but no, apparently she'd received an urgent call from Adam's GP. She'd been to visit Adam and Vera she told me, and after speaking to them, felt she would very much like to see me. She didn't say why, exactly, and I'm apprehensive about what this could mean for me, no question about that. Rightly or wrongly, I've strung a lot of people along in my attempts to get help for the lad. Schools and local authorities don't like being mucked about in that way. But I'm making no apology about it. None whatsoever. I will tell her so when she comes and then they can take whatever action they see fit.

But when I open the door, it is not Susan Gregory. I take a step back.

'Jen?'

Jenna looks pale and drawn. She looks terribly sad.

'I'd have rung beforehand, but I've misplaced my phone,' she stammers. 'I'm sorry.' She looks at her shoes, and then back at me. 'You seem a bit shocked to see me, Nate.'

361

'I'm not shocked.'

'And you look …' she stops, and I see her doing a double take, perhaps seeing how smartly I'm dressed, 'as if you might already be expecting someone?'

'I am.'

She looks disappointed. 'If you're expecting company then this is horrible timing, obviously. I'm really sorry, Nate, I'll …'

She's already backing off but I put out my hand to touch her arm, briefly.

'It's okay. Somebody is coming here, but … not yet, Jenna.'

'Not yet?'

'Not for an hour, yet.' I take her in cautiously. I haven't seen her since she stormed out of here on Monday and a lot has happened since then. For her too, I'm guessing. She's still as gorgeous as ever but there's no hiding that she's been through the mill since I saw her last. My heart sinks. Is it because of me? Is it because she's felt duty-bound to tell the school about me, what my real status is? If that's so I know it will have cost her, too. She won't have been happy to do that.

'It's okay.' I move back a little, making space for her to enter. 'You coming in, then?'

'You sure? Please don't feel that you have to …'

'I don't.'

Jen's almost hugging herself as she walks through the door and up the stairs, her eyes so full of remorse I wish I could put my arms around her, tell her that she doesn't need to fret. The woman from Children's Services will be en route by now. Whatever's coming my way as a result of what I did, I already know I'm going to have to account for it, it doesn't matter anymore. The only thing that matters now, is – Jenna is back.

'I'm so sorry, Nate.' She turns to me as soon as we're inside my flat. 'I wanted to let you know that.'

I indicate my sofa. *Will you sit down?* She gives a small, brief, shake of her head.

'Thank you, but no. I'm not staying.' I see her gaze go once again, almost involuntarily, to what I'm wearing: the starched, buttoned-up shirt, the smart chinos. 'You're looking good.' she says softly, a hint of regret in her voice. 'But you're expecting company and ...'

'She isn't due yet,' I repeat. *What if I could postpone the woman from Children's Services?* I can't, I know, but this timing sucks. 'Not for another hour.'

'Isn't she?' Jen sidles over to the edge of the couch and then, after a moment's hesitation, she sits down on the edge of it.

'Can I offer you some ...?'

'No,' she says abruptly. 'You're okay. I don't need anything and I don't want to put you out. I only came because I wanted to tell you I'm sorry.'

'And now you've said it, Jen.' Twice. But there was really no need to. I come over and lower myself gingerly onto the couch beside her, achingly aware of the empty seat between us.

'I wanted to apologise for walking out on you, the way I did,' she hurries on. 'You didn't deserve that.'

I give a small nod.

'Thank you.'

'I walked out in a panic,' she admits. 'I see now it was a brave thing, you did, even if it was a wrong thing. And that you did it for all the right reasons.'

'I did it for him.'

'I know.' She pulls in a breath. 'I only took it so badly because of my own past experiences, Nate.'

'I understand.'

'I've always done it. Got out of situations before the other person could abandon me.'

I blink.

'I'm sorry, did you just say "Before *they* could abandon ...?"'

'I took the train up to Hull after I left you on Monday,' she runs on in a small voice.

Okay. I sit back a little.

'You went back home to see your family?' I'm trying not to let the surprise register on my face. I know, more from all the things Jen hasn't said than what she has, that her relationship with her own people is strained.

'Only my sister was there. But she reminded me what we're like, us Tierneys. None of us too lucky in love, needless to say.' Jen gives a quiet laugh. 'And if you already know that it's all going to go wrong, then what's the point of …?' She doesn't finish that sentence. 'Oh, Nate. I can't tell you how many times I've imagined myself to be madly in love with a guy only to … to …' she trails off, staring at her hands, her face going very red. But I'm so struck by what she just said I can't think of anything else right now.

Did you imagine yourself to be in love with me, too?

'Only to …?' I prompt, not wanting her to stop speaking, wishing she'd carry on and say the rest of it, *how she'd been feeling about me,* before she found out about my real connection to Adam.

Jen throws up her hands a little.

'Only to have the guy cheat on me, or to find out later he'd been lying about something.'

'I'd never have cheated on you, Jen.' I move in a smidgeon closer. 'I'd never have lied to you, either.'

'I know that now.' Her voice is full of regret. 'And I realise you were never expecting me to change my mind about going to the States.'

I throw her a small smile.

'I can't believe you did that.' Especially, I can't believe she did it so she could be with *me.*

She pulls a rueful face.

'I can't believe I did it, either.'

'D'you regret it?'

'Not as much as I regret running out on you.'

I hold her gaze for a second.

'Jen, be honest with me,' I get out, hardly daring to hope. 'Are you saying now that you wish we could have …?' I glance at my watch, wondering how much time we've got left before this Susan

Gregory woman turns up and demands to know *what I thought I was doing, pretending to be the lad's father?*

'It's half past three,' Jen tell me hoarsely. She sits up a little straighter, now, her eyes narrowing slightly.

'Half past, thank you. It's just that I was …'

'You're waiting for someone else to show. I realise that.'

'I wasn't looking at my watch because I can't wait for her to get here, Jen!'

'Don't worry. It's not as if I'm here to try and resurrect any of what we had going,' Jenna rushes on, picking up her handbag.'

'Aren't you?'

The girl with the Titian hair sits back a little. For the first time since I've known her she has no immediate answer for me.

And then the penny drops.

'The woman I'm waiting for isn't a *date*, Jen.'

The look on her face is a picture but it's quickly followed up with an embarrassed cough as if she realises how relieved she must look.

'I came here to apologise,' she comes back stiffly. 'I already explained that.'

'You already did that right at the start.' I lean in a little closer and she doesn't try and move away. 'You know, you've helped me in so many ways. More than I can say, lovely girl, but you're not very good at saying sorry, are you?'

'I'm sorry if my *sorry* isn't good enough,' she says, huffily. But she sounds sad, really sad, and it dawns on me that maybe this is the real thing she's been running from all her life: not so much abandonment, as she thinks – but the fear that once something's gone wrong, she won't be able to find any way back?

She makes a half-hearted attempt to stand up but I tug at her hand.

'Don't fly away, Jenny-Wren. Don't do the same thing all over.'

'What do you …?'

'When things start to go wrong with people, you get out. By your own admission, you never stick around long enough to find out if things can be resolved.'

365

'What's wrong with that? I get out before they get another chance to hurt me, that's all.'

I give a small shake of my head.

'That's not the reason, Jen. All men get it wrong sometimes. Women too! Any man you're ever going to be with is going to hurt you at some point, and you'll do the same to him. I, for one, was hurting like hell after you walked out, Monday.'

Her eyes are glittering but she's still listening to me, for once, not going anywhere.

'Were you really?'

'More than I can tell you.'

And I see that I am right. She's actually terrified, this fierce and fearless one; terrified that when things go wrong, there won't be a way, and that a heartfelt, truly intended 'sorry' won't ever be enough to put it right.

But she's wrong.

'What else do you want me to do, Nate Hardman?'

'Just this. Stay.' When I lean in to cover Jen's mouth with my own, what I've been aching to do ever since she walked in, she doesn't resist and she doesn't try to leave and she doesn't have anything else to say.

At this moment, neither of us need to say anything.

Jenna

'No need to be so nervous, Nate.' We've been cuddling together on the sofa but he's just moved a little apart from me, his face set and serious.

'You sure about that?'

I sit up. It's five minutes to four. His visitor will be here any minute, so he might as well get his head in gear.

'That social worker lady isn't coming here to cart *you* off.'

He pulls a pained smile.

'What's she going to ask me, though? What if I answer all the wrong things and the boy ends up realising his worst nightmare?'

I consider that for a moment. Leaving aside the nightmare bit,

'What she wants to ask you will depend on why she's coming. You told me you went to see Adam's GP with Vera. You were also the person who alerted the police when he went missing last night – they'll be interested in exploring your relationship with the boy, I imagine.'

Nate practically cringes.

'And how exactly am I going to answer that one without landing myself in hot water, Jen?'

'I don't …'

The trill of his landline stops us both dead in our tracks.

'You think that could be her, ringing to cancel?' I breathe.

Nate shakes his head.

'Na. There's no way Susan Gregory is cancelling. She was adamant about me seeing her today as a matter of urgency. Besides, I *need* to see her.' His head drops into his hands for a moment and I sense his air of defeat. We both look towards the phone but neither of us makes a move. Is he going to let it go to answer-phone? It is, literally, his call.

'Someone needs to be talking about this kid,' he asserts now. '*Someone* needs to be sitting up and paying attention to all the shit that's going down in his life. He hasn't got anyone else to speak for him, Jen. I've got to be his voice.'

'You've already been more than a voice for him,' I remind Nate quietly. 'You've been ... you've been his dad, haven't you?'

'I wish I could have been his dad.' He looks up at me with haunted eyes. 'Wouldn't that have made the next part so much easier? He could have come to live here with me if the nan has to go into care.'

I nod at him now, feeling the smile growing inside me at how much this guy loves that little lad.

'You've got a big heart, Nate.'

'Maybe I ... don't have the biggest flat in the world, or the biggest pay cheque, to offer him. But having that boy around has totally changed my life.'

'I'm sure you've changed his.'

I glance at the phone, which is still ringing. Could it be the social worker, wanting to find out where exactly he lives, down the High Street? Nate doesn't seem too concerned about answering it, his thoughts still tangled elsewhere.

'When I found Adam on Rochester Bridge last night,' his voice is strangled, 'I can't tell you ... I saw my own life flash before me. I thought he was going to *jump*. And I knew ... if he jumped, I'd have to jump in after him.'

'Would you?' I shiver. Nate's only filled me in on the bridge episode briefly but it sounded hairy enough. 'You'd have gone in after him, really? Risked your own life?'

'When I saw him sitting there, I knew I'd have followed him in without a second thought if I had to. Adam deserves a chance, Jen. He's a good kid. He deserves to have someone there who'd risk everything for him.'

'Hey,' I say, as his face crumples, 'it's okay.'

'It's *not* okay though, is it?' Nate stares at the phone which is still, insistently, ringing. 'The poor lad's desperate not to go into care. It's why he came to me in the first place. It's what I picked up in his letter and then again, first time he came to the door, begging me to go to see you at the school. It's why I *pretended* to be his father, in the first place. However, when this woman ...' he's still looking at the phone, 'when she comes here to see me today, what d'you think she's going to make of that?'

I shrug.

'Maybe not what you think.'

'Give over. You know what they'll think the minute they find out what I did. I'm not even really a family friend.'

'Maybe you weren't at the beginning,' I point out. 'There's no one who wouldn't judge you to be one, now. Not after all you've done for him. *Nate*,' I coax gently. 'Don't you think you'd better pick that up? Just in case it's her?'

I watch as he reluctantly picks up the handset.

'Hello?' The expression on his face changes, swiftly, from one of reluctance, to one of horror. Shit. *What's happening now?* Nate looks towards the door.

She's out there, he indicates with his finger. He doesn't move.

'She's ...?' I get up, unsurely. Does he mean the social worker is? I never heard the bell going. Is she waiting downstairs and the doorbell's broken?

'Hello, there. Susan Gregory. Downstairs was open so I thought it would be okay to come up ...' The woman immediately on the other side of the flat door greets me with a firm, warm handshake the minute I open up.

'Oh.' I step back a little.

'Sorry to catch you by surprise. She glances down the stairwell. *Hell, did I leave the door open, when I came in?* "I used the phone in the end because nobody seemed to be able to hear my knocking up here?"

I look back towards Nate.

'Sorry,' he says in a thick voice. 'We didn't hear you knocking, there.' The look on his face, when he glances at me, asks the question; *how long has she been standing outside?*

'That's okay.' She ventures in a little. 'I didn't like to interrupt. The two of you did seem to be very deep in conversation.'

I can feel my face going pink, but Nate's a trooper.

'Hello, then. I'm Nate Hardman.' He's up in a trice to greet her. 'And this is ... Jenna Tierney. She's been teaching Adam at his school.'

'Pleased to meet you.' She's been addressing both of us but she turns to me now, 'Adams's teacher, you say? That's very helpful of you to be here. I'd very much appreciate a chance to chat with you too, if you're staying, that is?'

'Well I ... I could.' I look to Nate for confirmation. Does he want me here? He gives me a brief nod, but his attention's all on her, now. And since Susan Gregory has come in, she's barely taken her open, smiling eyes off him for one second. I don't know how much she's just overheard but the look on her face, not to put too fine a point on it, is nothing short of admiration. *Crap, though!* Did she hear what Nate said about him having pretended to be Adam's father? Did she hear what he said about him being prepared to jump off Rochester Bridge? I feel the backs of my knees go cold.

'Thank you so much for agreeing to see me at such short notice,' she says to Nate.

'You're very welcome.'

'And may I say, this is a very nice flat you've got here, Mr Hardman.' She's looking about, taking it all in with a clearly practised eye.

'Thank you. It's not that big, but it does the job.' I can feel the surprise in his answer, but he's probably thinking, like me, that

370

she's used to this kind of thing; small talk that eases people into a comfortable space. In a moment, she'll be segueing onto how he knows the child, maybe even – depending on how much she knows or has maybe just overheard – onto how well he actually knows the family, and so forth. How *would* the authorities be inclined to view what Nate did, in reality? She's beaming at him but when she knows the truth, she might take a dim view of it. I've been working to calm him down for the last twenty minutes, but now I feel a flash of worry, deep in my own gut.

'Near all local amenities too, *and* the school, I noticed that on the way down.' She's still smiling, as he offers her a seat.

'Would you mind very much if I asked you; has it got one bedroom, or two?'

Jenna

'Miss Tierney. Just finishing off the rota for Sports Day,' Mr Drummond is busy at his computer when I knock on his door. He looks up, a satisfied look on his face. 'Almost there, I think.'

'May I come in?'

'Certainly.' He indicates the chair opposite his desk, obviously curious. 'I heard from our school receptionist on Monday that you'd decided against leaving Rochester after all?'

'It's true.'

'If you're here for that job we were advertising, it's gone, I'm afraid.'

I bite my lip.

'I'm not here about the job, Mr Drummond.'

His fingers push the keyboard away from him, slightly.

'No? So, to what do we owe the pleasure?'

'I'm here about Adam Boxley.'

'Adam *Boxley*.' He pushes back in his computer chair, clearly agitated at even the mention of the name. 'I do believe he's not any of your concern, anymore, Miss Tierney.' His narrow, light blue eyes meet mine with a little more hostility in them now.

'And yet, I do still have concerns about him.'

'You and the world and his wife, Miss Tierney!' The Head gets up abruptly and goes to stand in front of an army-green metal cabinet file holder. From the back, his shoulders look all stiff and square to me. He looks overburdened and stubborn and unhelpful. 'Tell me. How is that lad still your business?'

I swallow.

'I think, you might soon have a bit of a problem on your hands, Mr Drummond.'

He swivels round, briefly pausing rummaging inside the cabinet. 'A problem. Regarding Adam?'

'You've got Sports Day coming up,' I remind him. 'He's determined to take part in it, but ...' I draw in a breath, anticipating how well The Head's going to take my next point. 'Those boys who've hurt him before have threatened to get revenge on him for telling on them. They mentioned the Sports Day in particular. I'm worried Adam's going to get hurt again.'

Am I wrong, or has his face just turned a little puce?

'I think that's most likely to be a lot of hot air on their part. I appreciate that you're worried about Adam. A whole host of people are suddenly worried about *Adam.*' Mr Drummond is clearly annoyed. 'I'll be frank with you, Miss Tierney. I have five – maybe six – days a week, that I allocate to running this school of 500 pupils, all of them equally deserving of my care and yet this week, this one lad has already taken up practically two and a half days of it!'

'I'm sorry,' I tell him evenly.

'And I have Sports Day to prepare for, as you just said.'

'I know. That's why I'm ...'

'You do realise, I haven't just had his GP ringing The Office with her concerns – and that's practically unheard of – I've had his social worker Susan Gregory breathing down my neck. I had his father who's just stepped out of the woodwork down here on Monday, getting him off the fixed period exclusion I put in place before the half-term and now you. Frankly, I'm done with it.'

'I can see why you'd like to be,' I agree. If all these issues are coming home to roost regarding the bullying Mr Drummond usually turns a blind eye to, I can totally see why he'd like to be *done* with it. But I'm not done with him, yet.

'You can see where I'm coming from, can't you?' He pulls out a folder with Adam's name on it. 'Look at the size of that file, Miss Tierney! All of it evidence we've had to pull together since Tuesday, for Susan Gregory's benefit.' When he speaks her name I can tell she's not his most favourite person in the world. 'Could have done with having *you* around this week,' he shoots at me now. 'You being the most recent teacher he's had contact with. Tell me.' He throws the unopened folder on his desk and returns to his seat, something of an air of defeat about his shoulders. 'What's going on here with that boy?'

'What's going on.' I look him straight in the eye. 'Is the last few weeks have been the first time in Adam's life anyone's ever sat up and really noticed he's there.'

He looks at me in surprise.

'Well. I'm sorry if you feel the school weren't doing a good enough job, before you appeared on the scene.'

'You weren't.'

'We may have overlooked a few things, granted.'

'You overlooked a lot of things, Mr Drummond. The fact that the child missed out on so many days schooling so he could look after his nan, for one. The fact that nobody ever returned any permission forms sent home for day-trips and outings so that he's missed out on practically *everything*. The fact the absence of a regular class teacher has meant no one noticed how far behind he was falling with his work. The fact that those bullies in Year Six could intimidate him for such a long time and no one ever saw or put a stop to it …'

'Steady on,' he says. 'We're doing all that we can now that the matter's been drawn to our attention.' He looks hurt. 'We may be guilty of some failings, but we can't be blamed for everything.' He pauses, and then he adds, 'I've got a whole file of statements put together by members of staff who've known him throughout his time with us and Boxley's always been a loner. He's a quiet lad, who's kept himself to himself by all accounts, making it all the more difficult for us to …'

'Hardly surprising under the circumstances, you'll agree?'

'Of course.' He clears his throat. 'And then again, his attendance record's not always been brilliant. Now of course we understand,' he concedes, 'the home issues that account for those little anomalies.'

'Home issues that were no fault of his own,' I assert. 'Issues that could have been picked up by any competent class teacher if he'd had one.'

'True.' His face darkens now. 'But don't let your fondness for the lad cloud your judgement completely, Miss Tierney. He's had his fair share of troubles, but if we're being completely honest here, he does have a tendency at times to *bring it upon himself, doesn't he?*'

'Excuse me?' I'm not here to fight with the man, but I can feel my face going red. 'Let's not even go there, Mr Drummond.'

The Head sits back in his chair, fingers clasped together in front of him.

'The lad's well known to be a petty thief, a magpie at best.'

'That's untrue. Adam is *not* a ...' I stare as he tips open the folder now and out fall all sorts of bits and bobs; a decorated curtain ring that I recognise from photos of 4C's Christmas play last year, a notepad with a picture of a blissful pigeon on it, monogrammed JT, that Alessandro's sister gave me last Christmas, a few other insignificant trinkets that I don't recognise and last but not least, my little travelling companion Bertie bear.

'Yours?' He's watching my face closely. 'I thought so.'

I pick ted up, automatically stroking his soft blue fur and a lump comes into my throat. Bertie Bear who's gone everywhere I've gone since the day I left home at sixteen; only thing I took with me, in fact, other than an open heart and a vow to live my life to the fullest, away from my dreary home in Hull. I brought him in one day for a Show And Tell lesson for the class.

What's he doing, stuck in a file in The Headmaster's office?

'You recognise at least some of these other items too, I take it?' I nod dumbly.

'Staff found this hoard of stolen stuff in Adam's locker before the end of half-term. I showed it to his social worker, naturally,'

The Head assures me. 'It's important she recognises that the lad's not a total innocent at the end of the day.'

I hold Bertie to my chest, feeling the sadness and the anger rise equally as it dawns on me; he's come to a full stop and so have I. Now that I've stopped running away from all those things I haven't wanted to face, what am I left with? The discomfort of having to face them, that's what.

'All this evidence you've been so busy putting together isn't for *Susan Gregory's* benefit.' I point at the folder, my finger trembling with anger. 'It isn't even for Adam's benefit, is it?'

'I'm not following you.'

'It's all for yours, Mr Drummond! You've failed this child and you're covering your own backs.'

The Head looks astounded.

'That is completely wrong, Miss Tierney.'

'All these are just petty, made-up allegations and attempts to besmirch him, that's all this is.'

'No.' He's shaking his head rapidly, gathering the rest of Adam's little hoard into a pile. I notice he doesn't put them back in the folder.

'No?'

'You've never approved of the way I've run my school, have you, Jenna?' His eyes are glittering dangerously. 'From the very first day you walked in here and I didn't react the way you wanted me to regarding the boys you kept waiting outside – you made your judgements there and then.'

'You're right. I didn't like what I saw,' I throw back at him. 'I thought you were only interested in your sporting heroes and you had no time at all for any of the lesser talented ones. I thought you were an overbearing, easily blind-sided man and every single thing I've learned about Adam's case since I've been here has borne that out.'

Mr Drummond's mouth drops open.

'*None* of these items are stolen, Mr Drummond.'

'I'm sorry? That ... that blue bear – that at least, is yours, I take it? And the monogrammed note pad?'

'I let Adam have them. He asked me for something that was mine, before I left. I gave him those things but none of you thought to ask about that, did you? You had to make him bad in some way because you failed him. You failed him, Mr Drummond, and it's about time you owned up to that, completely and unreservedly.'

The Head pauses in his stride and for the first time I see him actually taking something in. The information goes down with difficulty; like a snake swallowing a small pig, slowly, ostensibly painfully.

'Oh.' Mr Drummond says stiffly. 'In that case, I have maligned the lad on that score. He didn't steal the items?'

'No.'

'Then I will, of course, let his social worker know.' He leans forward, his hand to his mouth.

'Will you?' I breathe. I look up at him, feeling all my anger falling away as if by magic. He's *admitting* to his error? I hadn't expected that, somehow.

'You really think I've only got time for the sporting heroes?' he asks unexpectedly.

'You do prioritise them, and you could do with putting your head above the parapet at times, but ...' When I think back on all the activities the school's involved in, I know I've probably judged him harshly. 'You're all right. You *aren't* the total bureaucrat I took you to be when I first came here.'

'Wow.' He almost chokes. 'High praise, I think, coming from you.'

'I judged you too quickly. And I shouldn't have called you overbearing,' I allow. 'I apologise for that.'

He looks directly at me now.

'It's a long time since anyone called me out on anything. Maybe it was overdue?'

'Still, I shouldn't have been so rude.'

He waves my apology away with his hand and now I feel like a real heel. The man seems genuinely upset.

'And ... *thank you*,' I say, my voice a lot calmer. 'For what you've admitted to, today. That's important.'

He's still looking rather shell-shocked.

'Thank *you*,' he counters. 'For coming to me with the information that you have.'

'You mean about what those boys are planning?'

'Indeed. Your own personal thoughts on me I'm a little less grateful to hear.' He stands up. 'Thank you for trusting me with it.'

I swallow. Is that it? Am I supposed to leave, now? *Do I really trust him with it?*

'That won't have come easy to a person like you, I know.' The Head is smiling tightly.

'A person like ...?'

'Someone who doesn't conform naturally to the authority structures that must exist within any effective school establishment.'

I blink.

'I guess I don't,' I admit. That's true enough. If he knew my background he might understand why that is. 'I never saw much justice myself, in the schools I attended in my own youth.'

'And yet you elected to become a teacher?'

I shrug.

'I hoped to make a difference, once.'

'You could have, too.' He gives a small disparaging laugh. 'I know my traditional, old-school style of management doesn't sit well with your own views. You think I run a dodgy ship here, with bullies running amok at every turn?'

'Far from it,' I allow, now. 'Most of the children at St Anthony's are happy and settled, I've seen that for myself. It's just that ... with Miss Cheska being off so much last year, 4C have got neglected. The most vulnerable child of all in this school has fallen prey to that. Those older boys never touched him when I was on supply, you notice?'

He opens the door for me now.

'No, they didn't, did they?' He's looking at me thoughtfully. 'Perhaps you still could make a difference, Jenna? If you decided that was what you wanted to do?'

'I'm not sure that it is. Besides …' I hesitate, 'I thought you said that position was taken?'

He smiles. 'We've all been so busy. Who knows if that offer email got sent off to that other applicant this morning? With Sports Day coming up tomorrow, anything could happen, yet.'

It could. That's what I've been worried about.

But maybe it's time I stopped worrying.

Nate

'After I've spent half the night awake worrying about *that lot*, I guess we got lucky, after all.'

Adam indicates the Marshals Area behind us, where all the Year Sixes have been kitted out with yellow tunics, whistles, flags and measuring tapes – this year, they've all been declared 'referees'. I recognise a couple of Adam's enemies among the strutting yellow tunics.

'You did. They'll be too busy showing off how 'responsible' they are to get up to any mischief as far as you're concerned,' I tell him. Lucky break for us, that the Head made that decision, in the end. If Jenna had anything to do with it, she's nowhere in sight, but right now we've got a more pressing matter to worry about.

We need to make our way over to Area B. Our race is about to start.

'Your legs are making too big strides, Nate! I can't keep up.'

'Shall we take this a bit slower, then?' When I glance over at Adam's face, it's gone all red and earnest. I thought he wanted to win. Whoever dreamed up the idea of a parent-child three-legged race should be brought in front of a teacher's tribunal and court-marshalled. All right if your kid happens to be a giant and you're a four-foot midget, but with our disparity in height …

'If we take the race slower,' he hisses, 'we aren't going to win, are we?'

'Will it be the end of the world,' I ask cautiously, 'if we don't?'

'You know that it will be,' he growls mutinously. 'I *have* to win, today.'

'Why?'

'We've gotta win *because*,' Adam explains, exasperated. 'This is the only chance I'm ever going to get. You're here. Nan's here. Nobody's ever come to see me at a Sports Day before, Nate. *I've got to win.*'

Okay, so he's a bloke, like me. Winning is important to us, I understand that. I'd just prefer to see him chilled out a little more, actually enjoying this. But right now I don't think he is.

'We'll do our best, but I think the general idea is that you just have fun, Buddy.'

We've aligned ourselves carefully on the starting line. Eight other parent-child couples have hop-skipped themselves into place and when I check out the opposition, most of them have got big smiles on their faces.

'Lighten up, Kid.' I nudge him. 'My money's on that slim brunette with her lanky daughter on the end.'

Adam's looking around us, straining to see into the crowd. Looking for someone else? I know I am, but I don't spot her, either. Where's Jen got to, today? *Where's she got to?* She knew I was going to be here with Adam. She might have at least showed up to cheer for us. But we have no time to worry about that, now. Adam turns back to the front, his face set and determined.

'You reckon they'll win?'

'Size-wise, they're the most perfectly matched,' I point out.

'I think the beefy guy with his son – in the middle – they're the ones to watch.'

Glancing over, I see the kid could have a point.

'If we win, I will buy us each one of those ices from the cold drinks stand.'

'Thank you,' he says solemnly.

'If we don't win, I will buy us one anyway.'

'Okay, then.' My lad clenches his fists at his side. 'Let's *do* this.'

A tall girl blows the whistle. A smiling ginger boy drops the flag and now – we're off! A muted cheer goes up, a ripple of excitement spreading through the watching bystanders as the clear favourite, perfectly matched Lanky and her mum, take the lead and the race is on. Sweaty Beefy guy gives his son a dig in the ribs and they're inching a little closer to us even though we've made a brave start. It doesn't matter. Adam's legs and mine, uneven lengths and strengths, can still work well in tandem. Adam throws himself into greater speed to make up for his lack of stride, I match my stride to his shorter one, and after a while – we're into a rhythm! A crooked grin breaks over his determined face. I throw back my head and laugh. How long is it since I ran across a field of yellowing grass sprinkled with buttercups, the long afternoon blue and white and golden, the promise of a winner's medal at the end of a hundred yard's dash?

I don't know how long. Maybe I never did. Not with *anyone who mattered* there to note my prowess, but now Adam's here for me. I'm here for him. If we keep this up, I realise with a modicum of glee, we're even going to place second.

Just past the midway point, I cop of view of his nan, who's been pushed to the front. As we pass, Vera – seated like a queen on the fancy wheelchair provided by Adult Care Services especially for today – hoots loudly in our direction, waving a flag for the 'Year Four Three-Legged-Race Team'. I spy Susan Gregory, along with her colleague who's been pushing Nan's wheelchair, smiling in our direction. I see that Adam's spotted them too, and my heart swells with pride for him. Suddenly, I really want us to make second place. For him. For me. We won't make first, but second's respectable. Second is an honourable placement with a little room for improvement, right?

And then it happens. Just after we pass them. The kid had been relaxing, getting into his stride and starting to enjoy himself, but the sight of that little trio has fazed him. His expression changes. He starts to falter.

'Nate,' he says. 'What's she doing here?'

'Who?'

'Her. The social worker. What's she doing here?'

'Bud.' I puff. 'She's just come to help bring your nan along and to support you, that's all.'

'Why? I don't want her here. She's ruined it.'

'What d'you mean, she's …'

We stagger on a few more paces but his eyes are bulging. Is it the stress of the last few days, the difficulty of the race?

'Don't you get it?' He pulls at my arms suddenly, stopping us both mid-race. '*I don't want her here!*'

'You don't?' I come to a clumsy halt beside him, almost tripping over him now.

'*Argh!*' He grips at his ankle as his outer leg twists and we both fly, sprawling, onto the field. It's clearly over. This race is over for us.

'You okay, Buddy Boy?'

For a few seconds after he straightens up, extricating his leg from mine, Adam just sits there, rubbing his ankle, looking shocked. The retreating backs in front of us get further and further away. A few dandelion heads bounce across the grass. The crowd roars as Lanky and well-matched mum take it, as predicted.

When we limp over to the First Aid tent, it's shady and quiet inside. There's currently no one else there. I ease him onto a chair.

'She ruined it, Nate,' he says mutinously.

'How?' I've found a cool-aid bandage. 'Here. I'm just gonna apply this to your ankle to get the swelling down.'

'By *being* here.' He's deliberately avoiding my eye. 'You'd think she was the one who always took my nan out places, the way she was acting.'

'I'm not sure I understand what you mean.'

'Pushing Nan's chair, and getting her a cup of tea and such …'

'I'm sure those were just acts of kindness, no harm intended, Adam.' I shoot him a sideways glance. 'Why shouldn't she do those things for Vera?'

'Because ... because that's *my* job,' he blurts out.

I stop what I'm doing, wrapping an outer bandage round the cool bit.

'That's *been* your job,' I agree carefully. 'But all that's going to change now.' I tap him on the knee so he gives me some eye contact. 'You knew that. How else could things start to get better for you?'

'I don't know.' He hangs his head and I see a tear drop onto his nose. 'I'm going to *miss* her, Nate. She's the only person who's been there for me, all my life. And I'm worried that they won't look after her as well as I did, if I let them send her away.'

I take in a breath.

'It's gone well past the point of us having any choice on that score, Buddy. She *is* going into care. She needs to. You need her to. You've no need to feel guilty about it.'

I pull a tissue out of the box on the table and hand it to him.

'What if ... if I had never written you that letter, though?' He's looking at me with haunted eyes. 'You'd never have come into our lives. Nan and me – we'd have been able to stay together, wouldn't we?'

'I guess, that's true.' I tap his leg so he lifts it up onto the table to elevate it for a few minutes. 'But people would have found out, eventually, one way or the other.' I screw up my forehead, turning my face away. 'Only maybe, by then, it would have been too late for you.'

'Too late – how?'

'I had a brother once.' A thin pain shoots right across my head. 'We'll talk about him more another time, you and I, but for now I'll only say this; nobody ever noticed him, either. Only I did, and I wasn't in any position to help him. Nobody ever noticed my brother Mo had severe problems coping till it was way too late.'

'Your brother didn't make it,' he says. His brow is furrowed, putting two and two together. 'I suppose the day I first sent you that letter – I must have reminded you of him? When you read it, you must have been worried that maybe, I wouldn't make it, either?'

I don't answer that. I don't have to. He blows noisily into the tissue I've just handed him.

'In that case, I'm sorry for throwing the race, Nate. I could see that you really wanted to win.'

I give a short laugh.

'I did. But sometimes when you win – even when you win *big time*.' I throw him a significant look. 'Like, when you get that thing you've been longing and wishing for, forever … you have to be prepared to lose something important, too.'

'I have to lose … you mean, like me now? I have to give up being Nan's Carer. That's what you're saying, isn't it? I have to be prepared to stop being the person who she needs the most?'

Man, he's quick on the uptake, this kid.

'And in return I gain … a dad?'

'And I gain you.'

'Did you *want* me?' His eyes narrow. 'Was having *someone like me* around, the thing you'd been longing and dreaming for in your life, Nate?'

I stop and consider that for a bit, feeling the ache of disappointment in my stomach. It's a reprise of the feelings I've been pushing away all week. I haven't forgotten how to dream.

'No.' I need to be honest with him. 'You weren't, at all. My last girlfriend left me because I wouldn't settle down to have a family. I'm twenty-seven years old, and I still want a job that'll stimulate me and pay the bills. I want to travel more, and laugh more and go out and do all those crazy things you can only do before you get tied down with looking after a kid.'

Adam's eyes are opening wider in hurt and surprise.

'You *didn't* want to be a dad?' he stutters. He's imagined otherwise, clearly. He takes his foot down off the table, stands up now, and I catch a glint of hurt pride in his actions. Boy, he's a lot like Jenna, this one. They're going to get along famously once all these tangled knots are sorted.

'I didn't,' I admit. 'Not a hint of it. And then *you* came along.'

385

Adam's chin goes up a fraction. He lifts his foot, taking the weight off his ankle.

'I came along, and …?'

'And then everything changed.' I open out my hands. 'I started off meaning to help you and get out, get on with my life but … the more you came to matter, the more you helped to heal all the things that had gone wrong with *me*. The fact is,' my voice goes thick, now. 'I've come to love you, Adam Boxley. Like my own son. Like the child I never thought I wanted and yet … here I am. I do.'

He sits back down again.

'If you take me on,' he says thoughtfully, 'how're you going to fulfil all those other dreams you've just told me about, like – doing your war-reporting job and travelling and stuff? I'll tie you down, Nate. Even if I matter to you, after a while that's going to be a drag.' The kid looks forlorn. He knows what he's talking about. After all, he's had the care of his nan most of his life.

'I can't do some of those things – like the war reporting – I won't. My life's going to change, I know that.' I lean over and grab him by the arm. 'It's already changed beyond what I could imagine and d'you know what? I'm happy. I'm ready for it! I don't want my old life back, I want this new one with you in it.'

'Are they going to let you?' he asks cautiously.

'Your social worker has told me that she'd have no hesitation recommending they allow Vera's wish for me to take over your care to go ahead.'

I see him swallow. 'For real?'

'She made up her mind pretty rapidly. There's a gamut of formalities to run through; completion of a police check, disclosure of finances etc, but it's going to happen.'

'And …' he asks hesitantly. 'Nobody's mad at you for *pretending* to be my dad all that time?'

I shake my head. Miraculously, I am not in any trouble.

'Everyone's glossed the issue over,' I admit. I'm as surprised as he is, but, 'Susan Gregory accidentally overheard me speaking to

Jenna about you when she came to my flat – she realised I only ever wanted to help you and they're all confident that I acted in good faith. Jen's given me a glowing report, and as your nan and you are so keen, it's agreed I'd be the perfect candidate.'

'You are,' he says. He's not frowning anymore. He's only looking sad, and very relieved.

'Maybe one day when you and Jen get together, you can become my dad for real?'

I swallow. 'Maybe.'

'Where is she, anyway?'

I get up and tidy away the scissors and the remains of the bandage I just used, as much to get away from his scrutiny as anything else. Jenna found her phone – battery completely dead – in between the seat cushions of my couch but she hasn't answered the text I sent this morning. Maybe she hasn't charged it yet?

'I know she went to see The Head yesterday, Adam. But between all the visits and arrangements for you that've suddenly come my way, Jenna and I haven't had much chance to make contact.' I put my head down, aware of a growing disappointment.

I don't know where she is. I'd half expected – *hoped* – we might see Jenna here today, but she's full of surprises, a law unto herself, that one. Despite our reconciliation, right now I have no idea what her plans are; whether she means to stay, or whether she's preparing to take flight once again like the impetuous little bird that she is.

I am clear only on the thing that I have committed to do for Adam. As for what I'd love to happen between Jenna and me ...

The rest is up to her.

Jenna

'Hey, guys!' When I lift up the First Aid tent flap, the first thing that occurs to me is; *these two look so natural together.* A man and his son, that's what they could be: truly, biologically, the strength of love and affection between them, indisputable. I get a warm and fuzzy feeling seeing them, and it's immediately chased by a strange sense of emptiness that I cannot explain.

'Miss!' Adam is over the moon.

'Hey.' Nate's all smiles to see me, relieved. He's got his arm around Adam's shoulder, helping him to his feet. The lad looks sticky and hot and red about the eyes as if he's been crying. He fell during the race, I heard. He must have got hurt and Nate brought him in here to sort him out. Job done, it looks as if they were about to make their way out.

'So it's true.' I peer at Adam's foot. 'I heard you two had been in the wars.'

'This is nothing,' he reassures me staunchly.

I kneel down to inspect his bandaged ankle. His oversized PE shorts – I recognise them, on permanent loan to him from 'lost property' – are tattered at the seams, muddy from where he went down on the field. His T-shirt today smells vaguely musty, as if it's been sourced from the same pile, but despite all that there's still an air of something fresh about him. A sense that someone, at long last, is putting in the care and attention this child needs.

'I've been in the wars all my life, Miss.'

'You have,' I acknowledge, my throat aching to say it. 'But you're about to come through that, I hear?'

When I glance back over to Nate, I catch his dark brown eyes, thoughtful, on me. He's taking in my yellow 'Marshal' tunic, wondering if I'm back at the school, perhaps?

'How about you, Jen?' he asks me softly.

'I'm on volunteer duty only, I'm afraid. For my tardiness, they've put me in charge of the Bad Boys.' I laugh. 'Only they've been behaving impeccably, so I won't call them Bad Boys today. When they're not consumed with *competing*, they can show a different side to them altogether.'

'Still,' Adam mutters now, shuddering, 'I'm glad none of them will be around when I come back after September.'

'They won't.'

'... and you just missed our race, Miss!' Adam shares a glance with Nate.

'Sorry I was late, guys.' I shoot them a small, nervous smile. I have a confession to make. 'I popped into Jed Miller's before I came down here.'

'You went to the body art shop?' Nate's trying to hide his disappointment. 'I guess you'll be needing a new job if you've decided against coming back to the school, then?' Nate's taken the words out of Adam's mouth, I sense. Already those two are acting as a team. They're going to make a tight one, I can tell.

I let out a breath. I only made up my mind this morning, but now it's been decided they might as well know.

'On the contrary. I went in to apologise to him for letting his friend Christiane down after he put in that good word for me. Luckily, he was gracious about it. But my main news is something bigger than that.' I pause. '... I've agreed to stay on as a supply teacher till the end of this term, guys.'

'Oh. I'm *glad*, Jen.' Nate's face crumples in relief.

Adam doesn't say anything. He just wipes at his eyes fiercely with the back of his hand. Then he hobbles over to give me a hug, and for a long, long few minutes, we just stand there, swaying together, while the warm, damp patch of his silent tears grows larger on my sleeve.

'Thank you, Miss,' he mumbles gruffly into the top of my arm.

'Thank *you*, Adam.' The words are out before I even think them.

'For what?' His solemn round face looks up into mine, surprised. 'For *what?*'

'For … for *believing*,' I whisper into his ear, 'for not giving up the faith. For continuing to believe that your dream could come true and you'd find the parent that you needed. For believing.'

'Nate helped me with that,' he admits quietly.

'You helped him too, Adam. You've helped each other to find something very special.' We move apart a little, now, and as we do so, he notices the sticking plaster on my wrist.

'Oh, Miss. You hurt yourself too?'

'She hasn't hurt herself,' Nate realises, grinning. 'She's only gone in and had a tattoo done, haven't you, Jenna? You had that done while you were at Jed's?'

I smile, peeling back the plaster carefully to show them.

'I went for a classic, in the end.'

'Because a swallow always returns home, Jen?'

I nod. For the first time in my life, I feel I've got a place I really do want to call home. When I turn to Nate, despite the tiny feeling of emptiness that still persists in my own heart, I have to say it,

'You know, everyone should have what you two have. At least once in their lives, everyone should experience it.'

Nate opens up his arms to me. When I slide into them now, his kiss on my lips is sweet and open and unreserved.

'You feeling a little *left out*, Miss?' he murmurs into my ear.

'Maybe a little.' I smile at the ground.

'No need to be, though. If you're willing, there's plenty of room in our lives for one more.'

Nate looks up and Adam's standing at the tent flap now, his face a picture of determined consternation.

390

'*Oh, God ...*'

'You got something you want to add to that, Bud?'

'Only ... it looks as if Mrs Tallyman's getting ready to pack up.' Adam's hobbled outside, despite his hurt foot, looking worried.

Mrs Tallyman?

Nate shrugs at me, frowning slightly. He has no clue, either.

'You said if we won the race you'd buy us an ice lolly,' he reminds Nate. 'You promised you would buy us one if we didn't.'

Nate laughs now, deep in his belly.

'An ice lolly?' His face has broken into a smile. 'Even the walking wounded can struggle on for that.'

We all troop outside. By the 'Nice and Ice' table, Mrs Tallyman's already opening up another box full of choc-ices and lollies. Nate makes a *'Phew!'* gesture, wiping his brow.

'Sounds as if you were always onto a winner, there.' I nudge Adam, grinning.

'I think we all are, Miss.' Adam's rubbing his hands together, looking at the huge array of choice before him. This could take a while. 'There's plenty to go round.'

I smile at my Nate. My Keeper boyfriend, Nate, because this time I know it's for real, no more running away for me. I've done it. I've found the one. I've stopped looking.

And you know what?

I think that Adam's right.

Adam

Dear Nan,

I was so exited to see you last weekend in your new home with all your new old people friends. You said I had lost some wait. Now I live with Nate he makes me eat lots of veggies and stuff and we ~~work~~ walk a lot. You asked what happened to that tape Nate was making? His company cancelled the video-shorts programme in the end but he still got paid so that's okay. He erns money from home and he doesn't go to war zones anymore and he doesn't get panics anymore. I hope you do not, too.

I have a new freend! Her name is Anna May and she is in my class in year five and she comes from Spain. I went back to see our old house and her family lives there now. Nate teeses me but she is not a gurl-freend. She is only in the same class, 5T. Now Jenna is ~~tiching~~ teaching our class she says I have a chance to get into the Grammar school because of my good word power! She says the more letters I write, the better I will get, so I will be writing you a lot.

You asked where did I sleep in the last four months? Nate is okay sleeping in the sitting room so I can have the bed. He told me that Jenna is planning to move into a bigger place with him and me, soon. That is because (1) They are in love and (2) It will help his ~~appi~~ application to become my Special Guardian. He says that will be almost as good as being my real dad. But you and I know he already is even better than that.

Last of all, do you remember the big ginger tom cat that used to come in through our window all the time? Anna May's family have taken him in. He's gentler now. Anna says it is because he is more settled. He's happier. He's found his people and his forever home. I think she is right. And do you know what else I think, Nan?

I think that I have too ☺ ☺ ☺. Heart heart, Adam xxxx

The End

By the same author

Pandora's Box (Avon 2008)
Little Miracles (Avon 2009)
A Sister's Gift (Avon 2010)
Falling For You (Yule Press 2011)
Finding You – standalone sequel to Little Miracles
(Yule press 2014)

For more information about Giselle Green visit
www.Gisellegreen.com
Facebook page Giselle green Author
Twitter @gisellegreenUK